My stomach twisted ag
and longing burned through my
get out of the coffee shop before I did something stupid—like start screaming about how unfair it was that Logan was here with another girl. That a Reaper had tried to kill me twice now, and I'd almost been turned into puppy chow on the slopes by a Fenrir wolf. That I had a smartass magic sword that I didn't really know how to use and a goddess who'd chosen me to be her Champion, even though I was completely wrong for the job. That I wasn't a warrior like the other kids and never would be, no matter how hard I tried or how much I wanted to be like them. Not to mention the fact that my mom had been killed by a drunk driver the cops had never been able to find and that I still missed her so much I sometimes cried myself to sleep. Yeah, I had a lot to scream about.

Other Mythos Academy books by Jennifer Estep

Touch of Frost

First Frost

KISS OF FROST

A Mythos Academy Novel

Jennifer Estep

KENSINGTON PUBLISHING CORP.
www.kensingtonbooks.com

K TEEN BOOKS are published by

Kensington Publishing Corp.
119 West 40th Street
New York, NY 10018

ISBN-13: 978-0-7582-6694-1
ISBN-10: 0-7582-6694-4

First Kensington Trade Paperback Printing: December 2011
10   9   8   7   6   5   4

As always, to my mom, my grandma, and Andre

Acknowledgments

Any author will tell you that her book would not be possible without the hard work of many, many people. Here are some of the folks who helped bring Gwen Frost and the world of Mythos Academy to life:

Thanks to my agent, Annelise Robey, for all her helpful advice.

Thanks to my editor, Alicia Condon, for her sharp editorial eye and thoughtful suggestions. They always make the book so much better.

Thanks to everyone at Kensington who worked on the book.

Thanks to everyone who read the rough draft of *Kiss of Frost* and helped me with a plot point. Your comments were insightful and greatly appreciated.

And, finally, thanks to all the readers out there. Entertaining you is why I write books, and it's always an honor and a privilege. I hope you have as much fun reading about Gwen's adventures as I do writing them.

Happy reading!

Chapter 1

Logan Quinn was trying to kill me.

The Spartan relentlessly pursued me, cutting me off every single time I tried to duck around him and run away.

Swipe-swipe-swipe.

Logan swung his sword at me over and over again, the shining silver blade inching a little closer to my throat every single time. His muscles rippled underneath his tight long-sleeved T-shirt as he smoothly moved from one attack position to the next. A smile tugged up his lips, and his ice blue eyes practically glowed with the thrill of battle.

I did not glow with the thrill of battle. Cringe, yes. Glow, no.

Clang-clang-clang.

I brought up my own sword, trying to fend off Logan before he separated my head from my shoulders. Three times, I parried his blows, wincing whenever his sword hit mine, but the last time, I wasn't quite quick enough. Logan stepped forward, the edge of his sword a whisper away from kissing my throat before I could do much more than blink and wonder how it had gotten there to start with.

And Logan didn't stop there. He snapped his free wrist to one side and knocked my weapon out of my hand, sending it flying across the gym. My sword somersaulted several times in the air before landing point down in one of the thick mats that covered the gym floor.

"Dead again, Gypsy girl," Logan said in a soft voice. "That makes twelve kills in a row now."

I sighed. "I know. Believe me, I know. And I'm not any happier about it than you are."

Logan nodded, dropped the sword from my throat, and stepped back. Then he turned and looked over his shoulder at two other Spartan guys who were sprawled across the bleachers, alternately texting on their phones and watching us with bored disinterest.

"Time?" Logan asked.

Kenzie Tanaka hit a button on his phone. "Forty-five seconds. Up from thirty-five seconds the time before."

"Gwen's lasting a little longer at least," Oliver Hector chimed in. "Must be the Wonder Woman T-shirt finally adding to her awesome fighting skills."

My face flushed at his snide tone. Okay, so *maybe* I had worn my favorite long-sleeved superhero shirt this morning in hopes that it might bring me a little luck, which I seriously needed when it came to any kind of fight. But he didn't have to mock me about it, especially not in front of the others.

Oliver grinned and smirked at me. I crossed my arms over my chest and gave him a dirty look.

Kenzie looked at the other Spartan. "I think it's cool that Gwen likes superheroes."

Oliver frowned. He didn't like Kenzie sticking up for me, but he didn't say anything else. I didn't know what Oliver's deal was, but he always seemed to go out of his way to annoy me. Maybe he thought he was being charming or something. Some guys at Mythos Academy were like that—they thought being total jerks was super-cool. Whatever. I had zero interest in the Spartan that way. Oh, Oliver was cute enough with his sandy blond hair, forest green eyes, bronze skin, and lazy grin. So was Kenzie, with that glossy black hair and those dark eyes. Not to mention the obvious muscles the two of them had and the lean strength that was so evident in their bodies. The only problem was that the two Spartans weren't Logan Quinn.

Logan was the one that I was interested in—even if he had already broken my heart back in the fall.

Thinking about my stupid, hopeless, unreturned feelings for Logan soured my already grumpy mood, and I stalked across the mats toward my sword.

The gym at Mythos Academy was about five times the size of a regular one, with a ceiling that soared several hundred feet above my head. In some ways, it was completely normal. Bright banners marking all the various academy championships in fencing, archery, swimming, and other froufrou sports dangled from the rafters, while wooden bleachers jutted out from two of the walls. Mats covered the floor, hiding the basketball court from sight.

But then there were the weapons.

Racks and racks of them were stacked against another wall, going up so high, there was a ladder attached to one side to get to the weapons on the top rows. Swords, daggers, staffs, spears, bows, and quivers full of curved, wicked-looking arrows. All of them razor sharp and ready to be picked up and used by the students, most of whom took exceptional pride in showing off their prowess with the sharp, pointed edges.

The weapons were one of the ways in which Mythos Academy was anything *but* normal.

I reached for my sword, which was still wobbling back and forth, reminding me of my old piano teacher's metronome slowly ticking from side to side. I reached down, but before I could tug the sword out of the mat a round silver bulge on the hilt snapped open, revealing a narrowed, angry eye.

"Another bloody defeat," Vic muttered, his displeasure giving even more bite to his British accent. "Gwen Frost, you couldn't kill a Reaper to save your bloody life."

I narrowed my own eyes and glared at Vic, hoping he would get the message to *shut up already* before Logan and the others heard him. I didn't want to advertise the fact that I had a talking sword. I didn't want to advertise a lot of things about myself. Not at Mythos.

For his part, Vic glared right back at me, his eye a curious color that was somewhere between purple and gray. Vic wasn't alive, not exactly, but I'd come to think of him as that way. Vic was a simple enough sword—a long blade made out of silver metal. But what made the sword seem, well, human to me was the fact that the hilt was shaped like half of a man's face, complete with a nose, an ear, a mouth, and a round, bulging eye. All put together, it looked like a real person had somehow been encased there in the silver hilt. It all added up to Vic, whatever or whoever he really was.

Well, that and his bloodthirsty attitude. Vic wanted to kill things—Reapers, specifically. *Until we're both bathed in their blood and hungry for more!* he'd crowed to me more than once when I was alone in my dorm room practicing with him.

Please. The only things I could kill with ease were bugs. And even then only the tiny ones. The big ones crunched too much and made me feel all guilty and icked out. Doing the same to Reapers of Chaos, some seriously bad guys, was *totally* out of the question.

"What are you going to do when a real Reaper attacks you?" Vic demanded. "Run away and hope he doesn't chase after you?"

Actually, that sounded like an excellent plan to me, but I knew Vic wouldn't see it that way. Neither would Logan, Kenzie, or Oliver, since the guys were all Spartans, descended from a long line of magical, mythological warriors. Killing things was as natural as breathing to them. It was what they'd been trained to do since birth, along with all the other kids at the academy.

For the most part, the guys at Mythos were either Vikings or Romans, while the girls were Valkyries or Amazons. But tons of other ancient warrior types attended the academy, everyone from Samurais and Ninjas, to Celts, to the Spartans in front of me.

Killing was definitely *not* natural to me, but I'd been

thrust into this twisted world back at the start of the school year. That's when I'd first started attending Mythos, after a serious freak-out with my Gypsy magic back at my old public high school. Now the academy—with all its warrior whiz kids, scary Reaper bad guys, mythological monsters, and an angry, vengeful god—was a place that I just couldn't escape, no matter how much I would have liked to.

Especially since there was a goddess counting on me to do something about all the Bad, Bad Things out there in the world—and the ones hidden here on campus too.

"Shut up, Vic," I growled, tugging the sword free of the mat.

I felt Vic's mouth move underneath my palm like he was going to give me some more backtalk, but then he let out a loud *harrumph* and his eye snapped shut. I sighed again. Now, he was in one of his *moods,* which meant I was going to have to cajole him to open his eye and speak to me again later in the day. Maybe I'd turn on the TV in my dorm room and see if there was some kind of action-adventure movie playing. Watching the bad guys get theirs always seemed to bring Vic out of one of his funks, and the bloodier the movie, the better he liked it.

"Who are you talking to, Gwen?"

Oliver Hector's voice sounded right beside me, and I had to clamp my lips together to keep from shrieking in surprise. I hadn't heard the Spartan come up behind me.

"Nobody."

He gave me a look that said he thought I was a complete freak, then shook his head. "Come on. Logan wants you to practice shooting targets next."

I looked around, but Logan had disappeared while I'd been talking to Vic. So had Kenzie Tanaka. They'd probably gone to get an energy drink out of one of the vending machines outside the gym, leaving me alone with Oliver. Great.

Even grumpier than before, I stalked behind Oliver over to the other side of the gym, where an archery target had been set up. The Spartan headed for one of the weapons racks while I kept going toward the bleachers.

The four of us had dumped our bags on the bleachers when we'd first come into the gym at seven this morning. I'd only been going to Mythos a few months, and I hadn't had the lifelong warrior training that the other students had. Now, I was struggling to catch up, which meant schlepping over to the gym every morning for an hour's worth of work with Logan and his friends before my regular classes started.

Out of all the kids at the academy, the Spartans were the best warriors, and Professor Metis had thought that they could whip me into shape in no time flat. It wasn't working out that way, though. I just wasn't warrior material, no matter what some people—goddess included—thought.

I slid Vic into his black leather scabbard and laid him flat on one of the bleachers, so he wouldn't fall off. I'd already dropped the sword enough times today. Then I reached into my gray messenger bag for a mirror and brush, so I could pull my hair back into a tighter, neater

ponytail, since it had come undone while I'd been sparring with Logan.

I squinted at my reflection in the smooth glass. Wavy
brown hair, winter white skin dotted here and there
with a few freckles, and eyes that were a strange shade
of purple. *Violet eyes are smiling eyes,* my mom had always said. I thought of how easily Logan had kicked my
ass while we'd been training. Nope, I wasn't smiling
about anything this morning.

When I was done fixing my hair, I put the mirror and
brush back into my bag and threw it onto the bleachers.
In the process, my bag hit Oliver's and knocked his to
the floor because I was just that kind of total, uncoordinated klutz. And of course the top of his bag popped
open, and all kinds of stuff spilled out, tumbling over
the mats. Pens, pencils, books, his iPod, a laptop, some
silver throwing daggers.

Sighing, I got down on my knees and started scoop-
ing everything back into the bag, careful to use the edge
of my sleeve so as to not actually touch anything with
my bare fingers. I had no desire to see into the inner
workings of Oliver Hector's mind, but that's what
would happen if I wasn't careful.

I managed to get everything back into the bag except
for a thick red notebook. A couple of the metal rings
had been bent out of shape, and they snagged on the
fabric every time I tried to slide the notebook back into
the bag where it belonged. I just didn't have a long
enough sleeve to bend all the metal down, and I couldn't
get a good grip with the soft cotton anyway. Exasper-

ated, I took hold of the metal with my sleeve, so I wouldn't scrape my skin, then grabbed the bottom of the notebook with my bare hand.

The images hit me the second my fingers touched the red cover.

A picture of Oliver popped into my head, one of the Spartan leaning over the desk in his dorm room and writing in the notebook. One by one, the images flashed by, giving me a condensed, high-def version of Oliver alternately doodling, drawing, and scribbling furiously in the notebook. After a few seconds, the feelings kicked in, and I started experiencing Oliver's emotions, too. All the things he'd felt when he'd been writing in his notebook. The dull boredom of doing class assignments, the annoyed frustration of trying to understand some of the complicated homework, and then, surprisingly, a soft, dreamy fizz that warmed my whole body—

"What are you doing? That's mine," Oliver snapped in a harsh voice.

I shook off the images and feelings, and looked up. The Spartan stood over me, his features tight and pinched.

"Sorry," I snapped back. "I didn't think a guy like you would be so protective of his notebook. What's in here that's so supersecret? A list of everyone you've slept with? Let me guess. You don't want me to know who you've been hooking up with. You want to tell everyone yourself because that's what all the guys at Mythos do— brag about their stupid conquests, right?"

Oliver's face actually paled at my words. Seriously. He just went white with shock. For a second, I wondered why, but then I realized he must have heard about my psychometry—about my magic.

I wasn't a warrior like the other kids at Mythos—not exactly—but I wasn't completely without skills, either. I was a Gypsy, a person gifted with magic by one of the gods. In my case, that magic was psychometry, or the ability to touch an object and immediately know, see, and feel its history.

My Gypsy gift, my psychometry, was actually cooler—and a little scarier—than it sounded. Not only could I see who had once worn a bracelet or read a book, no matter how long ago it had been, but I also could feel that person's emotions. Everything she'd been thinking, feeling, and experiencing when she'd been wearing that bracelet or reading that book. Sometimes everything she'd ever felt, seen, or done over a whole lifetime, if her attachment to the object was strong enough. I could tell if a person had been happy or sad, good or bad, smart or dumb, or a thousand other things.

My magic let me know people's secrets—let me see and feel all the things they kept hidden from others and even themselves sometimes. All their conflicting emotions, all the sly things they'd done, all the things they only dreamed about doing in the deepest, blackest parts of their hearts.

Maybe it was dark and twisted of me, but I liked knowing other people's secrets. I liked the power that the knowledge gave me, especially since I didn't have any of the wicked cool fighting skills the other kids at Mythos did. Knowing other people's secrets was sort of an obsession of mine—one that had almost led to me getting killed a few weeks ago.

It was also the reason I held on to Oliver's notebook now. I'd totally expected the boredom and the frustration I'd sensed. Those were both emotions I'd felt many times before when I'd touched other kids' notebooks, computers, pens, and all the other ordinary, everyday objects they used to do their schoolwork.

But that warm, soft, fizzy feeling? Not so much. I knew what it was though: love. Or at least like—*serious* like. Oliver had a major, major crush on someone, enough to write about that person in his notebook, and I wanted to know who it was. Since, you know, secrets were my own form of crack.

I concentrated on the notebook again, on that soft, fizzy, hopeful feeling, and a hazy image started to form in my mind, someone with dark hair, black hair—

"I said that was mine," Oliver growled, yanking the notebook out of my hand and breaking my connection to it.

The half-formed image abruptly vanished, along with that warm, fizzy sensation. My fingers grabbed for the notebook, but I only came up with empty air. Another second, and I would have seen who Oliver's mystery crush was. But the Spartan held the notebook up out of my reach, then grabbed his bag and shoved the notebook inside it. He was in such a hurry that he ripped the side of the bag's fabric. Oliver glanced up at me to see if I'd noticed.

I smirked at him in the same cocky, knowing way he

had smirked at me a few minutes ago, when he'd been making fun of my T-shirt. Oliver's face darkened.

"What are you two doing?" Kenzie asked, coming out of one of the side doors and drinking from a bottle of water in his hand.

"Nothing," Oliver muttered, shooting me another cold look.

I rolled my eyes and ignored him. Since coming to Mythos, I'd almost been run through with a sword and mauled to death by a killer kitty cat. Dirty looks didn't faze me anymore.

"Where's Logan?" I asked.

"He'll be back in a minute. He said to get started without him," Kenzie said, his black eyes flicking back and forth between me and Oliver, wondering what was going on.

Oliver turned and stalked down to the other end of the bleachers, taking his bag along with him. Kenzie gave me another curious look, then went over to Oliver. The two of them started talking in low voices, with Oliver still glaring in my direction.

The Spartan was clearly angry at me for touching his precious notebook and teasing him about who his mystery crush might be. Whatever. I didn't care what Oliver thought about me. Besides, he'd started it by making fun of my T-shirt. I might not know how to sling a sword, but I could throw verbal daggers with the best of them.

After about a minute of talking, Kenzie and Oliver broke apart. They both headed toward the archery target, and Kenzie gestured for me to follow them. Apparently, I hadn't pissed them off enough to make them forget about the rest of our training session. Too bad.

Sighing, I got to my feet, ready to show the Spartans that I sucked just as much at using a bow as I did at swinging a sword.

Chapter 2

Thwang!

For the fifth time in as many tries, my arrow weakly thumped against the target, then bounced off and fell to the gym floor.

"No, no, no," Kenzie said, shaking his head. "How many times do I have to tell you? Using a bow is just like using a sword. You can't be timid about it, Gwen. You have to pull back the string and let the arrow go like you really mean it. Otherwise, you're not going to get enough power to make your arrow go through your target."

"Yeah, Gwen," Oliver sniped. "You want to kill Reapers, not make them die laughing at you."

I ignored Oliver's snide comment, focused on Kenzie's advice, and blew a loose strand of hair off my face. "Power. Mean it. Right."

I'd been practicing for the last fifteen minutes with a long, curved bow, while the Spartans had looked on and called out advice. Surprisingly, my aim was decent enough to let me hit the outer rim of the target, but I had yet to actually have an arrow stick in it. They all kept bouncing off. Kenzie claimed it was because I wasn't pulling the string back far enough and giving the arrow enough force to penetrate the target. I thought it was because I was just as bad at archery as I was at sword-play. I got good grades. Why did I have to be coordinated, too?

"Here," Kenzie said, handing me another arrow. "Let's try again."

Kenzie shook his head at Oliver, who snickered. I sighed and nocked the arrow.

One of the gym doors squeaked open, and Logan stepped back inside. But he wasn't alone—Savannah Warren was with him.

Savannah was a gorgeous Amazon, with intense green eyes and a mane of red hair that blazed down her back in a sunset of ringlets. She also happened to be Logan's current squeeze—one in a long, long line if you believed the gossip around campus.

Logan had a reputation for being one of the resident man-whores at Mythos Academy—the kind of guy that girls just couldn't resist and didn't really want to anyway. He certainly looked the part with his piercing, ice blue eyes; thick, ink black hair; and muscled body. He practically oozed bad-boy charm, even when wearing a T-shirt and sweatpants like he was now. One of the rumors that had gone around campus back in the fall was that Logan signed the mattress of every girl that he slept with at Mythos, just so he could keep them all straight.

Logan stood in the gym doorway, smiling down at Savannah. The Amazon toyed with his shirt, sliding her hand back and forth across his sculpted chest. My fingers tightened around the bow, and ugly, jealous anger burned in the pit of my stomach.

Logan and I had almost had a—a—*thing* a few weeks back. A freaking *moment*. Okay, several *moments*. The Spartan had gotten into the habit of saving my life, first when a Nemean prowler had tried to turn me into catnip, and then later on when a Valkyrie had wanted to kill me for messing up her evil plans. Bad-boy charm I could deal with, but saving my life? Twice? That was a little tougher to forget. I'd fallen hard for Logan as a result, even going so far as to ask him out.

He'd turned me down flat.

Logan had claimed that I didn't know what Spartans were really capable of, that I didn't know what *he* was capable of, and that he wasn't the hero I thought he was.

Whatever. If he didn't like me, he could have just said so. Instead he'd given me some lame excuse that he had a deep, dark secret that would scare me off. I'd once picked up a girl's hairbrush and had seen her stepfather sexually abusing her. I was willing to bet Logan's secret wasn't nearly as horrible as that, but nothing I'd said had convinced him otherwise. Nothing I'd said had convinced him to take a chance on me—on *us*.

"Gwen? You want to shoot that arrow sometime today?" Kenzie said. "We've only got fifteen minutes of practice time left."

"Sure," I muttered, turning toward the target.

Savannah's soft laughter drifted across the gym, making my anger burn a little hotter. If I'd been a Valkyrie, like my best friend, Daphne Cruz, princess pink sparks of magic would have been shooting out of my fingertips. That's what happened whenever Daphne got pissed about something—and I was plenty pissed at myself right now for still caring about Logan when he'd made it perfectly clear he didn't feel the same way about me.

I raised the arrow up to eye level and peered down the length of it at the target. Part of me was thinking about Logan, but the other part was thinking about Daphne and how she would have turned around and put an arrow in the Spartan's ass from all the way across the gym. Daphne was great with a bow. In fact, she was one of the best shots at Mythos and the captain of the girls' archery team. An image flickered in my mind then, one of Daphne using the bow, instead of me—

"Any time now, Gwen," Kenzie said in an impatient voice.

"Yeah, come on, Gwen, while we're all still young," Oliver sneered.

My anger flared up to supernova level at Oliver's snarky tone, so much so that I didn't think—I just let go.

THUNK!

The arrow hit the target dead center—perfectly in the middle of the black bull's-eye. And this time it stayed there instead of thumping off and falling to the floor.

Beside me, Kenzie blinked. "How did you do that?"

I frowned. "I don't know."

I really didn't. Yeah, I might have been hitting the target all along, but only the outside edge, and none of my other arrows had even come close to sticking in it. But this one? It had practically *skewered* the target, with only the back half of the shaft now visible.

"Well, whatever you were doing, do it again," Kenzie said, passing me another arrow.

"If you even can," Oliver chimed in.

I nocked another arrow and tried to remember what I'd just done. I'd been thinking about Daphne, of course, but it felt like more than that. It had almost seemed like I was . . . channeling her somehow. Or at least my memories of her.

My psychometry let me remember every single person and every single object I'd ever touched. Once I flashed on someone or something, those vibes, feelings, and emotions became part of me. I could think about those memories and call them up at will, replaying the images over and over again in my head with perfect color, picture, and sound every single time. That was one of the cool things about my magic. But the flip side to it and one of the not-so-cool things was that sometimes the memories just came out of nowhere and flooded my mind whether I wanted them to or not. Either way, it was like having a photographic memory, only a lot freakier—especially given some of the bad, bad stuff I'd seen.

But they weren't really *my* memories. When I'd let go of the arrow, I'd been thinking about Daphne's memories, what she'd done and how she'd felt. I'd picked up her bow in her dorm room last week and had gotten a whole bunch of flashes of the Valkyrie competing at various archery tournaments.

I thought about Daphne again, this time really focusing on her, picturing her at one of the competitions—
how she'd held her bow, how she'd lined up her arrow
and pulled back the string, the electric thrill of victory
she'd felt every time her arrow had hit the target dead
center. Then I lifted the bow and concentrated on my
own shot.

Once again, my own arrow zoomed straight into the
center of the target.

"All right," Kenzie said, clapping his hands. "It looks
like we're finally making progress with something."

He grinned at me, and I returned his smile, even
though I could see Oliver scowling behind him. I still
didn't understand exactly what I'd done, how I'd used
Daphne's memories to help myself, but at least I'd hit
the target again. Yeah, it was kind of weird, but in a
good way. It was certainly better than a lot of things I'd
experienced since coming to the academy.

I turned around to see if Logan had noticed my suc-
cess—and saw him French-kissing Savannah in the gym
doorway. The Amazon had her arms around his neck,
and Logan had his wrapped around her waist, pulling
her even closer to him. They kissed for another few seconds before Savannah drew back. She grabbed the front
of Logan's shirt and yanked him out of the gym. I didn't
know where they were headed, but it was obvious what
they were going to do—sneak in a make-out session before morning classes started.

Cold, bitter, aching hurt frosted my heart, piercing it
the way my arrow had the target a few seconds ago.

"Gwen?" Kenzie asked, his voice soft and kind.

For once, even Oliver was quiet, instead of stinging me with some barbed remark.

Not everyone at the academy knew about my massive crush on Logan, but it had no doubt become painfully obvious to Kenzie and Oliver, since they'd watched me train with Logan for weeks now. Plus, they'd just seen my reaction to him leaving me behind to go tongue wrestle with another girl.

"I'm fine," I snapped, hating the fact that they knew how much I cared about Logan, hating the fact that I still felt this way in the first place. "Let's keep practicing."

Kenzie handed me another arrow. He didn't say a word. Neither did Oliver.

Still channeling Daphne's memories and my own anger, I put five more arrows dead center into the target before training time was over.

"You *have* to come to Winter Carnival, Gwen. It's a Mythos Academy tradition. *Everybody* will be there."

I ignored Daphne and stabbed another miniscule piece of fruit in the delicate, white china bowl in front of me. The fruit was a vibrant yellow color, with a strange, pointed shape. Definitely not kiwi. Maybe a star fruit? I brought it up to my nose and sniffed, but all I could smell was the sharp, sweet tang of the honey-vanilla-lime dressing. The weird fruit didn't look like it would kill me if I ate it. Then again, a lot of things at the academy seemed far nicer than they really were.

Across from me, Daphne cut another dainty bite of

an egg white omelet topped with chunks of fresh, buttery lobster; sautéed spinach; and thick crumbles of Feta cheese. The Valkyrie was actually eating lobster for breakfast—and enjoying every single bite of it. Yucko.

Lobster was actually one of the tamer things served in the dining hall. Caviar, escargot, and veal were among the daily offerings for breakfast, lunch, and dinner, along with tons of other fancy, froufrou foods. Even the regular dishes—like lasagna, fried chicken, or the fruit salad I was eating—always featured weird ingredients, strange sauces, and bizarre toppings. But the other kids loved all the exotic foods, since they'd grown up eating the expensive entrées with their obscenely rich parents. The Mythos students scarfed down snails the way kids at my old public high school had inhaled greasy pizzas, crispy fries, and thick cheeseburgers.

The lack of simple, identifiable, *normal* food was one of the things I hated about the dining hall—and one of the many things I hated about Mythos Academy in general.

"Gwen? Are you even listening to me?" Daphne snapped her fingers in front of my face, causing pink sparks of magic to flutter around us like tiny fireflies.

"I don't have to listen," I said, putting my fork down in the bowl and pushing it, and the mystery fruit, away. "All you've been talking about for the last two weeks is this weekend getaway all the students are invited to."

"Not just any getaway," Daphne said. "*Winter Carnival.* Trust me. It's one of the best events of the year."

"Why?" I groused. "Because everyone gets to go to

some fancy ski resort for the weekend, where they can drink, smoke, and have sex with limited interference from the professors?"

Daphne grinned, her black eyes bright with excitement. "Exactly."

I didn't see how the carnival would be any different from what went on at the academy on a daily basis, but I didn't say anything. The kids might all be at Mythos to supposedly learn how to fight and use their magic to help protect the world, but they liked to party hard while they did it. Given the fact that everyone's parents were filthy, filthy rich, they could easily afford to. Apparently, back in the day, all the various gods and goddesses had rewarded their warriors with gold, silver, and diamonds the size of my fist. The wealth had trickled down and multiplied through the generations, which is why the Mythos students had the very best of everything, from designer clothes to expensive cars to custom-made jewelry and weapons.

Back at my old high school, a party had been a six-pack of wine coolers that somebody's college-age sister had bought on the sly. Here at Mythos, the kids whose parents owned Dionysian wineries sent them *cases* of the stuff.

"Come on," Daphne wheedled. "I'll need somebody to hold my hair back while I puke my guts out. Some of the parties can get pretty wild."

I raised an eyebrow. "Too wild for a mighty Valkyrie such as yourself to handle?"

Daphne grinned again. I snorted.

Like the other kids at Mythos, Daphne Cruz was the

great-great-whatever descendant of an ancient warrior. Oh, she looked like just another rich, spoiled princess, with her smooth, golden hair; perfect amber skin; expensive pink cashmere sweater; and even more expensive matching pink purse. Daphne was definitely a girly-girl, but she also happened to be a Valkyrie as well, which meant she was incredibly strong. Seriously. Like Hulk strong. Daphne could have torn apart the table we were sitting at with her bare hands and not even break a nail doing it.

Valkyries also had magic, hence all the sparks flickering around us and in other spots in the dining hall where the girls were sitting. Every time Daphne's French-manicured nails scraped against something or she got particularly emotional, little princess pink sparks would shoot off her fingertips and fill the air. Daphne had once told me that her fingers were like sparklers on the Fourth of July. I didn't mind the cracks and flashes of color, though. Sitting next to her was like being close to a rainbow. Well, if rainbows were solid pink. And volatile. Sometimes Daphne's temper flared up almost as much as the sparks did.

Daphne's magic hadn't quickened, or manifested, yet, but once it did, she'd have even more power. Valkyries had all sorts of magical abilities, like being able to heal people, control the weather, and even create illusions.

I shivered. I'd learned that last one the hard way a few weeks ago, when Jasmine Ashton, another one of the rich Valkyrie princesses at Mythos, had summoned up an illusion of a Nemean prowler to try to kill me. If you believed in an illusion, it could hurt you—even kill you—like the real thing. The prowler—a big, black, pantherlike monster—would have ripped me to shreds if Logan hadn't stabbed it to death, causing the illusion to vanish.

Maybe I had my own twisted kind of power today, because as soon as I thought about Logan, he stepped through the door of the dining hall—with Savannah right beside him. No doubt Logan had come here to grab some breakfast before classes started, just like I had. The Spartan had showered and changed since I'd last seen him in the gym, and his black hair was still damp. He'd traded in his T-shirt and sweatpants for acid-washed jeans, a blue sweater, and a black leather jacket that outlined his muscled shoulders. He looked totally sexy.

I watched Logan wind his way through the dining hall, past the oil paintings of various mythological feasts that covered the walls, and the polished suits of armor that stood guard beneath them. He led Savannah to a table not too far away from where Daphne and I were sitting. Like all the others, the table was covered with creamy white linens, dainty china, and a heavy crystal vase full of fresh poppies, hyacinths, and narcissus flowers.

The table also had the advantage of being right next to the open-air indoor garden that stood in the middle of the dining hall. Grape vines twisted through the area, winding their way over, around, and sometimes through the thick branches of the olive, orange, and almond trees planted in the black soil there. Marble statues of Demeter, Dionysus, and other gods and goddesses could be seen in various spots in the garden, their heads facing out and their eyes open, as though they were watching the students eat the bounty of the harvests they represented.

Logan and Savannah might as well have been eating in a romantic restaurant. The ambience was pretty much the same—especially given the dreamy way the two of them stared into each other's eyes.

Daphne realized that I wasn't paying attention to her anymore and turned around to see what I was looking at. Her pretty face softened with knowing sympathy, which made me feel even worse.

"Did I mention that it's not just Mythos students who will be at the carnival?" Daphne asked. "Lots of kids from the New York academy will be there too."

I blinked. "There are more academies out there? I thought this was the only school for warriors."

"Oh, no. There's a school up in New York and one out in Denver. Paris, London, Athens—there are lots of Mythos branches around the world, although the one here at Cypress Mountain is the biggest and the best."

"Really? Why's that?"

Daphne rolled her eyes. "Because it's the one we go to, silly. Plus, we've got the Library of Antiquities. None of the other branches has a library like ours, especially not one with as many artifacts."

At the academy, students learned about gods, goddesses, warriors, myths, magic, and monsters from every culture in the world—Greek, Norse, Roman, Japanese, Chinese, Native American, Egyptian, Indian, Russian, Irish, African, and all the others out there. I supposed it made sense there would be other branches, other schools, located throughout the world.

"Anyway," Daphne said. "My point is that there will be some new blood there. Some of the guys from the New York academy are supercute. I flirted with a couple of them myself during last year's carnival. Plus, most of their parents have mansions in the Hamptons, which is a great place to go for spring and summer breaks."

"Cute guys, huh?" I asked, still staring at Logan.

"*Tons* of them," Daphne promised. "I'm sure we can find you somebody to hook up with for the weekend. Somebody to take your mind off other . . . things."

I sighed. It had been weeks since I'd asked out Logan and he'd rejected me, but my feelings for him hadn't changed one bit. I didn't know what would take my mind off the sexy Spartan, except for maybe a total lobotomy.

"So what do you say, Gwen?" Daphne asked. "Are you ready to have some fun?"

Savannah threw back her head and laughed at something Logan said. The soft, happy sound zipped across the room like a spear, burying itself in my skull.

"I'll think about it," I promised my best friend.

Then I grabbed my stuff, got up, and left the dining hall, so I wouldn't have to see the happy couple eat breakfast together.

Chapter 3

Despite my sour mood, the day passed by with its usual mix of classes, lectures, and boring homework assignments. The last bell rang after sixth period, and I headed outside, along with the other students.

It was early December, and I pulled my purple plaid coat a little tighter around my body, trying to keep warm. Even though it was midafternoon, the sun's rays did little to penetrate the thick, heavy, gray clouds that cloaked the sky, and my breath frosted in the air, like a stream of icicles before flowing away to the ground. Winter had already spread its chilly blanket over North Carolina for the season. That's where the academy was located, in Cypress Mountain, a suburb tucked up in the mountains above the artsy town of Asheville.

You could tell Mythos was a place for rich kids just by walking around campus. All of the buildings were made out of old, dark, gray stone covered with curling coils of ivy, and every single one of the perfectly manicured lawns sported a thick layer of grass, despite the cold. Plus, the open quad that lay in the middle of campus looked like something you'd see in a brochure for an expensive college—lots of curving, cobblestone walkways; lots of iron benches; lots of shade trees.

In a way, Mythos Academy was a kind of college, since the students ranged from the first-years, who were sixteen, all the way up to the sixth-year kids, who were twenty-one. Since I was seventeen, I was a second-year student, which meant I had roughly four and a half more years to go before I'd graduate. Oh, goody.

The main quad spread out like a picnic blanket that had been thrown across the top of a grassy hill overlooking the rest of the lush academy grounds. I stepped onto one of the ash gray cobblestone paths that led down to the lower quads, where the student dorms and other smaller outbuildings dotted the landscape. All around me the other students headed down to their dorms or back up the hill to attend whatever after-school clubs, sports, or activities they were involved in. Not me, though. I hadn't joined any clubs, and I wasn't coordinated enough to play any sports, especially not at Mythos. Everyone was so much faster, stronger, and tougher than I was, thanks to their ancient warrior genes and the magic that went along with them.

I made a quick stop at my dorm—Styx Hall—to drop off Vic and some of my schoolbooks before heading out again. Instead of going back up to the main quad, I went the opposite direction toward the edge of campus, and I didn't stop walking until I reached the twelve-foot-high stone wall separating the academy from the

outside world. A closed gate stretched across the entrance, with two sphinxes perched on the wall on either
side, staring down at the black iron bars between them.

My steps slowed, then stopped altogether as I stared
up at the statues. The sphinxes were reportedly imbued
with some kind of magic mumbo jumbo, and only folks
who were supposed to be at the academy—students,
professors, and staff—could pass through the gate and
get by the sphinxes' watchful eyes. I didn't know exactly
what would happen if someone tried to force his way in
past the statues, but I felt like there was something underneath the smooth stone facades—something old and
violent that could erupt at any moment and gobble me
up if I so much as breathed wrong.

But it always seemed like there was a loophole when
it came to magic, and with the sphinxes, it was the fact
that they were designed to keep Reapers out—but not
students in. That's what Professor Metis had told me,
and I believed her, since the creatures hadn't come to life
and clawed me to death yet. Still, it always took me a
moment to suck up enough courage to dare to slip past
them.

I glanced around, but no one else was within sight
here at the edge of campus, which was just the way I
wanted it. I drew in a breath, then darted forward,
turned sideways, sucked in my stomach, and slipped
through a gap between the iron bars. Maybe it was just
my imagination, but I could feel the sphinxes' lidless
eyes on me, tracking my every awkward movement and
shallow breath. It only took a second for me to slide out

to the other side of the gate, but it felt much longer than that. I didn't look back at the statues. It was one thing to suspect there was something inside the stone watching me—it was another to see it for myself.

Students weren't supposed to leave the academy grounds during the week, since, you know, we were all supposed to be studying, training, and stuff. That's probably why I felt like the sphinxes were glaring at me, but I didn't care. Sneaking off campus was a pretty minor infraction compared to some of the other things that went on there.

Besides, if I didn't sneak out, I wouldn't be able to see my Grandma Frost.

I wasn't crazy about the fact that I'd started attending Mythos Academy back at the beginning of the school year, but even I had to admit that Cypress Mountain was a pretty suburb. Upscale shops lay on the other side of the road that curved past the academy, selling everything from books and coffee to designer clothing and custom-made jewelry and weapons. There was even a car dealership full of Aston Martins and Cadillacs, and another lot where the Mythos kids parked their expensive rides, since students' cars weren't allowed on campus during the week. But the most popular stores with the academy kids were the ones that sold wine, liquor, cigarettes, and condoms—and that wouldn't look too closely at your ID as long as you paid in cash, preferably hundreds.

I caught one of the afternoon buses that shuttled tourists down from Cypress Mountain to the city and back up again. Twenty minutes later, I got off in a residential neighborhood full of old, spacious homes, just a few streets over from downtown Asheville. I walked to the opposite end of the block, then hurried up the gray, concrete steps of a three-story house painted a light shade of lavender. A sign beside the front door read PSYCHIC READINGS HERE. The brass plate looked a little dull, so I polished it up a bit with the edge of my jacket sleeve before I used my key to let myself inside.

"Back here, pumpkin."

I'd barely closed the front door behind me when my grandma's voice drifted down the hallway. I couldn't see her from where I was, but it sounded like she was in the kitchen. Grandma Frost was a Gypsy, just like me, which meant that she also had a gift, that she had magic. In Grandma's case, she could see the future. In fact, that's how she made extra cash—by giving psychic readings here in her house. People came from near and far to get Geraldine Frost to read their fortunes. But unlike some of the conmen out there, Grandma didn't lie to anyone about what she saw. She always told people the truth, no matter how good, bad, or ugly it was.

I walked down the hallway and stepped into the kitchen. With its white tile floors and sky blue walls, the kitchen was a bright, cheery space and my favorite room in the whole house.

Grandma Frost stood in front of one of the counters, chopping up dried strawberries and dropping the ruby red pieces into a bowl of cookie dough. In addition to her psychic powers, Grandma also had some mad baking skills. I breathed in and could practically taste the dark chocolate, rich brown sugar, and bittersweet almond flavoring she'd already stirred into the batter. Yum.

Grandma must have just finished telling her fortunes for the day because she was still dressed in what she called her "Gypsy gear"—a white silk blouse, black pants, black slippers with curled toes, and most important, lots and lots of colorful scarves. The gauzy layers of lilac, gray, and emerald fabric fluttered around her body, while the gleaming silver coins on the ends of the scarves jingled and jangled together in a merry way. She also had a scarf wrapped over her head, hiding her iron gray hair from sight. Grandma had taken off the stacks of rings she usually wore on her fingers. The silver bands clumped together in a small patch of sunlight on the kitchen table, the jewels in them flashing and winking like faceted fireflies.

"You were expecting me," I said, slinging my messenger bag into a chair and eyeing the gooey batter with hungry interest. "Did you get a psychic flash that I was coming over?"

"Nah," Grandma Frost said, her violet eyes twinkling in her wrinkled face. "It's Wednesday. You always come to see me on Wednesdays, before you work your shift at the library. I finished a little early today, so I thought I'd make some cookies for you and Daphne."

I'd brought Daphne over and introduced the Valkyrie to my grandma a few weeks ago. The two of them had totally hit it off, thanks in part to the excellent applesauce cake Grandma had made that day. Daphne didn't have a raging sweet tooth like Grandma and I did, but the cake had still knocked off her pink argyle socks. Now, every time I came over here, Grandma always sent me back to Mythos with a treat for both me and Daphne, usually packed up in a tin shaped like a giant chocolate-chip cookie. The tin matched the cookie jar on the counter.

"So what's going on at school this week, pumpkin?" Grandma asked, dividing the batter into small, round balls and then sliding the cookies into the oven so they could bake.

I sat down at the table. "Not much. Classes, home-work, weapons training—the usual. Although Daphne keeps asking me to go with her to this thing called the Winter Carnival. The Powers That Were at the academy are taking all the kids over to one of the ski resorts. There are supposed to be carnival games and parties and stuff all weekend long."

"Oh?" Grandma said. "I remember that from your mom's days at the academy. She always seemed to have a lot of fun on those trips."

I shrugged. "Maybe the carnival will be fun, maybe not. I'm not even sure yet if I'm going or not."

Grandma looked over at me, but her violet eyes were suddenly blank and glassy, like she was seeing some-thing very far away instead of just me sitting in her kitchen.

"Well, I think you should go," she murmured in that odd, absentminded voice she used whenever she was staring at something only she could see. "Get away from the academy for a while."

She was having one of her visions. I sat there, still and quiet, while something old, powerful, and watchful swirled in the air around us. Something familiar and almost comforting. Something that made me think of a certain goddess I'd met not too long ago.

After a few seconds, Grandma's eyes snapped back into focus, and she smiled at me once more. The moment and her vision had passed, and the ancient, invisible force that had been stirring in the air around her was gone. Sometimes Grandma got all sorts of details when she had one of her visions, seeing the future with sharp, crystal clarity. Sometimes, though, her psychic flashes were vague and hazy, and she only got a general sense that something good or bad was going to happen, but not exactly what it was. This must have been one of those vague and hazy times, because she didn't say anything else about why I should go to the Winter Carnival or what might take place once I got there. Besides, Grandma had always told me that she wanted me to make my own choices and chart my own destiny, instead of acting on a possible future that might never come to pass in the first place. That's why she rarely shared the specific things she saw whenever she had a vision about me.

Grandma sat down beside me at the kitchen table while we waited for the chocolate-strawberry cookies to bake. "So, pumpkin, what are you on the trail of this week?" she asked, smiling. "Tracking down more lost cell phones and laptops for the other Mythos students?"

"Nah," I said. "Everyone's focused on the Winter

Carnival. Nobody's hired me to find anything for them this week."

Cell phones, laptops, wallets, purses, car keys, jewelry, discarded bras, and missing boxers—my psychometry magic helped me find all sorts of things that were lost, stolen, or otherwise missing. Of course, if the object wasn't where it was supposed to be, I couldn't actually touch it, but people left vibes everywhere they went and on everything they handled. Usually, all I had to do was run my fingers across a guy's desk or dig through a girl's purse to get an idea about where he'd last left his wallet or where she'd put down her cell phone. And if I didn't immediately flash on an item's location, then I kept touching that person's stuff until I did—or saw an image of who had swiped it. Most of the time, it was pretty easy for me to follow the trail of psychic bread crumbs to the missing item.

"And how are you feeling, pumpkin?" Grandma asked in a softer voice. "About everything? It's been several months now since . . . the accident."

I looked at her, wondering at the way she'd said "the accident," like the words had some hidden meaning, but Grandma's face was dark and sad. Besides, I knew what she was really asking: how was I handling my mom's death.

My dad, Tyr Forseti, had passed away from cancer when I was a kid. He and my mom, Grace, had been married, but she'd kept the last name of Frost and given it to me, as was the tradition for all the women in our family, since our Gypsy gifts, our powers, were passed down from mother to daughter.

I don't even remember my dad, but my mom had died back in the spring, and everything about her death was still sharp and fresh and painful. I had a lot of guilt—okay, a *ton* of guilt—over my mom's death, since I'd sort of caused it.

Back at my old high school, I'd picked up another girl's hairbrush after gym class. I'd figured I'd be safe enough using it, since it was just a hairbrush. Most people didn't have a lot of feelings about what they used to comb their hair.

I'd been wrong.

Instead, I'd immediately flashed on the hairbrush and had learned a sick, sick secret—that the girl's stepdad was sexually abusing her. The memories, images, and feelings had been so horrible that I'd had a total freak-out with my magic. I'd screamed and screamed and screamed before blacking out and later waking up in the hospital. I'd told my mom about what I'd seen, since she was a police detective. My mom had called me from the police station that night to say she'd arrested the girl's stepdad.

That had been the last time I'd ever spoken to her.

Mom's car had been T-boned by a drunk driver on her way home. Supposedly, she'd died instantly, and she'd been messed up so badly from the accident that the casket had been closed at her funeral. Hence, all my heart-shattering, soul-twisting guilt. I couldn't help but think that if I hadn't picked up that hairbrush, then my mom wouldn't have been out so late—and she would have never been killed.

I missed my mom like crazy, and I knew Grandma Frost did too, since it had always been just the three of us. That's why I risked the wrath of the professors and the other Powers That Were at Mythos to sneak off campus to come see her and that's why Grandma let me. Because we both wanted to spend as much time with each other as we could, just in case one of us was ever taken away as suddenly and cruelly as my mom had been—

Ding!

The timer sounded, interrupting my dark, guilty thoughts and saving me from answering her question. Grandma got up and slid the cookies out of the oven. The smells of melted sugar, sweet strawberries, and dark chocolate blasted into the kitchen, making everything feel warm, safe, and cozy. I didn't even wait for the cookies to cool before I snatched two off the baking sheet, broke them apart, and stuffed the pieces into my mouth. Yum. So good.

"Now you be sure and give some of these to Daphne," Grandma reminded me in a gentle voice, filling up my usual tin with the cookies. "I know she'll want some, too."

"Okay." That's what I said, but since I was still chewing, it sounded more like "Mmm-kay."

By the time Grandma had finished packing up the cookies, it was after five, which meant that I needed to leave so I could ride the bus back up to the academy. Nickamedes would be on my ass if I was even a minute late for my shift. In addition to going to classes and weapons training, I also had to work several hours a week at the Library of Antiquities as sort of an after-school job. Fun, fun.

I slid the container of cookies into my messenger bag, on top of the stack of comic books I was currently reading, then slung the strap over my head and across my chest.

"Love you, Grandma." I leaned down and kissed her wrinkled cheek.

"I love you too, pumpkin," she said, patting my hand one final time. "You be careful. It's a wicked old world out there."

I paused, wondering if Grandma Frost was having another one of her psychic flashes, if she was trying to warn me about something, but her violet eyes were calm, clear, and focused. Then again, I didn't really need Grandma to warn me. Thanks to my time at Mythos, I knew exactly what kind of scary things were out there—things like Reapers of Chaos, Nemean prowlers, and most especially, Loki.

"I will," I promised her. "I'll be careful."

With a third, still-warm cookie in my hand, I left Grandma Frost's house. The sun had given up trying to break through the clouds, and it had gotten even darker and colder while I'd been inside. I shoved the rest of the cookie into my mouth and stuck my hands deep into my jacket pockets, wishing I'd thought to wear gloves today. Of course, I supposed I could have worn gloves around the clock, to cut down on the flashes I got off other people and objects. But I already felt like enough of a freak as it was. Wearing elbow-length gloves all the time would *so* not help my social status at Mythos.

I walked to the end of the block, looked both ways to make sure the coast was clear, and stepped out into the street heading for the bus stop on the opposite side.

I didn't even see the car until it was right on top of me.

It was a big, black, expensive SUV with a shiny silver grille—and it was racing right toward me.

I froze in the middle of the street, not quite believing what I was seeing, not quite believing that the driver hadn't spotted me, that he wasn't going to blow the horn and slam on his brakes at any moment. Where had he come from? The street had been completely empty a second ago.

The SUV kept coming and coming, and the wheels kept churning and churning, gulping down all the pavement that separated us. The tinted windshield loomed up in my vision until it was all that I could see—a hungry black maw that was going to swallow me up whole, and then spit out my bloody, broken bones.

It seemed like forever, but after a second, my brain kicked in, screaming *Move! Move! Move!* I didn't have an Amazon's lightning-quick speed, but I managed to throw myself forward, my body slamming against a rusty pickup truck parked on the opposite side of the street.

The SUV roared past me, so close I felt the rush of air from its passing brush the back of my jacket. The vehicle zoomed down the street, zipped around the corner at the end of the block, and disappeared from view. The driver never slowed down—not even for a second.

With my mouth open, heart hammering, arms trembling, and legs shaking, I stared down the empty street and wondered whether or not the whole thing had been an accident—or something far more sinister.

Chapter 4

Heart still racing, I staggered onto the sidewalk and huddled against the steps of the home at the end of the block. I thought about sprinting back to my Grandma Frost's house and telling her what had happened, but there was nothing she could do. The SUV was probably long gone, and I hadn't gotten a look at the license plate.

The bus made my decision for me. Just as I'd taken a few tentative steps back to Grandma's house, the vehicle pulled up to the curb and the door opened. I bit my lip. As much as I wanted to run back to the safety of Grandma Frost's house, I didn't want to be late for my shift at the library either. Nickamedes already watched me like a hawk. I didn't want him to know the real reason I was late all the time. I don't know what I'd do if I couldn't see my grandma whenever I wanted to.

So I sighed and trudged onto the bus. I peered out the window the whole ride back up to Cypress Mountain, but I didn't see the black SUV that had almost mowed me down. No, that's not quite right. I saw lots of black cars—I just couldn't tell if the person who'd nearly plowed into me was driving any of them.

But what worried me most was the fact that I couldn't figure out whether or not it had been an accident.

The bus finally reached the top of Cypress Mountain and rumbled to a stop across from Mythos Academy. I got off, sprinted across the street, and slipped through the academy's iron gates, which were still closed and locked. For once, I was glad the sphinxes were there, perched on top of the wall and glaring down at me. Sure, the statues made me uneasy, but they were also supposed to keep the academy safe from Reapers. The sphinxes would keep whomever was after me from following me onto campus. At least, I hoped they would. But even that hope was better than nothing.

I stood there inside the gate, breathing hard and staring out at the street, wondering if I'd see a black SUV roll by. But the only vehicle in sight was the bus, which slowly lumbered away from the curb to start its trip back down to the city.

Maybe it had just been a careless driver after all. I hoped so—oh, how I hoped so.

"Come on, Gwen," I whispered to myself. "Get a grip."

It might have just been my imagination, but it seemed like the dull, brown, dried-up leaves in the trees above my head whispered back, even though I knew it was just the winter wind whipping through the branches.

Right?

* * *

Still nervous, I stuck my hands into my jacket pockets and hurried past the dorms and up the hill. If Mythos Academy had a black, beating heart, it would be the upper quad. Five main buildings ringed the area—English-history, math-science, the dining hall, the gym, and the library—all sitting at the edges of the quad, like the five points of a star.

Normally, in between and after the day's classes, students gathered on the quad to gossip, text on their cell phones, and see who was hooking up with whom. Not now, though. Since it was so cold, everyone was inside already, studying in the library, hanging out in their dorm rooms, or eating dinner in the dining hall. Usually, the emptiness of the quad wouldn't have bothered me, but tonight, it did.

The sun had already vanished for the day, letting the night's shadows ooze over everything, like black pools of blood. The trees on the quad were bare, except for a few stubborn leaves that rattled together like bones every time the wind touched them, and the swaying tangles of branches reminded me of skeletons strung together. Maybe I was still a little shaken up from almost getting run over. That had to be the reason I was thinking about things like blood, bones, and skeletons.

I shivered, tucked my head down into the collar of my jacket, and walked on.

The Library of Antiquities was the largest structure at the academy and took up a good chunk of the upper part of the quad, serving as the top point in the star of buildings. The library simply had the most of everything—the most floors, the most balconies, the most towers, the most parapets. All put together, the building reminded me of a sinister castle.

But the thing that creeped me out the most were the statues.

They could be found on all of the buildings at Mythos, but there were more of them on, around, and in the Library of Antiquities than on the rest of campus put together. Gryphons, gargoyles, Gorgons, dragons, a Minotaur, and other mythological creatures that I didn't even know the names for. The statues covered the library from the bottom balcony, which wrapped all the way around the building, to the top of the roof, with its towers and their swordlike points. And they weren't just simple stone figures. No, the statues all looked, well, *violent,* with big eyes, bigger teeth, and razor-sharp claws.

Maybe it was my Gypsy gift, but I always felt like the statues were watching me and tracking my steps with their open, angry eyes, just like the sphinxes at the front gate. That if I so much as brushed them with my fingertips, the cold monsters would somehow spring to life, leap out of their stone shells, and rip me to pieces.

It wasn't a good feeling.

I pulled my gaze away from the two gryphons positioned on either side of the gray stone steps and hurried into the building, through a short hallway, and past the open double doors that led into the library itself. Instead of walking down the wide, main aisle toward the study tables and offices, I turned and headed for a quiet area in the back.

My spot, as I'd come to think of it, wasn't much to

look at. Just another patch of floor in between the tall bookshelves that filled the library's many levels. Once, there had been a glass case here, one of hundreds that were scattered throughout the library and full of artifacts—weapons, jewelry, clothing, armor, and more—that had been used or worn over the years by various mythological gods, goddesses, heroes, villains, and monsters. Now, the case was gone, smashed to bits in my fight with Jasmine Ashton, although Vic, the sword who'd been inside it, was safe in my dorm room.

But the empty spot where the case had been wasn't the only thing of interest. I tilted my head, looking up at the person I'd come back here to see: Nike, the Greek goddess of victory.

Well, it wasn't really *her*, of course—just a thirty-foot-tall statue carved out of white marble. Statues of all the gods and goddesses from all the cultures of the world ringed the second-floor balcony. They were separated from each other by slender, fluted columns and stared down at the first floor of the library and all the students studying below. Every god and goddess you could think of was here. Norse ones, like Sol, Thor, and Freya. Greek ones, like Ares, Zeus, and Apollo. Egyptian ones, like Anubis, Ra, and Bastet. And tons more gods and goddesses who I'd never heard of before I'd come to Mythos.

The only one who wasn't represented in the circular pantheon was Loki, the Norse trickster and chaos god, and there was an empty spot where his statue would have been. Loki had done a lot of bad, bad stuff back in the day, like getting another god killed, trying to take over the world, and blah, blah, blah. They didn't build statues of you when you were the equivalent of a comic-book supervillain.

I'd met Nike a few weeks back, during the whole Jasmine situation. The goddess had appeared to me in the library and asked me to be her Champion, to be her hero here in the mortal realm, to help her fight Reapers of Chaos and other assorted bad guys.

The statue looked the same as Nike had the night she'd shown herself to me—hair falling past her shoulders; a long, flowing gown covering her strong, slender body; a crown of laurels resting on top of her head; feathery wings attached to her back. The goddess was the embodiment of victory, and she was cold, hard, fierce, and beautiful, all at the same time.

"Hi, Nike," I said in a low voice. "Hope you're having a good day up there on Mount Olympus or wherever you are. You know, eating lots of ambrosia, playing harps—things like that. Whatever goddesses do to have fun."

The statue didn't do or say anything, and I didn't really expect it to. Still, every time I came into the library, I stopped a moment to speak to the goddess. I didn't know if she actually heard me or not, but it made me feel a little better. Like maybe Nike was up there watching over me. Like maybe I was really worthy of the magic and trust she'd given to me.

Like maybe I really could do some good as her Champion.

I turned and headed for the center of the library. A long checkout counter split the main floor into two and separated one side of the enormous domed room from the other. A series of glassed-in offices lied behind the counter, while the open floor in front of it featured long tables for students to sit and study at. There was also a freestanding cart that sold coffee drinks, fruit smoothies, and sugary snacks. I breathed in, enjoying the warm, rich smell of the coffee mixing with the dry, slightly musty odor of the books.

The curved ceiling of the library arched high overhead, and it always seemed to me like the building was much taller than its seven floors, like the library just kept going up and up and up until it touched the clouds. Other students claimed there were amazing frescoes painted on the ceiling, ones that depicted various mythological battles and gleamed with gold, silver, and jewels, but I'd never been up to the top floor to look for myself. From down here, all I could see were shadows.

I'd barely put my messenger bag in a slot underneath the checkout counter when a door opened in the office complex behind me, and Nickamedes appeared.

"You're late, Gwendolyn," Nickamedes snapped, crossing his arms over his chest. "As usual."

Nickamedes was the head honcho at the Library of Antiquities. If you were just looking at him, you'd think that he was cute, handsome even, with his black hair and blue eyes. For a fortysomething-year-old guy, anyway. But then he opened his mouth, and you realized just how uptight, prissy, and snobby he really was. The library was Nickamedes's whole world, and he loved everything in here with an intense, devoted, detailed obsession. Well, everything but the students. Nickamedes didn't really like anyone touching his precious books and artifacts, not even for class assignments.

But the librarian was sort of stuck with me. Back when I'd first started going to the academy, Professor Metis had thought that working in the library would help me meet other kids and make friends. Not so much. Basically, I was Nickamedes's free slave labor—and there was nothing he enjoyed more than bossing me around.

Nickamedes had never really liked me and my smart mouth, but he'd come to actively hate me a few weeks ago. Jasmine Ashton had tried to kill me in the library, and, well, we'd torn up a lot of stuff during our struggle. Nickamedes despised anything that damaged his precious books. Seriously, the dude wouldn't even crack one of their spines. I'd done far worse than that. I'd pretty much trashed the entire first floor. In fact, I was still shelving books from where I'd shoved a case of them onto Jasmine to try to keep her from running me through with her sword.

"Well, Gwendolyn?" Nickamedes barked, tapping one of his long, pale fingers against his opposite elbow. "What do you have to say for yourself?"

I rolled my eyes. I couldn't exactly tell the librarian that I'd snuck off campus to go see my Grandma Frost, since that was against one of the Big Rules. But maybe I could sweeten up his sour mood. I rustled around in my bag, drew out the metal tin of cookies, popped off the top, and held it out to him. Surely the smell of chocolate would bring a smile to even his sharp, angular face.

"Cookie?" I asked in a hopeful voice.

Nickamedes's expression just darkened. "You brought unauthorized food into the library, Gwendolyn?"

I sighed, knowing that I was going to get the mother of all lectures now. *Ah, well,* I thought, biting into a cookie while Nickamedes glared at me. It had been worth a shot.

Chapter 5

After a five-minute, ear-blistering lecture from Nick-amedes about what food items could and could not be brought into the library, I got to work. Mostly, I sat behind the counter, checked out books, and looked up other ones in the computer system.

In addition to studying, the library was one of the main places on campus where students came to Hang Out and Be Seen. And that wasn't the only reason kids gathered here—lots of them liked to sneak off into the shadowy stacks to hook up. Occasionally, Nickamedes made me dust and clean the bookshelves, along with the glass artifact cases hidden back among the stacks. Every single time I'd find more used condoms than I did crumpled-up pieces of paper and lost pens. Yucko. I wouldn't want to do it in the library where anyone could walk by at any second, but at Mythos, it was considered some sort of thrill. Whatever.

Tonight, more kids than usual crowded into the library, since everyone was trying to get their homework done before taking off for the big weekend getaway. All the gossip was about the Winter Carnival. I heard more than a few excited comments as I moved through the library shelving books. Everyone seemed excited about making the trek over to one of the area ski resorts—and all the fun they had planned for when they got there.

"Did you hear? Samson Sorensen is throwing another *massive* party, just like he always does. There'll be at least five kegs there, maybe more."

"I know a guy who says he can get his hands on some primo pot."

"I wonder how many guys Morgan McDougall will sleep with during the weekend. Two? Twelve? Twenty?"

That last comment was made by Helena Paxton, an Amazon from my English lit class with sleek, caramel-colored hair and eyes. It was followed by a round of vicious snickers and sharp, sly looks over at Morgan, who was studying by herself at a table close to the checkout counter. With her black hair, hazel eyes, and curvy body, Morgan was one of the most gorgeous girls at Mythos—and she also happened to be the academy's most notorious slut. Seriously. Everyone knew that Morgan had been sleeping with Samson, even though he'd been dating her best friend, Jasmine, at the time.

"Well, my money's on twenty," Helena answered her own catty question. "Since Morgan likes to keep herself so busy."

More snickers filled the air. Morgan had her back to the group of Amazons, but I could see the anger and humiliation that flushed her face. She bent down over her books a little more, but she didn't give the other girls the satisfaction of turning around and glaring at them. Still,

I felt sorry for her. I knew what it was like to be an outcast.

Maybe it was almost getting run over by that SUV, but suddenly, I wasn't in the mood to be nice and quiet and blend into the background like I usually did, especially not when it came to the subject of Jasmine Ashton.

I stalked over to the table of giggling Amazons. "Hey," I snapped. "Why don't you guys shut up? Because you have no idea what Jasmine was really like. How mean and twisted and evil she really was. Trust me, Jasmine was not a sweet, innocent girl."

Jasmine might have been the prettiest, richest, and most popular girl in my second-year class, but the Valkyrie had also been a Reaper of Chaos. In fact, her whole family were Reapers, and Jasmine had faked her own death as part of a scheme to sacrifice Morgan to the evil god Loki.

Helena stopped laughing and looked at me. "And who are you?"

Another one of her friends spoke up. "The weird Gypsy girl. The one who found Jasmine after she was murdered."

The Amazon was right. I was the one who'd found Jasmine's body one night while I was working in the Library of Antiquities. I didn't know at the time that it was just an illusion, just a part of Jasmine's Valkyrie magic and her plan to make Morgan pay for screwing Samson behind her back.

I'd been stunned by Jasmine's supposed death and even more so by the other kids' blasé reaction to it.

Deaths weren't uncommon at Mythos, and practically all the students had had a family member or friend killed by Reapers, so Jasmine's supposed murder hadn't been as much of a shock to them as it had been to me. But I'd wanted to know exactly who'd killed Jasmine and why, so I'd started investigating her death with my psychometry magic. Of course, I'd figured out the truth too late, and Jasmine had almost sacrificed me, along with Morgan, to Loki. She would have, if Logan hadn't killed her first.

Professor Metis and the other Powers That Were at the academy had tried to keep the whole Jasmine thing quiet, but Metis had told me that the Valkyrie's family had somehow found out about my involvement in her death—and they blamed me for it.

Their logic seemed all twisted and wrong to me, since I hadn't actually, you know, *killed* Jasmine myself, but it was one of the reasons why I'd started weapons training with Logan and the other Spartans. So I could defend myself in case the Ashtons sent a Nemean prowler or some other nasty mythological monster after me—or perhaps even an SUV.

It wasn't out of the realm of possibility to think that Jasmine's family or one of their Reaper friends might have tried to run me down with a car instead of sending another killer kitty-cat prowler after me. I was willing to bet the Ashtons wouldn't be too concerned with how my murder actually happened.

The table of Amazons turned their full attention to me, their eyes sharp and narrow in their pretty faces. Their calculating looks reminded me of the sphinxes at the front gate. Then again, mean girls were monsters in their own way.

After a few seconds, Helena let out another laugh. "Whatever. We weren't talking to you, Gypsy, so why don't you run along and shelve some more books before Nickamedes comes out of his office and yells at you? No, wait. On the other hand, don't. I'd love to watch him scream at you again. Working in the library. That's so pathetic, just like your cheap clothes."

"My clothes aren't cheap," I growled, even though I knew I was fighting a losing battle the second the words came out of my mouth.

According to my Grandma Frost, we had plenty of money, but she and my mom had decided not to overindulge me, like the other warrior parents did to their kids. Since Reapers, and the death they brought with them, were a constant threat, almost all the parents spoiled their children rotten, giving them the finest things money could buy, just in case they—or their kids—died before their time. Which is why all the Amazons in front of me sported designer clothes, shoes, and purses, along with expensive jewelry.

Helena gave me a pitying look. "Oh, honey, no-name jeans and hoodies are the very definition of cheap. It's so sad you don't know that. Now, why don't you run along? The big girls are talking."

Her putdown delivered, Helena rolled her eyes and turned to her friends. And just like that, the other girls went back to their gossiping, ignoring me despite the fact that I was standing right in front of them. This time, my cheeks were the ones that flushed with anger, but there was nothing I could do but plod back over to the checkout counter.

I walked by Morgan's table, and my steps slowed as I studied the other girl. Sometimes I wondered exactly what Morgan remembered of that night in the library when Jasmine had tried to sacrifice her to Loki. Jasmine had dripped Morgan's blood into a powerful artifact called the Bowl of Tears, which had basically turned Morgan into a zombie while I'd fought the evil Valkyrie. Still, I thought Morgan knew something about what had really happened. She never said anything to me, but we had gym class together, and every once in a while I'd catch her staring at me, almost like she wanted to ask me something. But she always bit her lip and looked away.

Morgan saw me watching her. For a moment she looked at me, her eyes dark, haunted, and sad. Then she pressed her lips together and stared fixedly down at her book once more. Behind her, the Amazons let out another round of snickers, and Morgan's face started to burn again.

I couldn't help but feel sorry for her. Yeah, she'd screwed her best friend's boyfriend, but now she was all alone. I'd heard through the rumor mill that Morgan had broken up with Samson two weeks ago, and her old Valkyrie friends weren't speaking to her. Thanks to Daphne, the other Valkyries had discovered how Morgan and Jasmine had always made fun of them behind their backs. Kind of hard to be friends with someone who mocked you all the time.

Eventually, the Amazons quit laughing and got back

to their studying. Bits and pieces of other conversations drifted over to me from the various tables, but I ignored the whispers. I was still too busy thinking about the SUV that had almost pancaked me this afternoon. Had it been an accident? Or deliberate? Had Jasmine's parents decided to come after me after all? Or would the Ashtons send some other Reaper to kill me? I didn't know, and I had no way of finding out.

The worrying was driving me crazy.

Around seven o'clock, Daphne came into the library, along with her boyfriend, band geek Carson Callahan. I waved at them, but Nickamedes gave me such a venomous look that I didn't leave the counter to go talk to them, even though I really, really wanted to tell Daphne about the SUV. The Valkyrie was supposed to come over to my dorm room after my shift tonight anyway, so I'd just wait to tell her then. It wasn't the kind of thing I wanted to casually text her about.

Finally, at around eight thirty, the library started to clear out for the night. I packed up my own books, hoping that Nickamedes would let me leave early. But, being the giant pain in my ass that he was, the librarian pushed another cart of books over to me.

"I have a few more e-mails to send out before I close down the library," Nickamedes said. "I trust that you can shelve these books in the meantime, Gwendolyn, and not make any trouble while you're at it."

"Cross my heart." I made an exaggerated *X* over my chest. "No trouble at all."

The librarian gave me another cold, suspicious glare

before disappearing into the glass office complex. I stuck out my tongue at his retreating back. Yeah, I knew he was still pissed I'd wrecked the library, but that had been *weeks* ago, and I'd helped him clean up the damage. Nickamedes *so* needed to get over it. It wasn't like I'd decided to destroy his precious library on purpose— I'd just been trying to keep Jasmine from killing me. It wasn't my fault we'd knocked over thousands of books in the process.

I grabbed the old, rickety cart and pushed it into the stacks, having to fight against the loose wheel that always pulled to the right. I shelved books for the next twenty minutes, sliding all the thick volumes back into their proper places. Despite my psychometry, I didn't get much of a vibe off the books, since so many kids had thumbed through them over the years. They were just history books, used for research purposes and class assignments. Nobody had any other real interest in them. Usually, I didn't get much of a feeling off stuff that people used every day or items that had a specific purpose or function, like dishes, tables, or chairs.

I only got the whammies—the big, vivid, high-def flashes of images and feelings—when I touched an object that someone had a deep, personal attachment to, like a treasured family heirloom ring or a photo of the kid stepbrother who someone secretly despised.

When I'd first come to Mythos, I'd hated working in the library because, well, I'd hated pretty much everything about the academy. Especially the fact that I'd been taken out of my old school and away from all my old friends with no real explanation. But now I kind of liked roaming through the stacks—mainly because of all the cool artifacts on display.

It wasn't called the Library of Antiquities for nothing. Hundreds of glass cases could be found throughout the various floors of the library, each one containing an item that had once belonged to someone or something important in the mythological world. Like the shield that Achilles had used during the Trojan War, or the tattered shoes that Pysche had worn as she wandered the world in search of her husband, Eros, the Greek god of love. I peered into all the cases I passed, taking a minute to read the silver plaques stuck on the fronts or the small white cards tucked inside that told me what the objects were, who had used them, and what magic they might have.

I'd just finished reading about the loom Arachne had used to test her weaving skills against those of the Greek goddess Athena when something rustled in the next aisle over, and a flash of movement caught my eye.

"Hello?" I said, peering in that direction. "Is someone there?"

Yeah, calling out was probably the wrong thing to do, but I didn't want to step around the far end of the aisle and trip over a couple of kids doing the nasty. I'd done that twice last week, which had been two times too many.

"Hellooo," I said, pushing the cart toward the end of the aisle.

I wiggled the wheels back and forth, making them *squeak-squeak-squeak* even more than usual. Hopefully, if there were some kids going at it, they would hear the noise and have the good sense to pull their clothes back up—or down—where they belonged.

I pushed the cart past the end of the aisle and stepped out into the main library space. "The library's closing in a few minutes—"

An arrow zipped through the air and thunked into the bookcase beside my head.

It quivered there, wobbling back and forth ever so slightly, just like the ones I'd shot into the target in the gym this morning. A foot closer, and it would have drilled straight into my skull.

That's when my brain caught up with my eyes, and I realized that, you know, someone was actually *shooting at me.*

I immediately dropped to my knees and crabbed backward among the stacks, dragging the metal cart along with me and wincing at all the freaking noise it made. I didn't know if I was out of the archer's line of sight or not, but surely, he couldn't shoot at me through the cart—could he? Were there magical bows and arrows that could do that sort of thing?

Shit, shit, shit! Why did this always happen to me? You'd think the library would be one of the safest, most boring places at Mythos instead of one of the deadliest. This was the second time someone had tried to kill me in here. I *so* needed to work somewhere else on campus.

I huddled in the stacks, my back against a bookshelf, knees tucked into my chest, and the cart positioned in front of me. My breath puffed out of my mouth in sharp, short, ragged gasps. It took me several seconds and some deep, deep gulps of air before I was able to notice anything but the crazy *thump-thump-thump* of my heart and the blood roaring in my ears. I forced myself to focus, to listen, and to keep the panic to a minimum. You know, so I could maybe *hear* whether or not the mysterious archer was nocking another arrow in his bow and coming my way with it.

Silence—I heard nothing but absolute, still, dead freaking silence.

I stayed where I was. The seconds ticked by, going past one minute, then two, but I still didn't hear anything. Whoever the archer was, I hoped he was long gone by now, but I wasn't going to be stupid enough to just go about my business, like everything was normal. I might not be a highly trained warrior like all the other kids, but even I knew that assuming the bad guy was gone would be a quick, dumb way to die.

As quietly as I could, I shoved the metal cart away and crawled to the opposite end of the aisle, keeping close to the shelves and the floor. I paused there and listened some more. When I didn't hear anything, I slowly stuck my head around the corner.

Empty—the library was completely empty.

Nobody was studying at the tables. Nobody was packing up their stuff. Nobody was walking toward the double doors with a backpack slung over their shoulder. Even Mrs. Raven, the woman who manned the coffee cart, had already left for the night.

I bit my lip. Just because I didn't see anyone didn't mean the library was empty. That arrow had come from somewhere. Someone had shot it at me, and I had no way of knowing whether or not he was still in here—

A hand clamped down on my shoulder. I shrieked and threw myself to the left, banging my shoulder on the opposite bookshelf. I grabbed one of the thick books, whipped back my arm, and turned around on my knees, ready to throw the heavy volume at whomever was behind me, then surge to my feet and run like crazy.

Nickamedes stood in the middle of the aisle, his hands on his hips.

"Gwendolyn?" The librarian frowned. "Are you okay?"

I scrambled to my feet, for once extremely grateful to see him. So much so that I would have hugged him if it wouldn't have been just too weird. Nickamedes opened his mouth to say something else, but I held up my hand.

"Shh!" I hissed.

Nickamedes's confused frown turned into a glacial glare at my shushing, but I ignored him and concentrated. Once again, I didn't hear anything. No rustles, no whispers of clothing, no footsteps hurrying away.

"I ask again. Are you okay?" Nickamedes said in a snide tone. "Or are you having some sort of . . . episode?"

"No, no, I'm not okay," I said, moving past him and stalking to the end of the aisle. "I'm not okay because of that—"

I rounded the corner and pointed at the end of the bookshelf, but my words died on my lips.

The arrow was gone—vanished, like it had never even been there to start with.

"Gwendolyn? Is something the matter?" Nickamedes stepped out from the stacks behind me.

My mouth opened, closed, and opened again, but no words came out. *No, I'm not okay,* I wanted to say. *Someone just tried to put an arrow through my skull.*

But I couldn't tell him that. Not without proof. Nickamedes hated me. He'd never believe someone had just taken a shot at me in the library. And even if he did, well, he might not care all that much.

I clamped my lips together and stood there, anger, embarrassment, and fear making my cheeks burn.

Nickamedes raised his black eyebrows in a way that clearly said he thought I'd lost what little sense I had. "Well, I'm done with my e-mails. Go get your things together, and I'll turn off the lights and lock up for the night."

He walked back to his office, but I stayed where I was, feeling crazy, scared, and frustrated, all at the same time. I blew out a breath and turned back to the bookshelf, as if the arrow would somehow magically reappear. It didn't, of course, but I realized that maybe I hadn't been imagining things after all.

Because there was a nick in the wood that hadn't been there before.

The deep, ugly, starlike shape looked like it had grooved maybe four inches into the dark, glossy wood. Whoever had shot the arrow must have yanked it out while I'd been looking around the far side of the bookshelf. That was the only explanation I could come up with. But if that was the case, why hadn't he fired another arrow at me when I'd had my back turned? Had the archer heard Nickamedes moving around in his office and had been scared off? If so, I was going to have to start being a lot nicer to the uptight librarian—a whole lot nicer.

But right now I wanted answers, and I knew of one way to maybe get them. My hand trembling, I brought my fingers up to the groove. I hesitated a second, then pressed them to the splintered wood, knowing that my psychometry would kick in and show me exactly what had happened.

THUNK!

An image of the arrow slamming into the bookcase filled my mind—but nothing else. No clue as to who had shot it or why. Disappointing but not surprising. I'd need the actual arrow itself for that or the bow that it had been launched from. Those were the tools the archer had touched, the things he'd used when he'd tried to kill me. The bookshelf was just where the arrow had landed. That's why there weren't any emotions attached to it—just the sudden violence of the arrow slamming into the thick wood.

Frustrated, I dropped my hand.

"Gwendolyn!" Nickamedes called out to me from one of the doors in the glass office complex. "You either come get your bag right this second or leave it here for the night!"

There was nothing else I could do—not tonight, not without the bow, the arrow, or some other sort of proof—so I turned away from the splintered bookshelf and headed over to the checkout counter.

I grabbed my messenger bag and slung it over my

shoulder, but I wasn't really thinking about what I was doing. Instead, I was replaying the day's events in my head. First, the SUV, and now the arrow in the bookcase. It all added up to only one conclusion.

Someone was trying to kill me. But it wasn't in the gym this time, and it wasn't just for practice.

No—this time, it was for real.

Chapter 6

"Someone's trying to kill you? Really?" Daphne asked a half an hour later.

I shrugged. "Kill, maim, or injure. Isn't it all the same thing to Reapers?"

We were in my dorm room, eating the chocolate-strawberry cookies Grandma Frost had baked earlier today. Well, Daphne was eating the cookies. I didn't have an appetite for them. Knots still twisted and tangled together in my stomach from almost getting skewered in the library.

After Nickamedes had locked the front doors, I'd run all the way from the Library of Antiquities on the upper quad down to Styx Hall, where my dorm room was. With every step, I'd expected an arrow to zoom out of the shadows and rip through my heart.

But nothing had happened.

I'd made it to my dorm in one piece, used my student ID card to get inside, and had gone straight up to my room, which was stuck in a separate turret on the third floor. The room featured all your standard dorm furniture—a bed, a desk, some bookshelves, a TV, a small fridge—although I'd added my own personal touches. A couple of framed photos of my mom stood on my desk, along with a small statue of Nike. Vic, who was currently sleeping in his scabbard, hung on the wall above the desk, right next to my posters of Wonder Woman, Karma Girl, and The Killers.

Normally, I considered my dorm room a safe haven from the craziness that was Mythos Academy. Not tonight, though. I huddled on my knees on the floor, my purple and gray plaid comforter wrapped around me, and peered through the bottom of one of the picture windows set into the wall. There didn't *seem* to be anyone lurking on the dorm's lawn, but then again, it was pitch-black outside now.

"Why do you think it's a Reaper who tried to kill you?" Daphne asked.

"Who else could it be? Besides, Professor Metis told me that Jasmine's family might come after me because I was involved in her death."

"True," Daphne agreed. "You did spectacularly piss off her family. Not to mention Reapers in general."

The Valkyrie lounged on my bed, eating a cookie with one hand while she typed on her laptop with the other. The motion made the charms on the silver bracelet around her right wrist jangle together. Carson had bought the bracelet for Daphne weeks ago, back when he was trying to work up the courage to ask out the Valkyrie. Now, it was one of her most prized possessions.

"Reapers don't like it when one of their own dies," Daphne added. "Payback is, like, their life. Are you going to tell Professor Metis what happened?"

Metis was my myth-history professor, and she'd sort of become my mentor. She'd also been my mom's best friend, back when they'd both gone to Mythos. The professor had told me that my mom had saved her life more times than she could count and that she owed it to my mom to look out for me while I was here.

My eyes flicked to my desk, and I crawled over to it and grabbed a framed photo off the top. Two girls grinned up at me from underneath the glass, their arms around each other. My mom and Professor Metis, back when they'd been about my age.

Not too long ago, Metis had given me this photo of them as teenagers. Every time I slipped the picture out from behind the glass and ran my fingers over the slick paper, I felt all the love that my mom and Metis had had for each other. They'd been more like sisters than friends. Knowing someone else had cared about my mom as much as I did made me feel a little less alone and made my grief and guilt over her death a little easier to bear.

"What am I going to tell Metis?" I said, putting the photo back on the desk. "That somebody tried to run me over near my grandma's house and then took a shot at me in the library? I don't have any proof that either one actually happened. I didn't get a look at the license plate on the car, and I don't have the arrow. She might just think I was being paranoid."

"I don't think so," Daphne said, drumming her fingers on top of her keyboard and making pink sparks flicker in the air. "Metis is more understanding than most of the profs are. I think she'd believe you."

I shrugged. "Maybe, maybe not. You should have seen the look that Nickamedes gave me—like I'd just escaped from Ashland Asylum or something. Who knows? Maybe I have."

I tried to smile at my own stupid joke, but I couldn't quite make my lips turn up all the way. Knowing that someone was trying to kill me didn't put me in a smiling mood.

Daphne shook her head, her blond hair spilling over her shoulders. "I don't think you're crazy. If you think there's a Reaper after you, then there probably is. They pretty much live to kill us, you know, just like we do them."

"Great. Way to make me feel better."

Daphne rolled her black eyes. "Oh, suck it up, Gwen. It's not the end of the world. We're all here learning how to fight Reapers. You're just getting a crash course in it, that's all. Some of the kids would actually be jealous of you. The Spartans certainly would. Sometimes I think Logan and his friends would go off hunting Reapers if Coach Ajax and the other profs would let them."

In addition to being the best fighters at Mythos, the Spartans also had a reputation for being the most bloodthirsty. They actually liked to be in the thick of battle and killing things—it was part of their DNA or something. I guess that's just what happened when you could pick up normal, everyday objects—the cookies

Daphne was noshing on, the stapler on my desk, the small replica of Nike next to it—and automatically know how to kill people with them. Logan, Kenzie, and Oliver could grab any one of those things, kill me with it, and not think twice doing it. Seriously. That's the kind of freaky stuff they instinctively knew how to do.

"Well, it's a course I'm going to flunk," I groused. "Maybe I'll just hide up here in my room until Christmas break. Sooner or later, the Reaper will have to lose interest in me."

"Reapers *never* lose interest. Once you're on their hit list, they won't stop coming until you're dead—or they are." Daphne shook her head again. "And you can't stay here, especially not this weekend. Everyone's going to the Winter Carnival, even the professors and the academy staff. You'd be on campus all by yourself. If there *is* a Reaper out there gunning for you, you'd just give him an early Christmas present. You know what a total joke the dorm security is."

I sighed. "So what do you think I should do?"

"Talk to Metis," Daphne said. "Tell her what's going on and ask her if she's heard anything about Jasmine's family. If they're still in hiding or if the Pantheon has caught up to them yet and has thrown them in prison where they belong."

I nodded my head, and we were silent for a few moments.

"You know, it's just too bad that I didn't have a bow and arrow tonight," I finally groused. "I could have thought of you and defended myself against the Reaper."

"What do you mean?"

I told the Valkyrie how I'd done better during archery practice this morning just by thinking of her, by calling up the memories I had of her at the tournaments she'd won.

"Really? That's cool." Daphne tapped her fingers against her lips, deep in thought. "I wonder if you could do that with other things, too."

"What do you mean?"

She gestured at her bulging book bag on the floor. "I've been reading up on various magical theories and powers while I wait for my own magic to quicken. There are lots of stories about folks tapping into other people's powers. Most of them have some kind of mental magic, like you do. Telepathy or something that lets them see into other people's minds. So if you can call up the memories of my archery tournaments, who's to say you couldn't do that with other things? Or even with other people?"

I shrugged. "I don't know. I never thought of my magic like that before. Usually I just get flashes off objects. I don't actually *do* anything with the memories I see."

"Well, maybe you should try to, to see if it works," Daphne said. "Either way you might as well start packing your bags for the carnival. Because I'm not leaving you here by yourself, not with a Reaper lurking around. You're going to the carnival, even if I have to drag you kicking and screaming onto the bus myself."

Daphne's pretty features took on a determined, stubborn look, and more pink sparks of magic flickered in the air around her. We might have only been friends for a few weeks now, but I knew she meant what she said. And with her Valkyrie strength, she'd have no problem twisting my arm—literally—to get me to do exactly what she wanted.

"All right, all right," I groused again. "I'll talk to Metis tomorrow, and I'll go to the stupid Winter Carnival with you. Just don't expect me to like it."

Daphne grinned, and then stuffed another cookie into her mouth.

I stuck to my regular schedule the next day, Thursday; weapons training, bright and early, with Logan, Kenzie, and Oliver; breakfast in the dining hall with Daphne; then a full day of classes. I eyed all the other students, wondering which one of them might really be a Reaper, but no one paid me any more attention than usual. Which is to say, nobody noticed me at all. I wasn't exactly one of the popular kids, and I certainly wasn't pretty enough for the guys to check me out that way. Most people—like Helena Paxton and her snotty friends in the library last night—just thought of me as Gwen Frost, that weird Gypsy girl.

Finally, sixth period rolled around, and I slid into my seat in Professor Metis's myth-history class. Carson's desk was right in front of mine, and he turned around to talk to me. Carson was Daphne's boyfriend, but he was my friend, too, since I'd helped hook them up in the first place. He was just an all-around nice, sweet guy with a tall, lanky, six-foot frame and dusky brown hair and skin. He also happened to be a total band geek, and was the drum major for the Mythos Academy Marching Band, even though he was only seventeen and a second-year student, like me. Carson was a Celt, and had a magical talent for music, like some kind of warrior bard, although I'd never really asked him about it, what kind of power he had, or what he could do with it.

"Are you excited about the Winter Carnival?" Carson asked, pushing his black glasses up his nose and peering at me with his dark brown eyes. "This will be your first one, right, Gwen?"

"Yeah," I muttered. "And I'm just thrilled to death about it."

Carson frowned, picking up on my sour mood, but before he could say anything else, the bell rang, signaling the start of class. A few seconds later Professor Metis stepped into the room and closed the door behind her. Metis was of Greek descent, like so many of the kids and profs at Mythos. She was a short woman with a stocky body, bronze skin, and black hair that was always pulled back into a high, tight bun. Today she wore a heavy fisherman's sweater that was the same color green as her eyes behind her silver glasses.

"Good afternoon, everyone. Please open your books to page 251," Metis said. "Today we're going to focus on some of the creatures that aided Loki during the Chaos War, and some species that the Reapers still use today."

I winced. Monster talk, in other words. Definitely *not*

my favorite subject. Reapers were bad enough, but they were just people in the end. Okay, okay, people with magic, weapons, and seriously bad attitudes, but still, just people. It was the monsters—the mythological nightmares the Reapers trained to do their evil biddings—that really creeped me out. I'd been face-to-face with a Nemean prowler, and I'd seen exactly how big, long, and sharp the killer kitty-cat's teeth and claws were. It was like a black panther on steroids. Prowler super-, superdangerous. Gwen not so much. That was all I really needed to know.

But there was no getting out of class, so I cracked open my myth-history book to the appropriate page.

"Now," Professor Metis began, "you all know about the Reapers of Chaos, those who serve the evil god Loki, and how they and Loki tried to enslave everyone centuries ago. Their actions resulted in the long, bloody Chaos War, which had almost destroyed the entire world. Eventually, the members of Pantheon banded together to battle Loki and his Reapers. Nike, the Greek goddess of victory, defeated Loki in single combat, and she and the other gods trapped him in a magical, mythological prison far removed from the mortal realm."

Metis looked at first one student, then another, making sure we were all paying attention. "We've also talked about how the Reapers are trying to free Loki, so the god can plunge the world into a second Chaos War. . . ."

As the professor started her lecture, I once again thought about Jasmine Ashton and how she'd been a Reaper, along with the rest of her family. Before she'd died, Jasmine had told me there were other Reapers at the academy—something that made my stomach quiver with dread even now. It was bad enough to know Reapers existed in the first place. It was another scarier thing to realize you went to class with them and had no idea who they were—or when they might decide to try and kill you.

Reapers were the reason why all the kids were at Mythos to start with. The students were the descendants of all the ancient warriors who'd helped defeat Loki the first time around, and they were here in case the god ever got free again. All of the Mythos students had been training since birth to learn how to use whatever skills or magic they had, so they could fight Reapers. Of course, I wasn't a warrior like the other kids—not exactly—but I had my own magic: my psychometry, given to me by Nike herself.

I'd recently learned that all my ancestors had served Nike in some way, including my Grandma Frost and my mom, Grace. As a result, the goddess had gifted us with magic, which is what makes us Gypsies. My grandma had told me there were other Gypsies out there, other people with magic from the gods, but I'd never met any of them. I wasn't so sure I wanted to either, since Grandma Frost had told me that not all Gypsies were good—some were just as evil as the gods they served.

Now, I was Nike's Champion, picked by the goddess herself, and trying to carry on my family's tradition, with no real clue how I was supposed to keep Bad, Bad Things from happening to me or anyone else.

"... the more you know about the creatures that the Reapers use, the better you'll be able to protect yourself and your loved ones from them," Metis finished the opening part of her lecture.

I shook off my troubling thoughts and focused on Metis's words. For the next half hour, the professor talked about monsters—lots and lots of freaking monsters. Wyverns, basilisks, dragons, yetis, even gigantic birds named Black rocs. She called them all "creatures," like she was being politically correct or something, but really, they were monsters. Anything that had fangs longer than my fingers and that could breathe fire was *definitely* a monster.

"And on the next page we have one of the more interesting creatures—the Fenrir wolf," Metis said.

Books rustled as everyone flipped over to the next page, which featured a pen-and-ink drawing of the largest wolf I'd ever seen. Everything about it was just *big*—big eyes; big paws; big tail; and, of course, big, big teeth and claws. All the better to eat me with. Because what kind of monster would it be if it couldn't rip you to pieces and chew on your bones?

"These wolves are the descendants of Fenrir, the very first and most powerful wolf who fought alongside the members of the Pantheon during the Chaos War," Metis said. "Over the years, the Reapers have managed to trap most of the wolves, but a few of them can still be found in the wild today, including right here in the North Carolina mountains."

For a moment the drawing flickered on the page, and

the pen-and-ink wolf turned its head until it was staring straight at me. The black ink oozed down, then back up, and I realized the monster was smiling—and showing me each and every one of its needle-sharp teeth.

I shivered and looked away. Sometimes my Gypsy magic went a little haywire and made me see and feel things that weren't really there, even when I wasn't touching an object. Or maybe it was just my own warped imagination working overtime today. Either way, it was all I could do to keep from closing the book and throwing it across the room.

"What you need to understand is that these creatures didn't start out evil," Metis said, her soft green gaze going from one student's face to another. "The Reapers twisted them over the centuries, caged and tortured them until they turned into something else completely."

"Even the Nemean prowlers?" Carson asked from in front of me.

"Even the prowlers," Metis answered. "Although, keep in mind that while the Reapers have trained the creatures to kill, they still have free will in the end, just like we all do. There have been rare instances where prowlers, wolves, and other creatures have turned against the Reapers. Ultimately, it's up to the creatures as to whom they serve and what they do. Even the gods themselves can't force a person or creature to do something. We all have free will—we all make our own choices about the kinds of people we are and how we choose to live our lives."

Free will? Whatever. The Fenrir wolf grinning in my

book looked plenty evil to me, just like all the other monsters did. I didn't care if it had free will or not.

Metis asked us to turn the page and started talking about the next mythological nightmare. Monsters might not be my favorite topic, but I listened to every word the professor said, and took pages of notes. When I'd first come to the academy, I'd hated myth-history, but now it was my favorite class. At the beginning of the semester I didn't think that I had any connection to the warrior kids here. But now I knew that I did—and I wanted to be like them.

Maybe it was because my mom had been a police detective and had spent her life helping people before she'd died. Maybe it was because she and my Grandma Frost had both been Nike's Champions before me. Or maybe it was just everything I'd seen and heard since coming to Mythos. But I wanted to be a real warrior like the other students were. I wanted to be as fierce, strong, and brave as they were, as my mom and grandma had been. I wanted to keep the world and everyone in it safe from Reapers and Loki and monsters.

I wanted to do Big Things with my Gypsy gift, even if I didn't exactly know what those Big Things were just yet—or how I was even going to do them in the first place.

Class flew by, and it seemed like we'd only been talking a few minutes when the final bell of the day rang. I blinked and looked up from my notebook. All around me the other kids got to their feet, grabbed their books, and raced toward the door.

Carson threw his backpack over his shoulder and turned to look at me. "I guess I'll see you tomorrow out on the quad, when we all leave to go to the carnival."

"Yep," I said. "Bright and early in the freezing cold."

The band geek gave me a shy smile and left the room.

I took my sweet time stuffing my things into my messenger bag, so that everyone else had left by the time I was done, leaving me alone with Metis. I walked over to the podium where the professor was sliding her own papers into a battered leather briefcase. She looked up at the squeak of my sneakers on the floor.

"Hello, Gwen." Metis smiled at me. "How are you and Vic today?"

Like the other kids, I usually carried my own personal weapon with me during the day. It was just easier than having to walk all the way back to my dorm to get it before my fifth-period gym class. In my case, that weapon was Vic. The hilt of the silver sword stuck out of the top of my messenger bag. Vic's eye was closed, and I knew he was sleeping. Vic had told me more than once that he found the sound of Metis's soft voice quite soothing.

The professor knew all about Vic and the fact that the sword could talk because she was a Champion just like me. Metis served Athena, the Greek goddess of wisdom. She'd even showed me the weapon Athena had given her—a thick staff made out of a polished golden wood. All the Champions—good and bad—received a weapon from their respective god or goddess, and all of them were inscribed with some sort of saying relevant to that god or goddess. Only a Champion could read the words on her own weapon, though. Metis had once told me that the phrase "In wisdom, there is great strength" was carved into her staff, while Vic had his own saying etched into his blade—"Victory always."

"We're doing fine," I said.

"And how is your training with Logan going?"

"Um, good. Just . . . good."

"Good" if you considered the fact that I still couldn't survive more than a minute sparring with Logan. The Spartan had killed me fifteen times this morning before he'd finally taken pity on me and let me practice archery with Kenzie and Oliver. That, at least, I was getting a little better at. All I had to do was think of Daphne, and I could put the arrow into the center of the target every single time. I wondered if I could use my psychometry magic like that in other ways, as Daphne had suggested. I hadn't tried it yet, though. I'd been a little distracted by almost getting killed twice yesterday.

"Can I help you, Gwen?" Metis asked. "Is there something on your mind?"

I opened my mouth to tell Metis about the SUV that had almost run me over and the fact that someone had shot an arrow at me in the Library of Antiquities last night—but nothing came out.

I don't know why. I wanted to tell her what had happened. I *should* tell her. Metis was smart. She'd know what to do. She'd know how to help me.

But why can't you help yourself? a snide little voice

whispered in the back of my mind. *You're Nike's Champion. You should be able to take care of yourself. Everyone else around here can.*

It was true. Daphne had her Valkyrie strength and her awesome archery skills, and her magic would probably quicken and kick in any day now, giving her even more power, whatever it turned out to be. Logan, Kenzie, and Oliver had their mad Spartan weapons skills, and could kill Reapers with anything they picked up, no matter how harmless it actually was. Even Carson was better with a sword than I was, and he was the nicest, sweetest, gentlest guy at the academy.

The longer I was at Mythos, the more I wanted to be like them. Yeah, part of it was about fitting in and being something other than Gwen Frost, that freaky Gypsy girl. Part of it was also about being able to take care of myself, to defend myself against Reapers and monsters. But mostly I wanted to be the warrior that Nike thought I could be, the Champion that the goddess had chosen. I wanted to make my mom and my grandma and all the other Frost women who'd come before me proud.

"Gwen?" Metis asked again. "Are you okay?"

In that moment I made my decision. Yeah, maybe it was a little stupid, but I was going to keep my mouth shut about yesterday. I couldn't run to Metis for help every single time I had a problem. If there was a Reaper after me, then I was going to figure out who it was and take care of him myself. I had a talking sword, I had some fighting skills, and most important, I had my Gypsy gift.

I'd figure the rest of it out as I went along, just like I always did.

I gave her my very best I'm-not-up-to-anything smile. "I'm fine. I just wanted to tell you how excited I am about the Winter Carnival."

Metis frowned, like she didn't really believe that was all I wanted to say. I gave the professor another bright smile and hurried out of the room before she could ask me any more questions.

Chapter 7

Early the next morning, Friday, I stood out on the main upper quad, shivering in the cold along with the other students. Classes had been canceled for the day, and the professors were busy herding everyone toward the buses, which had been pulled into the parking lot behind the gym. The buses would haul us a few mountains over to Powder, the ski resort where the Winter Carnival was being held. Then the weekend fun would begin. Yippee-skippee.

I pulled my purple plaid coat tighter around me and shifted on my feet, trying to stay warm. Next to me, Daphne talked to Carson about the slopes they should hit once they got to the resort. The Valkyrie had on a pink designer snowsuit and a matching toboggan with a poofy white ball dangling off the end of it. That hat would have looked ridiculous on me, but it made Daphne seem quirky and cute. And of course everything from her outfit to her purse to her lip gloss went perfectly with the expensive luggage at her feet. Sometimes

I thought Daphne took the matchy-match look a little too far.

I'd stuffed my clothes for the weekend into an old gray duffel bag I'd dug out from the back of my closet. Jeans, hoodies, graphic T-shirts, sweaters. My wardrobe was way more downscale than Daphne's designer duds. I'd also brought along some of my favorite comic books, a stash of sugary snacks, and Vic—just in case the mystery Reaper tried to kill me again and I needed a sword before the weekend was through.

I wasn't the only kid with a weapon. Most everyone had a sword or a dagger or two stuffed into their luggage. I could tell by the way the metal *clink-clink-clink*ed together as the bags were loaded onto the bus. At Mythos, weapons were just another kind of accessory—a status symbol that let everyone else know what kind of warrior you were, what kind of magic you had, and how powerful you were.

Finally, we shuffled to the front of the line and boarded the bus. It wasn't your ordinary school bus. Oh, no. Nothing but the best would do for the rich kids at the academy. The bus was something a rock star would have, with plush, reclining seats and a flat-screen TV mounted above every third row. There was even a minibar in the very back, next to the restroom, although the profs onboard were making sure nobody was drinking anything stronger than soda—for now. I doubted the alcohol ban would last long, though, since I'd heard so many kids in the library talk about all the wild parties they planned to have before the weekend was over.

Daphne and Carson snagged two spots about halfway back on the bus, in one of the sections where four seats faced one another. They shared a quick kiss before Daphne pulled a map of the ski resort out of her over-size purse. The two of them bent their heads together and continued their previous discussion about which slopes they wanted to try out first.

I dropped into one of the seats facing them. We hadn't even left yet and I already felt like a third wheel. I sighed. I liked Daphne and Carson together—I really did. They made a cute couple, and they were good for each other. Daphne brought Carson out of his shell, while the band geek calmed the Valkyrie's quick temper. But seeing them together just reminded me of the fact that I didn't have a boyfriend—just a mad, mad crush on a guy who didn't like me back.

As if to prove my theory, Logan stepped onto the bus. The Spartan looked as scrumptious as ever in his black leather jacket, blue sweater, and faded jeans. For a moment I sat up straighter, hoping that maybe, just maybe, he'd see me, walk to the back, and take the seat next to mine. Yeah, I was really that pathetic.

Savannah boarded the bus right behind him, dashing my small, silly hope. Logan stuffed the Amazon's bag into one of the overhead compartments, and then the two of them sat down together. I had a perfect view of them from my seat. Great. Just great.

I got up, opened the bin where I'd stashed my own stuff, and pulled a stack of comic books and the tin with the last of Grandma Frost's chocolate-strawberry cook-ies out of my duffel bag. Then I plopped back down into my seat and resigned myself to reading about Wonder Woman, Batman, and other superheroes for the next two hours. Too bad the cookies wouldn't last nearly that long.

The first hour of the trip passed quietly, since everyone was still trying to wake up and recover from being dragged out of bed so early. By the start of the second hour, the conversation picked up, the noise level got louder, and more and more people started going to the bar in the back of the bus to get a drink or a snack. I moved over to the seat by the window, so my fingers wouldn't accidentally brush up against someone else's. I didn't want to flash on a guy walking by and see just how totally wasted he planned on getting this weekend.

I'd read about half of my comic books when Oliver dropped into the empty seat beside me.

"Hey, there, Gypsy girl," Oliver said, grinning.

I eyed him, wondering what he could possibly want. The Spartan and I had never talked outside of weapons training—not even once. I didn't know a lot about Oliver, just the things I'd overheard him talking to Logan and Kenzie about during our fighting sessions, but I doubted we had much in common. He loved gym class, and I did not. He knew how to use weapons, and I did not. He was a real bad-ass warrior, and I was not.

"Oliver," I said, then stuck my nose back into my comic book.

I expected him to get up and head over to his seat next to Kenzie, but instead, Oliver leaned over and peered at the colorful pages.

"Whatcha reading?" Oliver said, stretching out his fingers, like he was going to pluck the book out of my hands.

"None of your business. And *do not touch* my comic book," I snapped, moving it out of his reach. "I just got this issue last week, and I don't want you or anyone else contaminating it."

Oliver frowned. "Contaminate it? How could I do that?"

I sighed. I suppose I could have explained it to him, about how people touching and using objects was how they got emotions, images, and memories attached to them in the first place. But I just didn't feel like it. All I wanted was to be left alone until the bus got to the ski resort. Especially since I could hear Savannah's soft laughter, loud and clear, even though I was three rows back from her and Logan. The Amazon hadn't quit giggling since we'd left Mythos.

"You could contaminate it because you're *you*," I said.

Oliver's face tightened, and anger sparked in his green gaze. But I was angry too—at myself, mostly, because I couldn't get rid of these stupid feelings I had for Logan, even though he was sitting less than fifteen feet away, smiling at another girl.

As if on cue, Savannah chose that moment to let out another flirty giggle. It took me a moment to unclench my jaw.

"Why did you even sit down here?" I snapped again at the Spartan. "Because I know it wasn't just to talk to me. I touched your notebook, remember? I know you've got the hots for somebody at Mythos, and I know it's definitely not me. So do us both a favor and don't waste your time flirting with me or whatever you're trying to do."

By this point, Daphne and Carson had stopped talking and were staring at Oliver and me with open mouths.

For a moment hurt filled Oliver's eyes—along with something that looked like worry. I frowned. Why would the Spartan be worried? I wasn't saying anything we both didn't already know. Before I could figure out what was wrong with him, Oliver got to his feet, stormed up the aisle, and dropped into his seat next to Kenzie. He said something to Kenzie, and they both turned around and gave me dirty looks.

I glared right back at them. I didn't care if they were Logan's friends or not, they were being total jerks right now. Okay, okay, so maybe I was being bitchy myself, but Oliver had started it by sitting down and bugging me in the first place.

"What was that all about?" Daphne whispered. "Why were you so mean to him?"

I shrugged. "I don't know, and I don't care."

Three rows ahead of me, Savannah let out another giggle and laid her head on Logan's shoulder. I raised up my comic book, so I wouldn't have to look at them— and I didn't for the rest of the ride.

The Mythos Academy buses reached the resort a little after nine that morning. Despite the fact that I hadn't really wanted to come, I found myself staring out the window with all the other kids.

The Powder ski resort definitely lived up to its name. The ground had still been bare at the academy, but up here, it was all white. Snow stretched out in all directions, from the ten-foot-high drifts that ringed the parking lot to the ski runs on the hillsides to the jagged tip of the mountain and the others that surrounded it. The morning sun hit the snow just so, making it blaze like a carpet of diamonds that had been rolled over the entire mountain. Everything just *sparkled*.

Daphne, Carson, and I grabbed our luggage and got off the bus, along with everyone else. We had to wait around for a few minutes while the other buses unloaded, which gave me plenty of time to look around. We stood at the base of the mountain, with the various slopes rising like bigger and bigger ocean waves above us until they crashed into the dazzling blue of the sky. Ski lifts circled the steep, slick hills, like merry-go-rounds, hauling people up the mountain and back down again.

And that was just what I could see on this side of the complex. Down here, a variety of shops selling everything from hot chocolate to snowsuits to mountain crafts clustered together in a charming village. All of the buildings had an old-world, alpine look to them, with sharp, sloping roofs; bright, candy-colored paint; and cute, gingerbread trim. They'd all been decorated for Christmas, and thick boughs of holly, red velvet ribbons, and strings of twinkling lights stretched from one shop to the next. The whole village looked like a holiday painting. I half expected to see a Saint Bernard lope by, a barrel of whiskey attached to its neck, to complete the picture-postcard scene.

The biggest building by far was the resort hotel itself, which loomed over everything. The enormous thirteen-story structure looked like it had been carved out of the mountainside one brick at a time. The light gray stone blended in with the rest of the rugged landscape, while the long, narrow windows reflected the dazzling sparkle of the snow.

Apparently, though, the hotel wasn't quite big enough, because I saw people moving back and forth in a construction area attached to the right wing. Saws, drills, and more whined, and hoarse shouts drifted over to us. I hoped Daphne and I didn't get stuck in a room on that side of the resort with all the noise.

Finally, the professors got everyone rounded up and led us inside the hotel, which was in the center of the whole Powder complex. When I'd first come to Mythos, I thought the academy was totally pretentious, snobby, and froufrou with its suits of armor and old, expensive paintings. But this place put the academy to *shame*.

Everything about the hotel was massive, from the stone fireplace that took up one entire wall to the thick wooden beams that supported the roof to the diamond-shaped skylights set into the ceiling. An enormous chandelier made out of curved animal horns hung in the center of the lobby, while plush leather chairs and couches were scattered throughout the room, inviting folks to sit, chat, and feel the heat of the crackling fire. Bits of gold and silver leaf glinted here and there among the gray stone, while the hardwood floors gleamed like sheets of bronze underfoot. It was the nicest, fanciest, most expensive place I'd ever been to.

But even here I couldn't get away from the statues.

A thirty-foot-tall statue of a woman stood in the center of the lobby, her head and chin held high, her arms stretched up toward the sky. Strings of silver snowflakes had been wrapped around her body, making her look like she was summoning the beginnings of a blizzard. Skadi, the Norse goddess of winter. I recognized her from my myth-history book. Other smaller statues stood in the corners of the lobby and peeped out from recesses in the stone walls, like Ull, another Norse winter god, and Boreas, the Greek god of the North Wind.

Like the alpine village, the hotel had also been decorated for Christmas. Fat oranges and bags of figs gleamed like jewels in the silver bowls that had been placed at the statues' feet, right next to goblets filled with spiced mulberry wine. Holly had been shaped into crowns and ringed the heads of the various gods and goddesses while fat balls of mistletoe dangled from their cold fingers. Cedar and juniper trees covered with twinkling white lights clustered together in groups in the lobby, the fragrant scent of their needles mixing with the sweet smoke from the fire.

The crackling flames gave everything a soft, cheery glow, but I couldn't help but feel that the statues were all staring at me, just like the ones at the academy always did. I looked at Skadi. Maybe it was just my imagination in overdrive again, but the snowflakes twisted around her body seemed to wink at me one by one, like cold, cold eyes. I shivered and looked away.

"Isn't this place incredible?" Daphne asked from beside me.

"Yeah," I muttered. "Incredible."

Daphne smirked, not noticing my less-than-enthusiastic tone. "Told you. And just wait until you see the rooms. They're just as posh, and they even have a spa, too, where you can get all kinds of facials and other treatments. Watch my stuff, and I'll go get our room assignment and key cards so we can start exploring. Come on, Carson."

The two of them headed over and got in the line that had already formed by the front desk. Daphne and I would be sharing a room on one of the floors that had been designated girls only, while Carson would be bunking with one of his band buddies on one of the guys' floors.

The kids from the New York academy must have already arrived, because I only recognized about half of the students milling around the lobby. But really, they were all the same—warrior whiz kids dressed in the most expensive clothes their parents could buy. Sparks of magic cracked and flashed in the air as the students from the two schools mingled together, talking, laughing, and saying hello to old friends.

I dragged our bags over to one of the walls and stood there, just staring at everything and trying hard not to gawk. Despite the creepy statues, the hotel really was gorgeous. Back when my mom had been alive, we'd taken plenty of vacations, but we'd never stayed any-where as nice as this. Powder was the kind of place where everything was designer this and designer that, right down to the chocolate mints they put on your pil-lows at night.

"Pretty impressive, isn't it?" a low voice murmured beside me.

I turned my head and found myself staring at one of the cutest guys I'd ever seen. Seriously. He was just...perfect. White blond hair, intense blue eyes, fantastic cheekbones. And if all that wasn't enough, he had a great body, too. I could see his muscles, even under-neath the black turtleneck sweater he wore. He looked to be about my age or maybe a year or two older. At first, I didn't think he was talking to me—I mean, why would he?—but then, when he kept staring at me, I re-alized that he was.

"Yeah," I said, breathless. "It's amazing."

"So is the view from where I'm standing," the guy said.

And then he smiled at me.

It was like someone flipped a switch and suddenly turned on all the lights in the lobby—okay, okay, all the lights *everywhere*—because the guy went from cute to downright *gorgeous,* helped along by the two tiny dim-ples in his cheeks. Seriously, all that and dimples, too. He looked like a model who'd just stepped out of the page of some artsy fashion magazine. He was just that good-looking—the kind of guy you just couldn't help but stare at.

"You here for the Winter Carnival?" he asked.

I nodded. "Yeah. You?"

He nodded back. "The same. What's your name?"

It actually took me a second to remember it. "Gwen," I said. "Gwen Frost."

He smiled again. "Well, Gwen Frost, I'm Preston, from the New York academy. I take it you go to the one down here in the Carolinas? I know you don't go to my school, because I'm sure I would have noticed you before."

All I could do was just nod and try to keep my mouth from falling open. Was he—was he *flirting* with me? It sounded like it, but I wasn't completely sure. I hadn't had a lot of experience with this sort of thing. Before coming to Mythos, I'd had exactly one boyfriend for a grand total of three weeks. And now that I was at the academy, guys still weren't tripping over themselves to talk to me.

"I just started going to Mythos this year," I said. "This is my first Winter Carnival."

He nodded, like I'd just said something cool and interesting, instead of reciting stupid boring facts. We stood there in silence for a minute, while kids moved in the lobby around us, laughing, talking, and texting on their phones. I kept sneaking looks at Preston out of the corner of my eye, waiting for his girlfriend to show up. A guy that cute? He *had* to be with someone already.

But no one came over to us—no girls, no guys, no professors. And I started to wonder what it would be like to flirt back. Just a little bit.

Before I could open my mouth to try, I spotted Daphne waving at me. The Valkyrie had a couple of plastic key cards in her hands, and she started threading her way through the crowd in my direction. I waved back at her.

Preston glanced down and checked his watch. "Well, I gotta go. I'm sure my roommate's got our key cards by now."

I nodded, even though disappointment filled me. So he hadn't been flirting with me after all—he'd just been killing time until he could go up to his room. Of course he had. I should have known it was something like that from the start. Guys like him just didn't flirt with girls like me. I winced, thinking I'd probably come off like a total loser.

Preston stared at me, his blue eyes bright and warm in his handsome face. "I've got to hang out with some friends this afternoon, but I hear there's going to be an awesome party tonight over at the Solstice coffeehouse. Maybe I'll see you there?"

My heart stopped, sputtered, and then *thump-thump-thump*ed in my chest. Okay, okay, so he wasn't exactly asking me out, but it sounded like he wouldn't mind if he ran into me later either. And given my stupid, unrequited, disastrous crush on Logan, I'd take what I could get.

"Maybe," I said, trying to play it cool.

Preston smiled at me a final time, then headed across the lobby.

A few seconds later, Daphne broke free of the crowd and stepped over to me. When I didn't immediately turn toward her, the Valkyrie snapped her fingers in front of my face, making pink sparks flash everywhere and fall to the ground like raindrops.

"Earth to Gwen. What are you looking at?"

"Oh, just this guy I was talking to."

Daphne's black eyes narrowed. "What guy?"

I tried to point out Preston to her, but there were too many people between us and him, and he was walking away too fast for her to really see him.

"He looks cute," she said, standing on her tiptoes to try to get a better look. "At least from the back."

"Believe me," I murmured. "He is."

Daphne elbowed me in the side. "See? I told you there would be guys here from the New York academy, and you've met one already. And you didn't want to come."

I rolled my eyes. "Yeah, yeah. You're my genius best friend, always looking out for me."

"Damn straight," Daphne crowed. "Now, come on. Let's go dump our bags in our room. I told Carson that we'd meet him as soon as we could."

"Yes, master," I sniped.

We grabbed our luggage and headed toward one of the elevators. I looked for Preston, but I didn't see him in the crush of people hanging out in the lobby. Still, I couldn't help but think that maybe Daphne was right— finding a cute guy to take my mind off Logan was the best thing I could do this weekend.

Chapter 8

My hopeful mood lasted until Daphne and I met Carson in one of the ski shops off the hotel lobby. The two of them wandered up and down the crowded aisles, looking at all the equipment and trying to decide if they wanted to ski today or go tubing instead.

Like everything else I'd seen so far at Powder, the shop had the best of everything. All shapes, sizes, and styles of skis stood in racks against the wall, their bright, shiny surfaces as slick and smooth as glass. Puffy coats, pants, and gloves, all branded with designer logos, took up the middle of the shop, while sunglasses, hats, and scarves crowded together in a counter next to the back wall. Neon-colored inner tubes dangled from the ceiling, looking like oversize doughnuts.

I followed my friends through the shop, feeling small, shabby, and lost. I'd never really been an outdoorsy type, preferring to stay in my room and read comic books or watch television. All this nature was a little tough to take. Seriously. What was so fun about standing outside in the cold, trying not to fall and break your legs as you zoomed down a mountain?

Finally, Daphne and Carson picked out some skis, boots, and clothes and then looked at me, expecting me to do the same. Which meant that it was confession time.

"I, um, don't ski."

Daphne frowned. "What do you mean you don't ski?"

I cringed. "I mean, I don't know how to ski. I've never been. That's one of the reasons why I didn't really want to come to the resort this weekend."

Her mouth dropped open. "How can you live in the mountains and not know how to ski? Practically *everyone* at the academy comes to Powder or flies out to Aspen at least once or twice a year. . . ."

The Valkyrie's voice trailed off as she realized that I'd never been to Aspen either or to any of the other fancy places she had.

I stared at a pair of sunglasses and shifted on my feet, miserable embarrassment making my cheeks burn. The fact that the sunglasses had a twelve-hundred-dollar price tag on them didn't help matters. Most of the time, it didn't bother me that I didn't have the expensive clothes, cars, and jewelry the other kids had. I understood what my mom and grandma had been trying to do, how they'd been trying to give me a normal life for as long as possible and to teach me not to take money for granted. Besides, Grandma gave me an allowance, and I made plenty of cash on my own finding lost items for the Mythos kids. I had more than enough money to buy clothes, rent skis, and do whatever else I wanted to this weekend at Powder. But when Daphne talked about jetting off to the Hamptons or the Bahamas or wherever, yeah, sometimes I got a little jealous of all the interesting places she'd been to, all the things she'd done that I hadn't.

Carson gave me a knowing, sympathetic look, which only made me even more miserable. I didn't want my friends to feel sorry for me, and I definitely didn't want them to think of me as poor Gwen, that Gypsy girl who'd never been anywhere or done anything cool.

Daphne tapped her fingers against her lips, throwing pink sparks of magic everywhere. Thinking hard. "Okay, so you don't know how to ski, but maybe we can fix that. What if we try the archery thing?"

"What archery thing?" I asked, confused.

"Come on," she said. "I have an idea."

"This is a bad, bad idea," I muttered. "This is never going to work."

"Oh, suck it up, Gwen," Daphne said. "You haven't even tried it yet."

We'd left the shop thirty minutes ago and now stood on top of one of the beginner bunny slopes, outfitted with skis, boots, gloves, and goggles. Daphne looked cute in her pale pink ski suit, and Carson was perfectly at ease in his dark green one. I just felt like an oversize marshmallow. Seriously. The pants Daphne had picked out for me had so much air trapped in them that they made me feel twice my normal size, and the jacket puffed up so high that I had to keep my chin tucked down, just so I could see where I was going. The only thing good about the suit was the color, which was a pretty shade of purple.

The clothes were bad enough, but then there were the skis. I basically had two narrow, slick boards strapped to my feet, and I felt like I was going to fall down at any second. Not to mention the fact that I kept whacking myself in the legs with the stupid ski poles every time I moved. Getting on the chair lift to come up here had been an adventure by itself. And now Daphne actually expected me to take off down the hill.

Okay, okay, so it wasn't much of a slope. The hill flowed down at a gentle angle for several hundred feet before leveling out again. The area was deserted except for the three of us. Just like Daphne had said, everyone else at Mythos knew how to ski, and the other kids had gone up to the steeper, more difficult runs. Still, I was sure I could break something on the way down the bunny slope.

"Are you ready?" Daphne asked, pulling off one of her pink gloves.

"Sure," I muttered, and yanked off one of mine as well. "Might as well get it over with."

Then I reached out, clasped Daphne's hand, and waited for the images to come.

A few weeks ago, Daphne and I had sat down and done this very same thing. She was my best friend, after all, and we were always brushing up against each other.

Since I hadn't wanted my psychometry to kick every single time I accidentally touched her, I'd decided to just get it all over with in one major whammy.

It was another quirk of my magic. If I flashed on someone all at once, or often enough over a period of time, I sort of got used to their vibes and could touch them more freely. Oh, I'd still flash on Daphne if my skin was in contact with hers for more than a few minutes, but I wouldn't get a major whammy unless she was really upset or emotional about something.

So Daphne had come over to my dorm room one night, and we'd sat on my bed and clasped hands. She hadn't seen or felt anything, since she didn't have that kind of magic—touch magic, it was sometimes called.

But I had.

All sorts of images of the Valkyrie had filled my mind, everything from her growing up to her first day at Mythos to her French-kissing Carson after one of their recent dates. Yeah, that last one had kind of grossed me out a little.

And I'd felt all of Daphne's feelings, too—every last one of them. I'd felt how strong she was, how fierce, how brave, how loyal. And yeah, even how she could be a total, rich-girl snob and a major bitch from time to time. But all those images, all those feelings, good and bad, added up to Daphne—and I was glad she was my best friend.

"Are you seeing anything?" Daphne asked.

Carson looked back and forth between us.

"Not yet," I growled, tightening my grip on her hand

and closing my eyes. "Now quit talking and start concentrating."

"But you should be able to see *something* by now," Daphne said, totally not listening to me. "If you can use my memories to help you with archery, why can't you use them to help with something else? I know I'm right about this. I'm always right."

The reason we were standing on the bunny slope and holding hands in the first place was because of Daphne's *theory* about my psychometry—her idea that I could use my magic to pick up other memories and other skills from people, just like she'd talked about in my dorm room two nights ago. Basically, the Valkyrie figured if I could use my psychometry to tap into her archery prowess, then maybe I could pick up some of her skiing skills, too. That way, she, Carson, and I could go skiing together, instead of them leaving me behind on the bunny slope all by myself.

Daphne's theory made sense, I supposed. Thanks to my Gypsy gift, I remembered every single thing I'd ever seen from touching an object or another person—all the images, all the vibes, all the lights, sounds, and flashes of feeling. I'd just never really thought about using them in this specific way before, about trying to specifically call them up like this—

Suddenly an image popped into my head of Daphne standing on top of a tall slope. She let out a loud whoop, pushed off with her poles, and raced down the mountain. And I felt all the things that she had: her knees moving from side to side, the spray of snow against her legs, the cold air burning her lungs, even the blur of the ice-crusted pine trees as she zipped past them.

And then, as quickly as it had come, the image vanished, leaving nothing behind but the empty echo of the wind in my head.

I opened my eyes to find Daphne and Carson staring at me.

"Well?" Daphne asked. "Did it work?"

"We're about to find out," I said.

I let go of her hand, put my glove back on, and plodded over to the edge of the hill.

"Come on, Gwen. You can do it," Carson called out in an encouraging voice.

I didn't know about *that*, but I was going to at least try. And if I broke something on the way down, well, Daphne said the resort had awesome hot chocolate.

"Here goes nothing," I muttered, dug my poles into the snow, and pushed off.

And immediately wished that I hadn't. Everything happened so freaking *fast*. The snow was so packed and slick that it seemed like I was going a hundred miles an hour down the slope the second I took off. Plus, the sun glinted on the snow just so, throwing out dazzling sprays of light in every direction.

For a moment, hot, sweaty panic filled me, but I pushed it away and forced myself to focus, to call up Daphne's image, just like I had during archery practice with Kenzie and Oliver. I could do this. I *would* do this.

Daphne, Daphne, Daphne—I chanted the Valkyrie's name in my head and once again pictured her in her ski suit, sliding down that steep hill and loving every second of it.

In an instant everything changed.

My legs grew stronger and steadier underneath me. My arms dropped down to where they were supposed to go instead of wildly flailing around. My knees started moving from side to side to help control my speed, and I started leaning into the turns, such as they were on the bunny slope.

I drew in a breath and realized that skiing was kind of . . . fun.

Before I knew it, I was at the bottom of the hill. I moved the skis first right, then left, sending up a shower of snow and sliding to a stop, like I'd been on the slopes all my life instead of just a few minutes.

At the top of the hill, Daphne and Carson jumped up and down and screamed and waved at me. I lifted a shaky hand and waved back, a crazy grin on my face. I hadn't thought it would really work, but somehow, it had. It looked like there was a little more to my Gypsy gift than I'd thought. I'd have to tell Grandma Frost about it the next time I saw her, if she didn't already know. These days, Grandma always seemed to know more than she told me—about everything.

Daphne made a motion with her hand, pointing at the ski lift. She wanted me to ride back up there, probably so we go up to the next hill and see if I could do the same thing all over again. I waved back, telling her that I understood, and trudged off in that direction.

Several lifts snaked up the mountain at Powder, hauling students, profs, and everyone else up to the various ski, snowboard, and tubing runs, but there was only one lift at the base of the bunny slope. Since it didn't have nearly as many chairs on it as the others, I had to stand there and wait for it to come back around.

And that's when a low, ominous growl whispered behind me.

I froze, my blood suddenly as cold and icy as the surrounding snow. I knew that sort of growl. I'd heard it twice before in my life now, and both times, I'd almost died.

Riding over to the resort, meeting Preston, flashing on Daphne, trying to ski. I'd had a busy morning. So busy I'd forgotten about the fact that there was a Reaper who was trying to kill me—and that he just might send a monster to do the job.

I slowly turned around. At first I didn't see it, but then a movement in the thicket of pine trees at the far edge of the slope caught my eye. I strained to spot it in the shadows and then wished that I hadn't.

It looked like an overgrown wolf. Even though the creature was hunkered down in the snow, I could still see how very massive it was. It seemed to be roughly the same size as a Nemean prowler, with a body that would come up past my waist and was longer than I was tall. Something flicked in the trees behind it, and it took me a second to realize it was the creature's tail, slowly lashing from side to side and slapping snow everywhere.

Its fur was the color of crumbled ash—not quite black but not really gray either—and strands of red glinted in its thick, shaggy coat. The bloody tinge matched the color of the monster's eyes—a deep, dark, blistering red that seemed like it could burn right through anything, including me.

My breath caught in my throat. I'd only seen a drawing of it in my myth-history book, that weird, weird drawing that had moved and oozed ink all over the page, but I knew exactly what the monster was: a Fenrir wolf.

The wolf's lips drew back in a silent snarl, showing me its razor-sharp teeth. I knew that hidden somewhere in the shadows would be the creature's long, curved, black claws—ones that could tear through almost anything. Wood, skin, muscle, bone.

All put together, the Fenrir wolf was a nightmare come to life.

And now it was here to kill me.

Chapter 9

The Fenrir wolf let out a low, angry growl, and I slowly brought up my ski poles, holding them out in front of me. The thin, flimsy poles wouldn't do me much good against the wolf, but they were better than nothing. I knew better than to try to run. I wouldn't get two steps, not with the skis strapped to my feet, before the creature pounced on me and ripped me to shreds with its teeth and claws. Given the way it was licking its lips with its long, red tongue and staring at me with its bright, glowing eyes, the wolf would definitely enjoy that sort of thing.

This was the third time I'd been face-to-face with a mythological monster, and the only reason I'd survived the first two encounters was because Logan had stepped in to save me. But Logan wasn't here now, and I was all alone—

"Hey, guys! Over here! This lift isn't so crowded!"

A group of Mythos students zoomed into view, gliding over the snow and heading toward the ski lift. The wolf's gaze cut over to them, and it let out another low, ominous growl. While it was distracted, I took a step back, then another one, then another one, putting as much distance as possible between myself and the monster.

The wolf got to its feet and started stalking back and forth inside the thicket of trees. The other kids never even saw it as they stopped at the base of the lift and waited for the chairs to come down the mountain. The monster's gaze moved from them and then back to me, its eyes growing redder and angrier with each passing second, until it seemed like hungry flames flashed in the sockets were its eyes should be.

The wolf realized that I was moving away from it, but there was nothing the monster could do to stop me—not without showing itself. I didn't know how intelligent Fenrir wolves were, but this one must have instinctively known that it would be a bad idea to leap out into the middle of a group of kids. I might not be able to kill it, but the other Mythos students were warriors, trained to fight monsters. I had no doubt they could use their ski poles like spears to take down the creature.

Step by step, I backed up until I was standing on the edge of the group waiting for the chair lift. The other kids ignored me, of course, the way they always did. I kept watching the wolf the whole time, poles up and at the ready, just in case.

I thought about shouting out a warning to the others, but like running, I didn't think I'd even get to scream once before the wolf bounded out of the trees and tore open my throat with its claws. The Mythos kids might be warriors, but I didn't think they'd be fast enough to save me from the monster. I didn't even know if Logan was that good. Either way I wasn't about to bet my life on it—not now.

I didn't have to. The Fenrir wolf let out one final growl, then slid farther back into the trees and disappeared.

The chairs finally circled back around, and the other kids scrambled onto them. Legs shaking, I managed to slip-slide over and sit down on the final chair before it took off up the mountain. I leaned over the side and peered down into the trees, but I didn't spot the wolf anywhere beneath the thick tangles of snowy branches. It had vanished just as quickly as it had appeared.

But this wouldn't be the last time I saw it. The wolf would come for me sooner or later, lurking and hiding on the mountain until it got another shot at me, another chance to tear into me with its teeth and drag my body back to its Reaper master. I knew that, but I still couldn't stop the questions from filling my mind.

How was I going to kill it?

And who had sent it after me in the first place?

I was a little calmer by the time the chair lift reached the top of the slope. At least, I told myself that I was, even if my heart felt like it was going to pound out of my chest, and my palms were cold and clammy with sweat inside my puffy purple gloves.

Daphne and Carson were waiting for me. They sat at a wooden table that had been painted a bright, candy-apple red, and the glossy boards looked like blood resting on top of the snow. Or maybe it just seemed that way because I was still freaked out from seeing the Fenrir wolf.

My friends both clasped oversize mugs in their hands and slowly sipped the hot chocolate they'd bought from a guy in a concessions shack off to one side of the slope. Steam wisped up out of the mugs, the thin ribbons bringing the smells of warm milk, sweet cinnamon, and just a hint of tangy peppermint along with them. Normally, the rich aromas would have made me thirsty for my own mug of hot chocolate. Now, they just turned my stomach.

"Geez, Gwen. What took you so long?" Daphne said.

"Yeah, we thought maybe you'd fallen into a snowdrift or something," Carson joked.

"No," I said in a quiet voice. "But I saw a Fenrir wolf in the trees."

Instead of being scared by my confession, Daphne perked up. "Really? Cool! What did it look like? Was it really as big as a Nemean prowler? Did it have massive teeth?"

"Cool?" I asked, confused. "Why is that cool?"

Daphne and Carson exchanged a look, like they were in on some secret that I wasn't.

"Remember what Metis told us in class about how some of the Fenrir wolves still run around free in the wild?" Carson asked.

"Yeah. . . ."

"Well, the mountains around the ski resort are one of the places they live. A couple of kids saw some of the wolves last year, hanging around the resort. The kids tried to get close to the wolves, but they just disappeared into the trees."

"And it's not just wolves," Daphne added. "There are tons of wild animals around here. Sometimes we see bears or mountain lions or elk, right at the edges of the slopes."

My friends started talking about all the animals they'd seen last year and some of the cell phone videos and photos the other students had taken.

"But—"

I opened my mouth to tell them it wasn't just some wild Fenrir wolf that I'd seen, that it wasn't more scared of me than I was of it, that it had red eyes and had seemed to want to kill me more than anything else. But at the last second I changed my mind. Daphne and Carson looked so happy cozied up next to each other. I didn't want to ruin their day by going on and on about just how big, bad, and evil the wolf had seemed, especially when they weren't really concerned about me seeing the creature in the first place. I didn't want to be a total wimp—or worse, have my friends look at me like they didn't believe me. Besides, there was a small chance I was wrong about the wolf being here to kill me. Wild or not, the wolf was still a monster. Maybe they all had red eyes. Okay, okay, so I didn't really believe that, but it made me feel a smidge better.

Anyway, my friends had come here to have fun. If word got out there was a wolf with red eyes roaming around the mountain, the Powers That Were might cancel the whole Winter Carnival. Maybe it was selfish of me, but I didn't want to be known as Gwen Frost, that Gypsy girl who ruined everything. That would definitely make me more of a misfit freak than I already was.

But even more than that was the fact that I wanted to be like the other kids. I wanted to be a real warrior. If the wolf was here to kill me, then I wanted to take care of the monster myself. Kill it myself. Even if I had no idea exactly how I was going to do that.

So I made myself smile at my friends, even though my face felt frozen and numb. "Let's forget about the wolf, okay? What do you say we go on up to the next slope and see if I can work my Gypsy magic again?"

"Sounds like a plan to me," Carson said, pushing his black glasses up his nose and grinning.

"See? I told you it would work," Daphne said in a smug tone. "I always have the best ideas."

"Of course you do," Carson told her.

Daphne rolled her eyes and punched him lightly in the shoulder. Carson retaliated by trying to steal the Valkyrie's hot chocolate. She swatted his hand away, and the two of them started laughing and mock fighting.

Neither one of them saw the strained, fake smile drop from my lips or noticed that I didn't join in the fun.

For the rest of the afternoon, the three of us zoomed down the various ski slopes, then rode the chair lifts back up to the top again. All the while I kept an eye out for the Fenrir wolf, and I made sure that the three of us stayed far, far away from the trees. To my relief, I didn't spot the monster lurking in the snow-crusted pines.

The higher up the mountain we went, the more crowded the slopes were, and I relaxed a little bit. The wolf couldn't get to me out here, not with all the kids and profs around. That would be suicide for the monster. As long as I stayed with a crowd, I was safe.

For now.

To my surprise, I sort of got the hang of skiing. All I had to do was use my psychometry magic and think of Daphne skiing, and I could get down all the slopes, even the really steep ones that twisted and turned like crazy. But the second I let my concentration waver, the second I started worrying about the Fenrir wolf, my memories of Daphne vanished—along with my ability to tap into them.

I found that out the hard way—literally. One second I was swooshing over the snow just fine. The next I was looking for the wolf. And the one after that, I found myself face-first in a snowdrift and not quite sure how I had gotten there. I sat out the next few runs after that.

Finally, at around five, we called it quits for the day and skied down the mountain to the hotel. The three of us ate dinner in one of the resort restaurants, which was just as expensive as everything else. And just like at the academy, the food was all fancy, froufrou stuff, like frog legs, rabbit, and pan-seared tuna. Yucko. I settled for a filet mignon cheeseburger, Parmesan sweet potato fries, and a piece of baklava made with sourwood honey and topped with toasted, slivered almonds. The baklava wasn't nearly as good as what Grandma Frost made, but it was sugary sweet, so I scarfed it down anyway.

After dinner, the three of us split up. Carson went to

his room on the seventh floor, while Daphne and I headed up to ours on thirteen. Our room was on the side of the hotel that butted up against the new construction site, but the workers must have left for the weekend already, because I didn't hear any saws, hammers, or drills, and I hadn't noticed any noise while we'd been downstairs eating dinner.

Daphne and I hung out in our room for a while, unpacking our bags and gossiping about who we'd seen on the slopes, who they'd been with, and how many people would hook up with the kids from the New York academy. One couple I hadn't spotted had been Logan and Savannah. They were probably too busy sticking their tongues down each other's throats to go skiing. The thought didn't make me happy.

I flopped down on the bed and stared out the window. Since we were on the top floor, we had a great view of the surrounding mountains and the valleys that dipped down in between the jagged peaks. Snow, trees, and sky stretched out all the way to the horizon, blurring together in soft shades of purple, gray, and wintry silver. But the beautiful vista didn't soothe me. Not now. My thoughts turned back to the Fenrir wolf. I wondered where it was right now, if it was out there in the woods that surrounded the ski resort, if it was patiently waiting for another chance to attack me—

"What's wrong?" Daphne asked, staring at me in the mirror while she brushed out her golden hair. "You've been quiet all afternoon."

"Nothing," I lied. "I'm just tired. All that skiing wore me out."

"Tired? You can't be tired. We've got a party to go to, remember?"

I groaned and flopped back on the bed. "You can't be serious."

"Of course, I'm serious. Yeah, the skiing's nice and all, but we all really come here for the parties. They're *legendary*. Last year, somebody dared Morgan McDougall to go skinny-dipping in the hotel's indoor pool with a bunch of guys. And of course she did it—sober, no less. Everybody talked about it for *weeks*."

I grimaced. "Well, I'm not Morgan, and I'm definitely not the skinny-dipping type. I'm not sure I want to go."

Daphne put her hands on her hips and stalked over to me. Since I was lying with my head by the foot of the bed, she looked upside down to me. Pink sparks snapped and crackled around her fingertips like lightning. I sighed. Daphne always gave off more magic when she was upset, angry, or just plain annoyed. I was willing to bet she was feeling the last one right now, and I knew it was my fault. I hadn't exactly been a bucket of fun so far, and the Valkyrie was probably tired of having to coax me to do every little thing.

"Of course, you want to go," Daphne scoffed. "It's a *party*, Gwen. You know, a place where you go to have a good time."

I just shrugged. I didn't tell her I could have a perfectly good time in the room by myself with my comic books and sugar stash. That's pretty much how I'd spent every night when I'd first come to Mythos, since I hadn't had any friends at the academy.

Being alone didn't bother me. Part of me had been alone ever since my mom had died—alone, hollow, empty, and aching—and I knew part of me would always feel that way. The feelings might dull and dim with time, but they'd always be there. I'd always remember losing my mom—and always feel the gnawing pain of wishing she was still here with me.

"Well, what about that cute guy you talked to in the lobby? He said he was going to the Solstice party, didn't he?" Daphne said.

"Yeah."

"And he said maybe he'd see you there?"

"Yeah."

Daphne rolled her eyes. "Well, he can't *see* you if you don't actually *go to the party.*"

I opened my mouth, but I couldn't argue with her logic. Her point made, Daphne sniffed and stalked back over to the mirror. The Valkyrie put down her brush, plucked her raspberry-scented lip gloss out of the depths of her enormous Dooney & Bourke purse, and started working on her makeup.

I lay there on the bed, brooding. Yeah, I'd like to go to the party, see Preston, and have a good time, but I also couldn't forget that a Reaper was trying to kill me. First the SUV, then the arrow in the library, and now a Fenrir wolf in the snow. Whoever he was, he was definitely serious about wanting me dead, enough to try again here at the ski resort.

This trip was just for Mythos students and staff, both the ones here in North Carolina and those who'd come

down from New York, and Daphne had told me the resort was always closed to other guests during the Winter
Carnival weekend. That meant the Reaper had been at
the academy to start with and not just some random
bad guy who'd somehow gotten past the sphinxes on
the wall and snuck onto campus. My Reaper stalker
was either a student, a professor, or a staff member—
maybe even someone that I saw every single day. Helena
Paxton, that snotty Amazon girl from the library; Mr.
Llew, the calculus prof who bored me to tears with his
lectures; Coach Lir, who ran the swim teams and helped
out with the weapons training and other sports programs. The Reaper could be anyone.

Whoever he was, he was really starting to piss me off.
Yeah, Jasmine Ashton was dead because of me. I had
plenty of guilt over her death and the part I'd played in
it. But the Valkyrie had been two seconds away from
murdering me when Logan had put a spear through her
heart.

My mom had killed more than one bad guy while
she'd been a police detective. She'd told me once that it
wasn't right taking someone else's life, but sometimes it
was necessary to protect other people and yourself.
Logan had killed Jasmine to save me, even if Jasmine's
family didn't see it that way, even if the other Reapers
didn't see it that way.

The truth was, I wanted to know who was trying to
kill me, so I could take the Reaper down myself. Of
course, I wouldn't discover anything if I stayed here in
the room all night, even if it was definitely the safer op-

tion. No, the Reaper and his wolf were out there some-where, and it was time for me to find them. Or at least have enough fun to make me forget about them for the night. Right now, I wasn't too picky about which way things went.

I sat up and met Daphne's eyes in the mirror.

"All right," I said. "Let's party."

Chapter 10

"Parteeeee!" a Roman guy standing on top of a table screamed and raised his plastic cup of beer.

"Parteeeee!" all the other kids screamed, lifting up their own cups in response.

Then, with one thought, everyone chugged down whatever was in their cups. In my case, it was some kind of light-colored ale that tasted like sour grass as it slid down my throat. But I drank it anyway, if only to blend in. Nobody here was drinking soda tonight.

I wrinkled my nose. "Yucko. I can't believe people drink this stuff for *fun*."

"Not for fun," Carson said above the shouts, giving me a crooked grin and pushing his glasses up his nose. "Just to get drunk."

"And how do you know when you're drunk?"

His grin widened. "When it starts tasting good."

It was just after nine, and Carson, Daphne, and I were at one of the many student parties being held tonight as part of the Winter Carnival. This one was at

Solstice, which was one of the coffeehouses in the alpine village next to the hotel.

During the day, Solstice was actually a coffee shop, the kind of place that charged way too much for espressos, mochas, and lattes, not to mention the muffins, scones, and pound cakes that went along with them. Every once in a while, I got a whiff of the sugar and spices that had flavored the air earlier in the day, although now, the smells of perfume, beer, and smoke overpowered them.

Tonight, all of the tables had been pushed up against the walls to make room for a dance floor. Somebody had set up some strobe lights, and the music thumped with a low, steady bass beat through the sound system. Daphne had told me that Samson Sorensen's dad owned the whole Powder resort complex and always let the Viking have a party here at the coffee shop during the Winter Carnival—with absolutely no interference from the Mythos professors. Hence the insanely loud music and the row of kegs that squatted on the counter in plain view of the front windows. Not to mention the quick glows of orange-red lights in the crowd as some of the kids sucked down cigarettes or something even stronger and more illegal.

As for Samson, he stood in the middle of the coffee shop, a beer in one hand and his arm around a girl from the New York academy. The Viking accepted backslaps from all the guys for throwing such an awesome party, and the girl by his side looked up at him with adoring eyes. No wonder. With his sandy brown hair, hazel eyes, and dimples, Samson was one of the cutest guys at either school.

It wasn't that late, but more than a few kids were already totally wasted. One guy lay on top of the counter behind the row of kegs, his hand curled around one of them, like it was a stuffed animal he was clutching to his chest. A string of drool oozed out of the side of his open mouth. I could see it, because I was standing at the end of the counter where his head was. I thought he might be snoring, too, but the music was so loud that I couldn't really tell.

"Come on. Let's dance," Daphne said, grabbing Carson's hand.

He winced. "You should know by now that I don't dance."

She flashed him a confident, smirking smile. "Don't worry, babe. I'll make you look good. I always do."

Laughing, Carson let Daphne pull him out onto the dance floor. A second later, the two of them were grooving to the blaring music, with Daphne going about it much more smoothly than Carson, who was all flailing arms and jerky feet. If he wasn't careful, the band geek was going to stab someone in the eye with his elbow.

Of course, Daphne and Carson dancing left me standing by myself against the wall, with only Drool Guy for company. I eyed the unconscious kid, who smacked his lips, causing even more spit to trickle out of the side of his mouth. Disgusting.

I shifted away from the edge of the counter and scanned the crowd, just like I'd been doing ever since we'd gotten here an hour ago, but all I saw were drunk guys, dancing girls, and couples sticking their tongues down each other's throats. Nobody looked like she could be a Reaper in disguise, and nobody seemed like he wanted to kill me.

As soon as we'd stepped through the door, I knew that I wouldn't be able to do anything tonight to figure out who was after me. Not that I'd had a real plan to start with, other than to roam around, touch people and their stuff, and see if I got any psycho-killer vibes off anything. There were way too many kids packed into the coffee shop for me to touch every single one of them. Besides, I doubted that I'd see anything tonight through the beer-soaked haze.

I was still scanning the crowd when Logan walked through the door.

He looked as gorgeous as ever. His ink black hair glinted under the flashing lights, and his dark blue sweater brought out the exquisite, icy paleness of his eyes, while his leather jacket highlighted exactly how broad and strong his shoulders were. My breath caught in my throat, and my heart thrummed with painful awareness.

But of course he wasn't alone. Logan turned around and stretched out his hand. A second later, Savannah stepped through the door after him, her red hair gleaming like ribbons of copper streaming down her back. Logan bent down, and Savannah laughed at whatever he whispered into her ear.

They really did make a cute couple, both of them rich, powerful, and beautiful. I didn't know much about Savannah, besides the fact that she was an Amazon gifted with supernatural speed, but she really did seem to like Logan. I could tell by the way she smiled at him.

It was the same way *I* always smiled at him—with my heart in my eyes for everyone to see.

Logan must have sensed me staring at him, because he looked in my direction. He hesitated a second, then lifted his hand. I gritted my teeth, made myself smile, and waved back. Savannah peered around him, wondering who he was waving at. When she saw that it was me, her glossy lips flattened out. She grabbed the Spartan's arm and pulled him over to the other side of the coffee shop—as far away from me as she could get him and still be in the same room. Logan looked back at me a second, his eyes dark, then followed her.

My stomach twisted, and I suddenly wanted another beer, another ale, another *something* to get the bitter taste out of my mouth—and take away the sharp, hollow ache in my heart.

My plastic cup still in hand, I leaned over past Drool Guy and twisted the knob on the keg he was protecting. Nothing came out. Empty. Of course it was. Drool Guy had probably guzzled it all down hours ago. Since there wasn't another keg within arm's reach, I moved away from the wall and skirted through the crowd, careful to keep from touching anyone. I felt shitty enough already without flashing on someone and feeling his bender.

I tried a couple more kegs before I finally found one that still had something in it. I turned the knob, and a dark brown liquid filled my cup. I sniffed it suspiciously. It was darker than the ale I'd had before and smelled twice as sour, like someone had pissed in it. Maybe they had. Anything was possible at a Mythos party. I sighed and put the cup on the counter. I just couldn't chug down the mystery booze, no matter how much I might have liked to get drunk right now.

I turned around, looking for Daphne and Carson, but I didn't see them in the mass of thrashing bodies. Logan and Savannah stood about twenty feet off to my left, deep in conversation.

My stomach twisted again, and anger, frustration, and longing burned through my veins like acid. I had to get out of the coffee shop before I did something stupid—like start screaming about how unfair it was that Logan was here with another girl. That a Reaper had tried to kill me twice now, and I'd almost been turned into puppy chow on the slopes by a Fenrir wolf. That I had a smartass magical sword that I didn't really know how to use and a goddess who'd chosen me to be her Champion, even though I was completely wrong for the job. That I wasn't a warrior like the other kids and never would be, no matter how hard I tried or how much I wanted to be like them. Not to mention the fact that my mom had been killed by a drunk driver the cops had never been able to find and that I still missed her so much, I sometimes cried myself to sleep. Yeah, I had a lot to scream about.

I turned and headed for the door, not really caring who I bumped out of my way to get there. The coffeehouse suddenly felt as hot, small, and cramped as a cage.

Along the way, I passed Kenzie and Oliver. The Spartans guys were joined at the hip like always, although tonight, they were tag-teaming their prey. Kenzie was turned one way, chatting to Talia Pizarro, a tall, pretty Amazon with ebony skin, while Oliver was at his back, talking to a girl that I didn't recognize, some chick from the New York academy.

Oliver saw me looking at him, and his face tightened with anger. From the way he was glaring at me, it looked like he was still pissed I'd brushed him off on the bus ride over here this morning. Whatever. I still didn't know why he'd sat down beside me to start with. I certainly wasn't the person he had a crush on, so what was the point of trying to chat me up? I might not have gotten a crystal-clear picture of his mystery crush in my head when I'd accidentally touched Oliver's supersecret notebook during weapons training, but I'd seen enough to know it wasn't me.

Although the Spartan's hard stare made me wonder why he was talking to the other girl in the first place. After all, she had white blond hair, not black hair like Oliver's mystery crush had in my hazy flash.

I pushed away all thoughts of the Spartan and stepped outside. The night air felt cool and crisp against my cheeks, and a few flakes of snow fluttered in the air. A soft breeze carried a sharp metallic tang with it, whispering that even more of the white stuff was on the way. I looked up. There weren't any stars out tonight, but a silver sliver of the moon peeked down at me for a few seconds before the thick clouds swallowed it up again. The Christmas lights that had been strung up in the alpine village winked on and off, flashing red, green, and gold against the blackness of the night.

I leaned against the coffee shop window, tucked my hands into my jacket pockets, and just breathed. In and out, in and out, the way my mom had taught me to whenever I was feeling scared, panicked, or upset. The slow, steady rhythm soothed me, chasing away some of my anger, frustration, and heartache. The music from the party still thumped, but the sound was muffled out here—just a low, growling rumble through the brick and glass of the building.

My peace and quiet lasted maybe two minutes before a Valkyrie wearing a tight, white turtleneck sweater, a green leather miniskirt, and ridiculously high-heeled boots teetered outside, stumbled away about thirty feet, bent over, and puked up all the beer she'd just drunk. I wrinkled my nose. Ugh. I *so* did not need to see that.

She straightened up and wiped her mouth with the back of her hand, and I realized it was Morgan McDougall. The Valkyrie sensed me watching her and turned in my direction. We stood there staring at each other. Maybe it was just the flashing lights, but Morgan's face looked as green as her skirt and matching boots.

"Do you, uh, need some help?" I asked.

Morgan opened her mouth like she was going to say something, but then she clamped her lips together and shook her head. Without another word, she turned and tottered off toward the hotel, her stiletto boots digging into the snow like spikes.

Morgan puking her guts out seemed like a clear signal that it was time to leave. I turned around and glanced through the window. It took me a minute to spot Daphne and Carson, who were still dancing. Well,

Daphne was dancing. I wasn't quite sure what Carson was doing.

I thought about going inside and telling them that I was all partied out for the night. But I knew if I did that, Daphne would insist on leaving the party, so she and Carson could walk me back over to the hotel. She was just that good a friend, and so was Carson. The two of them had basically been babysitting me all day—they deserved to have a little time to themselves tonight.

Besides, there were plenty of other Mythos kids wandering around outside, laughing and talking and stumbling from one shop, or one party, to the next. I'd be safe enough walking back to the hotel by myself. I could see the entrance from here, lit up with strands of Christmas icicle lights. I doubted that even a Reaper would be stupid or brave enough to try to kill me in the middle of the alpine village, especially since it was full of drunk students.

My decision made, I pushed away from the building, heading back toward the hotel—and ran right into Preston.

One second, I was alone. The next, Preston appeared in front of me.

"Oof!"

I hit Preston square on and bounced back off his chest. And, of course, my boots skidded on a patch of black ice on the sidewalk. I would have fallen on my ass right in front of him if he hadn't leaned over and caught me, clutching me to his chest.

"Nice reflexes," I said, staring into his blue eyes.

He grinned. "Good to know all those long hours in the gym have finally paid off."

We stood there like that for another moment, the two of us frozen in this strange, intimate embrace. I cleared my throat and looked away. Preston got the message and pulled me back up onto my feet.

"Are you okay?" he asked in a concerned voice.

"I am now," I said, smiling at him.

Preston grinned at me again. "Good. You know, I was hoping I'd see you here tonight, Gwen."

Gwen. Even the way he said my name was sexy, as if his good looks and muscled body didn't make him cute enough already. Okay, okay, so maybe part of my heart stubbornly insisted that Preston's voice didn't have quite the same husky ring to it that Logan's did whenever the Spartan called me "Gypsy girl." But Logan was inside with another girl, and I was out here with Preston. Maybe Daphne was right. Maybe it was time to find someone to take my mind off Logan—and I thought Preston would do quite nicely.

"I was hoping that I'd see you, too," I said.

We stood there staring at each other. The glow from the coffee shop and the Christmas lights highlighted Preston's smooth skin and perfect features, making him look older, more handsome, and slightly dangerous. He just kept staring at me, as if he thought I was just as gorgeous as he was. I wasn't, of course, but I still liked the attention, even if a hot, furious blush worked its way into my cheeks as a result.

A few feet away, a couple who'd been making out on an iron bench next to the coffeehouse finally got up.

Their lips never broke contact as they walked toward the hotel.

Preston jerked his head in that direction. "Shall we?"

I nodded. We walked over and sat down on the bench. Preston leaned back and stretched his arm out across the top of the bench, almost like he was putting it around my shoulders. We both had on jackets, and he was wearing gloves, so there was no danger of me getting any kind of vibe off him. Still, I liked being close to him.

For a moment I wondered what would happen if I leaned over and brushed my fingers against Preston's face. What I would see and feel if I used my Gypsy gift to flash on him. Guys were so hard to read, especially supercute ones like Preston, and my magic was basically my own personal, built-in lie and bullshit detector. My psychometry would let me know what he really thought of me. If he thought I was pretty or funny or a total freak. If he really liked me or was thinking about someone else or was just sitting here with me because he thought he might get laid.

The temptation to find out the answers was so strong that it made my fingers twitch with anticipation, but I forced myself to stick my hands into my jacket pockets. I wasn't going to do that, I wasn't going to use my magic that way. I wasn't going to pull secrets out of people just because I had the power to do so, just because I wanted to know what they were up to. It was a decision I'd made a few weeks back, when I'd realized Logan had a secret he was hiding from me—one that was keeping us apart.

Besides, tonight I wanted something—something simple, easy, uncomplicated, and yeah, totally romantic, too. I thought that sitting on a bench with a cute guy and watching the flakes of snow gather in his white blond hair *definitely* qualified as romantic.

"So you go to Mythos down here in the South," Preston said. "What year are you?"

"Second-year. You?"

"Fourth," he said.

That would make him nineteen then, two years older than me. Not too old at all.

"So what are you?" I asked. "Spartan? Roman? Some other kind of warrior whiz kid?"

Preston shook his head, and his face seemed to darken for a moment before he answered me. "Nope, I'm just a Viking. I have a younger sister, too, but, of course, she's a Valkyrie."

I nodded. Siblings shared the same blood and heritage in warrior families, just like they did in normal mortal families, but the kids weren't always labeled as the same kind of warriors. Usually, the boys were Vikings, while the girls were Valkyries. Or if the boys were Romans, then the girls were Amazons. Then there were some warrior families where it was all the same, where both the boys and the girls were considered to be Spartans, Samurais, Ninjas, or whatever. Daphne had tried to explain it to me one day, but I hadn't really understood.

"And I'm definitely not a whiz kid," Preston continued. "At least not according to my parents whenever the academy e-mails them my grades. I'm currently flunking myth-history, just like I did last semester and the one before that."

"Aw, don't feel too bad," I said in a teasing tone. "I'm even worse off. I'm pretty much failing gym right now. Seriously, failing gym. How lame is that?"

We looked at each other, and we both started laughing. His deep, sexy voice, my lighter one. I liked the way they sounded together.

"So you're failing gym—why?" Preston asked. "Do they do something different down here at the Southern academy that they don't do up in New York?"

I shrugged. "Probably not. I'm just not all that coordinated. What about you?"

Preston shrugged as well. "I'm pretty good with a sword, but I kind of suck when it comes to some of the other weapons. And I absolutely despise archery. My aim is just never any good."

I flashed back to the arrow thunking into the bookcase a foot away from my head in the Library of Antiquities. "I don't like archery much either."

We just started talking after that, about the two academies and the differences between them, about our classes and professors, about music and movies and sports and books. I liked Preston. He was smart, funny, and charming—and so totally *gorgeous*.

Part of me still couldn't believe that he didn't have a girlfriend—and that he was hanging out with me instead of going into the coffee shop and finding someone cuter to flirt with. Someone like Morgan, who would have probably already asked him to go back to her room. But I wasn't about to complain. For once, I was having a good time, and I was going to enjoy it as long as it lasted.

We'd been sitting on the bench talking for about half an hour when the snow started to pick up, coming down in a thick shower of fat, fluffy flakes. For some reason, the snow made me think of Nike. It was cold, beautiful, and dangerous all at the same time, just like the goddess of victory.

A shiver swept through my body, and I realized that my nose and cheeks had gone numb from sitting outside. Preston noticed my shiver. He scooted closer, wrapped his arm around me, and stared into my eyes. For a second, I thought he might lean forward and kiss me. My heart thumped up into my throat in anticipation. Part of me wanted him to—and part of me still wished it was Logan out here with me instead.

"You want to get out of here?" Preston asked in a soft voice. "Maybe go somewhere warmer and . . . talk?"

I didn't know if he really meant talk, make out, or something else completely, but I'd be happy with any one of them. I smiled at him. "Let's go."

Chapter 11

Preston got to his feet and held out his hand. I slipped my bare fingers into his palm, enjoying the smooth feel of his glove on my skin. A second later, my pscyhometry kicked in and showed me an image of Preston sitting in a dark car and pulling on the black gloves.

No big whoop. It was exactly the kind of thing I'd expected to see, exactly the kind of thing I had seen hundreds of times before when touching someone's clothes. Usually, I barely noticed those sorts of flashes, although this time, I felt like there was more to the memory, something hovering right at the edge of my mind. Something important...

Before I could focus on it, Preston pulled me to the right. Instead of going toward the hotel, he was heading around the side of the building and the shadows there. My heart thumped even faster in my chest. If he took me back there and tried to kiss me, I was *so* going to let him—

The door to the coffee shop jangled opened, and Logan stepped outside.

Logan's sudden appearance startled me so much that I let go of Preston's hand. The beginning of the glove memory, whatever it had been, vanished as soon as I broke contact. And of course, I slipped on that stupid patch of black ice again. This time, I managed to catch myself before I fell on my ass.

Logan reached out a hand to help me, but I waved him off. One, because I'd embarrassed myself enough already. And two, because he wasn't wearing gloves. If I touched Logan's bare skin, I didn't know what kind of flash I'd get off him. I certainly didn't want to see him kissing Savannah or something else like that. I'd already witnessed *that* enough times in real life. Besides, I might discover how he felt about the Amazon, and if my magic told me that he really cared about her, well, that would only hurt me even more.

Logan saw my wary look at his outstretched fingers. His hand curled into a tight fist, and he dropped it to his side. Not too long ago, the Spartan had tried to kiss me, but just before our lips had touched, I'd realized I'd flash on him when he did—and that maybe I wouldn't like what I'd see.

I hadn't known Logan all that well back then, and I'd been afraid that I'd sense that he was laughing at me or just kissing me because he felt sorry for me, because he thought I was a total loser freak or would be an easy lay. He did have a reputation as a man-whore, after all, and those weren't exactly the sort of things you wanted to feel when you were making out with the cute guy you liked. I had some experience with that, since I'd once flashed on Drew Squires, my first and only boyfriend, and had realized that he was thinking about another girl while he was kissing me. I'd dumped Drew right then and there, but that still hadn't taken away my pain.

So I'd pulled back that night from Logan at the very last second—and I'd hurt his feelings because of it. He'd thought I hadn't wanted to kiss him because he was a Spartan, because they had a reputation for being so vicious and violent. I'd tried to explain about my psychometry magic, but he hadn't understood. From the dark expression on his face, it looked like he didn't understand right now either.

"Gypsy girl," Logan said, staring at Preston instead of me. "Who's your friend?"

"This is Preston. Preston, Logan. Logan goes to the North Carolina academy with me," I said.

Preston held out his hand, which Logan reluctantly took and shook. I'd thought this would be the end of things and that Logan would head back inside to the party and Savannah, but instead the Spartan crossed his arms over his chest and leaned against the side of the building. Like he expected Preston and me to stay put and talk to him or something. Weird. Very weird.

"Spartan?" Preston asked, eyeing Logan's relaxed stance.

Logan nodded. He didn't ask what Preston was, which I thought was kind of rude. I might not know all the ins and outs of Mythos Academy, but sharing what kind of warrior you were was one of the main conversation starters between the kids at the different branches. I'd heard tons of them ask each other that question up on the ski slopes today, and I'd chatted with a few of the

New York students myself. At least until they'd all started staring at me and asking me what kind of warrior a Gypsy really was and what kind of power I had.

It wasn't exactly a hush-hush secret that Gypsies were people gifted with magic by the gods, but it wasn't common knowledge either. Most of the kids and even some of the professors at Mythos thought I was just a different kind of warrior, which technically, I guess I was. I didn't really understand why so few people had heard of Gypsies before. It was something I kept meaning to ask Grandma Frost or Professor Metis about.

"Well, Logan," I said in a bright voice. "I'm sure you want to go back inside where it's warm. Preston and I were just leaving."

"Oh? Where were you going?" Logan asked. "Maybe I'll tag along. This party's getting a little tame. All the beer is gone already."

I frowned. Why would Logan want to go with Preston and me? I mean, hello, the two of us had been about to disappear into the shadows and totally make out. Logan had to have guessed that. He had plenty of experience in that area. Maybe it was the way the Spartan stared at Preston, with icy, narrowed eyes, but suddenly, the strangest thought filled my mind. Logan wasn't—he couldn't be—there was no way that he was *jealous*. Was he?

Preston looked at Logan, then back at me. His eyebrows shot up in his face. He realized something was going on between Logan and me. I wish he'd clue me in on exactly what it was, because I had no idea.

"Actually, I should go check on my friends. They're

over at another party across the village." Preston turned to me and grinned. "But I'd love to see you tomorrow. Maybe we can have lunch?"

My heart lifted, and a matching grin curved my lips. He wanted to see me again. Maybe he really did like me after all. I felt like doing a happy dance, but of course, I was way too cool for that. I'd at least wait until I got back to my hotel room, alone, where no one would see.

"It's a date," I said.

We pulled out our cell phones and swapped numbers.

"Just text me when you want to hook up, okay?" I told Preston.

He nodded, then gave me another killer smile. "I will. I had fun tonight, Gwen."

I smiled back at him. "Me, too."

For a second, Preston hesitated, like he was going to lean forward and kiss me on the cheek, but then his gaze cut to Logan, and he thought better of it. Preston nodded at me, stuffed his gloved hands into his jacket pockets, and set off across the alpine village.

As soon as he was out of sight, I whirled around and stabbed my finger at Logan, not quite poking him in the chest. "What the hell was that about?"

"What are you doing, Gypsy girl?" Logan asked in a soft voice, instead of answering my question. "You don't even know that guy."

My mouth dropped open, and anger burned through my veins, chasing away the chill of the falling snow. "Oh, cut the double-standard bullshit. I'd say I know just as much about Preston as you do about all the girls you've slept with. How many mattresses have you signed at Mythos, anyway? I'm willing to bet it's more than Preston has up in New York."

Logan's jaw tightened, but he didn't deny any of it. We both knew he had a reputation as a man-whore, whether or not it was actually true.

"What was I doing? I was trying to have some *fun*," I snapped. "That's what we're all here for this weekend, remember? To get totally drunk, wasted, and hook up with random kids from the other academy. According to Daphne, it's a yearly tradition. Besides, what do you care? You came here with Savannah tonight—not me."

Logan stared at me, emotions flickering in his bright blue gaze. "I do—I do care," he finally said, running his hand through his dark hair and melting the flakes of snow that had gathered there. "More than I should. Way more than I should."

These were the words I'd wanted him to say to me for weeks now, ever since I'd asked him out back in the fall. Even now, they made my whole body quiver with happiness. But I was so angry at him for coming between Preston and me—for butting in when he shouldn't have and ruining the moment. Who I talked to was none of his damn business. Ditto for who I made out with.

The happiness and anger battled for control in my chest like a pair of ancient Greco-Roman wrestlers. It didn't take long for the anger to put the happiness in a headlock.

"You care? Really? It sure doesn't seem like it to me, since every time I turn around, you're sticking your tongue down Savannah Warren's throat—right in front of me."

Logan grimaced. "You don't understand. I like Savannah just fine, but you're—you're different, Gypsy girl. Special. You always have been, ever since that first day when you ran into me out on the quad and gave me a piece of your mind."

I arched an eyebrow. "Different? Special? Really? If I'm so *special,* if I matter so *much* to you, then why did you turn me down when I wanted to go out? Huh, Logan? Why would you do that if you were *so* into me?"

He didn't answer, but I could see the anguish flickering in his eyes. The hurt in his face made me want to reach out, to comfort him somehow, but I pushed away the feeling and made my heart as cold as the snow falling around us. I had to be ruthless right now, just like he'd been when he told me that we couldn't be together, that we couldn't even go out on one simple date.

"Let me guess. You're still keeping that big, big secret from me. The one you think I can't handle. The one that will make me not like you anymore." I rolled my eyes. "Whatever. I don't want to understand you and your stupid, twisted logic anyway. Just leave me alone, Spartan, and I'll do the same to you."

I whirled around and stalked away, heading toward the hotel.

"Gwen. Stop. Please."

He called me by my name, which meant he was serious. That was the only time he used my name, instead of jokingly referring to me as "Gypsy girl," the nickname he'd given me the first day we'd met. For once, I was too pissed to care. I kept walking.

But Logan had other ideas. I hadn't taken three steps before he grabbed my arms and turned me around. Stupid Spartan reflexes. He was so much quicker than I was. It just wasn't fair, and his grip was too strong for me to easily break. Before I knew it, Logan had backed me up against the corner of the building. We stood in the shadows, out of sight of the windows and the bright glow of lights spilling out of the coffee shop.

Logan's face was close to mine—so close that his hot breath caressed my cheek. So close that I could see the silvery flecks in his ice blue eyes. So close that I could smell his faint, spicy scent. So close that I could feel the strength of him pressing against me, making me ache for something I knew would be scary and wonderful and heartbreaking all at the same time. Something that made me long to be alone in the dark with him, touching him skin to skin—with no secrets of any kind between us. Just feelings—all these *feelings*.

The flakes of snow kept pouring down, and clouds of frost filled the air between us, our breaths kissing back and forth. Looking at us from a distance, you would have probably thought we were a couple who'd snuck out of the party early to have a little quiet time together. But we weren't a couple, we weren't those happy people at all, and that realization made me miserable.

Because even now, I wanted him to kiss me—wanted him to want me just as much as I did him.

"Look, I'm sorry," Logan said in a low voice. "I just didn't like seeing you with that other guy. I saw the two of you talking through the window, and when you got up, I knew you were leaving with him."

"You're such a damn *hypocrite*. You had no right to come out here and get between us," I whispered in a fierce voice. "No right at all. Not while you're with Savannah."

"I know."

He didn't say anything else, and the snow continued to drift down, a curtain shutting out the rest of the world. Even the noise of the party seemed dim and distant now. Or maybe that was because Logan was filling up my senses until there wasn't room for anything else.

The seconds stretched out and turned into a minute, then two. Still, he didn't say anything—he just kept looking at me with his blue, blue gaze.

"Kiss me or let me go," I finally said in a miserable voice, hot tears stinging my eyes. "I don't care anymore."

Logan's face softened. "I never meant to hurt you. That's the last thing I would ever want to do. I care about you too much for that, Gwen."

Gwen. I closed my eyes at the sound of him saying my name. At the faint rumble of his deep, sexy voice. I couldn't bear to look at him. Maybe it was dark and twisted of me, but right now, for this one second, I wanted to pretend that we *were* a couple. That we really were out here in the dark—alone—together.

"Gwen," Logan repeated, a faint, pleading note in his voice.

I still didn't open my eyes. Silence. Then—

"Gwen." A husky whisper, full of all the longing I felt.

Logan's breath grew hotter on my face, and I knew

that his lips were inching toward mine. My fingers dug into his shoulders, and I waited for him to kiss me. For the images and feelings to fill my mind. For *Logan* to fill my mind until there was nothing else—

The door to the coffee shop banged against the side of the building. My eyes snapped open, but Logan had already drawn back. And there was this look on his face of . . . of *relief*. I knew it was because he hadn't kissed me. Because I hadn't touched him, hadn't flashed on him, which meant that his deep, dark secret—whatever it might be—was still safe.

Giggles filled the night air, along with flashing pink sparks. Daphne and Carson stumbled outside, both of them a little tipsy, and their arms wrapped around each other. Carson's glasses sat crooked on his face, and lip gloss shimmered on one of his cheeks. It looked like he and Daphne had been having a *very* good time inside at the party. The happy couple took one look at Logan and me, still locked together in the shadows, and their laughter cut off.

"Gwen?" Daphne asked, staring at the two of us. "Is something wrong?"

"Let go of me," I muttered in a low voice.

Logan dropped his arms and stepped back.

"No," I said, keeping my gaze fixed on my friends instead of looking at Logan. "Everything's fine. I'm ready to leave. Are you guys?"

The Valkyrie glanced at Carson, who nodded.

"Yeah. We're ready," Carson said.

"Good. Let's go."

I brushed by Logan, so close that I felt his breath kiss

my cheek once more, before breaking free and heading toward the hotel. Daphne and Carson scrambled to catch up with me. I didn't look back at Logan, even though I knew the Spartan was watching me the whole time.

I'd be damned if I let him see the tears in my eyes.

"Who does Logan Quinn think he is?" I fumed, stalking from one side of the hotel room to the other. "Can you believe him? He's got some nerve!"

Daphne rolled her eyes and hit a few buttons on her laptop. "Yeah, yeah. That's the same thing you've been saying for an hour now, Gwen. If you don't stop pacing, you're going to wear a hole in the carpet."

After my almost-kiss with Logan, I'd hurried back to the hotel as fast as I could, with Daphne and Carson right on my heels. They'd been worried about me, but I'd forced myself to put on a calm face, even though my emotions ate away at my heart like acid rain dripping everywhere. I'd already ruined their buzz from the party, so I told my friends that I was fine and was going to the room to take a shower. Then I'd gotten in the elevator and left them in the lobby so they could enjoy some time alone together.

Daphne had come up to our room an hour later, lips red, cheeks flushed, her magic crackling like crazy. She looked like a girl who'd just had a hot, intense, totally enjoyable make-out session with her boyfriend. I envied her. Oh, how I envied her.

I'd had some time to think while Daphne had been

with Carson, and I'd gone from heartbroken and melancholy to seriously pissed at the fact that Logan had the power to make me heartbroken and melancholy in the first place. Now, I was in a "bloody fit," as Vic would say.

I glanced over at the sword. Vic was safe and snug in his black leather scabbard, and I'd leaned him against the dresser within easy reach. The sword's eye was closed, and his mouth was relaxed in a way that meant he was sleeping. No surprise. Vic usually snoozed whenever Daphne came over to my dorm room. The sword claimed that all the "bloody girl talk" bored him.

"I can't believe the nerve of Logan," I muttered again and resumed my pacing. Since the room was so big, it took me several seconds to stalk from one side to the other.

Daphne pushed down the screen of her laptop and crossed her arms over her chest. Her pink Hello Kitty pajamas matched the stickers that decorated her computer case.

"So what are you going to do about it?" the Valkyrie asked. "Are you going to make a play for Logan and take him away from Savannah? The way he was staring at you outside the coffee shop, I think you could totally do that. He really does like you, you know. You should have seen the look on his face when he was holding you. It was *intense*. Even for a Spartan. I've seen some of them in full battle-rage mode who didn't look that focused."

"Well, he's got a funny way of showing it." I flopped

down onto the bed. "And I'm not going to take him away from Savannah. I'm not Morgan McDougall. I don't go around stealing other girls' boyfriends."

"Morgan doesn't exactly steal them," Daphne pointed out. "She just sleeps with them on the sly."

I thought about how sad Morgan had looked, first in the library earlier this week and then again tonight outside the coffee shop. I felt bad talking about the Valkyrie like she was just the school slut and nothing more. She had feelings, too, just like the rest of us did. "Whatever. The point is that I'm not like her, and I don't want to be. Not even for Logan freaking Quinn."

"So what are you going to do?" the Valkyrie asked again, opening her laptop once more.

I stared up at the ceiling. What *was* I going to do? Despite everything that had happened tonight, I still had a crazy, crazy crush on Logan. But nothing was ever going to come of it. For starters, he was dating another girl. Sure, Logan said that he cared about me, but he still had this big, bad secret he wanted to hide from me, something that just wasn't possible given my Gypsy gift. As soon as I touched him, my psychometry would kick in and show me his secret whether I wanted to see it or not. I didn't even have to kiss him—just holding his hand long enough would do the trick. Kind of hard to date a guy when you couldn't risk even touching him, especially when that guy was Logan, who I so badly wanted to touch—in all sorts of ways.

And then there was Preston. Before Logan had interrupted us, we'd been having fun getting to know each other. I liked Preston, and I thought he liked me, too—

at least enough to want to hang out with me this weekend. He had asked me to meet him for lunch tomorrow.

Maybe—maybe Preston could be my rebound guy.
Someone to help me get over this stupid, hopeless crush
I had on Logan. In fact, Preston would be a *perfect* rebound guy, since I wouldn't see him after the weekend
and the Winter Carnival were over. He'd go back to the
New York academy, and I'd go back to Mythos. So why
not have a little fun while we were both here together?

I raised myself up on my elbows. "What am I going
to do? I'm going to have lunch with Preston tomorrow
like he asked me to and forget Logan even exists."

Daphne grinned. "Now you're talking. You'll have to
introduce me to Preston. I really want to see for myself
how gorgeous he is."

"You didn't see him tonight? We were sitting right
outside the coffee shop."

Daphne shook her head. "Nope, I was too busy dancing with Carson and then keeping this trashy Amazon
from getting her hands on him. She was totally making
do-me eyes at Carson from across the room, and she
tried to horn in on us while we were dancing. Slut. She's
going to be sorry she did that, especially since she kept
on even after I told her that Carson was taken."

The Valkyrie hit some more keys on her laptop, her
black eyes glittering with anger. Pink sparks of magic
shot out of her fingertips, like mini streaks of lightning.

I frowned. "Is that what you're doing? Looking up
that other girl online?"

Daphne nodded. "The New York academy has a Web
site, just like we do, where students can blog and post

photos and stuff. Which is why you need to introduce me to your mystery guy. I looked, but there are no Prestons listed on the site. Apparently, your guy decided not to post his photo and set up his online student profile. Ah, there's the Amazon. Calinda Lopez."

Daphne's fingers picked up speed, and she started muttering under her breath. "Come on, baby. We can crack that pesky firewall...."

In addition to being a Valkyrie, Daphne also had some major computer skills. She was in the Tech Club at Mythos, which was really just an after-school group for all the budding hackers at the academy. In fact, Daphne had used her skills to help me break the password on Jasmine Ashton's laptop, back when I'd been investigating Jasmine's fake murder. That was how we'd become friends. Of course, I'd blackmailed Daphne into helping me to start with, but I thought it had all worked out okay in the end.

"Uh, what are you doing?"

Daphne shrugged. "Nothing much. Just erasing all of Calinda's good grades and replacing them with incompletes. Eventually, the administrators will figure out what happened, but I'm making it look like a computer error. Still, I imagine she'll get some nasty lectures from her profs and parents in the meantime."

I shook my head. "Remind me not to piss you off, because you're a total vindictive bitch when you're angry. There are supervillains in my comic books who could learn a thing or two from you."

The Valkyrie stuck out her tongue, then gave me a maniacal grin. "You'd better believe it, Gypsy."

Daphne focused on her laptop and went back to her Internet stalking, hacking, and general mayhem. I crawled under the covers and tucked my pillow underneath my head.

Preston, I thought. Tomorrow, I'd have lunch with Preston, and we'd have a great time together. We'd hang out and laugh and talk and just have fun. I thought about him then, about his blue eyes, his white blond hair, his cute dimples.

But no matter how much I tried to hold on to the image, no matter how hard I concentrated, Preston's face melted into Logan's the second I closed my eyes.

Chapter 12

The next day, Saturday, was the part of the weekend when there was actually a carnival set up as part of the Winter Carnival. Go figure.

Daphne yanked off the covers and pulled me out of bed way, *way* too early. Literally, she grabbed my ankle and used her Valkyrie strength to throw me over her shoulder and haul me into the shower. Sometimes, it really sucked having a best friend who could give the Hulk a run for his money in the weight-lifting department. Especially at seven in the morning.

I'd barely stepped out of the shower when Daphne threw some clothes at me and barked at me to get dressed—or else. Apparently, the carnival was her favorite part of the whole weekend, and she didn't want to miss a second of it, not even to get a few more hours of sleep. And she thought I was a freak.

Grumbling, I threw on some clothes, topped with a clean pair of ski pants and a matching jacket, both in a bright silver that Daphne had picked out for me at the shop yesterday. Boots, gloves, and a cute gray toboggan covered with tiny snowflakes completed my outfit. For once, Daphne actually decided to wear another color besides pink. Her ski suit was a powder blue that made her look like a real ice princess.

We met Carson downstairs in the one of the hotel restaurants. Apparently, the hotel didn't take breakfast quite as seriously as it did the other meals because there was actually some normal food set out as part of a massive buffet: tall stacks of buttermilk pancakes drizzled with apricot syrup, thick slabs of Canadian bacon, enormous omelets stuffed with cheese and colorful veggies. Yum. We washed everything down with spiced apple cider that was the perfect blend of sweet and tart. Then, just after nine, one of the chair lifts whisked us up the mountain and let us off at the carnival.

The Winter Carnival had been set up on a wide, level plateau situated between two of the ski slopes, about three-quarters of the way up the mountain. Ring tosses, duck shooting, milk bottle throws, even a couple of polar bear dunk tanks filled with ice water. Every kind of carnival game you could imagine was featured in the dozens of wooden booths that had been erected on the plateau for the day's event.

The small shacks looked like gingerbread houses with their bright, bold colors and crazy, candy-cane stripes. Glittery signs and streamers announcing the various prizes swooped from the corner of one booth to the next, while neon-colored stuffed animals fought for space on the shelves inside. Loud, cheery calliope music trilled through a portable sound system someone had dragged up the mountain, and heaters blasted away here and there in the snow, to help keep the chill at bay. The merchants from the shops in the alpine village had also made the trek up the mountain, setting up separate shacks and bringing their own high-end goods with them—jewelry, watches, designer clothes.

I thought the professors or the resort staff might perform some kind of ritual before the carnival opened. Light a fire, chant some magic mumbo jumbo, and thank the gods for watching over everyone on the mountain. That's what the profs had done a few weeks ago before the homecoming bonfire and dance back at the academy. Truth be told, I'd found it a little weird and creepy. But the kids had already started playing games, and the sounds of bells, whistles, and more trilled through the air. No ritual today then. Good.

But once again, I couldn't escape the statues. A large stone sculpture of Skadi, the Norse goddess of winter, stood in the middle of the carnival area, looking like a twin to the one inside the hotel lobby. Somehow, the goddess looked even fiercer up here on the mountain, in the midst of the snow, and it seemed like the statue radiated cold, despite the heaters tucked next to her feet. Statues of other gods and goddesses had also been planted in the snow here and there, their stone lips curled up into crazy smiles that matched the excitement of the day. I sighed and looked away from them.

It didn't take long for something else to catch my attention, though—the food. Cotton candy, kettle corn, caramel apples, corn dogs, deep-fried Twinkies. I spotted signs for all those treats, and each one made a grin spread a little wider across my face. For once, the food was actually normal, and I was *totally* getting my sugar rush on today. A warm, sweet, delicious aroma filled the air, and I breathed in. Were those funnel cakes I smelled? With powdered sugar and hot cherry sauce oozing off the top? My stomach rumbled in anticipation, even though we'd just eaten breakfast.

"Isn't it fabulous?" Daphne asked, her eyes glittering like black diamonds in her face. "Where do you think we should go first, Carson?"

The band geek put his arm around the Valkyrie and hugged her to his chest. "I think we should go over to the ring toss, so I can win you a stuffed animal. Or a dagger, whichever you prefer."

Daphne arched her eyebrows and gave him an amused smile. "Even though I can totally beat you whenever we play any kind of game in gym class?"

Carson blushed a little. "Yeah, well, I can try. Look how many tickets I bought. Surely, I can win something with them."

He pulled a wad of red tickets out of the pocket of his black ski pants. You had to buy tickets to play the various carnival games, and the proceeds went to help fund the whole weekend trip. Daphne and Carson had both whipped out their credit cards to get tickets for all the games as soon as we'd stepped off the chair lift. They'd dropped close to five hundred bucks each without batting an eye.

I hadn't bothered buying any tickets, though. I wasn't coordinated enough to play one of the games and actually win anything. Well, I might be able to win if there was some kind of archery game, and I channeled my memories of Daphne at her tournaments, just like I did during weapons training. But the Powers That Were at the academy would probably consider that to be cheating.

"Come on," Daphne said, grabbing my hand. "Enough standing around. Let's play some games!"

We wandered around the Winter Carnival for the next two hours, moving from one booth to another. It looked like everyone in the entire Powder complex had turned out for the event, and the whole mountain was crawling with kids, professors, and the resort staff.

I spotted Professor Metis running one of the ring toss games and cheerfully talking to all the students. Nickamedes stood next to her in the booth, handing out prizes to the winners, a pinched, sour expression on his face. No doubt the librarian was allergic to fresh air and sunshine. Sometimes I wondered if Nickamedes was actually a vampire, as pale and pasty as he was. I'd have to ask Daphne about the librarian, and if, you know, vampires actually existed in the first place. Despite all the things I'd learned in myth-history class, I was still a little unclear on all the different types of monsters out there. Okay, okay, on a lot of things, really.

Metis and Nickamedes weren't the only professors I saw. Mr. Llew, my calculus teacher; Mrs. Banba, the economics prof; Coach Lir, the lean, lanky swimming instructor—they were all helping out with the booths and games. Even Mrs. Raven, the library coffee cart lady was here, manning one of the cotton candy machines.

I had fun watching Daphne and Carson play all the carnival games, but it wasn't long before I noticed there was something a little . . . off about the contests. Like at the ring toss, where the kids threw spiked metal chains over the heads of Nemean prowlers instead of using simple rings and metal poles. Or over at the milk bottle toss, where the glass bottles all had grinning black masks painted on them to represent Reaper faces. And especially at the dunk tank, where the bulls'-eye reminded me of a drawing of Loki that I'd seen in my myth-history book, the one where the evil god's face was all twisted and melted from the snake venom that had dripped onto his handsome features for centuries. The venom continually spattering onto Loki had been part of his punishment the first time the other gods had locked him away, before he escaped and plunged the world into the Chaos War.

Then, there were the prizes. Carson hadn't been kidding when he said he could win Daphne a dagger. Most of the booths were crammed with stuffed animals and other oversize toys, but weapons gleamed on the shelves right alongside them—swords, staffs, crossbows, throwing stars, even a shield or two. And lots of kids chose the sharp, shiny weapons over the toys. But even when the students opted for the toys, they were still all wrong. Instead of fluffy pink bunnies and plush black bears, the stuffed animals were shaped like grinning gryphons or stoic sphinxes.

Once I started noticing all the stuff like that, I couldn't quit looking at it—and it seriously creeped me out. Who wanted to go to a carnival where the prizes could be used to murder you? Especially since I knew there was a real Reaper of Chaos lurking somewhere out here in the winter sunshine—one who wanted to kill me.

"Uh, what's with all the games?" I asked Carson at one point, while Daphne was busy shooting arrows through a metal ring that was barely bigger around than my wrist.

"What do you mean?" he mumbled, stuffing a wad of lime cotton candy into his mouth.

"I mean, why is everything decorated with Nemean prowlers and scary, twisted Reaper masks?"

Carson frowned. "What are you talking about, Gwen? The booths and games are decorated the same way they always are. I think they look great."

I opened my mouth to ask him another question, but I realized it was kind of pointless. To Carson, Nemean prowlers, Reaper masks, and bull's-eyes of Loki were completely normal. He'd never been to any other kind of carnival, out there in the regular mortal world, where kids had no idea that mythological monsters even existed or that there was an ancient struggle still being fought today in modern times. Then again, mortal carnivals usually had a clown or two. I supposed images of an evil god who wanted to break free of his mythological prison and enslave the whole world weren't any scarier than a guy wearing big red shoes, yellow plaid pants, and white face paint. Clowns had always creeped me out. They were *so* not funny.

Daphne put all her arrows through the ring and won a stuffed gryphon for Carson before we headed off to the next game.

I looked for Preston in the crowd, hoping that maybe we could hook up before lunch and I could introduce him to my friends, but I didn't see him anywhere. No surprise. So many people were crammed into the carnival space that it was hard enough to keep track of Daphne and Carson right beside me. I had my cell phone in my pocket though, waiting for him to text me. Or maybe I'd be brave and text him first. I hadn't decided yet.

One person I had no trouble spotting was Logan. The Spartan stood over at the strong man test, swinging a sledgehammer down onto a platform and making a weight shoot up a tall scale and ring a bell at the top. Big, burly Coach Ajax manned that game, his onyx skin glistening in the sunlight. With his arms crossed over his chest, the coach looked like a granite slab someone had planted on the mountainside, along with all the other statues.

Kenzie and Oliver were hanging out with Logan, all three of them taking turns with the sledgehammer. I glanced at the crowd of girls standing around giggling and watching them, but I didn't see Savannah anywhere. Maybe the Spartans were having a guys' day out or something. Whatever. I did not care what Logan was doing or who he was doing it with. I did not care. *I did not care.* Maybe if I told myself that enough times, it would actually be true. Yeah, right. Even I didn't believe that, and I was the one who was trying to lie to myself.

My cell phone buzzed in my jacket pocket, distracting me from my thoughts of Logan. I pulled it out and read the message. *Ready 4 lunch? Meet me @ hotel in 15 min. P.*

"Is that your mystery man?" Daphne asked, looking over my shoulder and squinting down at the screen.

I grinned at her. "Yes, it is. He wants to meet for lunch back at the hotel."

"Oh, okay, well, we'll go with you," Daphne said. "Just let Carson finish his game."

Carson was playing a whacked-out version of Whac-A-Mole, except he was trying to hit gargoyle heads as they popped up out of a metal table instead of, you know, moles. But he wasn't having much luck at it. A gargoyle popped up on the table, and Carson slammed his hammer straight down on top of it—and the thumb of his other hand, which had somehow gotten in the way. I winced. And I thought I was uncoordinated.

"Nah," I said, taking off my gloves and stuffing them into my pockets. "I know how much you love the carnival. You guys stay here. We'll catch up after lunch."

"Well, if you're sure . . ."

Daphne's voice trailed off, and she eyed Carson's hammer, no doubt thinking how much better she could do with it, especially with her Valkyrie strength. If Daphne whacked one of those gargoyles, I doubted it would rise back up. She could break the whole table with one blow if she wanted to.

"I'm sure," I said, texting Preston back and telling him that I was on my way down the mountain and would meet him in the lobby. "Go have fun. I'll be fine."

"And what about the Reaper?" Daphne asked in a low voice. "You haven't said anything, but I know you're still thinking about him, whoever he is. I would be. But Metis said she would take care of things, right?"

Daphne didn't know that I hadn't talked to Metis about the Reaper. Instead, I'd told my friend that the professor was looking into things. The vague answer had seemed to satisfy the Valkyrie. Plus, I hadn't said anything else to her about the Fenrir wolf that I'd seen in the trees yesterday and how I thought the creature wasn't just a wild wolf hanging around the mountain resort.

I shrugged. "Nothing's happened since we got here yesterday. Maybe he didn't make the trip to the resort. Or maybe he's having too good a time to want to kill me today."

I laughed at my lame joke, but Daphne didn't smile. She just looked at me, worry filling her face. She was right, though. I hadn't forgotten about the Reaper. In fact, that was one reason why I'd decided not to play any of the carnival games—so I could spy on the crowd instead.

I'd looked at everyone we'd passed today, all the other kids we'd talked to, all the profs manning the booths, all the hotel staff members making cotton candy and caramel apples. I'd even taken my gloves off and accidentally-on-purpose touched a few of them, just to see what kind of flashes I might get, just to see if I could figure out who the Reaper was. But I hadn't seen anything out of the ordinary. Everyone was focused on the carnival, all the games they wanted to play, and all the prizes they wanted to win.

"I'll take the chair lift and go straight down to the hotel," I said, crossing my heart with my finger. "Promise. I'll be fine. You'll see."

Daphne still hesitated. "Well, if you're sure . . ."

I gave her a little push. "I'm sure. Now, go take that hammer away from Carson before he hurts himself with it."

"Yeah," Daphne sighed. "He's not very good with it, is he? But luckily he more than makes up for it in other ways."

She gave me a knowing smirk, and I just rolled my eyes.

"So Carson's a great kisser. Whatever," I said, then grinned. "Although maybe if I'm lucky, I'll discover Preston has some similar talents after lunch."

I left Daphne and Carson at the carnival and headed back over to the chair lift. To my surprise, it wasn't operating, and the chairs dangled like wind chimes strung on the thick, black cables. A grizzled guy with a beard that reached down to his waist crouched by one of the steel stations that jutted up out of the snow. A hatch was open on the bottom of the station, and the guy clipped and twisted the wires inside, working on the electric circuits or whatever controlled the lift.

"Uh, excuse me, but why isn't the chair lift working right now?" I asked.

The guy pulled his head back out of the box and stared at me. His bushy white beard made him look like Santa Claus. "We've been having some electrical problems. Thought I'd take care of it while all you kids were busy playing your carnival games."

"Okay, so when are you going to be done? In a few minutes, maybe?"

The guy shook his head. "Nope. I've got at least another half hour's worth of work here. Probably closer to an hour."

Frustration filled me. I knew it wasn't the guy's fault he was doing his maintenance right now, it was just my bad luck.

"Well, how am I supposed to get back down to the hotel? I'm meeting someone for lunch."

He shrugged again. "I guess you'll have to walk down the slopes. That's what the other kids are doing."

He pointed, and sure enough, I saw a few figures at the very bottom of the mountain, walking through the alpine village and heading for the hotel. Tracks crisscrossed the snow where the other kids had wound their way down the steep slope.

"Thanks," I said.

The guy nodded, stuck his head back into the box, and started fiddling with all the wires inside again.

I should have headed toward the hotel immediately, but instead, I hesitated, my eyes scanning the snowy landscape, looking for the Fenrir wolf. I hadn't seen the monster since yesterday, but that didn't mean that it wasn't still lurking around the resort somewhere, waiting to pounce on me the second it got the chance.

My phone vibrated again, cutting into my thoughts, and I pulled it out of my pocket and read the message. *Here already. Waiting 4 U. P.*

I bit my lip and put my phone back into my pocket. I didn't want to stand up Preston, and I didn't want to text him some lame excuse about not wanting to walk down the mountain by myself, because there might be a mythological monster after me. He'd think I was crazy. Besides, there were tons of people on the mountain today making tons of noise. Surely, those things would be enough to make the wolf stay hidden wherever it was.

So I stepped into the tracks the other kids had made and set off down the mountain. Despite the fact the other students had plowed a path, the snow was still deep, coming up to midthigh on me in places. I floundered through it, doggedly going down the slope one slippery step at a time.

I moved as fast as I could, but it was slow going, and I was just debating whether or not I should text Preston to let him know I'd be late when I heard the sound I'd been dreading—the low, throaty growl of the Fenrir wolf.

The ominous sound slithered across the snow to me, and I froze, wondering where it had come from. I'd trudged about halfway down the mountain by this point, and the chair lift and the Winter Carnival were up and off to my left. Happy shrieks of laughter mixed with the loud calliope music on that side of the slope.

Okay, the wolf definitely wasn't over there. That only left one other option.

I slowly turned my head to the right, and there the creature was—crouched down in the snow just inside the tree line, like it had been yesterday when I'd first spotted it next to the bunny slope. I'd been so focused on meeting Preston and getting down the slope as fast as I could that I hadn't been paying attention to where I was going, just blindly following the tracks, and I'd drifted over toward the thicket of pine trees that covered this side of the mountain—and the Fenrir wolf.

It looked the same as I remembered—a big, powerful body covered with shaggy, ash-colored fur and burning crimson eyes that seemed to glow with a particular hatred for me. The wolf's lips drew back, exposing its many, many teeth, and it licked its lips with its long, red tongue before its chops drew back in something that looked like a supremely satisfied smile—just like the smile the drawing in my myth-history book had given me back at the academy.

Stupid, stupid, stupid, Gwen!

I cursed myself. How could I have been so freaking *stupid?* I knew I had to stay away from the trees, but I'd been so distracted by the thought of having lunch with a cute guy that I'd practically wandered over and given the wolf a pat on the head. Here you go, puppy dog. Here's a tasty treat just for *you.*

Before I could worry too much about the wolf and whether or not it was going to leap out of the trees and tear me into bite-size pieces, a tremendous roar ripped through the air, and the ground shook, like the mountain was the epicenter of a violent earthquake.

I fell on my ass in the snow and just sat there, stunned, while the ground bucked and heaved beneath me. Above my head, the chairs on the lift swung back and forth at sharp, crazy angles, *creak-creak-creak*ing with every tremor until I thought they might snap off the cables and come crashing down right on top of my head.

As suddenly as it had started, the intense shaking stopped, and I shook off my shock and scrambled to my feet. I shielded my eyes against the dazzling glare and looked up. Something must have exploded on top of the mountain, because I could see bright orange flames up there, licking at the sky like they wanted to burn all of the blue out of it.

I let out a tense breath. Whatever was going on, it was happening at the top of the mountain and not down here where I was at. . . .

That's when the rumbling started. This deep, violent, intense rumbling that rippled through the whole mountain, the roar of it drowning out everything else. I half expected the snow to split open under my feet and for me to start falling down, down, down into the middle of the earth.

And there was . . . there was . . . there was *something* coming down the mountain now. I squinted, trying to see exactly what it was. . . .

My breath caught in my throat, and I realized what the rumbling was.

The explosion that rocked the mountaintop hadn't just started a fire—it had also dislodged the snow.

Thousands and thousands of tons of it, all barreling toward me, until the towering, white, shadowy wave of it blotted out the sun.

An avalanche was tearing down the mountain—and I was right in the middle of its path.

Chapter 13

It took my brain maybe half a second to realize what was going on. That, yes, there was an avalanche on the mountain, that the snow was crashing down on itself with tremendous, unstoppable force—and that it was getting closer and closer with every breath I took.

I might not be the outdoorsy type, but I'd seen enough nature programs on television to realize I had two choices: stay where I was, get swept away by the avalanche, and die or make a run for the tree line and hope that the gnarled, knotty pines would shield me from the snow. Of course, the only problem with option number two was that the Fenrir wolf was waiting in the trees to rip me into bloody bits. Not much of a chance of me surviving either way, but the odds were slightly better with the wolf. People survived getting attacked by grizzly bears. A Fenrir wolf couldn't be much worse than that—right?

I was going to find out.

I picked up my feet and raced across the snow, running as fast as I could through the powder and heading straight for the tree line. The roar of the avalanche grew louder and louder until it drowned out everything else, even my own desperate, panicked breaths and the erratic *thump-thump-thump* of my heart. The air felt dense and heavy with snow, and I couldn't get enough oxygen into my lungs, but I kept running. I knew that if I stopped, even for a second, the avalanche would catch me and carry me away.

And then there was the wolf. It paced back and forth inside the thicket of trees, looking at me and then up at the snow that was probably going to bury us both.

I didn't have time to tiptoe around the creature or keep it from attacking me, so I threw myself into the trees and scrambled forward, trying to get into the very middle of the thicket. The wolf stayed where it was, watching me with its burning red eyes. They grew brighter and brighter as the snow rushed toward us and the landscape darkened.

I plopped down on my ass in front of the thickest, strongest tree I saw, ripped off my silver ski jacket, wrapped it around my waist, and used the sleeves to tie myself to the trunk. Then I curled my arms and legs around the sturdy trunk, ignoring the sharp, sticky needles that scratched my face and the pinecones that snagged in my hair. I anchored myself to the tree as best I could.

I was two feet away from the Fenrir wolf—well within killing distance. All it would have to do would be to lean forward and snap its jaws around my neck, and I'd be dead.

Instead of leaping on top of me, the wolf watched me

all the while, its pointed ears laid back flat against its enormous head. It had hunkered down in the snow just like I had. The wolf's mouth was open, and it was probably growling at me, although I couldn't hear it above the roar of the avalanche.

"This is not my fault, so don't kill me, okay?" I yelled to the creature, even though it was useless.

The wolf's red, narrowed eyes were the last thing I saw before the snow hit me, and the world went white.

Everything was just—*violent*. Roars and crashes and forces pulling me every which way, threatening to rip my arms and legs from around the tree trunk, threatening to sweep me away and bury me deep, deep down in the snow where no one would ever, ever find me.

I tightened my grip and held on.

I couldn't see, and I could barely breathe. There was just noise and pressure and stinging slaps of snow. I don't know how long I huddled there, my face mashed against the rough bark, my whole body pressed against the trunk, my arms aching from the effort of hanging onto the pine tree. My lungs burned from trying to suck down enough oxygen to stay conscious, and ice crystals pricked my face like thousands of tiny daggers. All the while, the snow slammed into me, a cold undertow trying to pull me down, down, down the mountain with it.

And then it stopped.

The roars, crashes, and forces slowed, sputtered, and then slid away all together. It had stopped—the avalanche had finally stopped.

I opened my aching eyes, but the world was still

white. Why? Why would everything still be white? My brain just did not want to work, and it took me a second to realize I was buried up to my neck in the snow, my face still digging into the trunk of the tree I'd tied myself to. For a moment I panicked, wondering how I was going to get out of here—and how long it would take before I froze to death.

I made myself think of my mom. She'd always told me to stop a second and take some deep breaths whenever I was panicked, scared, or upset. Yeah, I was definitely all of those things right now. But Mom had always said that no matter how bad things got, no matter how much trouble I was in, the worst thing to do was to panic on top of it. So I made myself focus on my memories of her and fixed the image of her face in my mind. Long, brown hair; warm violet eyes; a beautiful, wise smile. *Mom.*

I kept on breathing and thinking about her. The panic didn't completely fade away, since I was in some pretty serious trouble here, but it wasn't overwhelming me now either. I could manage it now. Slowly, reluctantly, I let go of my mom's image and let her face fade from my mind, feeling the sharp ache of her loss once more. Then I opened my eyes and started to move my arms and legs. Everything was still attached, even though I felt bruised, battered, and sore from head to toe.

The jacket I'd used to tie myself to the tree was long gone, ripped away by the snow. So were my cell phone and the gloves that I'd put in my pockets. I don't know how I'd held on to the trunk for as long as I had. Maybe because I'd known I simply had to in order to survive.

I clawed and pushed and heaved and pulled my way out of the snowbank, wriggling away from the tree that had saved my life. It was twisted and bent now, the needles long gone and the branches sheared off into broken, spearlike pieces. All the other pines in the thicket looked the same, like they'd all been scalped. Once I was free, I lay there in the snow, panting, just grateful I was still alive. . . .

A soft, almost whimpering sound whispered through the crushed trees.

The wolf!

I'd completely forgotten about it in the roaring confusion of the avalanche. My head snapped around, looking for the creature, waiting for it to leap out of a snowbank and claw me to death.

I spotted it lying on its side about ten feet away from me—with blood on the snow all around it. I looked closer and realized that a long, jagged branch stuck out of one of the wolf's legs, like an arrow. The force of the avalanche must have thrown the monster against a tree and shoved the branch through its leg, although I didn't know how the snow hadn't carried the wolf away completely. I supposed that was just a monster for you—surviving no matter what.

The wolf saw me staring at it and let out another low, pitiful, pain-filled whimper. It looked at me with its red, red eyes and twitched its injured leg in my direction, almost like it wanted me to somehow . . . help it.

I bit my lip, wondering if this was some sort of trick. Despite Metis's lecture in myth-history class, I didn't know much about Fenrir wolves. Well, okay, I knew this particular wolf would have killed me if the avalanche hadn't caught us both. That it had been ordered to kill me by its Reaper master.

The smart thing to do would have been to crawl away from it as quick as I could, to get to my feet, stumble out of the crushed thicket, and hope there was someone on the way to rescue me. But I couldn't just leave the wolf here like that. Not all wounded, bloody, broken-looking, and crying like a puppy who'd just lost its mother. My mom would have tried to help it, even if it was a monster, even if it had been sent to kill her. That was just the kind of person she'd been—and it was the kind of person I wanted to be, too.

"Nike," I whispered. "If you're watching me right now, I would really, really appreciate it if you would keep that thing from eating me."

There was no answer, of course. According to everything that Metis had told us in myth-history class, the gods rarely appeared to mortals—and even when they did, it was strictly on their terms. After the end of the Chaos War, the gods had made a pact not to interfere in mortal affairs, so they wouldn't destroy the world with their magic and meddling, and they stuck to the agreement for the most part, letting their Champions do their dirty work for them. But asking Nike for help made me feel a little better, even if I knew that she wouldn't magically pop into view and solve all my problems.

Crazy—what I was about to do was absolutely crazy. But I did it anyway.

I drew in a breath and crawled across the snow to the Fenrir wolf. The creature watched me with its red eyes, although its gaze was now dark and dull with pain. I stopped about a foot away from it, looking at the wound. The branch wasn't all that big, but it had to hurt, stuck through the wolf's leg that like, just the way it had hurt when I'd accidentally rammed a needle through my finger while trying to sew a button on a shirt once.

Hands shaking, I reached forward and grabbed hold of the branch. I didn't get much of a vibe off the broken piece—it was just wood, after all—but the wolf let out a low, warning growl. For a second, I thought it was going to reach up with its other paw and rip my throat open with its sharp, black claws. Instead, the creature put its head back down, burying its muzzle in the snow, and closed its eyes, bracing itself for what it knew I was going to do.

"Here goes nothing," I muttered.

I shoved the branch through the wolf's leg. It took all the strength and bravery I had to force the wood through the creature's muscle and out the other side, but I did it. Then I grabbed the bloody stick and threw it as far away as I could. The broken branch hit one of the flattened trees and fluttered to the snow.

The Fenrir wolf let out a horrible, horrible howl, and before I could blink, I was on my back in the snow, with the monster on top of me, its paws as heavy as lead weights on my chest. I froze, staring up into its bloodred eyes. The wolf leaned closer, its breath hot, heavy, and sour on my face. I tensed, waiting for it to sink its teeth into me. . . .

The wolf leaned forward and licked my cold cheek.

Its tongue was wet, heavy, and as rough as sandpaper against my skin, but the wolf's touch was gentle enough. My psychometry kicked in the second it licked me, and I got a series of flashes off it, mostly of the avalanche and all the snow slamming into its body just like it had mine. But there was also a warmer, softer feeling in the mix, a sense that the wolf was actually . . . grateful to me for getting the branch out of its leg. For helping it when I could have just crawled away and left it here alone and injured in the snow.

The wolf stared down at me, paws still on my chest, its shaggy tail thumping from side to side and spraying us both with snow. It seemed like . . . it expected me to *do* something. Maybe my mind was completely gone, because there was only one thing I could think of right now that might satisfy it. I reached up and awkwardly patted the side of its head, since that was all I could reach.

"Nice puppy," I whispered, and passed out.

Chapter 14

"Gwen! Gwen Frost!"

Someone shouting my name snapped me out of the blackness that I'd been drifting along in. I opened my eyes and realized that I was still outside on my back in what was left of the crushed, snowy thicket.

But I wasn't cold.

Sometime while I'd been unconscious, the Fenrir wolf had lain down lengthwise next to me. It was longer than I was tall, and it had wrapped its thick, shaggy tail around my legs, like I was a cute, wayward puppy that it was cuddling with. I turned my head and almost bumped my nose into the wolf's. The creature blinked at me, like it had been asleep, too, then yawned, showing me each and every one of its sharp, pointed teeth. It could have seriously used a breath mint.

Snuggling with a wolf? That was kind of weird. All right, really weird. But since the creature hadn't tried to, you know, *eat me,* I wasn't going to complain. Not one little bit. Still, I slowly scooted away from it. No point in tempting fate, the gods, or whatever crazy thing was at work here.

"Gwen!" the shout came again. This time I realized it was a man's voice. "Can you hear me?"

"Over here!" I shouted back, although my voice came out as more of a low, strained rasp. "I'm over here!"

Silence. For a second I wondered if he'd even heard my hoarse cry, but then—

"I heard her! She's alive!"

Scuffles sounded, and through the pulverized pine trees, I spotted someone in a black jacket running toward me, sending up sprays of snow in every direction. I turned and looked back at the wolf.

"I think you'd better go now," I said. "They wouldn't like you being here."

I don't know if the Fenrir wolf understood my words or not, but the creature rose to its feet. I noticed that its right ear had a bloody, jagged V in it, like a piece of it had been torn off during the avalanche. The creature leaned down and gently butted me with its head. I hesitated, then reached up and stroked its silky ear. My psychometry kicked in, and once again, the wolf's warm gratitude filled my mind. Maybe it was my imagination, but the wolf almost seemed to—to *rumble* with pleasure at me petting it. Yeah, that was kind of weird, too, especially since I'd never thought of the wolf as anything but a mythological monster, a nightmare come to life.

"Gwen!" the shout came again, closer and louder this time.

The wolf let out another happy rumble, then loped off through the trees, heading away from the sound of the approaching voice. It limped a little on its injured leg, but it still moved quicker than I could ever dream of.

I put my head back down on the snow and tried to ignore the tremors that shook my body and the fact that my teeth clattered together like dried up bones. I'd just petted a Fenrir wolf—and *lived*. How twisted was that? Daphne would have probably thought it was wicked cool. I was just happy I'd survived.

Without the wolf to help keep me warm, the cold quickly seeped into my body. I knew I should fight the icy numbness, but I just didn't have the strength. Not right now. I'd just started to drift off to sleep again when Coach Ajax burst into the thicket, his big, burly body tearing through the broken trees like they weren't even there. He dropped to one knee in the snow beside me.

"Gwen?" he asked in a tight, concerned voice. "Are you all right?"

"I've definitely been better," I said, and passed out again.

I was out of it for a while after that. I tried to stay awake, really, I did. You would think it would have been easy, given all the shouting, noise, and general commotion. But time after time, my eyes slid shut, and I just didn't have the energy to stop them. All I got to see of my dramatic rescue were these little snapshots whenever I woke up for a minute or two.

Coach Ajax carrying me out of the trees and putting me on a stretcher that was attached to the back of a snowmobile. Professor Metis wrapping me in warm thermal blankets to help get my body temperature back up where it should be. Even Nickamedes was there, throwing the snowmobile into gear and racing down the mountain faster than I thought the librarian would ever dare to drive.

Finally, though, the cold, wind, and noise faded away, replaced by soft, soothing, quiet warmth. I dreamed then—strange dreams about all sorts of things. Well, they weren't really *dreams* so much as disjointed images and old memories, not all of which were my own.

I'd had these sorts of dreams before. Thanks to my Gypsy gift, I never forgot anything that I saw or felt when I touched an object and got a vibe off it. Sometimes, when I went to sleep, my mind randomly surfed through other people's memories, other people's feelings. Usually I saw things that I'd already experienced, thanks to my magic. Other times the images were completely new. I didn't always notice every little thing when I touched an object and flashed on it. But all the information was floating around in my mind, and sometimes my subconscious kicked in and showed me what I'd missed.

Either way, it was like watching a movie in my head, and more often than not, I felt like Alice roaming through Wonderland and staring at all the curious things around her.

This time was no different. One after another, various

flickers, flashes, and flares of memory filled my mind. The arrow quivering in the bookcase beside my head at the Library of Antiquities. The shriek of the calliope music from the Winter Carnival turning into the roar of the avalanche. The Fenrir wolf sitting in the snow staring at me with its red, red eyes. Even my mom, climbing into her car.

Somehow I knew this last memory was from the night my mom had been killed by a drunk driver—and I was watching her get into her car for the very last time before the accident. But the really bizarre thing was that it was a memory I shouldn't even have. I hadn't been there the night my mom had left the police station—or touched anything that would give me a vibe about the accident. At least, not that I knew of, and I think I would have remembered *that,* even in my weird, twisted dreams.

"Mom?" I mumbled.

My mom opened her car door and slid inside. Cold, sweaty panic filled me, and I suddenly couldn't breathe. I had to stop her. I had to tell her to stay at the police station and not drive home tonight. If only she would stay put, she wouldn't be T-boned by that damn drunk driver. She wouldn't die and leave me and Grandma Frost by ourselves.

I raced toward my mom, my sneakers smacking against the cracked pavement, but the closer I got to her car, the fuzzier the image got, until the vehicle just faded away completely—with my mom still inside it. I stopped, gasping for air, and my heart throbbed with a dull, familiar, bitter ache. I whirled around and around, but there was no one else in the parking lot—and nothing but blackness all around me. Why did my mom always keep leaving me? Why couldn't she stay with me for just a little while? Why was I always the one who was left behind?

"I think she's finally coming out of it." A soft voice interrupted my dream.

The blackness vanished, and my eyes fluttered open.

I was lying on a hard, lumpy hospital bed. To my left, a complicated-looking machine chirped out a steady tune in time to the green, squiggly lines that skipped up and down on a monitor. My heart rate, I supposed. Blankets covered me from neck to ankle, and I felt several heating pads trapped between my back and the bed. I tried to move and found that I was wrapped up tighter than a mummy. It took me several seconds to wiggle my hands out of the tight cocoon and sit up.

Everything in the room was white—white walls, white floors, white ceiling, even the blankets piled on top of me were white. The lack of color worried me, and for a second I thought I was still stuck in the snow-bank before I was able to shake off my confusion.

My eyes skipped around the rest of the room, but there wasn't much to see—except for the statue. The stone figure perched on a long table directly across from my bed, turned so its eyes stared straight into mine. It was the same statue of Skadi that I'd noticed in the lobby and then earlier today at the outdoor carnival. Only this time, the Norse winter goddess's lips curved down, as though she was disappointed I'd survived the avalanche and was here in the infirmary, instead of buried in a cold, snowy grave. I pulled the blankets back up to my chin and looked away.

Footsteps scuffed on the floor, and Professor Metis stepped into the room. Faint lines grooved into her forehead, and weary worry darkened her green eyes. The professor looked all tired and used up, like she'd been the one out in the avalanche instead of me.

"How are you feeling, Gwen?" Metis asked in a soft voice.

"Fine," I said. "I feel fine."

The weird thing was that I really did feel fine. All the aches, pains, bruises, and scratches I'd gotten during the avalanche had vanished. In fact, I felt like I could hop out of bed right now and do a round of weapons training with the Spartans—and win. Which totally wasn't like me at all.

"Of course you feel fine, Gwendolyn," Nickamedes said in a snide tone, entering the room behind the professor. "Since Aurora just spent the better part of an hour healing you."

Aurora? It took me a second to realize that he meant Professor Metis. Aurora, so that was her first name. Pretty. I liked it.

"Did you—did you touch me?" I asked her. "When you healed me?"

If she had, it might help explain all the crazy dreams I'd had. Although I still wasn't sure where that memory of my mom had come from. Could it have been from

Metis? She and my mom had been best friends when they were kids, so she had to have tons of memories of my mom. But the images I'd seen had been from the night my mom had died, when her car had been hit by a drunk driver. Surely, Metis would have told me if she'd been there that night. What reason would she have to keep it a secret? My head started to ache from trying to figure everything out.

Metis shook her head. "I didn't know if you'd want that or not, Gwen, given your psychometry, so I didn't actually touch you. It's more difficult, but I can heal people just by being in close proximity to them, sort of by pushing my aura into theirs and feeding them my energy until they're well again."

The way she described it made me think of Daphne and the pink sparks that always flashed around her fingertips. The Valkyrie had once told me that the color of her magic was tied to her aura and personality. I wondered if Daphne would have the same healing power that Metis did when the Valkyrie's magic finally quickened.

"So what happened?" I asked. "Up on the mountain?"

"What do you remember?" Metis asked, her voice much softer and kinder than Nickamedes's was.

I thought back. "Well, the chair lift was on the fritz, and I was slogging down the slope to the hotel when I heard some kind of explosion. I looked up, and there were flames dancing all over the top of the mountain. Then, a few seconds later, the avalanche started, and all the snow began sliding down the mountain, coming right at me."

I shuddered and hugged my arms around myself, as if that would somehow banish the horrible memory from my mind. I wouldn't need my Gypsy gift to recall the avalanche. No matter how many other bad things happened to me, I'd remember the roar of the snow for the rest of my life. The shadow of it blocking out everything else, and the cold, cruel force of it trying to pull me under and bury me—forever.

Across from me, I noticed the statue of Skadi was now smiling, as if the stone figure could somehow hear what I was thinking. *Creepy.*

Then another awful thought filled my mind. "No one else was hurt, were they? By the avalanche?"

"No," Metis said. "All the other students were either at the carnival or at the hotel. You were the only one walking down the slope at the time."

I sighed with relief. No one else had gotten hurt. Good. That was good.

Metis and Nickamedes looked at each other. The librarian raised his black eyebrows, like he was asking the professor a question. Metis shook her head the tiniest bit, telling the librarian no to whatever it was he wanted.

"What?" I asked. "What's going on? The two of you aren't telling me something. Teachers and parents *always* have that guilty look when they're holding something back."

Metis drew in a breath. "You're right, Gwen. I really don't know how to say this, but there is some . . . evidence that the avalanche wasn't an accident."

I frowned. "What are you talking about? Sure, I saw

the flames and heard the explosion or whatever, but there has to be some kind of explanation right? The chair lift catching on fire or something?"

Nickamedes stared at me, his eyes as cold and hard as chips of ice. "Oh, there's an explanation, all right, Gwendolyn. Mainly, that someone caused the avalanche—on purpose."

Chapter 15

Despite all the craziness that had been going on the past few days, Nickamedes's words still stunned me.

"You think it was—it was *deliberate?*" I asked, cold dread pooling in the bottom of my stomach. "Why?"

Nickamedes stared down his nose at me. "Mountains do not blow themselves up, Gwendolyn. After we got you down here safely to the infirmary, Ajax and I went back up the mountain. We found some burn marks and other things that indicate that someone deliberately set off an explosion at the top of the mountain, which was what caused the avalanche."

The Reaper. I knew it was the mysterious Reaper who was trying to kill me. First, the SUV outside my Grandma Frost's house, then the arrow in the library, and now, the Fenrir wolf and the avalanche. Somehow, the Reaper had seen me leave the carnival and start down the mountain. I didn't know if he'd planned the explosion and the avalanche in advance or not, but he'd seen an opportunity to kill me, and he'd taken it.

And he'd almost succeeded. If I'd hadn't run for the

pine trees, if I'd been just a second or two slower in getting there, if I hadn't tied myself to the tree . . .

If, if, if.

If any of those things had gone wrong, the avalanche would have swept me away—forever.

What was even worse was the fact that this time the Reaper hadn't cared who else he might have hurt. If there had been anyone else going down the mountain the same time I had been, if Daphne and Carson had decided to have lunch with Preston and me . . . My stomach twisted, and I thought I was going to be sick.

The door to the infirmary banged open, and Daphne barged inside, pink sparks of magic flashing around her, like a thousand tiny fireflies winking on and off.

"Sorry, Aurora," Coach Ajax said, sticking his head into the room. "I couldn't keep her out any longer."

"Gwen!" Daphne said, rushing over to me.

She bumped Nickamedes out of the way, her Valkyrie strength pushing the librarian back several steps. He gave her a sour look, and his mouth pinched down into a frown.

Daphne grabbed my hand, and her concern for me flooded my body. It was a nice feeling—in a panicked, anxious kind of way.

"I'm fine," I said, squeezing her hand tight. "Really, I'm fine."

Her face relaxed a little bit. "You'd damn well better be. You're my best friend."

"And you're mine," I whispered back, hot tears stinging my eyes. "You're my best friend, too."

Daphne gripped my hand even tighter, her Valkyrie

strength crunching my bones together, but I didn't pull away. I knew I'd have bruises tomorrow, but I didn't care. Right now, I was happy to let her warm, happy relief flood my body. We stayed like that for a few seconds, before the Valkyrie's gaze flicked around the room.

"What's going on?" she asked. "What's with the big professor powwow?"

Metis smoothed a stray piece of her black hair back into her bun. "Nickamedes and I were just filling Gwen in on what happened during the avalanche and what we think might have caused it."

"You mean the *explosion*," Daphne corrected her. "Somebody totally set a bomb off on top of the mountain, didn't they? I mean, the flames were just shooting up and up into the air like they were never going to stop."

Nickamedes and Metis exchanged another look, obviously debating how much they wanted to tell Daphne— and whether they thought the Valkyrie would spread the gossip around to all the other students. But they decided to trust her or just realized that I would tell her later anyway, because Nickamedes finally nodded.

"Yes, we do believe it was some kind of deliberate explosion meant to specifically cause the avalanche," the librarian said.

Daphne rolled her eyes. "Well, of course, it was. When Reapers try to kill people, they always bring out the big guns."

*   *   *

Busted. I was totally, completely busted.

I knew the second the words came out of Daphne's mouth that there was no taking them back—or wiggling my way out of an explanation.

"Reapers?" Nickamedes asked in a sharp tone. "What Reapers?"

Daphne frowned, a puzzled expression on her pretty face. "*The* Reaper. The one who's trying to kill Gwen. The one who almost ran her over with a car and then took a shot at her in the Library of Antiquities the other night . . ."

The Valkyrie's voice drifted off as she realized just how intently Nickamedes and Metis were staring at her. She looked at them a second before turning her gaze to me. "You didn't tell them about the Reaper? You told me you were going to talk to Metis!"

"And I changed my mind," I muttered. "I have the right to do that, you know. Free will and all. We talked about it just the other day in myth-history class."

Daphne put her hands on her hips and glared at me. The pink sparks flashing around her fingertips crackled and coalesced into tiny streaks of lightning, showing me just how pissed she was at me right now.

"And *I* told *you* that you don't mess around when it comes to Reapers, especially when one of them is trying to kill you," the Valkyrie snapped.

Metis stepped around the hospital bed and put a hand on Daphne's arm. "I think the two of you need to tell us what's going on. Right now."

Yep, there was no way out of this—not with the professor staring at me, her green eyes sharp and narrow behind her silver glasses. And especially not with Nickamedes glaring at me, his own gaze as blue and cold as the snow on the mountain.

I sighed and told them the whole story, from almost being run over outside Grandma Frost's house to the arrow in the library to the Fenrir wolf that had been lurking around the ski resort and finally, to the avalanche. When I was finished, Metis called Coach Ajax into the room and made me repeat the whole thing over again to him.

"Why didn't you tell anyone about this before?" Ajax asked when I was finished.

I shifted in the bed, feeling the weight of the professors' accusing stares on my chest, as hard and heavy as the wolf's paws had been earlier. "Because I didn't have any proof. Nobody saw the car, the arrow, or even the Fenrir wolf but me. I didn't want you all to think I was being hysterical or paranoid or something."

Nickamedes crossed his arms over his chest. "Do you know how much danger you've put everyone in, Gwendolyn? If you even *suspected* that a Reaper of Chaos was running around the academy, you should have told one of your professors immediately. Not stupidly thought that you could handle it by yourself."

I really, really wanted to point out the small fact that the mystery Reaper hadn't actually, you know, *killed me yet*. That in my own way, I had handled it. At least, enough to stay alive these past few days. But then I looked at Metis. I didn't have to touch her or use my

Gypsy gift to see the disappointment and reproach in her face. She was upset I hadn't trusted her enough to tell her about the Reaper. Somehow that made me feel worse than anything else, even almost getting buried by the avalanche.

"I'm going to call your grandmother and tell her what's happened," Metis said in a low voice. "I'm sure she'll want to talk to you."

I was sure she would too. Grandma Frost didn't get angry at me often, but when she did, watch out. My grandma was probably going to be majorly pissed I hadn't told her what was going on. Though, in my defense, nothing had actually happened until after I'd left her house.

"Most important, you are not to leave the hotel until either we get this whole thing sorted out or head back to the academy tomorrow night," Nickamedes said. "I mean it, Gwendolyn. You are not to set one foot outside this building. Do you understand me?"

I gave him a sullen look.

"*Do you understand me?*" The librarian's harsh tone had so much acid in it that it actually made me flinch.

"Yes, sir," I muttered.

Nickamedes gave me another stern glare, but he didn't say anything else. He wanted to, though. Anger made his face even pastier than normal. Instead of yelling at me some more, Nickamedes turned to Ajax, and the two of them, along with Metis, moved to the other side of the infirmary and started talking in low voices. Probably trying to figure out who the Reaper might be and how they could track down him and the Fenrir wolf. Daphne stayed by my side at the bed.

"Sorry," she whispered. "I really didn't mean to rat you out."

I sighed. "I know. And you were right. I should have told Metis what was going on after class the other day, and I should have told you and Carson that I didn't think it was just a wild Fenrir wolf I'd seen. I hate to admit it, but Nickamedes and the other profs have a right to be pissed. I put myself in danger, and everyone else here, too."

"So why didn't you tell them about the Reaper? Or at least get me and Carson to believe you about the wolf?"

I threw my hands up. "Because I go to a school for warrior whiz kids. Everyone else at Mythos can take care of themselves, including you and Carson. I just wanted to be able to do the same. I bet if there was a Reaper after Logan or one of the other Spartans, the profs wouldn't make such a big deal about it. They certainly wouldn't make Logan hide in the hotel like he was a kid. Ajax would probably give him a weapon and let Logan hunt down the Reaper by himself."

Red-hot shame and miserable embarrassment tangled up together in tight knots in my stomach, overcoming the uneasy guilt I felt at keeping quiet. That was one reason why I'd hated the academy so much when I'd started going there—because everyone was so much *better* at everything than I was. So much braver, tougher, smarter, stronger. I was a weak little freak in comparison to everyone else at Mythos Academy, with only my Gypsy gift to rely on.

"But you haven't had the training the rest of us

have," Daphne pointed out. "Your mom and your grandma sheltered you from all that stuff. I started using a bow when I was three years old. It took me a long time to learn how to use it and all the other weapons we train with—and even longer to think I could actually hurt someone with them."

"Do you think you could do it?" I asked. "Do you think you could kill a Reaper if you had to?"

The Valkyrie thought about it. "I think so, after everything I've seen—all the other kids, parents, and professors who have been murdered by them over the years. I hope so, because I know that if I didn't kill the Reaper, then he would kill me—without hesitating."

Even though I was still lying under the thermal blankets, Daphne's words made me shiver, because I knew they were true. Anybody who'd gone to all the trouble to start an *avalanche* wouldn't hesitate to run me through with a sword if he got the chance.

"Just do what the profs want and stay in the hotel until we head back to the academy, okay, Gwen?" Daphne said, her black eyes full of concern. "I don't want you to get hurt, and I know Metis and the others don't either. Not even Nickamedes, even if he doesn't act like it."

I could have argued with her about the librarian, but I just blew out a breath and nodded. "Yeah, I'll be a good girl from now on."

Daphne smiled and took my hand again. "Good."

I smiled back, even though the fingers on my other hand were firmly crossed. Yeah, maybe it was silly, but crossing my fingers made me feel a little better about lying to my best friend. But in this case, it was necessary. Because not only was I freaked out about what had happened today, but I was seriously pissed off about it, too.

Maybe I hadn't had the warrior training the other kids had. Maybe I wasn't as good with a sword as Daphne, Logan, and the other students were. Maybe I wasn't as strong or quick or tough or brave. But I had my psychometry magic, and I was Nike's freaking *Champion*. Those things had to count for something. Otherwise, what was the point of me being at Mythos Academy in the first place?

But the most important thing was the fact that the Reaper was after *me*. He wanted to kill *me*. Not anyone else, just *me*.

I might not be able to put an arrow through his heart, but I was Gwen Frost, that weird Gypsy girl who touched stuff and saw things. I used my magic to find things that were lost and to learn people's secrets. Well, the Reaper's real identity was just something else to uncover, just another puzzle to solve, just another secret waiting to be revealed.

No matter what I'd promised Metis, Nickamedes, and even Daphne, I was going to do everything in my power to find out who the Reaper was and take him down—before he tried to kill me again.

Chapter 16

Professor Metis, Nickamedes, and Coach Ajax finished up their hushed talk and left the infirmary, probably to start tracking down the Reaper. Daphne went out with them, so she could let Carson know that I was fine. I didn't ask the Valkyrie if she was going to talk to Logan—or if the Spartan had even asked her whether I was okay or not. I didn't want to know if he hadn't.

Half an hour later, Metis came back into the infirmary and handed me a cell phone, since my own had been swept away by the snow. "Your grandmother, as promised."

"Thank you," I said. "And I'm sorry for, well, everything. But mainly for not telling you about the Reaper in the first place. You told me a while back you'd always look out for me, because of your friendship with my mom. I should have trusted you the way she would have."

Metis looked at me a second, then gave me a curt nod. Her face was still tight with worry, but her green gaze was a little softer than it had been before. She might not like it, but I think Metis understood why I hadn't told her about the Reaper. I hoped so anyway. I also hoped she could forgive me for keeping my mouth shut—and the other things I planned on doing to discover the Reaper's real identity, just as soon as she and the Powers That Were let me out of this hospital bed.

The professor stepped back outside and shut the infirmary door behind her, giving me some privacy.

I raised the phone to my ear. "Hi, Grandma."

"Hi, pumpkin," Grandma Frost's voice flooded the line, as warm, soft, and comforting as a hug. "Are you okay?"

"I'm fine. Really, I am."

"Tell me what happened."

I drew in a breath and told Grandma everything that had happened since I'd left her house on Wednesday afternoon. When I finished, she stayed quiet for a few seconds.

"Do you want me to come get you, pumpkin? Bring you home with me?" she asked, worry making her voice sound low and strained.

Part of me really, really wanted to say yes. To let Grandma Frost come get me and take me back to her house, just like she had when I was a little girl and I'd woken up scared and crying in the middle of the night the first time I slept over at a friend's house when my mom was out of town.

But the other part of me wondered how much danger I would be putting my grandma in if I let her do that. Word would get out if I'd left the hotel before the other kids, and it wouldn't be too hard for the Reaper to track me back to my grandma's house. He already knew where it was since that was where he'd tried to kill me in the first place.

Besides, I wasn't a little girl, and I didn't want to act or be treated like one. Yeah, I was only seventeen, but I'd grown up a lot since coming to Mythos. Like it or not, Reapers, mythological monsters, and the evil god Loki were part of my life now. I couldn't just pretend they didn't exist anymore. If I didn't stand up for myself against them now, if I didn't try to fight back against the Reaper who was trying to kill me, I didn't know if I'd ever be able to—and Nike would have placed her trust in me for nothing.

I wanted to be worthy of the faith the goddess of victory had in me—and all the other Frost women who had been Nike's Champions over the years. I wanted to fight against the bad guys and the darkness in them that I'd seen.

"I want to stay here at the resort," I finally said. "But I'm not going to lie to you. I want to stay, so I can figure out what's going on and who the Reaper really is before he hurts someone else."

Grandma Frost let out a long, weary sigh, like she'd known that's what I was going to say all along. Maybe she had, given her Gypsy gift of seeing the future. "I don't like it, but I understand, Gwen."

I blinked. Grandma hardly ever called me Gwen. I was always "pumpkin" to her.

She let out a sharp, rueful laugh. "You're growing up,

just the same way your mom did: wanting to help people, just like she did. Wanting to be worthy of the Gypsy magic that Nike has entrusted our family with."

"Yeah," I said. "I do. How did you know?"

"Because I felt the same when I was your age, and I'm not going to stand in your way now. Just be careful, Gwen. More careful than you've ever been before because I—I don't want to lose you." Her voice cracked on the last two words. "I don't think I could bear to lose you like I did your mom."

"I'll be careful," I whispered back. "More careful than you can imagine."

"I love you, pumpkin," Grandma said. "You call me whenever you need me. Any time, day or night, and I'll come running."

All the emotions I was feeling clogged up my throat, making it hard to talk, but I forced out the words. "I know you will, and I love you, too."

"Bye, pumpkin."

"Bye, Grandma."

She hung up. I ended the call and curled up into a small ball on the hospital bed. Despite the fact that I knew I was doing the right thing by staying at the resort, I couldn't keep the tears from leaking out of the corners of my eyes—and wishing that I could go back to just being Grandma's little girl again.

Late that afternoon, the professors finally let me leave the infirmary and go back to my room with Daphne on the thirteenth floor of the resort. Coach Ajax put his heavy hand on my shoulder and walked me through the hotel lobby, like I was some kind of invalid—or crimi-nal. I couldn't decide which one was more embarrass-ing.

Quite a crowd had gathered there to witness my walk of shame. Well, that and the fact that they were stuck inside the hotel until the Powers That Were at the resort made sure the slopes had stabilized and were safe once more. Of course, pretty much all the Mythos kids had seen the avalanche come hurtling down the mountain toward me during the carnival. And if they hadn't, then their friends had texted them all the juicy details, along with the cell phone photos they'd snapped during the avalanche.

Still, it was kind of weird having everyone stare at me, since, you know, most of the students at the acad-emy barely acknowledged my existence, unless they were mocking me or wanted to hire me to find something they'd lost. But I shouldn't have been worried about being the center of attention. Once the kids in the lobby realized I was fine, they all turned away and started gos-siping and texting on their phones again.

Everyone except for Logan.

The Spartan stood by a coffee cart in the lobby, with Kenzie and Oliver by his side. Logan's gaze met mine across the massive room. I hadn't noticed how tense he'd been before, but seeing that I was okay must have taken some kind of burden off his shoulders, because he visibly relaxed. One moment he looked all dark and dangerous and on edge and keyed up for battle. The next he was just Logan again—fun, flirty, sexy Logan. Once the Spartan relaxed, so did Kenzie and even

Oliver, who for once didn't give me a dirty look. Instead, Oliver actually looked . . . concerned, like he'd been worried about me too. Strange.

But really, I only had eyes for Logan. The intense expression on his face made my heart quiver and my whole body sing. Nobody could fake that kind of concern—*nobody*. Maybe he really did care about me after all. Maybe Logan really did feel the same way about me that I felt about him. . . .

Then Savannah stepped around the cart, holding two cups of steaming hot chocolate in her hands. She headed straight for Logan. Even though he didn't turn around and look at her, I realized nothing had changed at all. He was still with Savannah, and I was still being lovestruck and stupid.

Disgusted, I looked away. A flash of movement caught my eye, and I spotted Preston waving at me. He leaned up against the far wall of the hotel lobby, half hidden behind a cedar tree and well away from all the other kids who'd come to gawk at me. Ajax stopped a second to talk to Coach Lir. Preston waved at me again, and I used Ajax's distraction to slip away and walk over to him.

"Hi, there," I said.

"Hi." Preston's face was tight with worry. "How are you? I heard what happened. I'm so sorry, Gwen. That must have been awful. I was down here waiting for you, and there was just this tremendous noise. I looked out the window and saw the avalanche rushing down the mountain. I can't imagine how terrible it was for you to be in the middle of it."

I shrugged. I didn't really want to talk about it right

now, and I definitely didn't want Preston to think of me as the girl who got caught in the avalanche. No, I wanted him to think of me as Gwen, the cute girl he'd just met. A Reaper might be trying to kill me, but I'd be damned if he'd ruin this for me, too.

"Since we never got to have lunch, do you want to do something tomorrow?" Preston asked. "Maybe go skiing or something? If you feel like it?"

My heart lifted at his words, but then I remembered that I was under house arrest, so to speak. I sighed. "I'd love to, but the profs want me to stay in the hotel tomorrow . . . just in case I'm more shook up than I'm letting on."

I winced at the lie. That sounded totally lame, but I supposed it was better than telling Preston the truth about the Reaper. Even though we were only going to be at the resort another day, I didn't want to scare him off.

His face darkened with disappointment. "Oh."

"But maybe we could have lunch tomorrow?" I suggested. "We wouldn't have to leave the hotel to do that."

Preston thought about it a second, and his face brightened. "Sure. That'll work. I'll text you again in the morning, and we'll figure out the details, okay?"

I smiled at him. "It's a date. Again. This time, I promise I'll keep it."

He let out a little laugh. "Don't worry. I know you will, Gwen. I'll make sure of it. I won't let you get away again."

A flash of movement caught my eye, and I realized

Ajax had finished up his conversation and was walking through the lobby looking for me. "Well, I have to go. I'll see you tomorrow, okay?"

Preston nodded. "You can count on it."

He gave me a quick smile, then left the lobby, keeping to the edges of the crowd as he headed down the hallway where some of the restaurants were located, as well as the new construction site. Preston was probably going to have dinner with his friends. I thought it was really cool that he'd come down here to see how I was doing. Most guys wouldn't have bothered to, not for a girl they'd just met yesterday.

Coach Ajax finally spotted me and came over. "Who were you talking to? I didn't get a good look at him."

"Oh, just a guy I met from the New York academy."

"Well, come on then," Ajax rumbled. "Metis and Nickamedes want you tucked in your room for the rest of the night, and so do I."

Ajax rode up with me in the elevator and walked me down the hall to my room. He even made sure Daphne was waiting inside and that the room was free of Reapers before he left.

To my surprise, Daphne had taken Vic out of his scabbard and laid him out flat on my bed. I flopped down beside the sword, and his twilight-colored eye snapped open.

"You're supposed to take me with you when you go off having adventures, Gwen," Vic said in his British accent. "Not get to have all the bloody fun by yourself."

"Trust me, Vic, surviving the avalanche wasn't much

fun. Neither was shoving a tree branch through a Fenrir wolf's leg."

"What?!" Vic and Daphne shrieked in unison.

I sat there on the bed and told them about the wolf and how it had actually seemed to . . . like me after I helped it. That was the only part of the story I hadn't shared with Metis and the other profs, instead saying that I'd thought the wolf had been carried away by the snow. Maybe it was crazy, but I didn't want them to hunt down the wolf and kill it, even though I knew that's what they were determined to do. Sure, maybe the creature had wanted to make me a chew toy to start with, but I didn't think it would hurt me now. Maybe. Probably. Well, okay, I really had no idea what the wolf would or wouldn't do, but I didn't want to be the cause of its death.

Daphne shook her head, her blond hair spilling over her shoulders. "You've been watching too many Disney movies, Gwen. Fenrir wolves are trained to kill—that's all they know how to do. That's all they're good for."

"Well, if they can be trained to kill, then they can be trained to do other things, right?" I insisted in a stubborn tone. "I mean, they're not *born* bad, are they? Metis said they weren't necessarily evil, that they have free will, just like we do."

Daphne looked at me like I was spouting nonsense. Maybe I was. "Yeah, maybe Fenrir wolves have free will, but the Reapers have tortured all the goodness out of them, just like they have the Nemean prowlers, Black rocs, and all the other creatures they use. Face it, Gwen.

That wolf was trained by a Reaper, which makes it just as twisted and evil as the Reaper is."

"Yep," Vic chimed in. "Twisted, evil, and deserving of death. If you'd had me with you, then I could have taken care of the oversized puppy all by myself."

I rolled my eyes, but the sword didn't notice. Neither did the Valkyrie. Instead, Daphne and Vic stared arguing about who was more evil, the Reapers or the mythological creatures they trained, and the best ways to kill them all. I tuned them out. They hadn't been there, and they hadn't seen how much pain the wolf had been in. They hadn't felt its emotions the way I had. No matter what they claimed, the creature wasn't all evil. Somewhere underneath all those teeth and claws was a heart that beat just like mine. No, the wolf wasn't a complete monster, even if its Reaper master had trained it to be that way.

Once Daphne and Vic quit arguing, the three of us spent the next hour lounging around and talking. Well, the Valkyrie did most of the talking, telling me about how she and the other kids at the Winter Carnival had heard the explosion and then seen the avalanche rush down the mountain toward me. Since the carnival had been set up back on the plateau, everyone there had been well out of the path of the roaring snow.

"Everyone was seriously freaked out," Daphne said. "Including Logan."

My heart skipped a beat, even though I kept my face calm. "Really? I find that hard to believe."

"Oh yeah," the Valkyrie said. "He totally wanted to

go with Ajax and start looking for you. Carson and I did too, but Metis and the other profs wouldn't let us. They kept everyone at the carnival until the snow had settled. But Logan, man, I thought he was actually going to punch Nickamedes at one point. The two of them were screaming at each other, and Kenzie and Oliver had to grab hold of Logan to keep him from going after the librarian."

I laughed. "Now that I would have liked to have seen. Yeah, maybe Logan was worried about me. I mean, we are friends, in a weird sort of way. But it doesn't matter, because I saw him hanging out with Savannah down in the lobby a few minutes ago, just like always. So nothing's changed. Besides, I ran into Preston downstairs. We're going to have lunch tomorrow, and I'm going to forget all about Logan—at least for the rest of the weekend."

Daphne opened her mouth, but her phone started vibrating on the nightstand. She bent over to see who was texting her. She hit a few buttons, and a guilty look filled her pretty face.

"So, that was Carson and . . . there's this party tonight," Daphne said, not quite looking at me.

"And let me guess. I can't go because it's out in the alpine village somewhere and I'm not supposed to leave the hotel, right?"

Daphne winced and nodded.

"Go," I said. "Have fun with your boyfriend. I'm going to stay right here with Vic, read my comic books, and eat junk food for the rest of the night."

"Are you sure?" Daphne asked, biting her glossy lip. "I don't mind staying here with you and just hanging out. . . ."

"Go," I repeated in a firm voice. "Go to the party, get drunk, and totally make out with Carson. I'll be fine. I promise. Believe me, after what happened today, I have zero desire to party tonight."

It took some more prodding on my part, but eventually, Daphne brushed out her hair, put on some more lip gloss, and left to go hook up with Carson. As soon as the door locked behind her, I walked over to my gray duffel bag and pulled out a pen and notebook. Then I settled myself on the bed, with Vic propped up on a pillow beside me.

"What are you doing?" the sword asked. "Because that doesn't look like a comic book to me."

"Nothing much," I said. "Just trying to figure out who wants me dead."

Chapter 17

For a moment, Vic peered at me with his one eye, then his slash of a mouth curved back into a full-on smile. I almost thought he would have nodded in approval if he could actually, you know, move his half of a head.

"*Finally,* Gypsy," he chirped in his English accent. "I was wondering how long you were going to let something like that slide. It's a major breach of etiquette you know, not striking back at your enemies in a timely fashion."

Etiquette? What kind of etiquette was there in someone trying to murder me? Sometimes I just didn't understand Vic at all. I shook my head.

"It's not that I've been *letting it slide* exactly," I said. "It's just that I don't have much to go on. I couldn't see who was driving the car that tried to hit me, and I didn't get the license plate. The same thing happened in the library. I didn't see who fired the arrow, and I didn't get much of a vibe on the hole it left behind in the bookshelf. And yeah, I touched the Fenrir wolf, but not long enough to really get a major whammy off it or see who its master is. Mostly, the wolf was still thinking about the avalanche, just like I was."

"So what are you going to do?" Vic asked.

I shrugged. "I thought I'd make a list of everyone who might have a grudge against me and go from there. It always works on TV."

Vic rolled his eye. "Why are you playing bloody detective again instead of just going out there and using me to get some answers? Put me up against someone's throat, and I'll make him start talking real quick."

I arched an eyebrow and gave the sword a look.

"What?" he growled. "It'd be much more fun than listening to you and the Valkyrie natter on about what some other bloody girl was *wearing.*"

"Shut up, Vic," I said. "I need to think."

The sword let out a loud harrumph and snapped his eye shut, his mouth turning down into a pout. And people thought teenagers were moody. Please. We had nothing on ancient, bloodthirsty, talking swords.

Vic kept his eye shut, enjoying his snit, so I sat there on the bed and started making my list. It took me about five seconds. What can I say? It was a short list with only one name on it: Jasmine Ashton's family. Okay, okay, so it wasn't really a *name,* but the Ashtons were the only ones with any reason to kill me. At least, that I knew of.

Since my list idea wasn't working, I decided to go back to the beginning and see if I could remember anything strange or weird, anything out of place, anything out of the ordinary. But really, there was nothing. It had just been a regular week at Mythos Academy until someone had tried to kill me.

Well, sure, I was here at the Winter Carnival at a super-fancy resort, and I was having lunch tomorrow with a cute guy. Both of those were out of the ordinary, but not in a bad way. I needed to think harder, needed to go back to the day this had all started. Wednesday. Three days ago. What had happened then? Maybe I'd done something to set off the Reaper, or maybe I'd pissed off someone else entirely. I closed my eyes and concentrated.

Okay, let's see. After weapons training with Logan, Kenzie, and Oliver in the gym, I'd gone to my classes that morning, even scoring an A+ on my English lit paper. We'd had to write about the influence of myth on superheroes and modern culture, a topic that I'd totally nailed, since I was such a comic book and fantasy geek. I'd had lunch with Daphne and Carson in the dining hall, then after my afternoon classes, I'd snuck off campus to go see Grandma Frost. After I'd visited my grandma, I'd ridden the bus back to the academy and had worked my usual shift at the Library of Antiquities.

There was nothing there. Nothing special, nothing unusual, nothing out of the ordinary. Well, besides the SUV almost mowing me down and the arrow almost splitting my skull open. I hadn't even touched anything unusual that day or gotten any real vibes with my psychometry magic, except for the fuzzy flash I'd seen of Oliver's crush when I'd picked up his notebook that morning in the gym.

My eyes snapped open. Oliver's notebook. Of course.

How could I have been so stupid? Oliver had totally freaked when I'd picked up his notebook, and he'd realized I was getting a flash off it. I'd thought it was just because he didn't want me to know who he was crushing on and all the teasing that would go along with that.

But what if maybe—just *maybe*—he had something else to hide. Like the fact that he was really a Reaper of Chaos. I'd felt Oliver's emotions when I'd touched his notebook. He'd been everything from bored to angry to lusting after his crush. He could have totally had some psycho-killer vibes or evil plans hidden in there, too. I just hadn't held on to the notebook long enough to get the lowdown on them.

The more I thought about it, the more it made sense. It would also explain why Oliver had sat down next to me on the bus ride over to the resort and all the dirty looks he'd been shooting my way in the meantime. The Spartan had been fishing yesterday morning on the bus, trying to figure out exactly what I'd seen when I'd touched his notebook and who I might have told about it.

Except now it seemed like he wasn't going to take a chance that I hadn't seen anything since, you know, he'd tried to kill me four times already. Oliver definitely wanted me to keep quiet about whatever was in that notebook. What else could be in there that was worth killing for if it wasn't information that he was a Reaper or some stupid plan he'd cooked up to serve Loki?

I had to get my hands on that notebook. That was the only way I was going to figure out what Oliver was up to—and why he felt that he needed to kill me to cover it up.

Now, all I had to do was figure out how to swipe the notebook from him—and not get murdered in the meantime.

The next morning, Daphne, Carson, and I grabbed some toasted cranberry-orange bagels, wild blueberry muffins, cream cheese Danish, and cherry-pomegranate juice from one of the hotel restaurants, then seated ourselves on a sofa in front of the massive stone fireplace in the lobby. The flames cracked and popped like fireworks, while the heat from the mini-explosions warmed the whole area. The sweet smell of cedar woodchips tickled my nose.

I gobbled down the chewy bagels, scrumptious muffins, and tart juice in record time, eager to get on with my plans for the day. Daphne and Carson just picked at their food, though. The Valkyrie hadn't stumbled back to our room until almost one o'clock this morning, and both she and Carson had a decidedly sick, green tinge to their faces. It must have been one intense party for them both to still be this hungover.

Daphne stuffed the remains of her half-eaten bagel back into the paper bag it had come in and put it on the table at her right elbow. "If I eat one more bite of that, I'm going to be sick."

"Me, too," Carson mumbled, staring down into his cup of juice. "Why did I drink so much last night?"

"It must have tasted really, really good, considering

how wasted the two of you still look," I said in a sarcastic tone.

"Please, Gwen," the band geek whispered. "Don't talk so loud. My head is killing me."

Daphne and Carson both shot me looks that were equal parts annoyance and misery. Yeah, I was totally laughing at them, but they would have been doing the same to me if I'd been the one with the raging hangover.

"I think I should go back to my room, fall onto the bed, and hope I don't die before lunchtime," Carson mumbled again.

"Me, too," Daphne muttered.

"You can't do that," I said, my voice sharpening.

Daphne had on oversize sunglasses to block the light in the lobby, and she squinted over the tops of them at me. "Why not?"

Because if she and Carson were in the hotel all day, then I wouldn't be able to go through with my plan to snatch Oliver's notebook and see exactly what secrets it contained. Despite being hungover, my friends would insist on helping me—or worse, telling Professor Metis about my suspicions. That was something I didn't want to do without concrete proof, or at least knowing that I'd seen Oliver's true intentions for myself using my Gypsy gift. Of course, I couldn't exactly tell the two of them that, though.

Besides, I'd already gotten myself into enough trouble by not telling the profs about the Reaper and Fenrir wolf. And yeah, maybe part of me still wanted to take care of this myself, but I also didn't want to drag my friends down with me—or put them in danger if my suspicions turned out to be correct.

"Because we're leaving tonight to go back to the academy, and you haven't hit half the slopes you wanted to, much less gone tubing," I said. "Besides, the fresh air and sunshine will do you good. Once you get out there, you won't even remember how much you had to drink last night."

Carson groaned. "Believe me, I'll remember."

It took some not-so-subtle nudging on my part, but Daphne and Carson finally headed out to go skiing. Of course, the slopes directly above the hotel were still off limits because of the avalanche, but there were some runs on the far side of the mountain that hadn't been affected and were open to students. The three of us agreed to hook up after lunch. Hopefully, I could introduce them to Preston then. In the meantime, though, I had work to do—and a Reaper to catch.

As soon as Daphne and Carson were out the door, I went over to the registration desk on the far side of the lobby. There were a couple of clerks working, and I headed toward a college-age girl. She looked up as I approached and smiled at me.

"How can I help you this morning?" she asked in a bright, friendly tone.

"Uh, this is really, really embarrassing," I said, not quite looking at the clerk and shuffling on my feet. "But I, uh, left my phone in somebody else's room last night. After one of the parties. You know what I mean?"

Understanding flashed in her eyes.

"Anyway, I know the guy's name, but I can't remember his room number. I had a little more to drink than I should have, and some of last night is a little . . . blurry." I let out a nervous giggle, like I was a total ditz. "I was wondering if you could tell me what room he's in."

"I'm not supposed to give out information about other guests at the hotel," the clerk said in a neutral tone. "Especially not to students."

I winced. "I know, believe me, I know. But my parents just bought me that phone last week, and they will *kill* me if I lose another one. It was like super-, super-expensive. It's not my fault I dropped the last two in the sink. People totally need to quit texting me while I'm in the bathroom touching up my makeup. I only have two hands."

She shook her head. "Look, I'm really sorry about your phone, but I can't help you."

I bit back a growl. I needed to know what room Oliver was in, and I couldn't exactly go up to the Spartan and ask him. I opened my mouth to plead with the clerk some more when a voice spoke up behind me.

"Actually, Valerie, it's my phone that got lost. Gwen was nice enough to come over here and ask about it for me."

Morgan McDougall stepped up beside me, looking gorgeous in a form-fitting, mint green snowsuit. I eyed the other girl, wondering what she was doing—and why she was trying to help me.

The clerk's face creased into a smile. "Oh, hi, Morgan. I haven't seen you around much this weekend."

The Valkyrie shrugged. "I've been busy—like usual.

Lots of fresh blood at the New York academy this year, if you know what I mean."

She winked at the clerk, and both of them dissolved into a fit of giggles. I just stood there, feeling awkward and stupid.

"Anyway," Morgan said, pulling a hundred-dollar bill out of the pocket of her snowsuit and sliding it across the counter. The motion made green sparks of magic shoot off the Valkyrie's fingertips. "Do you think you can help me out? Because Gwen's right. My parents will kill me if I lose another phone this year."

The clerk took the money as smoothly as the Valkyrie had offered it and gave her another smile. "What's his name?"

Morgan raised her eyebrows and looked at me. "Yes, what *was* his name, Gwen? I can't remember."

"Oliver," I said. "Oliver Hector."

Morgan's eyebrows shot up a little higher on her face, and she gave me a really weird look, but she didn't say anything. The clerk, Valerie, hit a few buttons on her computer and told us that Oliver was in room 822. Morgan thanked her, and the two of us strolled away from the registration desk. I waited until we were halfway across the lobby, right next to the statue of Skadi, before I turned and looked at her.

"Why did you do that?" I asked.

Morgan shrugged. "There are some advantages to being the school slut."

For a moment the Valkyrie stared at me, a strange light flaring in her hazel eyes, almost like she wanted to say something to me, wanted to talk to me about something. I wondered if it was about what had happened the night Jasmine had almost sacrificed her in the Library of Antiquities.

But then Morgan clamped her lips shut. She stalked off across the lobby and headed outside—alone.

Strange. Very strange. But the Valkyrie had gotten me the information I needed. I supposed I should be grateful to her for that, although I still couldn't imagine why she'd helped me in the first place. Yeah, maybe I'd saved her from being murdered by her best friend, but I didn't know if Morgan even remembered what had happened that night. Maybe she'd figured out some of what had gone down, though. That was the only reason I could think of to explain all the strange looks she gave me.

But what Morgan did or didn't know wasn't important, not right now, so I pushed away all thoughts of the Valkyrie. It was time to gear up for the next phase of my plan. Now that I knew which room Oliver was in, I just needed to swipe his key card—or his roommate's.

Chapter 18

Kenzie Tanaka never saw me coming.

Thanks to all the texts the students constantly sent out on the Mythos network, I was able to track him down in one of the hotel restaurants. The Spartan was having what looked like a very private, very *cozy* breakfast with Talia Pizarro when I walked by and accidentally-on-purpose spilled my extra-large spiced apple cider all over their blueberry, ricotta-cheese pancakes and strawberry shortcake waffles.

"Oops! I'm so sorry!" I said, bumping the table with my hip and making the cider slop everywhere.

Both Kenzie and Talia shoved their chairs back and leapt to their feet, Talia quite a bit faster than Kenzie, since she had her Amazon superspeed working for her.

"Geez, Gwen!" Talia snapped. "Watch where you're going!"

"Sorry, sorry, it's my fault. Totally my fault. Here, let me clean it up."

I used the napkins I'd gotten along with the cider and

started dabbing at the puddles of liquid on the table. Kenzie and Talia stepped back and checked to make sure they hadn't gotten any of the sticky cider on their clothes. I moved from one side of the table to the other, bumping the chair Kenzie had thrown his leather jacket over and making the garment fall to the floor.

I fussed over the cider on the table for a couple of minutes, working until it was all cleaned up and chattering on the whole time about how sorry I was for ruining their breakfast. Talia rolled her dark eyes at Kenzie, and he shook his head in return. I'd totally annoyed them, which was exactly what I'd wanted to do. Annoyed people didn't pay much attention to details, like the fact that I slipped my right hand into one of the pockets on Kenzie's jacket while I used my left hand to wipe cider out of the chairs.

Finally, I finished cleaning up and gave them another sheepish smile. Then I leaned down, grabbed Kenzie's jacket, and handed it to him.

"Come on, Talia," Kenzie said, glaring at me as he grabbed his leather jacket and put it on. "Let's get out of here before Gwen decides to spill something else on us."

I gave them another apologetic smile as they stormed away. The two of them didn't see me stick my hand into the pocket of my purple hoodie and draw out a small, white, plastic card.

From our time training together, I knew that Kenzie always kept his wallet in his right jacket pocket, and it hadn't been too much of a stretch to think he'd put his key card in there too. For once, I'd actually gotten lucky, and the card had just been loose in the pocket, instead of tucked away inside his wallet.

"Room 822, here I come," I whispered.

I discreetly trailed Kenzie and Talia back to the hotel lobby and stepped behind a cedar tree, so they wouldn't see me. Oliver was waiting by the main door for them, just like I'd hoped he would be. I needed both of the Spartans to be out of the room while I searched it.

"What took you guys so long?" Oliver asked, frowning. "We were supposed to leave for the slopes five minutes ago."

I didn't hear Kenzie's reply, but I didn't really need to. I could imagine what he was saying about me right now. Gwen Frost, that clumsy Gypsy girl. The three of them walked outside and headed toward the alpine village. I eased over to the door and peered through the glass. If they were going skiing, I doubted they'd be coming back anytime soon. Good. I turned and headed for the elevators.

Before I went to Oliver's room, I had one more thing to do. I rode the elevator up to the thirteenth floor, went into my own room, and grabbed Vic off the bed. Whether or not Oliver was a Reaper, someone had almost killed me four times now, and I wanted to be prepared in case he tried again. Besides, it would be just my luck that Oliver would come back to his room for some reason before I'd found the notebook. Whatever happened, I figured it would be better to have the sword with me than not.

Vic's eye snapped open when I picked up the black leather scabbard with him in it.

"I know that maniacal twinkle in your eye. You're up to something, Gwen," he said. "What is it? And is there any chance I'll get to kill something today? Like a Reaper, perhaps?"

"If everything goes to plan, then no, you won't get to kill something today," I said, unzipping my hoodie. "But we might be able to catch the guy who's been try-ing to murder me."

Vic snorted. "Always a bleeding pacifist. Well, you can wake me if there's any killing to be done. Other-wise, I'm going back to my nap."

His eye snapped shut.

I strapped Vic and his scabbard to my waist, then zipped my purple hoodie back up. The fabric came down past my waist, hiding the top half of the sword and Vic's gleaming hilt from sight. The bottom half of the scabbard dangled next to my left leg, but since the jeans I had on were as black as it was, the scabbard wasn't too noticeable. Besides, all the other kids had packed their weapons, and I doubted anyone would look twice at mine. Still, if the Reaper did come after me again, maybe he wouldn't realize that I was wearing a sword until it was too late—for him.

I stared at myself in the mirror. Wavy, dark brown hair; winter white skin; a few freckles splashed across my cheeks; purple eyes; and a sword strapped to my waist. Maybe it was weird, but I didn't feel like I really looked like myself today. Right now, I resembled some-one else entirely—someone strong, someone confident, someone ready to kick a little Reaper ass. I shook my head, and the image and feeling faded, replaced by my same old boring face, wobbly nerves, and twisted insecurities.

But I'd come this far, and I wasn't about to back out now. Oliver Hector had a secret, and I was going to find out what it was—and why he was trying to kill me because of it.

"Here goes nothing," I whispered to my reflection, and left the room.

I got back in the elevator and rode down to the eighth floor. I stepped outside the doors and stood there a second, listening. The whole floor was quiet, and only the hum of the snack and ice machines interrupted the silence. Everyone was either still sleeping off their hangovers in their rooms or out on the slopes enjoying a final day of skiing and snowboarding before heading back to the academy. Either way, I wouldn't get a better chance than this.

I strode down the hall with purpose, like I was supposed to be on this floor, even though it was guys only, a lame attempt by the profs to keep the weekend sex to a minimum. Room 822 was about halfway down the hall. I slid the key card in the slot, waited for the green light to flash, opened the door, and stepped inside.

Kenzie and Oliver's room was a mirror image of the one Daphne and I were sharing. There was two of everything, from big, soft beds to nightstands to mirrors mounted on the walls. Clothes and shoes were strewn everywhere, and I couldn't tell which side of the room belonged to Kenzie and which side was Oliver's. Jeans, shirts, socks—from the looks of things, the Spartans had brought enough threads with them for an entire week, instead of just a weekend. And I'd thought Daphne had overpacked.

Since I couldn't tell whose stuff was where, I crouched down by the foot of the bed closest to the door, reached out, and touched the suitcase there. My Gypsy gift kicked in, and an image of Kenzie stuffing clothes into it filled my mind. Okay, so this was his side then, which meant Oliver's stuff was piled around the bed closest to the window.

I moved over to that side of the room, picking my way through the piles of crumpled clothes on the floor. Then I bent down and started going through Oliver's suitcase. I used the edge of my hoodie sleeve to flip open the top and peered inside. Clothes, clothes, and more clothes filled the space, along with a couple of pairs of slightly smelly boots.

I went through the suitcase, opening up all the zippered pockets and looking inside. No notebook. I got up and stepped inside the bathroom. A couple of shaving kits sat on the counter, but there was nothing interesting in them, except for the lemon-scented cologne Oliver had in his. It smelled nice. Certainly better than the Spartan's boots.

Since the notebook wasn't in the bathroom or Oliver's suitcase, that meant it was hidden somewhere in the mess in the rest of the room—if he'd even brought it with him to start with. I hoped he had. Only one way to find out.

I moved from one side of the room to the other, going through all the piles of clothes, Kenzie's and Oliver's alike. They both had packed plenty of stuff for the weekend, and there were more shirts, shoes, and jeans on one side of the hotel room than I had in my entire closet back at the academy.

"Guys," I muttered. "Why do they have to be so sloppy?"

The minutes ticked by, and I still couldn't find the notebook. I was beginning to think Oliver had left it at the academy when I untangled the sheets at the foot of his bed as a last resort, thinking he might have scribbled in it last night before he went to sleep. The red notebook slid out of the sheets and flopped to the floor.

"Jackpot," I whispered.

I used the edge of my hoodie sleeve to pick up the notebook, then sat down on the bed and put it in my lap. It looked the same as I remembered—just an ordinary red notebook with a couple of the metal rings bent out of shape. It certainly didn't look like it held anything particularly evil or sinister. But Oliver was hiding *something,* and this was my best chance of finding out what it was before he tried to kill me again.

So I drew in a breath, pushed up my sleeves, and wrapped my bare hands around the notebook. Then I sat there and waited for the images and feelings to flood my mind.

Chapter 19

For a half a second nothing happened, but then my psychometry kicked in, and images of Oliver filled my
mind. Mostly, there were the same images I'd seen the
first time I'd picked up the notebook Wednesday morning during weapons training. Oliver sitting at the desk
in his dorm room, scribbling on the pages, and the Spartan hunched over the notebook, doodling in class while
his professors lectured. I also got the same flashes of
feelings that I had before, boredom and frustration from
doing homework mixed with occasional spurts of anger
and angst.

Then that warm, soft, fizzy feeling started way, way
down deep in the pit of my stomach. I concentrated, focusing on that particular vibe, trying to call up all the
images that went with it. Everything and everyone
Oliver associated with that specific feeling. A hazy figure began to take shape in my mind, one with black hair
and eyes. I shut out everything else, so I could bring the
haze into supersharp focus and see exactly who Oliver
had such a massive crush on—

Kenzie's face popped into my head.

I gasped in surprise, but the sensations didn't stop there. It was like I'd opened a floodgate. All these emotions just poured into me. I saw and felt everything Oliver did toward his friend. All the good times they'd had together growing up. All the admiration and loyalty between them. All the small ways Oliver's feelings had started to deepen into something that went way beyond friendship. All the giddy joy just being with Kenzie made him feel. All the anger and soul-crushing despair that Kenzie would never like him back the same way. And then, at the very end, all the frustration and fear that I would tell Kenzie how Oliver really felt about him and ruin their friendship—ruin everything good they had between them.

My heart alternately soared up and plummeted down as I rode the roller coaster of Oliver's emotions until I thought it would pop right out of my chest. Finally, though, the emotions flickered, then faded away, telling me that I'd seen and felt everything I could from the notebook.

My eyes snapped open. The notebook slipped from my fingers, and I sagged down onto the bed, a little overwhelmed by everything I'd just seen. I drew in several deep breaths, waiting for the intense emotions and feelings to fade.

So Oliver was in love—or at least serious, serious like—just as I'd thought he was, but instead of crushing on a girl, Oliver had feelings for Kenzie, his best friend and fellow Spartan. That was it? That was Oliver's big secret?

Yeah, it was a pretty major secret, but I couldn't help but feel a little disappointed. It didn't matter to me who Oliver was crushing on. People liked who they liked, and I thought we all should just get over it already. As long as people were happy with who they were, that was all that mattered.

But knowing Oliver's secret didn't help me answer any of my other questions. Like whether or not he was a Reaper and had tried to kill me. I felt like I was still missing something, so I picked up the notebook again. This time I flipped through it page by page, trying to read Oliver's scribbled handwriting. But there was nothing on the pages I hadn't already seen and felt. Lots of class notes, lots of doodles, lots of really cool portraits of Kenzie. Whatever else he was, Oliver was an artist with some wicked talent.

What I didn't find was anything that told me one way or the other if Oliver was the Reaper who'd been gunning for me. I'd gotten all that I could from the notebook, so I stuffed it back down into the sheets were I'd found it. Then I stood in the center of the room, wondering if there was anything else in here that I could get a vibe off of, anything else that could tell me whether or not my suspicions about Oliver were right.

My searching gaze landed on some keys on Oliver's nightstand. I walked over, leaned down, and looked at them. I didn't know much about car keys, but I recognized the symbol for a Cadillac when I saw one. I'd seen this kind of key dozens of times at Mythos and had found lost sets of them a dozen times more, since so many of the academy students had big, fancy cars they took out on the weekends—like Cadillac Escalades.

My breath caught in my throat, and I thought back to that day outside my Grandma Frost's house. The SUV that had almost hit me had been big, black, and expensive. That was all I really remembered about the vehicle. It could have been an Escalade, or it could have been something else. Only one way to find out.

My heart racing, I picked up the keys and wrapped my fingers around the one for the Cadillac. The metal key felt cold and smooth in my palm, and the images started almost immediately. Flickers and flashes of various trips Oliver had taken, most of them with Kenzie sitting in the passenger's seat, the two of them listening to the radio. Sometimes Logan lounged in the back, hanging out with his friends.

I concentrated, going deeper, and calling up every image, every memory associated with the key. After a few seconds, the images changed, and the scene shifted. Oliver sat in his SUV parked on a residential street. I got the sense he was nervous and waiting for something—or someone. He looked through the tinted windshield, his eyes on a lavender-painted house at the end of the block.

It was like I was watching a scary movie from the killer's point of view. After a moment, I saw myself open the door of Grandma Frost's house and come outside, heading toward the bus stop. Oliver cranked the engine, put the SUV into gear, and steered it away from the curb. I stepped out into the street, and he accelerated, putting his foot all the way down on the gas—

My eyes snapped open again, and I had to sit back down on the bed a second time. I knew what had happened from there. Oliver had almost run me down. I was willing to bet if I touched the Spartan's bow, wherever it was, I'd get a flash of him aiming it at me in the Library of Antiquities.

Yeah, maybe I'd thought Oliver had tried to kill me, but my stomach still twisted with the certain knowledge, and a bitter, bitter taste filled my mouth. Oliver Hector had tried to kill me. Well, had tried to run me down with his SUV at the very least. But why? Because he'd thought I'd tell Kenzie about Oliver's crush on him? Or because Oliver was a Reaper? I didn't know, and my head started pounding as my troubled thoughts spun around and around.

Whether he was a Reaper or not, Oliver wanted me dead. The real question now was this: What was I going to do about it?

I put Oliver's keys back where they belonged and laid Kenzie's key card on his nightstand to make him think he'd just forgotten it this morning. Then I left the Spartans' room and pulled the door shut behind me.

I stood there in the hallway, thinking about everything I'd just seen and felt and wondering what I should do next. Metis, I thought. I should go tell Professor Metis what I'd learned. Yeah, she'd be pissed that I'd broken into Oliver's room, but she'd listen when I told her what I'd seen when I'd picked up his car keys. She'd believe me when I told her he'd tried to run me down.

While I was standing there wondering if Metis was

even in the hotel this morning and how quickly I could find her, the elevator at the end of the hallway pinged. The doors opened, and Oliver stepped out.

Our gazes locked, and Oliver started, like he was surprised to see me on the guys-only floor. Then he realized exactly whose room I was standing outside. His face paled, then his eyes narrowed. Oliver took a step toward me.

I turned and ran.

Yeah, maybe I was a coward, but Oliver had tried to kill me at least once that I knew of. Given the angry expression on his face, it wasn't too much of a stretch to think that me snooping around in his room would seriously piss him off, maybe even enough for him to try again—right here, right now.

"Gwen! Stop!"

There wasn't an elevator at this end of the hallway, so I slammed through a door and into the emergency stairwell. Down, down, down, I hurried as fast as I could. Footsteps echoed on the stairs above my head, growing louder and louder with every second. The Spartan was gaining on me.

"Gwen Frost!" Oliver called out again, his voice bouncing all the way down to the ground floor and then ricocheting back to the top of the stairwell.

I didn't answer him. I couldn't outrun Oliver, but maybe, just maybe, I could lose him. On the fifth floor, I stopped long enough to shove open the door, like I'd left the stairs and stepped out onto that floor. Then I crept down to the fourth-floor landing and stopped, trying to listen to what Oliver was doing despite the blood roaring in my ears and the rapid *thump-thump-thump* of my heart.

His footsteps slowed, then stopped. He paused, and for a few seconds, there was nothing but silence. I stood as still as possible, scarcely daring to breathe for fear the Spartan might hear me. For all I knew, Oliver had enhanced senses, like so many of the other warrior whiz kids did. I knew he was wondering whether I'd really gone through the door or was just trying to trick him. Oliver went for the door. I heard him open it and step out into the hallway.

I started sprinting down the stairs again. I tried to listen and run at the same time, but I didn't hear any more footsteps ringing out on the steps above me. Maybe I'd lost him. I hoped so. I reached the bottom of the stairwell and pushed through the door, expecting it to open up somewhere in the resort hotel's massive lobby.

I stepped out into the construction zone. Plywood, sawhorses, power tools, and plastic tarps filled the space in front of me. There were no lights down here, just eerie shadows cast by what little sunshine trickled in through the gaps in the boards that were nailed up where the windows were supposed to go. The dark, sinister gloom covered everything, like a thick, suffocating blanket. I shivered.

Daphne had told me the resort was adding on a new wing, and I'd seen the construction myself from the outside when we'd first gotten here Friday morning. Somehow I'd walked right into the middle of it by going down the emergency stairs instead of taking the elevator. I peered into the gloom. How was I supposed to get out of here? I couldn't go back up the stairs, not without risking running into Oliver, and I didn't see any doors or exits nearby. All I could do was go forward and try to find a way out of the construction maze.

I picked my way through the semidarkness, trying to make as little noise as possible. I winced every time my sneakers scuffed up against something in the shadows. Sawdust puffed up with every step I took, making my nose twitch. I put my hoodie sleeve up against my nose, so I wouldn't sneeze and give myself away, just in case Oliver had followed me down here.

I don't know how long I wandered around, but it seemed like I was moving in circles. That, or the resort expansion was just much, much bigger than I realized, and I hadn't reached the end of it yet.

I stopped in front of one of the windows. This one hadn't been boarded up as tightly as the others, and a couple of cracks of sunlight slipped through, along with a blast of cold, wintry air. I put my back to the window and stood there a second, looking around and trying to get my bearings. Okay, this looked like it was one of the exterior walls, so if I just followed it, I should be able to get out of here sooner or later. That made sense, right?

Besides, tons of footprints marred the sawdust, probably from all the construction workers. I'd seen them, too, on Friday morning, although they must have quit work for the weekend, since I didn't hear any hammers banging or drills whining. I squatted down and peered at the faint marks, trying to see which direction the footprints went. Maybe I could pretend they were the Yellow Brick Road and follow them right out of here.

I froze, staring at one of the prints on the floor. It wasn't a boot print or even one made by a sneaker or some other kind of shoe. No, this print hadn't been made by anyone walking around down here. It was shaped like an animal's paw, one that was bigger than my hand, with four toe pads and four sharp claws on the ends of them. I might not be a nature-loving girl, but I'd seen that kind of paw print twice before: once in my myth-history book and yesterday in the snow after the avalanche had almost swept me away.

The Fenrir wolf had been down here. Recently, from the looks of it. And where the wolf was, the Reaper wouldn't be far behind.

Just as that chilling thought occurred to me, I noticed an odd shape out of the corner of my eye, something that didn't match the rest of the construction equipment. It took me a few seconds of squinting, but I finally realized what the shape was: a sleeping bag. And that wasn't all. A couple of flashlights rested on top of it, along some empty bottles of Perrier and crumpled bags that smelled of cold, greasy food. It wasn't hard to figure out that someone had been hiding down here with the wolf.

I thought I'd been so clever getting away from Oliver, but I'd walked right into the middle of his supersecret lair in the construction zone.

Stupid, stupid, stupid Gwen!

Panic filled me, and I cursed myself. I had to get out of here—now. Before Oliver found me and sicced his killer puppy dog on me again. I wouldn't escape, not again, not from both of them, not down here in the dark.

I hurried through the construction zone as fast as I could, hurtling over all the tools, boards, and bags of cement, not caring how much noise I made. Escape was the only thing on my mind, burning away everything else.

Finally, just when I wanted to scream with frustration that I was never getting out of the maze, I realized it was getting lighter—and that there was the outline of a door up ahead.

Relief cooled my panic, and I let out a tense breath. As soon as I stepped through that door, I'd be safe. I'd run around the hotel, back to the lobby; find Professor Metis, Coach Ajax, or even Nickamedes; and tell them what was going on. Then they would track down the Reaper and deal with him.

My eyes fixed on the door, I stepped around a wheelbarrow and ran right into Oliver.

Chapter 20

I hit the Spartan's chest and bounced off, shrieking. And I kept right on back-back-backing up until my body was flat against one of the plywood-covered windows.

My hand dropped to my waist, pushing up the bottom of my hoodie and fumbling for the scabbard that was strapped there. After a second my fingers curled around Vic's hilt. If the Spartan tried anything, anything at all, I'd pull the sword and defend myself with it—or at least try to.

Oliver held out his hands and stepped toward me. "Gwen, it's okay. I didn't mean to scare you. I just want to talk to you."

"Talk?" I snapped, keeping my back to the wall, one hand on Vic's hilt as I edged away from him. "Talk about what? How you tried to mow me down with your SUV earlier this week? Or maybe you'd like to talk about how you took a shot at me with your bow and arrow in the Library of Antiquities?"

Guilt filled his face. "Look, I can explain all that."

"Really? Like you can explain the avalanche you

caused yesterday? The one that almost buried me on this damn mountain forever? Because I'd really, really like to hear you explain that one."

Oliver frowned. "Avalanche? I didn't cause the avalanche, Gwen."

"I don't believe you. I don't believe a word that's coming out of your mouth. You're a Reaper of Chaos, and you're trying to kill me. That's all I need to know."

Oliver stared at me, worry etching deep lines into his forehead. "I'm not a Reaper! Why would you even think that?"

"Oh, I don't know," I said in a sarcastic tone. "Maybe it has something to do with the fact that you've tried to kill me *four times now.*"

"I wasn't trying to kill you," Oliver said. "Not with my car and not in the library. I was just trying to scare you a little."

My eyebrows shot up in my face. "Scare me? Why?"

"Because of Kenzie," Oliver growled in a frustrated tone. "And what you saw when you touched my notebook. Logan told us about your psychometry magic and how you can learn people's secrets just by touching stuff that belongs to them. You said something about my crush, and I knew that you knew about Kenzie. I didn't want you telling anyone, so I did all that other stuff to distract you. I wasn't really trying to hurt you, Gwen. I swear."

His mouth twisted a little. "Logan would kill me if I ever hurt you on purpose. Hell, he'd kill me now if he realized what I've done so far."

Oliver looked and sounded sincere, but I didn't know

if I believed him or not. A few weeks ago, I'd thought Jasmine had been brutally murdered, but it had all just been an illusion the crazy Valkyrie had created. Who was to say Oliver wasn't playing me the same way Jasmine had?

I tiptoed along the wall, creeping closer to the door, until I was forced to step around another wheelbarrow. I put it between me and the Spartan. Now, my back was to the door, and I kept my gaze fixed on Oliver, just in case he tried to rush after me. I still had my hand on Vic's hilt, although I doubted I would pull the sword now. I could run faster if I wasn't carrying him in my hand.

"I'm going to walk out that door and find Professor Metis," I told Oliver. "You can explain it all to her."

I took one step back toward the door, then another, then another. More frustration filled the Spartan's face, and his hands curled into fists, but he didn't make a move to follow me. Maybe he was telling the truth, maybe he wasn't a Reaper, but I couldn't take a chance he wasn't. Besides, he'd already copped to the fact that he'd come after me with his SUV and fired that arrow at my head. What kind of guy did stuff like that? Okay, okay, so maybe all the Mythos kids were a little twisted and violent that way, and maybe I was, too, since I'd just broken into the Spartan's room on a hunch. But I certainly didn't want to be trapped alone with him in the dark, with no one around to hear me scream.

Oliver opened his mouth, like he was going to say something. Then his eyes widened. "Look out—"

A crossbow bolt zipped by my ear and sank into the Spartan's left shoulder. Blood sprayed through the air. Oliver screamed with pain and collapsed onto the concrete floor, clawing at the bolt. I whirled around.

A figure stood behind me. He must have slipped in through the door while I'd been talking to Oliver. Shadows cloaked his face, but I could clearly see the crossbow in his hand—the one that he'd just loaded with a fresh bolt. He gestured with the weapon, and I put my hands up and slowly backed around the wheelbarrow until I stood next to Oliver, who was writhing on the floor in pain.

"Stop," the shadowy figure commanded.

I gasped. I recognized that voice, knew exactly who it belonged to. But why would he be here? And why would he shoot Oliver?

Preston stepped into a slice of sunlight and leveled his crossbow at me. "You're not going anywhere, Gypsy."

This time, my eyes were the ones that widened. "Preston?" I asked. "What's going on? What are you doing?"

"I think it's rather obvious. I'm here to kill you." His handsome face twisted into a sneer. "Just like you killed my little sister. And my name's not Preston. Well, not exactly. Preston's my middle name, you see. Julian Preston Ashton."

"Your sister?" I whispered, ice filling up my stomach. "Jasmine was your sister?"

Professor Metis had warned me that Jasmine's family blamed me for her death, that they might come after me. Jasmine herself had told me that she and the rest of her family were Reapers. Now one of them had come to collect.

"Don't you say her name!" Preston screamed. "Don't you dare say her name, you Gypsy bitch!"

Preston leveled the crossbow at my face, and for a second I thought he was going to pull the trigger. But then he calmed down and lowered the weapon a few inches—aiming it at my heart instead. Not much of an improvement.

"Did you really think you could kill my sister—kill an Ashton, kill a Reaper—and get away with it?" Preston snarled.

I swallowed, but a hard lump of fear filled my throat. "Jasmine—Jasmine tried to kill me first. I just defended myself."

I didn't say anything about the fact that Logan was really the one who'd killed Jasmine, that the Spartan had been the one to put a spear through her chest. I didn't want to put him in danger, too. Besides, Preston wouldn't believe me anyway.

Preston laughed, and the harsh, mocking sound fluttered against the walls, somehow darkening the shadows all around us. "I don't care what you did. You killed my sister, and now you're going to pay for it."

He cocked his head to one side, studying me. "All that's left is to decide how much I want to make you suffer in the meantime."

His words chilled me to the bone, because I knew he meant them. He was just as determined to kill me as Jasmine had been to sacrifice Morgan to Loki. I wondered if Preston would do the same thing to me. If he would stake me out down here in the sawdust and concrete, chant some magic mumbo jumbo, and dedicate my death to the evil god he served before he put a crossbow bolt through my skull.

The sick, horrid thought made me want to vomit, but I forced myself to just breathe—in and out, in and out, like my mom had taught me. I couldn't give in to the panic. If I did that, I was already dead. Calm, I had to stay calm, and I had to *think*. That was the only way I was going to get out of this alive.

My eyes flicked down, but Oliver had quit screaming. Now, the Spartan lay quiet and still at my feet. A wide pool of blood had formed under his left shoulder, mixing with the sawdust on the floor. I didn't know if the Spartan was dead or not, and I didn't dare bend down to check. Not with Preston still aiming his crossbow at me.

"Don't worry about him," Preston sneered. "Like I told you before, archery's not really my thing, but that's a pretty nasty wound. If he's not dead by the time I'm done with you, I'll put another bolt through his skull and finish him off. Actually, this will work out even better than I'd planned. I'll make it look like the two of you fought and killed each other. That way, no one will be chasing me after the fact."

Think, Gwen, think!

Okay, so Oliver couldn't help, since he was so badly injured, but I had to do something to try and save us. I had to keep Preston talking while I figured out some sort of plan.

"Why now?" I asked, wetting my lips. "Why did you decide to kill me now? Why wait all these weeks?"

Preston's face tightened with anger. "Because after Jasmine's death, after they found out that the Ashtons are Reapers, the members of the Pantheon started hunting for us, so they could throw us into one of their pathetic little prisons. I had to leave school in Athens, and my parents had to go into hiding. Besides, I couldn't get to you at the academy. I'd visited Jasmine there before, and I couldn't take a chance that someone would recognize me. Like your friend Daphne."

All sorts of images from the past two days filled my mind. Preston always standing next to the lobby wall. Me never seeing him with anyone else, even though he always claimed he was meeting friends. The fact that he always disappeared whenever Daphne and Carson showed up. The Valkyrie telling me that she didn't see his profile and picture with the rest of the student photos on the New York academy's Web site.

Something whispered at my feet, and I spotted Oliver slowly, slowly sliding his hand down along the floor. Relief flooded my body, chasing away some of the cold dread. The Spartan wasn't dead yet, even though his eyes were closed and he was acting like he was.

I focused my attention on Preston again, determined to keep the Reaper talking for as long as possible. Determined to keep him looking at me and not Oliver. I didn't know what the Spartan was up to, but I was going to give him a chance to do it.

"So it was all a lie, then," I said, rocking forward on my heels, so Preston wouldn't notice the fact that Oliver was digging in his jacket pocket for something. "You flirting and chatting me up all those times, asking me to lunch. You've been trying to get me alone all weekend, just so you could kill me. And you've been staying down here, too, haven't you? Here in the construction site, since all the rooms were rented out to Mythos students and staff for the weekend."

Preston nodded. "Yeah, pretty much. I was going to kill you that first night, right outside the party, but then your little Spartan boyfriend came outside and got in the middle of things."

I wrapped my arms around my chest, feeling numb and frozen inside. Every word Preston said only added to the ice running through my veins. I remembered how happy I'd been that Preston had been flirting with me that night, how eager I'd been to follow him around the side of the building so we could make out. Preston might have kissed me, but he would have followed it up by shoving a dagger through my heart. I'd been so pissed at Logan for butting in, but the Spartan had saved my life. If I got out of this alive, I was going to tell Logan as much, and that I was sorry for—for *everything*.

"And the avalanche?" I asked. "You texted me and asked me to meet you at the hotel, so what exactly—you could make sure I was going down the mountain at the right time?"

"Well, yeah." Preston rolled his eyes. "I only had enough explosives for one try at that. I didn't want to waste them."

"And the Fenrir wolf?"

He shrugged. "I had it follow you around the slopes and keep an eye on you. I figured that if the avalanche didn't get you, then the wolf would finish the job. But the stupid dog got hurt instead."

Preston glanced to his left and let out a sharp whistle. A shadow I hadn't noticed before detached itself from the wall and came over to him. The Fenrir wolf walked with a noticeable limp, although a bandage covered its leg where the tree branch had skewered it. Preston's doing, I supposed. As weird as it was, I was glad to see that the wolf was okay. It wasn't the creature's fault Preston was a Reaper maniac who wanted to murder me.

"Useless dog," Preston snarled.

The wolf lowered its head, but I saw its red eyes narrow the tiniest bit. I didn't know how much of Preston's words the creature understood, but the wolf didn't seem to like the Reaper any more than I did. So why did it obey him? What kind of hold did Preston have over it?

While Preston glared at the creature, I glanced down at Oliver. Somehow the Spartan had gotten his cell phone out of his jacket pocket. His pain-filled eyes fluttered open, and he looked at me. I nodded, telling him to do whatever he was trying to do. That I'd keep Preston crowing for as long as I could. Bloody fingers shaking, Oliver punched a button on the phone, then another one. I stepped in front of him, so Preston wouldn't see the light from the screen glowing in the semidarkness.

"How did you even know I'd be here at the ski resort to start with?" I asked. "You took a big risk coming all the way here from wherever you were hiding."

He shrugged. "Everyone always comes to the Winter Carnival. It's a Mythos Academy tradition."

I could have laughed at the irony. Daphne had said those very same words to me earlier this week, but I hadn't really believed her—or known that such a tradition was probably going to be the death of me. On the floor, Oliver hit some more buttons on his phone.

Desperate to give him more time, I looked back up at Preston. "But what about—"

"Enough!" Preston snapped. "Stop talking. Your whiny sniveling is driving me crazy. Face it, Gypsy. The Spartan's dying, and you're down here all alone with me and the wolf. You're not getting out of here alive."

Preston stared at me, his blue eyes glinting with hate, his handsome face twisted into something black, ugly, and evil. Then he raised the crossbow until it was level with my head and pulled the trigger.

Chapter 21

Everything happened at once.

I dove to my right, Preston pulled the trigger on the crossbow, and the Fenrir wolf bumped into his side, making Preston stumble. I don't know if the creature did it on purpose or not, if it was trying to help me or not, but the wolf screwed up the Reaper's aim and the bolt zipped over my head and disappeared into the semidarkness.

I scrambled to my feet. For a second I thought about running, about getting as far away from Preston as I could. Then my gaze dropped to the floor, where Oliver still lay, more and more blood pooling underneath him as he fumbled with his phone. Yeah, maybe the Spartan had scared me, but I couldn't leave him down here, helpless and defenseless with a barbed bolt sticking out of his shoulder.

So I did the only thing I could think of: I withdrew Vic out of the leather scabbard strapped to my waist.

"Well, it's about bloody time," Vic muttered, glaring

at me with his purplish eye. "I was wondering if you'd forgotten about me, Gwen."

Yeah, I kind of had a little bit, but I wasn't going to admit that to him.

"What was I supposed to do? Whip you out right in front of Preston?" I hissed. "My hands were up in the air, in case you didn't notice. And hello, he had a crossbow aimed at my head. Crossbow beats sword in that case."

Vic just sniffed.

"Oh, look, the Gypsy has a sword," Preston said in an amused voice. "Good thing I do too."

The distinctive, raspy whisper of metal sliding free of a scabbard made my heart drop like a stone in my chest. I whirled around and raised Vic. Preston had climbed back to his feet and drawn his own sword. He must have been wearing the weapon underneath his long, flowing, black coat. The edge of the blade touched one of the cracks of sunlight. Maybe it was my imagination, but the metal seemed to wink at me, even as it took on a bloody, reddish tinge. I shivered and tightened my grip on Vic.

Preston walked closer and closer to me, picking his way through the construction debris and nonchalantly swinging his sword from side to side. "You know, I'm kind of glad I missed you with that bolt," he hissed. "It'll be so much more fun to cut you into pieces."

I really, *really* wanted to scream, drop Vic, turn, and run. But I couldn't leave Oliver to the Reaper's mercy. Besides, Preston would just stab me from behind anyway. All I could do was stand and fight—or at least try to.

I glanced past Preston, wondering what the Fenrir wolf was doing. The creature sat upright on its haunches, like it was an ancient statue that had been frozen in place, like one of the gryphons outside the Library of Antiquities. Its red eyes met mine. Something like sadness flickered in its gaze, and it let out a low whimper. I might have helped the wolf during the avalanche, but I knew I couldn't count on it to come to my rescue. Not again, not here, not against its master. Spoiling Preston's aim was the only aid the wolf was going to give me. I'd just have to make sure it was enough.

Preston looked at me, taking in my stance and focusing on the sword bobbing up and down in my trembling hands. A cruel, cruel grin curved his face. And then he attacked.

Clang-clang-clang!

Preston launched himself at me, his moves a shadowy blur in the semidarkness. Maybe some of my weapons training had finally sunk in, because I was able to deflect his blows. But Preston was two years older than I was, six inches taller, and totally ripped with muscle. Not to mention the fact he was a Viking. He was stronger than I was—so much *stronger*—and his blows jarred me from my wrist, all the way up to my shoulder. Every stinging, ringing clash of his sword threatened to rip Vic out of my hands. I could feel Vic's mouth moving underneath my palm, trying to shout out words of encouragement, but I had such a death grip on the hilt that my hands muffled his voice.

"Not bad—for a five-year-old who just got her first toy sword to play with," Preston sneered. "I can't believe you're supposed to be Nike's Champion. Start saying your prayers to that stupid goddess you serve, Gypsy, because you won't last another minute."

I blinked. "How do you know I'm Nike's Champion? I never told you that."

Daphne, Professor Metis, and Grandma Frost were the only people who knew the truth. Well, them and Vic, of course.

Preston's eyes narrowed, and something red and evil sparked to life in the depths of his gaze. "Oh, we know all about you, Gwen Frost, and what you're supposed to do."

What I was supposed to do? What the hell was he talking about? I didn't have time to think about it before he charged me again.

Clang-clang-clang!

I managed to block all of his attacks once more, although I was panting from the effort. Sweat slicked my palms, and my arms felt heavy and slow, like lead weights attached to my shoulders. I didn't know how much longer I could stop Preston from running me through with his sword. He was right. I wouldn't last another minute.

He came at me a third time, his sword whistling through the air, getting closer and closer to my neck with every single blow until—

CLANG!

Preston finally broke through my defenses. He smashed his weapon into mine so hard that I lost my grip on Vic, and the sword sailed off into the shadows.

"Gwen! Gwen!" Vic shouted, his voice getting fainter and more frantic the farther he slid into the darkness.

I started to lunge after him, but Preston grabbed me by my hair. I shrieked and then punched and clawed at him, but he just laughed at my weak blows. Preston jerked me back, then threw me forward. I tripped over one of the bags of cement on the floor and hit the wall hard. My legs slid out from under me, and I landed in a heap.

Before I could even think about moving, Preston was on top of me, his sword an inch away from my throat. I kept my head perfectly still, scarcely daring to breathe.

"Like I said," Preston sneered. "Didn't even last a minute."

A flash of movement caught my eye, and a shadow broke free of the wall, creeping closer and closer to Preston.

The Reaper stared down at me and frowned. "What are you smiling at? I'm about to slit your throat, you stupid Gypsy."

"Nothing much," I drawled. "Just my hero."

Logan erupted out of the darkness. The Spartan slammed into Preston, knocking the Reaper and his sword away from me. The two of them fell to the floor, punching, kicking, and rolling over everything in their path. Oliver must have texted Logan and told him what was going on. That was the only reason I could think of as to why he would be down here right now. Despite the fact that Oliver had done his best to scare me, I was *totally* forgiving him for everything.

"Vic!" I shouted.

"Here! Over here!"

I scrambled to my feet and followed the sound of the sword's voice. I plucked Vic out of the pile of sawdust he'd landed in. Out of the corner of my eye, I spotted a hammer lying on one of the sawhorses, so I grabbed it, too, then turned and ran back the other way, so I could help Logan.

The Reaper and the Spartan had both gotten back on their feet and were slowly circling each other. Eyes narrow, faces tight, lips drawn back in silent snarls. Logan had his fists up, while Preston was doing that annoying, wavy-wavy thing with his sword again.

Smack! Smack! Clang!

The two of them clashed together. Logan landed two solid punches to Preston's face, but the Reaper lashed out with his sword, making Logan jump back. And on it went. The more I watched, the more worried I got. Preston had his Viking strength to rely on, and he was a good fighter, almost as good as Logan. I hadn't been at Mythos Academy long, but even I could tell that.

Plus, Preston had a sword and Logan didn't. That was what was tipping the scales in the Reaper's favor. Logan just couldn't get in close enough to do much damage to Preston, not without getting cut up in the process. I stood there and bit my lip, swallowing my screams, not daring to do or say anything that would distract Logan.

Smack! Smack! Clang!

The two of them came together again, and Preston sliced his sword through the air. This time, Logan wasn't quite quick enough, and the blade cut across his left leg, opening up a deep, deep wound. He stumbled back, and Preston raised his sword for the killing strike.

"Logan!" I screamed.

Adrenaline, concern, and fear for Logan surged through my veins, blocking out everything else. I didn't think—I just acted. I charged in between them, raised my sword, and swung it at Preston. Of course, he blocked my clumsy blow.

Preston laughed at me. "Sorry, Gypsy. I'm going to kill your boyfriend, and then I'm going to kill you—and there's nothing you can do to stop me."

"Shut up, Reaper," I snarled.

And that's when I snapped up my left hand and smashed him in the face with the hammer I'd grabbed. Preston screamed and stumbled back. I followed him and hit him again, cracking the hammer across his skull as hard as I could. He tripped over a couple of two-by-fours and fell face-first onto a pile of cement bags.

I didn't look to see how badly I'd hurt him before I dropped the hammer and raced back to Logan's side. He had dropped to a knee on the floor beside Oliver. Logan put his hand under Oliver's shoulder, trying to help his friend get to his feet, but Logan was just too weak to do it with the deep cut in his leg.

"Leave me," Oliver whispered, his face white, the tendons in his neck tight with pain. "Go. Save yourselves."

"Spartans never leave each other behind," Logan rasped, and tried to lift his friend again. "*Never*, remember?"

Once more, he failed. In the middle of the pile of cement bags, Preston let out a low groan. The Fenrir wolf stayed where it was in front of the door, blocking our escape and watching all of us with its glowing red eyes.

"Make him go, Gwen," Oliver said, pleading with me. "Or the Reaper will kill us all."

Logan grabbed for his friend again, but Oliver slapped his hands away and flopped back down onto the floor. He shut his eyes and let his head loll to one side. Playing dead, which was the only thing he could do right now, the only way he could protect himself.

Preston groaned again. The Reaper got up onto his hands and knees.

"Come on! Come on! Come on!" I shouted at Logan.

I put my arm under Logan's shoulder and got him on his feet. Then I dragged the Spartan away from Oliver, Preston, and the wolf, heading back into the gloom of the construction site.

I didn't know how long we hurried through the site, navigating around all the piles of tools and lumber and moving from one half-finished hallway to the next. All I could think about was getting Logan away from Preston before the Reaper killed him or sicced the Fenrir wolf on both of us. The Spartan limped along beside me, and I took as much of his weight as I could on my left shoulder. I carried Vic in my other hand.

"Stop, Gwen, stop!" Logan finally said. "I have to stop and tie off the wound. I'm losing too much blood."

I didn't want to stop for anything, but I knew that he was right. So I helped him sit down on a couple of bags of cement that had been stacked up on top of each other. I unzipped my hoodie and took it off, passing it over to him.

Logan grabbed the jacket and used Vic to tear the fabric into a couple of long strips. He quickly wrapped them around his leg, tying them off with a series of tight knots. Blood from the gash had already soaked his jeans, turning them more black than blue. My stomach twisted. So much blood.

"Can you go on?" I whispered. "We have to get out of here."

"I think so."

Logan tried to stand and immediately sat down again, biting back a scream of pain. Sweat rolled down his forehead, and his lips were a thin white stain in his face. The fabric strips he'd just tied around his leg were already turning an ugly brown as the blood seeped into them.

"I'm sorry," he rasped. "I don't think I can walk any farther. Go on, Gwen. Get out of here. Run. Before he finds us both."

I shook my head. "We already left Oliver behind. I'm not leaving you, too."

Logan grabbed my shoulders and shook me. "Listen to me! This isn't like that night in the Library of Antiquities. I had weapons then. All we have now is your sword, and I'm stuck with a bum leg. There's no way I can beat Preston like this. He's almost as good as I am, and we all know it."

"Listen to the Spartan, Gwen," Vic chimed in. "Go and get help. I'll stay here with him. We'll give you time to get away."

"Shut up, Vic," I snapped. "I'm not going anywhere. Be quiet and let me think a second."

Logan frowned and looked around, probably wondering who I was talking to since he didn't know about Vic. I ignored the Spartan and his confusion. Instead, I paced back and forth, my sneakers sending up puffs of sawdust into the shadows. Thinking. Logan couldn't beat Preston, not now, not with his leg cut up, and I simply didn't have the skills to go toe-to-toe with the Reaper and win. Preston had said that I was like a five-year-old with a toy sword, and he was right.

So what were we going to do? If only I'd been the one that Preston had injured instead of Logan. I could have just given Vic to Logan and let the Spartan use all of his years of training, knowledge, and fighting skills to beat the Reaper. If I'd had more training, if I knew how to actually use a sword myself, then I would have taken on Preston in a heartbeat. But I didn't, and there was just no getting around that.

If you can use my memories to help you with archery,

*why can't you use them to help with something else? I
know I'm right about this. I'm always right.*

Daphne's words whispered in my mind, and I flashed
back to that first day in the gym when I'd thought about
the Valkyrie, when I'd called up her memories and used
them to put my arrows into the center of the target. I'd
done the same thing again on Friday, when I'd flashed
on Daphne skiing and used those images to help myself
get down first the bunny slope and then the higher ones.
A crazy, crazy idea came to me then, a way that I could
keep Logan and me from getting killed, maybe the *only*
way that I could keep that from happening.

I crouched down in front of Logan. "Listen, we both
know that you can't fight Preston with your wounded
leg, and I can't beat him by myself. But maybe we can
stop him—together."

"What do you mean?"

I quickly told Logan about this new thing I'd learned
how to do with my psychometry.

"So you want to touch me and take my memories of
all the battles I've been in and all the weapons training
I've had. Then you want to use them to fight Preston
yourself?" Logan asked after I explained everything.

I winced. It sounded completely nutso when he said it
out loud like that. "More or less."

Logan thought about it a second. "I think that's one
of the craziest things I've ever heard—and one of the
most brilliant. Let's do it."

I blinked. "You . . . believe me? You really think it
will work?"

"I think you're one of the smartest, bravest people I know," Logan said. "I trust you, Gypsy girl. If you think it will work, then I know it will."

Certainty blazed in his ice blue gaze, and his voice rang with an absolute, unwavering trust. The Spartan's rock-steady belief in me, that I could actually use my magic to get us out of this mess, made hot tears sting my eyes. Emotion clogged my throat, making it hard to breathe. I nodded and stretched out my hand toward his.

Logan held up his own hand, signaling me to stop. He looked at me a second, then gave me a crooked grin. "Come on, Gypsy girl. I'm bleeding to death here, in case you haven't noticed. At least make it worth my while and kiss me before I die."

Despite the situation, my heart lifted at his words, and I found myself grinning back at him. I wanted to kiss him. I wanted that more than *anything*, especially since this might be the last chance I ever got to do it. But I wanted to make sure Logan knew what he was doing—and what might happen when I touched him.

"Are you sure?" I whispered. "I don't—I don't know what I might see, and I know there are some parts of yourself that you want to stay . . . hidden. That you have . . . secrets you want to keep to yourself."

Logan nodded. "I'm sure."

I stared at him. "It'll be okay, I promise. No matter what I see or feel. You'll still be Logan, and I'll still be your Gypsy girl."

He stared back at me, his eyes as bright as blue stars

in his rugged, pain-filled face. "I know it will, Gwen. I know it will. Now shut up and kiss me before I pass out."

"Well, when you put it like that, how can a girl possibly resist?" I quipped back.

Before I could think too much about what I was about to do, I leaned forward and pressed my lips to his.

Chapter 22

The feelings and images immediately overwhelmed me.

Touching Logan, feeling his skin against mine, flashing on him with my magic. It was all just—just—*electric*. He was so strong, so full of life, so fun and crazy and irrepressible. The Spartan's strength flooded my heart and mind, even as his arms crept around my waist and drew me closer. His spirit gave my own new power, energy, and hope.

Logan's lips were firm against my own, and the kiss was everything I'd ever dreamed it would be. Warm, caring, and sexy. I opened my mouth, and our tongues touched, slowly stroking against each other. For a moment I just let myself enjoy the kiss, just let myself relish the feel of his hot mouth on mine, the feel of his hard, muscled body pressed against mine.

Being this close to Logan made me dizzy and breathless, but I forced myself to focus. I concentrated on the Spartan, going beyond that crazy jumble of desire and longing, and looking for the memories I needed to help us both survive. I could feel Logan concentrating too, trying to call up every bit of his fighting and weapons knowledge and bring it to the surface of his mind, so I'd be able to see it, remember it, use it.

My plan worked.

The memories poured into my mind, and hundreds of images flashed by, one after another. Logan using swords, staffs, spears, and weapons I didn't even know the names for. The Spartan sparring with other Mythos students in gym class and almost always winning. Him battling kids outside of the gym, for real, and winning all of those matches, too. Even Logan fighting the Nemean prowler in the Library of Antiquities the night Jasmine had tried to kill me. Logan's strength roared to the surface then, along with his ferocity and pride at overcoming something as dangerous as the prowler.

It was like a light snapped on inside my head. Suddenly, I saw everything I'd been doing wrong during our mock fights in the gym. All the sloppy mistakes I'd made, all the obvious weaknesses I had, all the easy ways Logan had been able to "kill" me time after time. And I realized what I had to do to beat Preston, what I had to do to save us both.

I was just about to pull away when the memories of Logan fighting faded away, and a different one popped into my head. I should have ended the kiss then, but I didn't. Even though I knew it was wrong of me, I still wanted to see the image. I wanted to know everything there was to know about Logan. I wanted to learn what deep, dark secret he'd been so desperate to hide from me.

In this memory, Logan was a little boy, only around

five years old. Even back then, he was cute, with big blue eyes and a tousled mop of black hair. But the memory wasn't a happy one—not at all. Logan huddled on the floor of a large closet, hidden in the very back, behind a rack of clothes. Screams sounded just outside the closed door, and shadows twisted and writhed on the other side of the wide slats. Logan clutched a small metal sword in his hands, but he wasn't using it. He wanted to, though. The urge to run out of the closet made his heart pound, but he was so afraid of the screams, so scared of the shadows, that he felt frozen in place.

The image abruptly shifted and bled into another memory. Logan stood over two bodies, a woman and a girl who was a few years older than he was. *His mother and his sister,* a voice whispered in my mind. They were dead, their throats cut, and blood covered the floor all around them, coating their faces. So much blood. Logan still clutched his sword in his hand. Angry, he threw it away, then lay down in between his mother and sister, not caring that he was getting their blood all over him. Tears streaked over his small, pale face, and then, he started to scream.

Logan drew back, breaking the kiss, breaking our connection. I would have fallen over, if he hadn't caught me and cradled me in his arms.

"Gwen?" Logan whispered against my cheek. "Are you okay? What did you see?"

I saw why part of you is so sad, I thought. *Why you won't let me get close to you, because you once lost the people you cared about the most.* But I didn't say the words. I just . . . couldn't. Not now. Later. We'd . . . talk about it later. If we had a later.

I shook my head and drew back, looking into his rugged face. "I'll give you this, Spartan. You sure can kiss. Feel free to lay one on me anytime you want to."

For a second relief flashed in his eyes—relief that I hadn't discovered his secret. That I hadn't seen the blood and bodies that haunted him so. Then Logan grinned.

"Well, I do aim to please," he drawled. "You should see what I can do with my hands. And other parts of my body."

I rolled my eyes. "Seriously? You've been cut open like a fish, there's a psycho-killer Reaper after us, and you're still hitting me up for sex?"

Logan shrugged, but the devilish light didn't fade from his gaze. "Hey, you can't blame a guy for trying."

"Right. We'll talk about that later. Now, come on," I said. "I have an idea."

I stood behind the doorway and waited for Preston Ashton to come and kill me.

I didn't have long to wait. I'd barely gotten into position when footsteps scuffled, and a shadow appeared at the far end of the half-finished hallway.

"Gypsy . . ." Preston's voice echoed through the semi-dark construction site. "Oh, Gypsy . . . I'm coming to kill you. . . ."

I gritted my teeth and gripped Vic tighter. I knew Preston was trying to scare me, but I could still hear the crazy in his voice, loud and clear. How had I ever thought he was cute? He *so* needed to be locked up in an insane asylum somewhere. Too bad Batman wasn't here to come and drag his ass off to Arkham.

I looked over at Logan, who leaned against one of the walls, hidden in the shadows. The Spartan clutched a loose brick in his hand, the only weapon we'd been able to find in the construction debris, since I'd dropped the hammer earlier. I nodded at him, and he nodded back. Showtime.

"Here goes nothing," I whispered.

"Cut him to bits!" Vic crowed. "And feed me the pieces! It's been a long time since I've dined on Reaper blood." Underneath my palm, the sword's lips smacked together in anticipation.

"Let's just hope I win. Now, shut up, Vic. I need to concentrate."

I drew in a breath and stepped out into the hallway, so Preston could see me.

The Reaper spotted me at once, and a mocking smile curved his lips. "Coming out in hopes that I'll kill you quick? I hate to disappoint you, but that's not going to happen, Gypsy. Not now."

He stepped closer, and I realized that blood covered the lower half of his face. I must have done more damage with that hammer than I'd thought. Preston's nose had swelled up to twice its normal size, and black and purple streaks radiated out from it like sunbeams.

But his eyes were what really creeped me out. They glowed a wicked, wicked red. It looked like someone had filled Preston's eyes with dozens of matches and then lit them all at once. Crimson flames danced in his gaze, burning so hot and bright I thought he might just shoot fire out of his eyeballs and fry me where I stood.

Jasmine's eyes had looked exactly the same way when she'd tried to kill me in the Library of Antiquities. Preston must be channeling Loki, tapping into the evil god's magic or whatever Reapers of Chaos did when they were intent on killing their enemies.

But I had Logan to channel and all his fighting memories to tap into. It would be enough to save us both. It was going to have to be.

"You want a fight?" I called out. "Then come and get it, you arrogant, snot-nosed punk."

I didn't have to taunt him twice. Preston screamed with rage and raced down the hallway toward me. I turned and ran to the far end and into an open area, drawing him out past Logan's hiding spot. The plan was simple. I'd keep Preston busy, and as soon as Logan got the chance, the Spartan would lurch up behind the Reaper and brain him with the brick he was holding until Preston was unconscious. All I had to do was not get killed in the meantime.

I whirled around, moved Vic into position, and summoned up all of the memories of Logan that I had. Preston broke free of the hallway, raised his sword over his head, and brought it down at me.

CLANG!

Preston had struck with all his Viking strength and skill, trying to split my skull in two with one blow. The force of his vicious attack rocked me back, but I thought of Logan, called up my memories of him, and managed to hang on to Vic.

And so we fought.

Back and forth we moved in the chaos of the construction site. Screaming, snarling, and trying to hack each other into bloody pieces, just like Vic wanted. Preston was in a *frenzy* now, his eyes getting redder, brighter, and angrier with every passing second. Even with my memories of Logan, it was all I could do to keep the Reaper from shoving his sword through my heart. And Preston and I were locked so close together that Logan couldn't jump into the mix with his cut leg— not without getting sliced to ribbons by one of us. If I was going to beat the Reaper, I was going to have to do it myself.

I reached for my Gypsy gift again, and I thought about Logan. I focused on how fierce he was, how strong, how he never gave up no matter what. I flipped through my memories of all the battles he'd ever been in, and I concentrated on that sweet, electric thrill of victory he felt every time he won. I called up image after image of Logan until the Spartan's face was all I could see, and his emotions were all I could feel—until Logan was all that I *was*.

And then I attacked.

Clang! Clang! Clang!

I stepped forward, swinging my sword in a rapid series of moves.

Thrust, thrust, thrust.

Preston managed to block my blows, but he did

something he hadn't done before: He stepped back instead of forward.

For the first time worry flickered in his gaze, right along with his burning hate for me. "How did you suddenly get so much better with that sword?"

"I'm a Gypsy," I snarled. "Nike's freaking *Champion*. Blessed and gifted with magic by the goddess herself. And Nike is victory itself, remember? That's who and what she is."

"So what?" Preston muttered.

"So I found a way to beat you, dumbass. I found a way to *win*."

Okay, so maybe I was only winning because I was tapping into Logan's memories and fighting skills, but the smack talk was all me.

Preston opened his mouth to say something else, but I didn't give him the chance. I pressed my advantage, going at him with everything I had, with every sneaky trick Logan knew and a couple of even dirtier ones I'd thought of myself.

On my first blow, I nicked his arm.

On the second, I sliced Vic across his stomach.

And on the third, I knocked Preston's sword from his hand.

Preston bent down, scrambling for his weapon, but I didn't stop my attack. I drew my leg back and slammed my foot into his face. Something crunched underneath my sneaker, and the Reaper screamed.

In another second, it was over. Preston lay sprawled flat on his back on the floor, and I had Vic up against his throat.

"Now that's what I'm talking about!" Vic crowed, his eye glowing like a purple moon in the shadows.

Vic's voice brought me back to myself, and I blinked a few times. I felt a little dazed and disoriented. Maybe it was because I'd been concentrating so hard on Logan's memories, but even though I'd just been fighting Preston, it was hard for me to remember exactly what had happened, exactly how I'd beaten him.

Preston glared up at me. That eerie, flashing, fiery hate still burned in his crimson eyes, even though his face was bloody and bruised, and his nose broken. "Go ahead, Gypsy. Kill me. I dare you to."

I moved Vic a fraction of an inch, but it was enough to break the skin on Preston's neck. A single drop of blood rolled down his throat.

"Do it," he hissed. "Kill me!"

I wanted to—I really, *really* wanted to. For everything he'd done to me, for how he'd hurt Logan, Oliver, and even the Fenrir wolf. But Preston was injured and unarmed now. He wasn't a threat to me anymore, and killing him now would make me no better than he was. Besides, I had a sneaking suspicion of what he really wanted anyway.

"Why?" I asked. "So you can dedicate your death to Loki and make him stronger, right? That's what Reapers do. They sacrifice other people and even themselves to their god, trying to help him break out of that magical prison he's trapped in. Kind of a whacked out thing to do if you ask me. I wouldn't want to serve a god like that."

"And it's *working*," Preston hissed. "The seals are all

but broken, and it won't be much longer before we find the key to unlock the last one. Soon, Loki will be free, and his Chaos will reign once more. And when that happens, you will rue the day you were ever born, Gypsy. You and Nike and all the other members of the pathetic Pantheon."

Seals? A key? I didn't know if Preston was spouting total bullshit or if he actually knew what he was talking about. Maybe it was his twisted face, or the red fire flickering where his eyes should be, but a cold shiver slithered up my spine.

"You'd better finish me now, Gypsy," Preston snarled. "Or I'll get free one day, and I'll go kill that doddering old grandmother you love so much."

I'd never known my dad, and I'd already lost my mom to a drunk driver. I couldn't lose my grandma, too. I just—couldn't. Rage exploded in my heart then—cold, black rage that the Reaper would dare to threaten my Grandma Frost—and sharp, bitter fear that he might somehow make good on his terrible promise. My whole body vibrated with the force of the two warring emotions. It took a few seconds, but the rage won out.

My hands tightened around Vic, and I pressed the sword deeper into Preston's neck, until his blood looked like crimson teardrops *drip-drip-dripp*ing onto the concrete floor.

"Come on, Gypsy," Preston muttered. "Do it!"

Footsteps scuffed in the sawdust, and Logan limped over to stand beside me.

"Gwen," Logan said in a soft voice. "Gwen."

There was no judgment in his voice, no reproach, no

condemnation, and I knew the Spartan would go along with whatever I decided to do. If I killed Preston, Logan would stand here and watch me do it. And I wanted to do it so *badly*. My hands trembled from the urge to just end Preston and the threats he'd made against my grandma.

But I didn't want Logan to see me as that kind of person—someone who could kill in cold blood—and I didn't want to be that kind of person myself. I didn't want to be a monster. For the first time, I truly understood what that was.

I let out a tense, ragged breath and pulled the sword away from Preston's throat.

"I'm okay now," I whispered. "I'm okay."

Logan reached out and put his hand on my shoulder. "I'm glad," he whispered back.

Chapter 23

Scarcely a minute had passed after I lowered the sword before shouts started echoing through the semidark construction site.

"Gwen! Logan! Oliver!"

"Over here!" Logan yelled back.

A few seconds later, a flashlight cut a bright path through the gloom and landed on my face. I squinted against the harsh glare, keeping my sword and eyes trained on Preston, not daring to let myself be distracted by the fact that we were about to have company. I might not have killed Preston, but if the Reaper moved an inch now, I'd cut him and worry about the consequences later. He'd do the same to me, try to kill me any way he could, no matter what. Something else Daphne had been right about.

To my surprise, Nickamedes stepped out of the shadows, a sword clutched in one hand and a flashlight in the other. The librarian's black eyebrows shot up at the sight of me standing over Preston, the Reaper's blood covering both of us like we'd been playing paintball instead of fighting to the death.

"Are you two all right?" Nickamedes asked, looking at Logan.

"We're fine, more or less," Logan replied. "I've got a bad gash on my thigh, and Gypsy girl's got some bumps and bruises. What about Oliver?"

Oliver. My breath caught in my throat. I'd been so busy fighting Preston that I'd forgotten about the other injured Spartan—and the fact that we'd had to leave him behind at the mercy of the Reaper and the Fenrir wolf. Even though I knew it had been the only choice at the time, guilt and shame burned in my heart. If Preston had killed Oliver, I didn't know what I'd do.

"Ajax found Oliver and took him to Aurora in the infirmary," Nickamedes said. "He should be fine, once she gets that bolt out of his shoulder and stops the bleeding."

I let out a breath I didn't even realize I'd been holding in.

Relief filled Logan's face. "Good." He looked away from the librarian. "I didn't want to leave him. You have to believe me. I would never leave someone behind. Not again. I wanted to stand and fight."

Misery made Logan's shoulders sag, and his voice was so soft I had to strain to hear it.

"I know you didn't, and so does Oliver." Nickamedes stepped closer to the Spartan and put a hand on his shoulder. "I'm glad you're okay. You had me worried, Logan."

I'd thought I was done being surprised for the day, but I didn't expect the casual, easy familiarity the two of them seemed to have with each other. The way they were talking, you'd think they were actually . . . friends or something. *Family even,* a small voice whispered from the back of my mind. For the first time, I noticed how similar the two of them looked—and how they both had the same black hair and ice blue eyes.

Logan and Nickamedes? Family? That was a little hard to wrap my brain around, especially since I'd never heard one mention anything about the other. Besides, Nickamedes was just too prissy to be related to someone as easygoing as Logan.

As if to prove my point, Nickamedes turned to glare at me, his eyes sharp and narrowed in his pale face.

"Two students severely injured, you yourself covered in blood, a Reaper on the premises, a Fenrir wolf running around loose somewhere, and extensive property damage to the resort. Well?" Nickamedes snapped. "What do you have to say for yourself, Gwendolyn?"

I thought for a second, then grinned at him. "I followed your directions exactly. I never set one foot outside the hotel."

I thought the librarian was going to reach over and strangle me right then and there.

An hour later, I sat on a bed in the resort infirmary watching Professor Metis finish healing Oliver. Metis had already fixed the gash in Logan's leg, and the Spartan was in the next room, telling Coach Ajax and Nickamedes what had happened for the tenth time. Like

Logan had said, I'd only gotten a few bumps and bruises, and my injuries weren't severe enough to require healing. But I'd stayed behind in the infirmary anyway. I needed to talk to Oliver—about a lot of things.

"There," Metis said. "All done."

She dropped her hands from Oliver's shoulder, and the warm, healing, golden glow that had enveloped his body slowly disappeared. Metis had already pulled the bolt out of his shoulder, and the skin there was smooth, whole, and unbroken once more. Oliver's face was still pale and sweaty from all the pain he'd experienced, but if I hadn't seen the Spartan writhing on the floor in the construction site, I wouldn't have known anything much had even happened to him.

Metis looked first at me, then at Oliver. Her green eyes were dark and thoughtful behind her silver glasses. She could tell something was going on between the two of us, but I didn't volunteer any information, and neither did he.

"I'll leave the two of you alone for a few minutes," she finally said, after it became apparent Oliver and I weren't going to talk in front of her.

"Thanks, professor," I said in a soft voice. "I think we'd both appreciate that."

Metis nodded, then left the room and closed the door behind her. Oliver and I didn't speak for a few moments.

"So, here we are," I said, staring at the Spartan who was half lying, half sitting on the next bed over.

He sighed. "Yeah. Lucky us."

More seconds ticked by in silence. On the table against the wall, the miniature statue of Skadi stared at us, her features neutral for once.

"Do you want to tell me about it?" I finally asked in a soft voice.

Oliver winced. "I guess I owe you that much, don't I?"

I shrugged.

Oliver sighed again, then sat all the way up on the bed. He swung his legs over the side so that he was facing me. Then he straightened his shoulders and looked at me.

"So I'm gay, and I'm in love with my best friend, who is not gay and has no idea how I feel about him. But you know all that already. You have ever since you picked up my notebook in the gym."

I shook my head. "No, I didn't. I got a feeling you had a serious crush on somebody, but I didn't realize who it was. You yanked the notebook out of my hands before I could see that it was Kenzie."

Oliver frowned. "But I thought you knew. You said all that stuff about me not wanting anyone to know who I wanted to hook up with. And then on the bus ride over here, you said that I'd...contaminate your stuff if I so much as touched it. I thought you were talking about me being gay."

Pain filled his green eyes. Oliver dropped his gaze from mine and picked at a loose thread on one of the bed sheets.

You could contaminate it because you're you, my own cold, nasty voice whispered in my mind. I'd been talking about something else entirely, and I'd said the words without thinking, without realizing how Oliver would interpret them.

"I was talking about my comic books," I said, trying to explain. "Whenever people touch stuff, they can leave part of themselves behind—their thoughts, feelings, memories. My psychometry magic lets me see, feel, and experience those things like they're my own memories, my own emotions. That's why I don't like people touching my things—because they can leave bitter, ugly pieces of themselves behind. Plus, I thought you were teasing me or something. I just wanted you to go away."

I winced. "Shit. I was a complete bitch, wasn't I? You probably think I'm a total bigot."

This time, Oliver shrugged. We fell silent for a few seconds.

"So why did you try to run me down outside my grandma's house? Why shoot that arrow at me in the library?" I asked.

"It's complicated," he said. "My parents know I'm gay, and they've been great about it. Really, really supportive. Logan and Kenzie know, too, and they're cool with it. They wouldn't be my friends otherwise. Pretty much everyone at Mythos knows. I'm not trying to hide it, but I don't shout it from the rooftops either, you know? I figure it's nobody's business but mine."

I nodded. I understood what he was talking about. I did the same thing with my Gypsy gift. Yeah, the other Mythos kids knew I had the power to find lost items, but I didn't stand out on the quad and brag about it between classes either.

I thought about that strange look Morgan had given me in the lobby when I'd told the clerk that I wanted to know what room Oliver was in. The Valkyrie knew Oliver was gay—that's why Morgan had thought it was weird that I'd go to his room or that I'd said that she'd hooked up with him.

Oliver drew in a breath. "But Kenzie doesn't know how I feel about *him*. I think Logan suspects, but he'd never say anything to Kenzie. Logan's too good a friend to do that. But I didn't know what you would do, Gwen. I didn't want you to tell anyone, especially not Kenzie."

"But why not just tell Kenzie how you feel?" I asked in a soft tone, even though I already knew what his answer would be.

Oliver shook his head. "Because Kenzie's my best friend, and I don't want to ruin our friendship. It's one of the best things in my life. Kenzie's not gay, so he's never going to feel the same way about me that I do about him. When I realized you knew about my feelings for him, I just . . . panicked, and I thought that if maybe I gave you something else to think about, then you'd forget all about me and my secret."

Oliver and I were more alike than he realized. I hated the fact that my feelings for Logan were so obvious to everyone. If I could have, I would have hidden them, especially since I had no idea how Logan really felt about me. Even back at my old school, I'd mostly kept my crushes to myself instead of immediately telling all my friends, because I knew how easy it was for one person to slip up and let a secret like that out of the bag. And if my crush didn't like me back, well, that's when things got humiliating, like they had with Logan. I could only imagine how much worse the situation would have been if Logan and I had been as close as Oliver and Kenzie were. So yeah, I could totally understand where Oliver was coming from about wanting to keep his feelings to himself.

He drew in a breath. "Plus, I didn't want to be the juicy gossip of the week at the academy or make Kenzie that either. That would just hurt both of us. I've got enough to deal with as it is now—being gay, being a Spartan, learning how to fight Reapers. I don't need people snickering and texting about me behind my back, because I'm in love with my best friend on top of everything else, you know?"

I did know. I'd been miserable when I'd first come to the academy because I hadn't fit in, because I'd felt so desperately out of place. Even after I'd become friends with Daphne and Carson, there were days when I still felt that way—like all anyone saw when they looked at me was Gwen Frost, that freaky Gypsy girl who touched stuff and saw things. Yeah, I knew how Oliver felt.

"I know what you're going through," I said. "But don't you think that the car and the arrow were a little . . . extreme? You could have just asked me not to say anything to Kenzie. I would have kept quiet about something that important to you."

Oliver winced. "I know, but I was mean to you that

morning in the gym, making fun of you. I thought that you'd tell Kenzie, even if I asked you not to. Let's face it. Getting payback is like the school sport at Mythos."

"Why were you so snarky to me? I wondered about that."

"Because Kenzie said he thought it was cool you liked superheroes. He's been dropping hints for a couple of weeks now that he's into someone. I thought it might be you, and I was jealous. That's why I made fun of your shirt."

"But Talia Pizarro was the girl Kenzie really liked instead."

Oliver nodded and drew in another breath. "Plus, Logan had told me and Kenzie that you'd had some run-ins with Reapers and that was why we were training you, in case they came after you again. I know I overreacted, but scaring you and making you think there was another Reaper after you just seemed like the easiest, quickest way to make you forget about my crush on Kenzie."

Oliver stared at me, his green eyes bright and earnest in his face. "But I wasn't trying to hurt you. Not really. If you hadn't jumped out of the way of my Escalade, I was going to swerve to the other side of the street, and I made sure I put the arrow at least a foot away from your head in the library. I was just trying to scare you. That's all, Gwen. I swear."

His logic made sense, in a weird sort of way. Oliver had just wanted to give me something else to think about besides the fact that he was in love with someone who would probably never return his feelings. It was my own fault I'd jumped to the wrong conclusions and had been stupid enough not to see Preston for the villain that he really was.

It was just like when I'd asked Carson about all the freaky games and decorations at the carnival. Carson hadn't seen anything wrong with the Reaper masks and Nemean prowlers because they were a part of the world that he'd grown up in. Those things were normal to Carson, just like fighting and scaring your enemy were normal to a fierce Spartan warrior like Oliver. Just like Daphne hacking into a computer system and messing with another girl's grades or me breaking into people's rooms and trying to learn all their secrets was normal to us. Maybe we all just did things that seemed perfectly reasonable to us at the time, even if deep down we knew that these things were wrong, or that other people wouldn't understand or agree with us.

I shook my head. "Well, you did a good job. I thought there was a Reaper trying to kill me because of what happened to Jasmine."

Oliver's gaze sharpened. "What did you have to do with Jasmine?"

I sat there and told him all about Jasmine faking her own murder, trying to sacrifice Morgan to Loki, and how I'd gotten caught up in the middle of it all. The Spartan had just told me his secret. I figured it was only fair to tell one of mine. Besides, Oliver had helped save me by texting Logan and telling him we were in trouble. Then, after Preston had stormed off after me and Logan, Oliver had texted Nickamedes and the other professors and told them what was going on. Maybe he hadn't used his Spartan fighting skills, but Oliver was still a hero.

Oliver looked at me with new interest after I finished my story. "Logan always said you were kick-ass, but I didn't really believe him—until now."

"Why? Because most of the time I don't know the end of a sword from the back of my hand?"

"Something like that."

We grinned at each other.

After a moment, my smile faded. This time, I was the one who looked down and picked at the bed sheet. "So . . . Logan thinks that I'm kick-ass?"

Oliver winced. "I'm, uh, really not supposed to say anything about that."

I stared at him with narrowed eyes. "Spill it, Spartan."

For a second I thought he wasn't going to answer me, but then he sighed. "Yeah, Logan thinks that you're kick-ass. He talks about you all the time. The boy is totally obsessed with you, Gwen."

"So why is he with Savannah instead of me?" The jagged edges of my heart scraped together in my chest as I asked the question, but I wanted to know why—I *needed* to know why.

"Logan has a problem with letting girls get close to him. I mean, really, really close to him and not just for—" Oliver bit off his words.

"Sex?" I asked in a wry tone.

He blushed a little. "Yeah, sex. I think you scare Logan, because he already cares so much about you. If he let you get closer to him, he'd be a total goner."

I didn't ask Oliver why Logan wouldn't let a girl get

close to him. I knew the answer had something to do with that horrible memory I'd seen—the one of a young Logan standing over the dead, bloody bodies of his mother and sister.

"So . . . are we cool?" Oliver said, interrupting my thoughts.

"About you scaring the shit out of me?"

He gulped and nodded.

I grinned. "Yeah, we're cool."

Oliver hesitated. "And about Kenzie and how I feel about him—"

This time, I cut him off. "It's your secret. You keep it as long as you need to, and I'll do the same. But if you ever need somebody to talk to, I'm here. I'm pretty good at listening." My grin widened. "Since, you know, I'm all kick-ass and stuff."

Oliver snorted and rolled his eyes, like he wished he'd never told me that. Yeah, I was *totally* going to get some mileage out of Logan's comment. After a moment, Oliver stretched out his closed fist toward me.

"Friends?" he asked in a quiet voice.

It occurred to me then that something unexpected and good had come out of this whole mess. I wouldn't want to face down another Reaper anytime soon. Okay, okay, I wouldn't want to battle another Reaper *ever,* but this time, I thought the battle had been worth the reward.

I leaned forward and bumped my fist against Oliver's. "Definitely friends."

Chapter 24

Oliver and I left the infirmary and went out to face the others.

Professor Metis, Coach Ajax, and Nickamedes wanted to question both of us, along with Logan, about what had happened in the construction site, so we all trooped into an office next to the infirmary. The grilling went on for about an hour. I told the whole story three times, from beginning to end, with a few small changes. Namely, that Preston had confessed to trying to run me over and shooting the arrow at me in the Library of Antiquities.

Under the table, out of sight of the profs, Oliver held out his fist to me again. I bumped it with mine once more, letting him know we were good. Logan stared at us, wondering what we were doing, but neither one of us looked at him. I'd promised Oliver I'd keep his secret, and I planned to make good on my vow. And I was okay with blaming Preston for everything, since, you know, the Reaper had tried to kill all three of us.

Finally, the professors wound down with their questions, and I asked the one—the *only* one—that I thought really mattered.

"What's going to happen to Preston?" I asked.

After Ajax had taken Oliver to the infirmary, the coach had come back down to the construction site and helped Nickamedes slap a set of magically reinforced handcuffs on Preston, who'd been cursing all the while. I'd watched the two profs haul away the Reaper. I didn't know where they'd taken Preston, and I didn't really care. All I wanted was to make sure he'd never see the light of day again—or get a chance to make good on his horrible threat.

You'd better finish me now, Gypsy. Or I'll get free one day, and I'll go kill that doddering old grandmother you love so much. Preston's cold, sneering voice rang in my head.

I shivered and wrapped my arms around myself. That wasn't going to happen, I vowed. Nobody was hurting my Grandma Frost. No matter what I had to do to stop it.

Metis, Ajax, and Nickamedes exchanged a look.

"He'll be locked up at Mythos until we can question him," Metis said. "We want to find out as much as we can about the other Reapers he's been working with and what their plans are."

My mouth dropped open. "There's a prison? At the freaking *academy*?"

Nickamedes winced. "Please, Gwendolyn. Keep the shrieking to a minimum. Of course, there's a prison on the academy grounds. This isn't the first time that Reapers, Fenrir wolves, and the like have tried to kill students. We have to have some place to put them until they can be shipped elsewhere to a more permanent facility."

Not too long ago, Jasmine's death had clued me in to the fact that there was a morgue at the academy to store student bodies, just in case kids got killed by Reapers. Now, I'd learned there was also a prison hidden somewhere amid the gray stone buildings, manicured lawns, and lifelike statues. I wondered what other nasty little secrets there were at Mythos. A cemetery? A crematorium? Or something even worse?

Eventually, the professors ran out of questions and sent Logan, Oliver, and me off to our rooms to get cleaned up. We'd just entered the hotel lobby when the front doors opened, and Daphne and Carson stepped inside. They were laughing, their cheeks flushed from the cold. Daphne spotted me and dragged Carson over to the three of us.

"Gwen! You won't believe what an awesome time we had today. It's too bad you were locked up here in the hotel. . . ."

The Valkyrie's voice trailed off, and her eyes widened as she took in my ripped, bloody clothes; dirty face; and rumpled, flyaway hair. Her gaze flicked to Oliver and Logan, who were just as filthy as I was.

"What happened to you?" She jerked her head at Oliver and Logan. "And them?"

"It's a long story," I said, linking my arm through hers. "But you didn't really think I was just going to sit around the hotel all day long and do nothing, did you?"

*   *   *

After I showered and changed into some clean clothes, I filled Daphne and Carson in on everything that had happened while they'd been off skiing.

"Great," the Valkyrie muttered, her black gaze accusing. "You go off chasing Reapers and forget to invite us. What kind of best friend are you, Gwen?"

I tried to convince Daphne that facing down Preston in the dark had been anything but fun, but she wouldn't believe me. And she thought I was a freak sometimes. Please.

I also called my Grandma Frost. Professor Metis had ordered me to, but I would have done it anyway, just to hear my grandma's voice. Just so I could make sure she was okay and that Preston or one of his Reaper friends hadn't found a way to hurt her like Preston had promised me he would. I didn't know what I would do if I lost my Grandma the way I had my mom.

This time, I couldn't convince Grandma Frost not to come to the resort. She showed up at Powder late that afternoon and drove me back across the mountains to her house in Asheville. Metis said that I could spend the night there in my old room before going back to the academy in the morning. Despite the fact that I'd almost died, the Powers That Were at Mythos still expected me to get up bright and early Monday morning for weapons training, classes, and homework. Life was *so* not fair sometimes.

Grandma fussed over me the rest of the evening, and I let her. It was nice to be taken care of after everything that had happened. Grandma Frost cooked one of my favorite meals for dinner: thick, juicy, mesquite steaks;

mashed potatoes with loads of cheese and sour cream; honey-coated carrots; and rich, chewy, sourdough rolls slathered with cinnamon butter. She even made my favorite pineapple-lime cheesecake for dessert. By the time we got done with the tropical treat, there was only a sliver left in the pan.

Grandma Frost came into my room late that night and sat on the edge of the bed. Concern filled her violet eyes, and her face seemed to have a few more wrinkles grooved into it than I remembered her having the last time I saw her.

"How are you holding up, pumpkin?" she asked.

"Okay, I guess," I said. "Just trying to process everything, you know?"

On the ride home, I'd told Grandma everything that had happened—from picking up Oliver's notebook to the Spartan trying to scare me with his car and the arrow to the avalanche and everything that had gone down with Preston in the construction site.

"What do you think happened to the Fenrir wolf?" I asked. "Do you think it's okay?"

The profs might have rounded up Preston, but they hadn't been able to find the wolf anywhere. Oliver had said the wolf had rammed open the door and bolted through it as soon as Preston had gone after me and Logan. The professors had lost the creature's trail in the snowy woods outside the resort. Maybe it was silly, but part of me hoped the professors didn't find it, that the wolf had gone deep into the mountains where it could finally be free of the Reapers.

"I'm sure it will be fine," Grandma said, trying to reassure me. "It's a wild animal, one that was never meant to be tortured or twisted by the Reapers. I'm sure it will be much happier in the forest than it ever has been before. There are other wolves that roam the mountains, and it might find a pack of them to join. Who knows? You might just see it again someday."

Her eyes took on an empty, glassy look for a second, and I wondered if she was seeing the wolf, if she was getting a glimpse of its future—or maybe even mine, too. But then the moment passed, and her eyes cleared once more.

I hesitated. "And what about my Gypsy gift? And what I can do with it now? Why do you think I have this new power?"

"You're seventeen, Gwen," Grandma Frost said. "You're not quite full grown yet, and neither is your magic. It's evolving and changing, just like you are. It will only continue to get stronger, just like you will. When I was your age, I was lucky if I could tell what time it was, much less see the future. But my magic got more and more powerful over the years, just like your mom's did—and just like yours will, too."

She drew in a breath. "And your psychometry isn't the end of your powers—it's just the beginning. You have what the old timers call touch magic. It's very rare and powerful. You always say that you touch stuff and see things, and that's true. But touch magic works both ways."

I frowned. "What does that mean?"

"It means that when you touch something, the object influences you—you see the memories and emotions attached to it. But the flip side of that is you should be able to influence the object or person you're touching as well. You should be able to feed that person your memories and emotions—and maybe more. At least, that's the theory. There's no telling what you'll be able to do with it someday. All you have to remember is to use your Gypsy gift wisely—help others, and yourself if you need it, and you'll be fine."

Somehow Grandma always knew just what to say to keep me from feeling like a freak, although I made a mental note to look up *touch magic* the next time I was in the Library of Antiquities. If there was more to my psychometry than just flashing on objects and people or using those memories, then I wanted to know what it was, so I could learn how to do it to protect myself—and Grandma Frost, too.

She reached out and clasped my hand, rubbing it in her spotted, wrinkled one, and I felt the warmth of her love wash over me, driving away everything that was cold, dark, and scary. At least for tonight.

"I just want to let you know how proud I am of you, pumpkin—and how proud your mom would be, too."

"Why?" I asked. "All I really did was almost get myself killed, along with Oliver and Logan."

My heart pounded again at the memory of Preston's burning red eyes and the evil sneer that had twisted his face. We'd all come so close to dying—*so close*. No matter what the others said, I knew it was my fault. Yeah, we'd all come through it okay, but that didn't ease my guilt about putting Oliver and Logan in danger and the horrible wounds they'd suffered because of me.

Grandma shook her head. "You stood by Oliver when it really counted and Logan, too. You figured out how to use your magic to save yourself and your friends. That makes you strong and smart, Gwen, and I couldn't be prouder of you. Now, get some rest. You've had a long day. We'll talk more in the morning before you go back to the academy."

She drew the quilt up to my neck, kissed my cheek, and left the room, shutting the door behind her.

You'd better finish me now, Gypsy. Or I'll get free one day, and I'll go kill that doddering old grandmother you love so much.

Preston's words rippled through my head again, a black echo that wouldn't fade away. I shivered and turned off the light by the bed, trying to put the Reaper's awful promise out of my mind. Preston was locked up where he couldn't hurt me anymore, and he was never, ever getting out.

I told myself that over and over again, but it was still a long, long time before I went to sleep.

Chapter 25

Life went back to normal. Well, as normal as it could be, given the fact that I went to Mythos Academy. I went to class, snuck off campus to see Grandma Frost, and worked my shifts at the Library of Antiquities, just like usual.

One thing that was different was weapons training. It was a lot more fun these days. Oliver and I had become real friends, and even Kenzie was starting to warm up to me, despite the fact that I'd ruined his breakfast with Talia. Kenzie and Talia were now officially dating and extremely hot and heavy. Sometimes Kenzie would sneak out of weapons training early to go meet the Amazon for breakfast. The Spartan never noticed the sad, longing looks Oliver gave him. I wished things could have been different for Oliver, and I hoped he found someone to take his mind off Kenzie. I knew how much unrequited love sucked, and I didn't want my new friend to feel the same hopelessness that I did.

I was doing better during training, too. Now I could make it a whole minute before Logan mock killed me with his sword, and I could hit the edge of the target with my arrows every single time. I tried not to use my memories of Logan and Daphne during training, though. I wanted to know how to defend myself for real and not have to rely on my Gypsy gift and someone else's skills and memories to get me through another battle with a Reaper. It was slow going, but I felt like I was finally starting to learn how to be a real warrior.

And then, of course, there was Logan.

We hadn't really talked since we'd kissed in the construction site. Sure, we did weapons training together and joked around, but neither one of us had mentioned *the kiss*—the one that had made me feel so many wonderful things. I wasn't sure how to bring it up or even what to say. So I kept my mouth shut, and Logan did the same.

Every once in a while, though, I'd catch him staring at me, a worried look in his blue eyes. I knew Logan wanted to ask me what I'd seen when I'd kissed him, but I wasn't sure what I should tell him. *I saw you crying over two dead bodies* didn't exactly make for great romantic talk.

The days slipped by, until there were just a few more before the academy let out for the long holiday break. All the Mythos kids were going home to spend Christmas and New Year's with their families, and I was looking forward to having a simple holiday with Grandma Frost and Vic. I'd even bought the sword a little red Santa hat to wear, although I expected him to put up a fuss about it.

"Bloody holidays," Vic muttered to me one night in

my dorm room. "We should be out fighting Reapers instead of thinking about stuffing ourselves with ham and pie."

I, for one, was looking forward to Grandma Frost's cooking, as well as a little peace and quiet, but I couldn't tell him that. If anything, Vic had become even more bloodthirsty since the fight with Preston. Apparently, I'd done so well during the battle that Vic now had some far-fetched hope that I'd turn out to be "a right proper brawler after all."

I just rolled my eyes, turned up the television a little louder in my dorm room, and let the sword rant.

Two days later, the final bell rang, signaling the end of myth-history, my last class of the day. I stuffed my books into my messenger bag and started to file out of the room with the other kids, but Professor Metis stepped in front of me and gestured for me to stay behind.

"I need you to come with me, Gwen," Metis said. "Right now, please."

Icy dread filled my stomach at her serious tone and the grim look on her face. "What's wrong? Did something happen to my grandma?"

She shook her head. "No, your grandma's fine, but I need your help with something else."

Mystified and still a little worried, I followed Metis out of the building. We stepped out onto the upper quad. Snow flurries had been flying through the air all day, and now, the fat flakes drifted down, dusting the ground like powdered sugar. Despite the cold, students still hung out on the quad, clustered together in tight groups, texting on their cell phones as best they could with their gloved fingers.

I thought we might be going to the Library of Antiquities to speak to Nickamedes about something or maybe even to the gym to talk to Coach Ajax, but instead, Metis cut across the quad. I followed her, and the two of us headed over to the math-science building. Like all the other structures at Mythos, the building was covered with statues of gryphons, gargoyles, and other mythological creatures, looking hard and sinister underneath their thickening coats of snow. As always, the creatures' eyes seemed to follow my every move, as though they were just waiting to shake off the snow, break free of their stony shells, and attack me. I shivered; pulled my gaze away from a pair of snarling, fanged gargoyles mounted on either side of the stone steps; and hurried after the professor.

Metis led me inside the building. Instead of going into one of the classrooms or up to a lab on another floor, I followed the professor down several flights of stairs. Down, down, down we went until it seemed like we were going into the belly of the academy. Every once in a while, when we came to a door, Metis would stop and either punch in a code on an electronic keypad or mumble a few words in a language I didn't understand.

I didn't know how far underground we were, but we'd passed the last classroom three floors ago. There were just as many lights on down here as in the rest of the building, but for some reason, the shadows seemed darker, longer, and deeper, like blood slowly oozing across the floor. Maybe it was silly of me, but I took care not to step in the shadows, just in case there was something hiding in them that I couldn't see.

Finally, on the bottom floor, Metis walked down a long hallway and stopped outside a strange door. Unlike the other metal ones we'd passed, this door was made out of the same dark gray stone as the rest of the building. Iron bars thicker than my wrist crisscrossed in a tic-tac-toe pattern over the stone, and two giant sphinxes had been carved into the surface. The creatures stared at each other, just like the pair above the main academy gate, and I got the sense that this was definitely a door designed to keep something *in*.

The professor stared at the door a moment, as if the sphinxes might turn their heads and reveal some secret to her. But the statues remained fixed where they were, so she looked at me.

"I guess I should tell you where we are," Metis said.

"The Mythos Academy prison, right?" I asked. "I saw the sign for the morgue on the floor above this one, so I'm guessing this is the prison that Nickamedes was talking about at the ski resort."

Metis tried to smile, but her lips twisted into more of a grimace. "Correct. This is where we keep Reapers, Nemean prowlers, and other threats to students before they're shipped off to a more permanent facility."

I stared at the reinforced door and the staring pair of sphinxes. My stomach twisted. Somehow, I knew exactly why Metis had brought me down here today. "Preston Ashton's still here, isn't he?"

Metis nodded. "Unfortunately, yes. We've been questioning him ever since we brought him back from the resort, but Preston has been...less than forthcoming about what the Reapers are up to. I was hoping you might be able to help us, Gwen." She hesitated. "I was hoping you'd be willing to use your psychometry on him."

I heard what she said, but for a second, her words didn't actually register. Then they sank in, and my stomach twisted even more. My knees felt like they were going to go out from under me, and I staggered back a few steps. I started to put my hand against the wall to steady myself, but thought better of it. I had no idea what kind of memories I'd see down here, but I doubted they'd be happy ones.

"You want me to—to *touch* him?" I whispered.

Metis nodded again. "We've tried everything we can think of, but Preston won't talk to us, and so far, he's been resistant to all the magic we've thrown at him. With you, he doesn't have to talk. You can see his memories whether he wants you to or not."

"So what? You want me to dig around in his brain and see what I can come up with?" I asked. "What if there isn't anything to find? What if he doesn't know anything about what the Reapers are planning? Yeah, Preston's one of them, but he mainly wanted to kill me because he was Jasmine's brother, and he thinks I murdered his sister."

Metis's face hardened until her features looked as cold and remote as those of the sphinxes on the door in front of us. "Then at least we'll know that, and we can put him in a real prison where he belongs. But if the Reapers are planning something, like we think they are, then we're all at risk. And this is a chance to strike back against them—the first good chance we've had in a long time. Please, Gwen, I know I'm asking a lot, but we've run out of options here."

I knew Metis wouldn't ask me to do this if there was any way to avoid it. She'd promised my mom she'd look out for me. More than that, she was just too good a person to ask me to do something like this unless it really was a last resort. As much as I wanted to, I couldn't say no. Not if there was a chance of stopping the Reapers and saving other people, no matter how slim it was. My mom would have done the same thing if she was here, if she'd had the kind of magic that I did.

I blew out a breath. "All right. I'll do it."

"Thank you, Gwen. This means more to the Pantheon than you know."

Metis drew an old-fashioned skeleton key out of her pocket and slid it into the lock on the door. It turned with an ear-splitting screech. For a moment it seemed like the sphinxes looked in her direction, narrowing their eyes and judging whether or not the professor had the right to be down here. Apparently, they were satisfied she did, because the professor yanked open the heavy door and stepped through to the other side. I hesitated a second, then followed her.

The prison was larger than I'd thought it would be, given the fact that we were so far underground. It was shaped like a dome, just like the Library of Antiquities was, although with a much lower ceiling. I glanced up, but no gold or jewels adorned the top of the dome. Instead, an enormous hand holding a set of balanced scales had been carved into the rock. I shivered. Somehow, that was creepier than if the faces of all the gods and goddesses in the Pantheon had been up there, glaring down at me.

The glassed-in cells were arranged in a circle, rising up three stories, and forming the walls of the prison. They were all empty, but a stone table stood in the center of the open space, directly below the carving of the hand and the scales.

That's where Preston sat, his hands shackled to the table and his legs anchored to the floor beneath it. Coach Ajax stood on one side of him, while Nickamedes hovered on the other. Preston's head hung down, and he stared at the floor.

And there was one more person in the prison: Mrs. Raven, the lady who manned the coffee cart in the library. She sat at a desk just inside the door, thumbing through a celebrity gossip magazine. I'd never paid much attention to her while I was working in the library, but now that I did, I realized that she was an old woman, even older than Grandma Frost. Everything about her was extreme and opposite. Her hair was completely white, although her eyes were as black as coal. Her skin was even paler than mine, yet wrinkles painted thick black streaks all over her face. Her fingers were long and slender, but old, faded scars marred her hands and arms. She wore a long, flowing, white gown made of a fine silk, and black combats boots adorned her feet. I noticed those in particular since she had them propped up on the desk and was leaning back in her chair. Weird. Even for Mythos.

"Why is Mrs. Raven here?" I whispered to Metis. "Shouldn't she be in the library handing out snacks or something?"

"She helps guard the prison whenever we have someone who needs to be watched," Metis whispered back. "She's part of the academy's security council, along with Nickamedes, Ajax, and myself. And it's just Raven—no Mrs."

I eyed Mrs., er, Raven and her bizarre figure. I supposed there was more to her than met the eye, just like the sphinxes on the door. Although I had no idea what that something more could possibly be.

Both Ajax and Nickamedes looked as grim as Metis did. Raven stared at me a few seconds, her eyes dark and curious, before going back to her magazine. Metis gestured for me to follow her. I swallowed and headed toward the center of the room.

Preston looked up at the whisper of our footsteps on the stone floor. His blue eyes narrowed at the sight of me.

"Why, Gypsy, so nice of you to come visit me. I would stand but . . ." He lifted his hands and rattled the chains at me.

I flinched at the harsh, ringing sound of the metal clanking together.

"There's no way he can break those chains," Ajax said in his deep, gruff voice. "They're magically reinforced. There's no way he can hurt you, Gwen. We've made sure of that."

I wanted to tell him that Preston had already hurt me, that his threat against my Grandma Frost haunted my dreams, but I kept my mouth shut. Now was definitely not the time to confess how wimpy I really was.

I crept closer, staring at Preston. White blond hair, blue eyes, great body. He looked just as handsome as he had the ski resort, despite the orange jumpsuit and paper shoes he wore. But the faintest flicker of red burned deep in his gaze. I wondered if the professors could see it, too. I didn't know how I'd missed it before.

An empty chair stood on the other side of the table from Preston, and Metis pulled it out for me. I undid the strap of my gray messenger bag from around my shoulder and set it on the floor. Then I sank down into the chair, trying to keep my hands from visibly shaking. The stone chair felt as cold as ice against my back.

"Take your time, Gwen," Metis said in a kind voice. "There's no rush. Whenever you're ready."

Preston's lips thinned out into an amused smile. "Ah, so they've brought you in to try to break me. Oh, Gypsy, trust me when I tell you that you won't like what you'll see if you use your psychometry on me."

I blinked. How did Preston know about my magic? I'd never told him about my Gypsy gift, but he was talking as if he knew all about it. *Oh, we know all about you, Gwen Frost, and what you're supposed to do.* Preston had said those words to me in the gloom of the construction site. I hadn't thought much about them then, but now they filled me with worry. What did the Reapers know about my magic that I didn't? What could I possibly do with it that would interest them?

Preston kept staring at me, expecting me to say something.

"I don't like breathing the same air as you," I finally snapped back. "But I make do."

I stared at his hands resting on top of the table. They were just hands, I told myself. Hands that belonged to an evil, psycho-killer Reaper, but just hands nonetheless. Five fingers on either one. I could do this. I could handle this.

I drew in a breath and let it out. Then I reached over and grabbed his hand, wanting to get this over with as quickly as possible. Wanting to get Metis the information she needed so I could leave this awful place and never see Preston again.

The feelings and images flooded my mind the second my skin touched the Reaper's. Even though I didn't want to, I gritted my teeth, closed my eyes, and let the memories carry me away.

Maybe it was all my years of tracking down lost objects, of touching desks, purses, and wallets and trying to get specific vibes off them, so I could locate the phones, jewelry, and laptops that people had misplaced or others had stolen. But going into Preston's mind was

easier than I'd thought it would be. I could feel him trying to block me, trying to think of nothing at all, just a
blank wall of white, but I went deeper, slipping past the
emptiness he tried to fill his mind with.

I saw so many things—so many horrible, horrible
things. Preston fighting, Preston killing other people,
other kids, even whipping the Fenrir wolf until its back
was red with blood. And Preston wasn't alone while he
did these things. Jasmine was right there with him most
of the time. Laughing, smiling, and killing alongside her
brother. I could feel how much Preston had loved her,
how happy he had been that she was just as vicious as
he was, just as devoted to Loki. They were like two
sides of the same evil coin, mirroring each other in almost every way. And I felt his burning pain, his deep anguish, when he learned that his little sister was dead. It
would have made me feel sorry for him if I hadn't seen
all the other evil things that he'd done, all the people
he'd tortured and killed.

Each and every thing I saw turned my stomach, but I
kept looking, searching for something I could tell Metis,
something that would help her and the others stop
whatever the Reapers of Chaos were planning.

Through it all, I was aware of a pair of burning red
eyes following me. The eyes jumped from memory to
memory just like I did, watching me all the while. I
knew who they belonged to now: Loki. His Reapers
were the evil god's window to the mortal realm, a way
he could see out of his magical prison, and I could almost feel him glaring at me from inside Preston's brain.
I told myself over and over again that the eyes couldn't

hurt me, that Loki was locked away where he couldn't touch me, but the thought didn't comfort me as much as it should have.

I was about to give up, let go of Preston's hand, open my eyes, and tell Metis that I wasn't getting anything useful from him, when an image of Preston pulling on a pair of gloves popped into my head. It was the same memory I'd gotten when I'd touched his gloved hand outside the Solstice coffee shop that night in the alpine village. It seemed strange, given all the other more violent and disturbing things that I'd witnessed so far. Curious, I concentrated on that memory, digging it out of the depths of his brain like a miner prospecting for gold, shining it up, and pulling it into sharper focus. Suddenly I was completely in the memory, seeing everything from Preston's point of view.

He sat in the driver's seat of an SUV, pulling on the gloves. Once that was done, he looked in the rearview mirror at the person sitting in the back of the vehicle. Shadows cloaked the inside of the car, so I couldn't tell who was there, although I got the impression it was a girl about my age. Whoever she was, Preston knew her—and was afraid of her. A tingle of fear tickled his spine just from looking at her. Weird. What kind of person would frighten a Reaper like Preston?

"Are you sure she's still in the police station?" the girl asked in a low, soft voice.

"I called and asked for her five minutes ago," Preston said. "She's still in there. See? There she is, coming out right now."

Preston turned his head, and I saw who he was talking about. Brown hair, violet eyes, beautiful smile. My mom stepped out of the back door of the police station.

Oh no, I thought, somehow knowing what was coming next. *No, no, no.*

My mom strode across the parking lot and got into her car, just like she had in the dream I'd had of her at the ski resort. I'd wondered where the awful memory had come from, and now I knew. It had been an image, a feeling, associated with Preston's glove, one that my psychometry and my subconscious had picked up on, even if I hadn't immediately seen it when I'd touched his glove.

"I thought you said the daughter would be with her," Preston asked. "We could kill them both tonight and be done with this whole thing."

The girl shrugged. "So the daughter's not here. So what? We have our orders. We disable the mom and question her about the dagger and where she hid it. That's what's important tonight. Now let's go."

Dagger? What dagger? What were they talking about? Why would my mom have a dagger, much less hide it?

I lost my focus, and the memory blurred and shifted before I was able to latch onto it again. Now the SUV idled at a dark intersection, its lights off. Preston's head was turned, looking out the window.

"Here she comes. Get ready," the girl ordered from the backseat. "Now . . . go!"

Preston smashed his foot down on the gas, and the SUV hurtled out of the dark toward my mom's car. She never even saw it coming. The sound of metal screeching and glass breaking roared in my ears, as though I'd really been there when Preston had rammed his vehicle into hers.

I drew in a ragged breath, and the memory blurred again. Now my mom was out of the car and lying on her back on the blacktop. A light rain had started to fall, but it couldn't hide the fact that blood covered her whole body—her legs, her chest, her face. The ends of her broken bones poked against the skin of her arms, and her breath came in shallow rasps. Dying—my mom was dying.

The girl stood in front of Preston, a sword glinting in her hand as she towered over my mom. She was wearing a hoodie, just like I did all the time. Except the girl's hood was up to protect her from the rain, so I couldn't even see the back of her head, much less her face.

"Where's the dagger?" the girl snarled. "Where did you hide it?"

My mom smiled at the Reaper girl. "Someplace you'll never think to look."

"Fool. There's no place you can hide it that we won't find it. It's only a matter of time."

"I'm not a fool," my mom said, raising her head. Despite her injuries, pride blazed in her violet eyes. "I was a Champion in my time, and I've served my goddess well. There is comfort in that, even now, at the end."

Nike. My mom was talking about Nike. She must have hidden the mystery dagger—or whatever it was—on the goddess's orders. But why? And why did the Reapers want to get their hands on it so badly?

"So am I," the girl snapped. "I'm Loki's Champion,

and he's decided it's time for you to die. Tell me where the dagger is, and I'll make it quick. Otherwise . . ."

She swung her sword in a menacing arc, and raindrops hissed against the blade.

"I'm dying anyway," my mom said, coughing up a mouthful of blood. "So do your worst, Reaper. Because in a few minutes, I'll be beyond your reach."

"But your precious daughter won't be, and you won't be able to protect her from me," the girl said. "What's her name again?"

"Gwen," my mom whispered. "My lovely, lovely Gwen. There was so much I wanted to tell you, so much I wanted to teach you. . . ."

Her voice trailed off, and tears streamed down her face, mixing with the cold, cold rain. My mom started mumbling then, about all the things she'd wished she'd said to me. I was so shocked by what I was seeing that I couldn't quite focus on what she was saying. Her voice grew raspier, and her words more incoherent, until the only thing she muttered was "Gwen, Gwen, I love you, Gwen. . . ."

"She's not going to talk," Preston said. "Finish her, and let's go before another car comes along."

"Oh, very well," the girl huffed.

She gripped her sword and raised it over her head. She turned toward Preston, and I saw a smile curve her lips despite the shadows that cloaked her face. Then she brought the weapon down with a vicious slash. I shoved the memory away the second before the sword plunged into my mom's heart.

My mom hadn't been killed by some anonymous drunk driver like I'd thought. No, she'd been *murdered*— murdered by Preston and the Reaper girl.

I opened my eyes, wrenched my hand away from his, and sprang up out of my chair, stumbling away until my back was pressed up against one of the glass walls of the cells. I was only about a foot away from Raven and her desk.

"I told you that you wouldn't like what you saw, Gypsy," Preston sneered. "Tell me, how did it feel to see your own mother murdered right before your very eyes?"

Everyone froze for a second, then they all turned to look at me. Metis shocked, Coach Ajax angry and disgusted, Nickamedes with a pitying expression on his face. Even Raven looked up from her gossip magazine, a haunted look in her eyes.

"Just wait," Preston sneered. "Because I'll be doing the same thing to you real soon, Gypsy."

I opened my mouth, but no words came out. I couldn't speak, I couldn't scream, I couldn't even breathe. Everything just *hurt*. Every cell, every nerve, every broken, bloody bit of my shattered heart.

Desperate, I turned to Metis, searching for some kind of comfort, some kind of reassurance. Instead, what I saw was guilt. Sometimes if a memory was vivid enough, if an emotion was strong enough, I didn't have to touch an object or person to get a vibe off them. Guilt filled the professor's green eyes, and her whole body radiated with it, like heat boiling off the sun, burning me to the bone.

"You knew my mom was murdered," I whispered. "This whole time, you *knew*."

"Gwen—" Metis started, stepping toward me.

I turned and ran from the prison, but I didn't even make it to the door before Preston's mocking laughter started ringing in my ears.

Chapter 26

I sprinted out of the prison and back up the many flights of stairs. Somehow all the doors opened at my touch, despite the fact that I didn't know the codes or the magic mumbo jumbo. Or maybe Metis just hadn't locked them behind her. Either way, I stumbled out of the math-science building and into the cold. And then I just *ran,* desperate to get as far away from Preston and the awful thing I'd seen, the awful thing he'd helped the Reaper girl to do my mom.

They'd followed her home from work that night. They'd caused the car accident. They'd murdered her. They'd taken her away from me. Not a drunk driver. The casket at her funeral had been closed because the Reaper girl had murdered her, and Grandma Frost hadn't wanted me to see my mom like that.

Grandma. She had to have known about my mom's murder, just like Metis. When I'd first come to the academy, I'd asked Grandma over and over again why I had to go to school at Mythos. I'd thought it had been because I'd had a freak-out with my magic. Now I knew the real reason why: Reapers had murdered my mom, and Metis and Grandma Frost had been afraid they'd do the same thing to me. So they'd shipped me off to Mythos, so Metis could keep an eye on me, thinking I'd be safe on campus, that the magic protecting the grounds would protect me as well. They just hadn't realized how dangerous the academy would turn out to be for me.

But as hard as I tried, as fast as my legs pumped, I couldn't outrun the memories—because they were mine now, too. I couldn't unsee them, and I couldn't forget them—ever. My psychometry wouldn't let me.

For the very first time, I thought of my Gypsy gift as a curse.

I don't remember exactly how, but I wound up in the Library of Antiquities. Students and staff crowded into the first floor of the library, clustered around the study tables and checkout counter. I kept to the back wall and raced past the bookshelves and glass cases full of artifacts. For once, I was glad the other kids never paid any attention to me. I didn't want anyone to see me like this, much less start gossiping and texting about it on their stupid cell phones.

I didn't stop running until I sprinted up the stairs and reached the second floor, where all the statues of the gods and goddesses were arranged in an enormous circle on the balcony. Nobody else was up here, and the silence pressed against my face like a blanket, smothering me. Or maybe that was because I was out of breath from my frantic run.

My footsteps finally slowed, then stopped, in front of Nike's statue. The Greek goddess of victory towered thirty feet tall, like all the other statues, her feathery wings just peeking out from behind her back, her proud gaze fixed on something only she could see.

"Why?" I whispered. "Why did they have to kill my mom?"

Nike's face remained cold and impassive. I didn't know why I'd come here, what I'd thought would happen, but the grief overwhelmed me, weighing me down until I couldn't take another step.

I curled up into a ball at the goddess's feet and wept.

I don't know how long I cried—the eerie, still silence of the second floor swallowed up my sobs—but at some point, my exhaustion overpowered everything else, and I fell asleep right there in the library. I woke up, stiff and sore from my awkward position, my eyes crusty with dried tears, and my heart just—just *sick* with what I'd seen in Preston's mind. His awful, awful memories of my mother's murder.

It took me two minutes to realize the statue was gone.

I'd collapsed in a heap at Nike's feet, but now only empty air filled the space where the goddess's statue had been. I jumped to my feet and looked around, but all the other statues were still in their places along the second floor balcony, all turned the same way, staring down into the first floor of the Library of Antiquities. Only Nike was missing. I took a few steps back from the spot where she'd been—

"Hello, Gwendolyn," a soft voice called out to me.

Somehow I managed not to scream. Instead, I slowly turned around, and there she was—Nike. She looked the same as she had the last time I'd seen her, the night Jasmine had tried to murder me in the library.

Nike might have been the Greek goddess of victory, but she was also the most beautiful woman I'd ever seen. Her hair slipped past her shoulders, the soft brown waves shimmering with a metallic, bronze sheen. An elegant gown in a soft lilac color rippled around her body like water, while a thin silver belt looped around her waist. The belt matched the crown of silver flowers that ringed her head—laurels, the symbol for victory. Soft, feathery wings arched up from the goddess's back, making her look as if she could take flight at any moment.

Nike was pretty enough, but the thing that made her striking to me was the sheer power that radiated off her—cold, beautiful, and terrible all at the same time.

"Okay," I said. "We're doing that weird dream world thing again, aren't we? Where we're in the library but not really there at all? That's why there aren't any students studying on the first floor right now?"

It was the same thing that had happened the last time I'd spoken to the goddess. One minute I'd been in the library, fighting Jasmine. The next I'd still been in the library, but everyone and everything else had disappeared except for me, the goddess, and Vic.

Nike laughed and stepped closer to me. "Something like that."

The goddess's eyes met mine, and I felt I could stare

into her gaze forever. Her eyes were a curious shade, not quite purple, but not quite gray either, just like Vic's eye was. Her gaze made me think of the soft color of twilight, that instant of time just before darkness came and covered the land in blackness for the night.

Maybe I should have been more humbled, maybe I should have been more respectful, but now that the goddess was here in front of me, I couldn't help asking the questions that burned in my heart.

"Why did the Reapers kill my mom? What did they want? What are they up to? How can I stop them? What am I supposed to *do* now?"

Nike's face was kind, but sadness tugged down her mouth. "Walk with me, Gwendolyn."

I fell in step beside the goddess, and we started strolling around the balcony, passing the other statues of the gods and goddesses from all the various cultures of the world. Maybe it was my Gypsy gift or maybe it was only my imagination, but it seemed that all the stone figures stared at me, their heads swiveling around one by one to watch us circle the balcony. I shivered and wrapped my arms around myself, dropping my gaze from the statues. I didn't know what I'd see if I kept looking at them. Part of me didn't want to know.

Finally, Nike spoke. "Long ago, after Loki was defeated in the final battle of the Chaos War, the other gods and I combined our powers and locked Loki away from the mortal realm, trapping him in another realm, another dimension. In a sort of prison, if you will."

"Kind of like this library is a mirror image of the real one that I'm sleeping in right now . . . or whatever?"

She nodded. "The gods placed seven seals on Loki's prison, using various artifacts and other magical safeguards to keep him contained."

The goddess stopped and looked at me. "Six of those seals have been broken. And when the last one, the seventh seal breaks, Loki will be free once more."

The seals are all but broken, and it won't be much longer before we find the key to unlock the last one. Soon, Loki will be free, and his Chaos will reign once more. And when that happens, you will rue the day you were ever born, Gypsy. You and Nike and all the other members of the pathetic Pantheon.

Preston's words echoed in my head. Back at the ski resort, I'd wondered if the Reaper knew what he was talking about or if he was just crazy. I really, really wished he had just been crazy.

I drew in a ragged breath. "But—but how is that even possible? You're so *strong.* I can feel the power rolling off you in waves. Surely, you and the other gods together have enough magic to fix the seals."

Nike shook her head. "It took all the magic we had to create the artifacts and seals in the first place and trap Loki with them. Centuries have passed, and some of the gods still haven't recovered from the ordeal."

"But how did the seals even get broken in the first place?" I asked.

"By Loki's followers," Nike said. "They found the artifacts and other items we used, took them from the Champions who were guarding them, and destroyed them. They also weakened and eventually broke through some of the other safeguards with their blood sacrifices.

Blood has great power you see, especially a Champion's blood, since she has been blessed by her god or goddess. Every time a Reaper kills and dedicates that spilled blood to Loki, the god of chaos becomes a little stronger and gets a little closer to breaking free of his prison."

Daphne and Grandma Frost had both told me that being a Champion was dangerous, that it was as good as having a target on your back, and that Reapers would do anything to kill Champions. Know I knew why. Because my blood had power—more power than I'd ever dreamed of. More power than I'd ever wanted. I shivered.

Nike walked on, passing a statue of Athena, the Greek goddess of wisdom. I thought about Metis then, about how the professor was Athena's Champion. I wondered if Metis knew about the broken seals—and the fact that Loki was *thisfreakingclose* to being free again.

"So what can I do?" I asked. "Is there any way to keep the last seal from being broken?"

"The last seal, the strongest seal, was an artifact that was entrusted to my Champion," Nike said, not quite answering my question. "Over the years, it has been passed down from one of my Champions to the other, from your first ancestor all the way down to your mother, Grace Frost."

Suddenly, the words Preston had said in his memories made perfect sense to me.

"A dagger," I whispered. "The artifact, the one that's the last seal on Loki's prison, is a dagger. That's why the

Reapers killed my mom—because she hid the dagger and wouldn't tell them where it was, and they need it to free Loki."

Nike nodded. "Correct. It's called the Helheim Dagger, because it has the power to open a portal to Helheim, the underground netherworld where the other gods and I trapped Loki."

"Do you know where the dagger is?" I asked. "Where my mom hid it?"

Nike shook her head. "After the last battle of the Chaos War, all the gods made a pact not to become involved in mortal affairs. We would have torn the world apart otherwise until there was nothing left. That's why the seals and other safeguards were given to our Champions and other trusted warriors to hide and protect as best they could. The seals were designed to stay in the mortal world, so no god could touch or break them. But, of course, the Reapers have been relentlessly searching for them ever since Loki was imprisoned. One by one, they've found the artifacts, and now, only the dagger is left."

"And nobody knows where the Helheim Dagger is but my mom, and she can't tell anyone because she's dead." Bitterness filled my empty, aching heart.

"I'm truly sorry, Gwendolyn," Nike said in a sad voice. "But Champions are often called upon to make sacrifices. Your mother gave her life to keep Loki imprisoned, and she saved countless other lives doing that. Every day Loki remains trapped is another day the world isn't on the brink of war. Your mother died protecting others, which is the bravest, noblest thing a Champion can do."

I understood what my mom had done and why, but that didn't make it any easier to bear. It didn't make my heart hurt any less.

"What am I supposed to do now?" I whispered, feeling like I was coming apart from the inside out.

"These things never stay hidden forever," Nike said, once again not quite answering my question. "There's too much power attached to the dagger, and there are too many Reapers looking for it. One of them will eventually find the dagger and use it to free Loki."

I looked at the goddess. "You want me to find the dagger first, don't you? And what, hide it somewhere else? What good will that do? Won't the Reapers just keep looking for it?"

Nike nodded again. "They will. Even now, they are using their blood sacrifices to try to break through the cloaking spell your mother put on the dagger to hide it. Once the spell is gone, they'll be able to divine its general location and start searching for it. You need to find the dagger, hide it somewhere else, and put a new, stronger cloaking spell on it. Your Professor Metis should be able to help you with that, along with the Spartan librarian, Nickamedes."

Well, that made sense. If there was anyone here at Mythos who could help keep the dagger out of the Reapers' hands, it was Metis. But Nickamedes? Really? And he was a Spartan? My brain rattled around inside my skull a little at that revelation. But then, I thought about seeing Logan and Nickamedes together at the ski resort. If they were related like I suspected, it made sense that Nickamedes was a Spartan, just like Logan was.

"Your mother hid the dagger well, and every day the Reapers don't find it is a small victory for the members of the Pantheon—and the world," Nike continued. "But time is running out, and the cloaking spell won't hold much longer. The Pantheon needs more time to prepare for what's coming."

"And what would that be?"

The goddess stared at me with her twilight eyes. She didn't say anything, but somehow, I knew the answer to my question. Chaos. War. Death. Destruction. Loki breaking free of his prison and trying to take over the world again. Bad, Bad Things all around.

"But how am I supposed to find the dagger?" I asked. "My mom was smart—the smartest person I knew. If the Reapers haven't been able to find the dagger where she hid it, what makes you think I can?"

Nike smiled. "Because you're my Champion, Gwendolyn, and I have faith in you, just as I did in your mother before you."

As much as I appreciated the goddess's confidence, it wasn't exactly the most helpful thing in the world right now. "But can't you help me at all? Give me a clue or something? Someplace to start at least? What am I supposed to *do* now?"

It was the same question I'd asked her a minute ago, and for the third time, she didn't exactly answer me.

"I can't tell you that. All I can do is appear to you now and then to advise you, Gwendolyn. Nothing more. That is the agreement the gods made with respect to our Champions. The battle is between you and the Reapers. The rest is up to you. The choices are yours to make. Neither I nor any of the other gods can *ever* make you do anything you don't want to," Nike said. "Every creature, mortal and god alike, has free will. It's what we choose to do with that will that defines us, that makes us who we are, good or bad. Remember that."

It was the same speech Metis had given a few weeks ago in myth-history class, but it didn't make me feel any better now than it had then. Yeah, free will was great and all, but I didn't see how it would help me defeat a Reaper—or Loki, if the evil god ever got free.

By this point, we'd circled all the way around the balcony. The goddess stepped back up onto the pedestal where her statue stood in the library's pantheon.

"You have served me well so far, Gwendolyn Frost," Nike said. "You have used your wits and your magic wisely. I hope you continue to do so—for all our sakes."

The goddess leaned down and kissed me on the cheek. For a moment her power washed over me—that cold, beautiful, terrible power that made her who and what she was. My own blood turned to ice, just like it had the last time she'd kissed me here in the library, and I felt something shift inside myself. Something settling into a new place, bringing new strength, courage, and determination along with it. The feeling didn't frighten me like it had before. Not anymore.

The goddess stepped back. She gave me a final, soft

smile before her body started shimmering and melting like early morning twilight being banished by the breaking dawn.

I blinked, and Nike was gone, replaced by her white marble statue once more.

Chapter 27

"Gwen?" a soft voice called out to me. "Gwen, wake up."

A hand gently shook my shoulder, snapping me out of—of wherever I'd been. I opened my eyes to find Logan crouching in front of me, his ice blue gaze full of concern.

"Hey, are you okay?" he asked. "Nickamedes told me what happened with Preston. He and the others were worried about you. They're out looking for you, along with Daphne, Carson, and Oliver."

I let out a bitter laugh. "I must have really freaked them out if Nickamedes was worried about me."

I leaned my head back against the base of Nike's statue. Logan looked at me a second, then sat down on the cold floor beside me.

"You want to tell me what happened? What you saw?" he asked in a quiet voice.

I needed to talk to someone about what I'd seen when I'd touched Preston, when I'd looked into his horrible memories. I couldn't think of anyone better than Logan. After all, I'd seen the Spartan's memories, too, when I'd kissed him—I knew he'd understand.

"Yeah, I'd like to talk about it," I said. "But to really understand it, first I have to tell you some other things about me. Things you don't know."

"Like what?"

I drew in a breath. "Like the fact that I'm Nike's Champion."

I sat there and told Logan everything, starting from the first time I saw Nike that night in the library when we'd both been fighting Jasmine and her Nemean prowler. The Spartan didn't say a word while I talked. He just sat there and let me get it all out, let me get all my fears, feelings, and hurts out there in the open. And I told him *everything*—about seeing my mom's murder through Preston's eyes, that Metis and my Grandma Frost had known about it the whole time, that they'd kept the truth from me, what Nike had told me about the broken seals on Loki's prison, how my mom had hidden the Helheim Dagger, and that Nike had asked me to find and protect the dagger from the Reapers who were looking for it.

After I was done, Logan sat there for a minute, thinking. Then he grinned at me. "You really have a talking sword?"

I rolled my eyes. "Trust you to be a total Spartan weapons geek and focus on Vic."

I leaned over and lightly punched him in the shoulder. But we both laughed, and I felt just a smidge better.

"I'm sorry about your mom," Logan said in a quiet tone. "I know—I know what it's like to lose your family, to lose someone you care about so much."

The image of him as a boy standing over those two bloody bodies filled my mind, but I didn't say anything. Instead, I looked at Logan, wanting him to tell me what had happened that day, how he'd lost his mother and sister, and why he thought knowing about it would make me think less of him. Would make me think he wasn't the hero I knew him to be.

He didn't say a word.

Logan opened his mouth, like he was going to tell me, but then he shut it again and looked away, a haunted, guilty expression on his face. I stared down at his bare hand, which was just an inch away from mine. I knew if I touched him right now, if I reached over and took his hand in mine, my psychometry would kick in. And then I would see and feel what Logan was remembering right now—and I'd finally discover his secret. Why and how he'd lost his family—and the reason it was keeping us apart. The reason it made the Spartan doubt himself and who and what he was.

I cared about Logan so *much,* and the temptation to do it was so *strong.*

But then I remembered what both Professor Metis and Nike had said about free will, about how the choices we made defined who we were. I didn't want to use my magic to find out Logan's secret. I wanted him to trust me enough to tell me about it, just the way I trusted him. And if I had to wait a little while longer for him to do that, then that was okay. My feelings for him weren't going to change, my caring about him no matter what wasn't going to change.

"I'm glad you came looking for me," I finally said. "Here tonight and back at the ski resort."

Logan gave me a crooked grin. "I'll always come looking for you, Gypsy girl."

He hesitated, then reached over and put his arm around me. I leaned my head on his shoulder, and he tightened his other arm around me, careful not to touch my bare skin.

We stayed like that for a long, long time.

The next day after classes, I slipped off campus and went to visit Grandma Frost. We sat on opposite sides of the table in the kitchen, but for once, the bright furnishings failed to cheer me up, and the scrumptious raspberry pound cake that Grandma had just baked sat uncut and untouched between us. She knew why I was here. After Logan had found me in the library, I'd talked to Metis and told the professor exactly what I'd seen when I'd touched Preston's hand, all the talk about the Helheim Dagger and all the awful, awful memories that I'd witnessed of him and the Reaper girl murdering my mom. Metis had called my grandma and told her everything. Now I wanted answers—about a lot of things.

"I want to know what you know about Mom's death," I finally said, my throat closing up. "About her murder."

Grandma stared at me. Then she sighed. "Gwen—"

"You might as well tell me," I interrupted her. "It's kind of hard to keep secrets from a girl with psychometry magic, don't you think? Especially since Metis asked me to use that magic to dig through Preston's brain in the first place."

She winced, but she couldn't argue with me. Not about this.

"How did you find out what really happened to Mom? Or have you always known?"

Grandma fiddled with the silver coins on the edge of one of her purple scarves. "Your mom was late coming home that night. Much, much later than she said she was going to be. I started to have this feeling that something bad had happened to her, one of my psychic flashes—this cold, aching dread in my heart that just wouldn't go away. So I called Professor Metis and asked her to go out and look for Grace. Even though your mom and I had left the warrior world behind, we were still in contact with Aurora. I'd seen an image of a car in the rain, so I was able to tell Aurora where to start looking. She did as I asked, and eventually, she found your mom. . . ."

Her voice trailed off for a moment, tears shimmering in her eyes, and I remembered that Grandma had lost her only daughter and that she'd loved my mom just as much as I had. Suddenly, I realized how awful that night had been for her, too—especially since she'd seen part of it, thanks to her Gypsy gift.

Grandma drew in a breath. "Aurora came to the house, but I knew what she was going to say even before she told me: Grace had been murdered by Reapers. We thought it was just payback from the Reapers. We didn't know exactly why they'd targeted your mom until now."

"But Metis knew, too? That Mom had been murdered this whole time?"

She nodded. "We both thought it was best to keep the truth from you, pumpkin. Your mom . . . wouldn't have wanted you to see her like that. She wouldn't have wanted you to remember her like that. Never like that."

"But why keep lying to me? Especially after I started going to Mythos?" I asked.

"Because you didn't know anything about Reapers, Loki, and the Chaos War. Your mom and I shielded you from that world, and Aurora and I thought it would be better to ease you into things, rather than hit you with everything all at once. That's why I've let you keep visiting me, even though I worry about you leaving campus." Grandma Frost sighed. "But mostly I didn't want you to hate Mythos or who and what you are because of what happened to your mom."

I snorted. I'd hated *everything* after my mom had died, especially the fact that I'd had to leave my old school and my old friends behind and start going to Mythos.

"Where you ever going to tell me?" I asked. "You and Metis?"

Grandma shrugged. "We hadn't thought that far ahead. We were mainly focused on making sure that you were safe at the academy. But things haven't exactly worked out like we'd planned."

No, they hadn't. I'd been almost killed by Reapers

twice now, and I imagined that I'd be in even more danger when I started searching for the Helheim Dagger—and the Reaper girl. Loki's Champion. She was looking for the dagger too. I knew she was.

"What about the dagger?" I asked. "Did you know that Mom had hidden it? Do you know where it is?"

Grandma Frost shook her head. "No. I knew about the dagger's existence, but that's all. I had no idea that Nike had asked Grace to hide it, and I have no idea where your mom would have left it. I would tell you if I did, pumpkin. I swear I would."

Grandma reached over and placed her hand on top of mine. A surge of truth filled me at the touch of her fingers against mine, along with all the love she had for me. The gentle warmth wrapped around me like a blanket, as if it could protect me from all the bad, scary, evil things out there in the world. Now, though, I knew that not even Grandma's love could do that.

"I hope you can understand why we kept it from you," she said in a low voice, her violet eyes dark in her wrinkled face. "It's hard enough to lose someone you care about. Having your mom die in a car accident seemed like it would be kinder to you than the truth. Easier to bear."

The funny thing was that I did understand. Grandma Frost and Professor Metis had just been trying to protect me. But I was Nike's Champion now, and the goddess had given me an important mission. They couldn't protect me anymore, even if I'd wanted them to. And yeah, part of me really wanted them to. Part of me wanted to go back to the beginning of the year, when my mom had still been alive, and just stay there forever. Part of me would always want that, but it wasn't meant to be—and that was the hardest thing of all to accept.

"I understand why you did it," I said in a quiet voice. "But you can't keep lying and not tell me things because they might hurt me. The Reapers are going to come for me no matter what you do. Keeping secrets from me is only going to make it that much harder for me to fight them."

"I know, pumpkin," Grandma said. "I just wanted you to feel safe for as long as I could. No more secrets, I promise."

Once again, I felt the truthfulness of her words move through me, and I knew we were going to be okay. We would get through everything that was to come just like we had my mom's death—together. As a family.

Despite the pain I felt over learning what had really happened to my mom, I squeezed Grandma's hand and smiled at her. "You know, that cake you made looks awfully good."

Grandma grinned back at me. "Well, let's dish us up some pieces and see just how tasty it really is. What do you say?"

This time, my smile was a little brighter. "Sounds like a plan to me."

I ate a piece of cake with Grandma, who wrapped up the rest of the treat for me to share with Daphne, and rode the afternoon bus back to the academy. Half an hour later, I found myself back in the creepy prison in the math-science building. I stood there staring at the stone-and-iron door, trying to stay cold and calm.

"Are you sure that you want to do this, Gwen?" Professor Metis asked, putting her hand on my shoulder. "You don't have to. After what you saw yesterday, I wouldn't blame you. Neither will Ajax or Nickamedes."

She'd tried to hide it, but I'd seen how worried the professor was about the possibility of the Reapers finding the Helheim Dagger and freeing Loki—and I knew what I had to do. If there was even a chance that Preston knew something that would help me find where my mom had hidden the dagger, then I had to take it. That meant I had to touch him again, had to dig into his memories once more—no matter how many ugly things I might see.

"I'm sure," I said. "I want to do this. I feel like I'm *supposed* to do this. Besides, self-sacrifice is what being a Champion is all about, right?"

Metis gave me a sad smile. In that moment, I got the feeling she knew a lot more about self-sacrifice than I did.

"Before we go in, there's one thing that I need you to do," I said. "Don't keep any more secrets from me, okay?"

The professor raised her eyebrows. "That works both ways, Gwen. Don't go chasing off after any more Reapers by yourself. Agreed?"

I sighed and nodded at her. "Agreed."

I jerked my head at the door and the two sphinxes who were staring at me once more, listening to every word we said. "Now, can we get this over with before I lose my nerve?"

Metis unlocked the door with her skeleton key, and we stepped inside the prison. Preston sat chained to the table in the center of the dome, right under the carving of the hand holding the set of scales. Coach Ajax and Nickamedes flanked him just as before, and Raven sat at her desk, her combat boots propped up on top of it, flipping through another gossip magazine.

Once again, the Reaper looked up at the sound of my footsteps on the floor.

"Back for more, Gypsy?" Preston sneered and held out his hands to me, palms up. "Go ahead. Use your magic on me. I'll be happy to watch you run crying from the room again."

I kept my face cold and impassive, although my stomach twisted and vomit rose in my throat at his mocking words. I could do this. I *would* do this—for Nike, for my mom, and for me, too.

I sat down across from Preston and stared him straight in the eyes. That burn of red still flickered in his gaze, but this time, I knew there was fire in my eyes as well—cold, purple fire.

"Listen up, you arrogant punk," I snapped. "The only one who's going to be crying is you, when I dig through your memories and use them to round up all your little Reaper friends, including the girl who killed my mom. I'll be coming down here and doing that again and again, every single day if I have to, until I get every last one of them. Until I've seen every last evil thing you've ever done in your miserable life."

The sneer slid off Preston's handsome face. His mouth tightened with worry, and for a moment, panic sparked in his gaze instead of hatred. Yeah, I'll admit that flash of fear made me happy. In my own way, I supposed I was just as dark and twisted as Preston was, except I was going to use that part of me to help other people, not hurt them like he and the other Reapers had.

"And you know what the worst part is, Preston? The very worst part?"

"What?" he asked, his voice cracking on that single word.

I leaned forward, keeping my gaze on his. "There's absolutely nothing you can do to stop me."

I don't know what Preston saw in my face then, what coldness might have filled my eyes, but whatever it was, it penetrated the Reaper's sullen demeanor. His mouth dropped open, and then, he started screaming.

"No," he said, trying to twist away from me. "No, no, no!"

I ignored his screams, grabbed his hands, and reached for his memories.

Chapter 28

"Are you sure you're going to be okay over the holidays?" Daphne asked.

It was the last day of the fall semester. Classes had ended a couple of hours ago, and now, I was in Daphne's room, lounging on her bed and watching her pack up her stuff to go home for the winter break. I didn't really know why my best friend was bothering to sort through her closet, since three-quarters of the stuff inside was pink, just like the rest of her room. She could just close her eyes, grab some sweaters and pants, and they would all match. But, of course, the Valkyrie wouldn't agree with me on that point.

"I'll be fine," I said for the tenth time in as many minutes.

"Are you sure?" she persisted. "You're not going to snap and go all Reaper, are you? Now that you're plowing through Preston's memories?"

I'd been going to the prison for a few days now, using my Gypsy gift to find out everything Preston knew about the Reapers, what they were up to, and where they were hiding. It hadn't been fun. Most of Preston's memories involved hurting other people—killing them and sacrificing them to Loki.

But try as I might, I hadn't been able to discover the most important secret of all: who Loki's Champion was. The Reaper who'd been in the back of the SUV with Preston the night they'd plowed into my mom's car, the one even he was afraid of. The girl who'd killed my mom. It seemed like they'd always met at night the few times that they'd been face-to-face, and in all of Preston's memories, she was always in the shadows with her face hidden. He didn't seem to know who she really was. The fact that I couldn't figure out her real identity was beyond frustrating. It was driving me crazy.

Professor Metis, Coach Ajax, and Nickamedes knew about the Reaper girl and what she'd done to my mom, but I hadn't exactly told them that I was peering into every corner of Preston's brain, trying to find out who she really was. I knew what they'd say—that tracking down Loki's Champion just so I could kill her the same way she'd murdered my mom was wrong and would make me no better than she was. Whatever. The Reaper girl had killed my mom, and she was going to pay for that. There was nothing else to talk about as far as I was concerned.

Daphne and Vic certainly agreed with me on this point. In fact, Vic had spent an hour enthusiastically describing all the various ways he could be used to torture the Reaper girl. I didn't know about all *that,* but I'd be just fine with her dying—and me being the cause of it.

Still, despite the fact that I hadn't discovered the Reaper girl's identity yet, I felt like I was doing something good with my magic, that I was making a difference. Metis told me that members of the Pantheon had used some of the information I'd gotten from Preston to capture several Reapers, and were hot on the trail of even more. So I thought Nike would have approved of what I was doing—and my mom, too.

"I'll be fine," I said. "I won't be seeing Preston again until after the break. I'm going to go to Grandma Frost's house and just chill out over the holidays. Eat junk food, watch television, read my new stash of comic books. There will be absolutely no thinking about Preston, his horrible memories, Reapers, or anything else like that."

"All right," Daphne said, finally satisfied. "But you call me every day."

I rolled my eyes. "Well, yeah. I want to know all about your Christmas—and what your parents think of Carson."

Daphne and Carson were taking the major, major step of introducing each other to their parents. Daphne was going home with Carson for a few days before Christmas, then he was coming over to her house after New Year's. After that, Daphne was going to come spend a few days with me and Grandma Frost before classes started again at the academy.

The Valkyrie bit her lip, and pink sparks of magic flashed around her fingertips. "I hope his parents like me."

"I'm sure they will," I said. "What's not to like?"

Daphne narrowed her eyes, plucked one of her pillows off the bed, and threw it at me. "Your sarcasm is noted."

I grinned. "And you love me for it."

I helped Daphne carry her ridiculously stuffed, ridiculously heavy suitcases out of her room, down the steps, and outside Valhalla Hall. Kids streamed out of all of the dorms at this point, bags in one hand and cell phones in the other. Golf carts zipped over the cobblestone paths, hauling students up the hill, past the main quad, and over to the parking lot behind the gym, where a variety of private towncars waited to drive them home or to the airport.

Carson waited out front, along with Oliver and Logan. While Logan helped Carson and Daphne load her bags onto one of the golf carts, I drifted over to Oliver's side.

"I hope you have a good holiday," I said. "Going home to see your parents?"

The Spartan nodded. "Yep. You going to your grandma's?"

I nodded.

Oliver grinned. "Try not to fall for any Reaper guys while you're away, okay?"

I rolled my eyes. "Just as long as you don't try to run down or shoot arrows at any Gypsy girls. Do we have a deal?"

"I don't know," Oliver murmured. "I kind of like

scaring Gypsy girls. It's a lot more fun than myth-history class."

I punched the Spartan in the shoulder, and he just laughed.

"What about Kenzie?" I asked in a low voice only he could hear. "You going to see him over the break?"

Oliver shook his head. "He wanted to hang out, but I told him that I'd be too busy with family stuff. I think it's better if I don't see him for a while. Give me a chance to get over him, you know?"

I nodded again. I did know. "Maybe you'll meet somebody new over the holidays."

Oliver smiled, but his green eyes were dark and sad. "Here's hoping anyway."

Carson and Logan finished loading Daphne's luggage. The Valkyrie came over and hugged me tight, cracking my back with her enormous strength, then hopped into the back of the cart with Carson. Oliver jumped into the driver's seat, and the three of them waved good-bye before Oliver hit the gas and the cart took off toward upper quad.

That left Logan and me alone, standing outside Valhalla Hall. Students moved all around us, talking, texting, and laughing, but everyone was so focused on going home that no one paid any attention to us.

I wasn't quite sure what to say to the Spartan. We hadn't really talked since he'd found me a few days ago in the library, and we still hadn't discussed *the kiss*. I didn't know what was going on between us, but I knew I'd miss him like crazy over the next few weeks.

"So . . . I should probably get going," I said. "I need to go grab my stuff out of my room and catch the afternoon bus down the mountain."

Logan nodded. "Me, too. My uncle has a car waiting up at the gym to take us home."

"Nickamedes, right? He's your uncle?"

The Spartan blinked. "How did you . . . ?"

"I saw the two of you at the ski resort, remember? And I realized just how much you look alike." I shrugged. "And the way you talked to him, it was like the two of you knew each other very, very well. Like you were family. It wasn't too hard to figure out. Why didn't you ever say anything to me?"

This time, Logan shrugged. "It's . . . complicated. Nickamedes and my dad don't exactly get along."

He didn't explain any more, but after a moment, he grinned. "Besides, you've met Nickamedes. Would you claim him as a relative? Especially if he worked at your school?"

I thought about the prissy librarian and how his mouth always turned down whenever he saw me. "Point taken."

"Anyway, before I go meet him, I wanted to give you this."

Logan reached into his black leather jacket and drew out a small box wrapped in silver paper. A faint flush crept up his neck, and he wouldn't look at me. "I, uh, got you something. For Christmas. I hope that's okay."

"Oh. *Oh.* You—you didn't have to do that." My heart soared in my chest for about half a second before I winced. "I didn't get anything for you. I'm so sorry. If

I'd known—I mean, if I even thought for a *second* you were going to get me something—"

"Just open it, okay?" the Spartan said, interrupting me.

Logan held out the small box. I hesitated, then took it, careful not to brush my fingers against his. I held it in my palm a second, but I didn't get any real vibes off the silver wrapping paper, so I tore it off with my nails. Beneath the paper was a marble box that was a lovely shade of lilac. Once again, I held on to the box a moment, but the only flash I got off it was of Logan wrapping the paper around it. So I cracked the lid open, and my breath caught in my throat.

A gorgeous silver necklace was nestled on top of the black velvet inside the box. It looked like something a goddess would wear—all these delicate silver wires strung together. But the coolest part was that the six strands joined together, their jewel-tipped points forming a specific shape—a snowflake. The diamonds that made up the six rays of the delicate snowflake glinted in the winter sun.

After I got over my initial shock and the dazzle of the diamonds, I let out a little laugh.

Logan frowned. "What's so funny? Don't you—don't you like it?"

"Oh, no! It's beautiful. I love it, really, I do. It's just funny. My grandma and I always get each other something with snowflakes on it for Christmas. It's just part of having Frost as a last name, I suppose. I bought her a cookie jar shaped like a giant blue snowflake when Daphne and I went shopping the other day. And now, you give me this." I drew in a breath. "But it's too much. I can't accept this—"

"Yes, you can," Logan said, cutting me off again. "Think of it as an apology for me being such a dick with Savannah and everything."

His eyes locked with mine. "I've been meaning to tell you for a while now, but Savannah and I broke up while we were at the ski resort—the night after I talked to you outside the coffee shop."

He didn't have to tell me because I already knew. The news had spread around the academy the Monday morning after the Winter Carnival that Logan had broken up with Savannah. It had gone viral in about ten seconds, getting texted from one person's phone to the other. That's why Savannah hadn't been with Logan during the Saturday carnival on the mountain. I'd seen her close to him in the lobby after the avalanche, but Daphne had found out that Savannah had just been getting hot chocolate for her and Talia—not hanging out with Logan.

Nobody seemed to know the exact reason why they'd broken up, although Savannah shot daggers at me with her eyes every time she saw me. So did Talia. Even though Logan and I weren't exactly together, it was obvious Savannah thought I had something to do with their breakup and had spread the word around to her friends. Maybe I had. The thought made me happy and guilty at the same time. I wanted Logan, but I hadn't wanted him to hurt Savannah either.

But the Spartan was here, now, standing right in front of me, and I wasn't about to miss this opportunity.

I swallowed the lump in my throat. "You know how much I . . . care about you. You breaking up with Savannah . . . What does that mean . . . for us?" I couldn't keep the faint whisper of hope out of my voice.

Logan stared at me, his blue eyes dark and serious, and I knew he was thinking about his secret again, and whether he could trust me with it or not. What I would think about it. But then the moment passed, and he grinned once more. "It means I'll be seeing you after Christmas break, Gypsy girl. Try not to get into too much trouble in the meantime, okay?"

Then he leaned over and kissed me. It was just a brief touch, just a quick caress of his lips on mine, but I still felt the firmness of his mouth, still felt the warmth of his body against my own, still felt his breath mixing with mine, both of them mingling in the clouds of frost between us.

Logan drew back. He winked at me, then turned and walked away.

All I could do was smile and watch him go, wishing the holiday break was over with already.

Since all my friends had left, I went back to my own dorm room in Styx Hall to get my stuff and head down the mountain to Grandma Frost's house. The first thing I did when I got back to the room was stand in front of the mirror on the wall and put on the necklace Logan had just given me.

I hooked the chain together and stroked the diamond snowflake with my fingertips. Then, I closed my hand over the delicate silver strands and concentrated. It only took a second for the images and feelings to fill my mind.

Logan seeing me at the Winter Carnival and eyeing the snowflake toboggan I'd had on that day. The horror he'd felt when he'd realized I was in the path of the avalanche. Him watching me run from the snow and wishing he could do something, anything, to help me. The cold fear that had filled him when he'd gotten Oliver's text that I was in trouble. His determination to save me from Preston no matter what. The fierce pride he'd felt as he watched me use Vic to fight Preston—and win.

There were some happier memories, too. Logan prowling through a jewelry shop, trying to find just the right gift for me. Him seeing the necklace and thinking it reminded him of me. The Spartan hoping I would like it. Logan holding me, first that night outside the coffee shop at the ski resort and then again in the library. And finally, our desperate kiss that day in the construction site, the one that had let me tap into the Spartan's fighting skills.

Through all the memories, good and bad, I felt what Logan did every time he saw or thought about me—that soft, warm, fizzy feeling that only meant one thing.

Logan Quinn really did care about me.

"He likes me," I whispered. "He really does like me."

At the sound of my voice, Vic opened his eye. I'd propped the sword up on my desk, and his face was just level with mine.

"That's a shiny little bauble," Vic said, staring at the necklace."Looks like the Spartan boy has good taste."

"How do you know Logan gave it to me?"

Vic snorted. "I might be old and cranky, but I'm not bloody *stupid*. The boy is crazy about you. Anyone can see that. It certainly took you long enough to figure it out."

"Shut up, Vic," I said, but there was a smile on my face.

I moved around my dorm room, stuffing clothes and comic books into my duffel bags. One of the last things I picked up to take with me was the small statue of Nike I kept on my desk. The winged figure of the goddess looked exactly the same as her statue in the library. Maybe it was silly, but the cheap replica made me feel a little closer to her, made me feel like I could somehow find the Helheim Dagger and keep it safe from the Reapers.

"Have a good Christmas, goddess," I told the statue, then stuffed it into my bag.

Finally, there were only two more things left to pack—the photos of my mom. I slid the one of her and Metis into my bag. I picked up the second glass frame and stared at the picture of my mom by herself, taken a few months before her murder. Brown hair, violet eyes, beautiful face. She peered up at me, a small smile curving her lips.

This would be my first Christmas without her, I realized with a jolt. The first Christmas she wouldn't be there to open presents with me and Grandma Frost. The first Christmas she wouldn't be around to laugh and talk and joke with the two of us. My chest ached in a familiar, bitter way, but I pushed the feeling aside and focused on my anger—the anger that had grown and grown like a poisonous flower blooming inside my heart, ever since I'd found out what had really happened to my mom.

I didn't know how, I didn't know when, but I was going to find Loki's Champion, the Reaper girl who'd killed my mom—and I was going to shove a sword through her heart. Logan had told Oliver that I was totally kick-ass. I figured it was time for me to live up to the Spartan's words.

But first there would be Christmas with Grandma Frost and Vic. I put the photo of my mom into my bag, nestled right next to the statue of Nike. Then I rummaged through my desk, grabbed the miniature red Santa hat I'd bought for Vic, and stuck it on the hilt of the talking sword.

"You ready to go get that Christmas ham and pie?" I asked. "Grandma Frost called me this morning. She's been baking cookies all day just for the two of us."

"I *suppose* that a brief holiday wouldn't hurt," Vic grumbled. "Although you're going to practice with me every day, Gwen. You're finally starting to get the hang of me, and I won't have you backsliding and forgetting what little you've learned, just because school's out. We've got Reapers to kill, you know."

"Don't you worry," I said. "We're going to kill Reapers until we're both bathed in their blood and hungry for more."

Vic arced his one eyebrow. "That's my line."

"Yeah," I said. "And it's a good one. Now come on, we've got a bus to catch."

I slung my bags over my shoulder and grabbed Vic. I took one more glance in the mirror at the snowflake necklace Logan had given me. Maybe it was just my imagination, but the diamonds seemed to sparkle with an inner fire, blazing as bright as my feelings for the Spartan did—and would over the long winter break. The pure, hopeful light made me smile as I left my dorm room and headed home to Grandma Frost for the holidays.

BEYOND
THE
STORY

Gwen's Thoughts on the Schedule
for the Winter Carnival

Friday

7 a.m.: Depart Mythos Academy. Oh goody. I get to be dragged out of bed before the crack of dawn—in the bitter cold, no less.

9 a.m.: Arrive at Powder ski resort. If I have to schlep over to the resort, I at least hope that the rooms are nice.

10 a.m. to 5 p.m.: Students check in and enjoy a day on the slopes. Maybe the other students will. I've never been skiing before and don't have any desire to start now.

7 p.m.: Social time in the alpine village. In other words, the students party hard with minimal interference from the professors.

Saturday

8 a.m. to 10 a.m.: Breakfast buffet will be served. I hope they have some normal food here, unlike the dining hall back at the academy.

10 a.m. to 5 p.m.: The Winter Carnival will be held. Daphne tells me this is an actual carnival with games and prizes and stuff. This might actually be fun.

7 p.m.: Social time in the alpine village. More parties, more drinking and smoking, and more kids hooking up.

Sunday

8 a.m. to 10 a.m.: Breakfast buffet will be served. Maybe they'll at least have pancakes and waffles . . . Oh, and bacon!

10 a.m. to 5 p.m.: Students enjoy a final day on the slopes. Maybe the other students will. Not me.

8 p.m.: Students board the bus for the return trip. Time to schlep back to the academy. Oh, goody.

10 p.m.: Arrive at Mythos Academy. We'll get back to the academy just in time for curfew, and we don't even get a day off before we have to go back to class in the morning. That's *so* not fair. . . .

Mythos Academy Warriors
and Their Magic

The students at Mythos Academy are the descendants of ancient warriors, and they are at the academy to learn how to fight and use weapons, along with whatever magic or other skills that they might have. Here's a little more about the warrior whiz kids, as Gwen calls them:

Amazons and Valkyries: Most of the girls at Mythos are either Amazons or Valkyries. Amazons are gifted with supernatural quickness. In gym class during mock fights, they look like blurs more than anything else. Valkyries are incredibly strong. Also, bright, colorful sparks of magic can often be seen shooting out of Valkyries' fingertips.

Romans and Vikings: Most of the guys at Mythos Academy are either Romans or Vikings. Romans are superquick, just like Amazons, while Vikings are superstrong, just like Valkyries.

Siblings: Brothers and sisters born to the same parents will have similar abilities and magic, but they're sometimes classified as different types of warriors. For example, if the girls in a family are Amazons, then the boys will be Romans. If the girls in a family are Valkyries, then the boys will be Vikings.

However, in other families, brothers and sisters are considered to be the same kind of warriors, like those born to Spartan, Samurai, or Ninja parents. The boys and girls are both considered to Spartans, Samurais, or Ninjas.

More Magic: As if being superstrong or superquick wasn't good enough, the students at Mythos Academy also have other types of magic. They can do everything from heal injuries to control the weather to create life-like illusions with their bare hands. Many of the students have enhanced senses as well. The powers vary from student to student, but as a general rule, everyone is dangerous and deadly in their own special way.

Spartans: Spartans are among the rarest of the warrior whiz kids, and there are only a few at Mythos Academy. But Spartans are the most dangerous and deadliest of all the warriors because they have the ability to pick up any weapon—or any *thing*—and automatically know how to use and even kill someone with it. Even Reapers of Chaos are afraid to battle Spartans in a fair fight. But then again, Reapers rarely fight fair. . . .

Gypsies: Gypsies are just as rare as Spartans. Gypsies are those who have been gifted with magic by the gods. But not all Gypsies are good. Some are just as evil as the gods they serve. Gwen is a Gypsy who is gifted with psychometry magic, or the ability to know, see, and feel an object's history just by touching it. Gwen's magic comes from Nike, the Greek goddess of victory.

**Want to know more about Mythos Academy?
Read on and take a tour of the campus.**

The heart of Mythos Academy is made up of five buildings that are clustered together like the loose points of a star on the upper quad. They are the Library of Antiquities, the gym, the dining hall, the English-history building, and the math-science building.

The Library of Antiquities: The library is the largest building on campus. In addition to books, the library also houses artifacts—weapons, jewelry, clothes, armor, and more—that were once used by ancient warriors, gods, goddesses, and mythological creatures. Some of the artifacts have a lot of power, and the Reapers of Chaos would love to get their hands on them to use them for Bad, Bad Things.

The Gym: The gym is the second largest building at Mythos. In addition to a pool, basketball court, and more, the gym also features racks of weapons, including swords, staffs, and more, that the students use during mock fights. At Mythos, gym class is really weapons training, and students are graded on how well they can fight—something that Gwen thinks she's not very good at.

The Dining Hall: The dining hall is the third largest building at Mythos. With its white linens, fancy china, and open-air indoor garden, the dining hall looks more like a five-star restaurant than a student cafeteria. The dining hall is famous for all the fancy, froufrou foods that it serves on a daily basis, like liver, veal, and escargot. Yucko, as Gwen would say.

The English-History Building: Students attend English, myth-history, geography, art, and other classes in this building. Professor Metis's office is also in this building.

The Math-Science Building: Students attend math, science, and other classes in this building. But there are more than just classrooms here. This building also features a morgue and a prison deep underground. Creepy, huh?

The Student Dorms: The student dorms are located down the hill from the upper quad, along with several other smaller outbuildings. Guys and girls live in separate dorms, although that doesn't keep them from hooking up on a regular basis.

The Statues: Statues of mythological creatures—like gryphons, garygoles, and more—can be found on all the academy buildings, although the library has the most statues. Gwen thinks that the statues are all super creepy, especially since they always seem to be watching her. . . .

Who's Who at Mythos Academy— The Students

Gwen (Gwendolyn) Frost: Gwen is a Gypsy girl with the gift of psychometry magic, or the ability to know an object's history just by touching it. Gwen's a little dark and twisted in that she likes her magic and the fact that it lets her know other people's secrets—no matter how hard they try to hide them. She also has a major sweet tooth, loves to read comic books, and wears jeans, T-shirts, hoodies, and sneakers almost everywhere she goes.

Daphne Cruz: Daphne is a Valkyrie and a renowned archer. She's also has some wicked computer skills and loves designer clothes and expensive purses. Daphne is also rather obsessed with the color pink. She wears it more often than not, and her entire dorm room is done in various shades of pink.

Logan Quinn: This seriously cute and seriously deadly Spartan is the best fighter at Mythos Academy—and someone who Gwen just can't stop thinking about. But Logan has a secret that he doesn't want anyone to know—especially not Gwen.

Carson Callahan: Carson is the head of the Mythos Academy Marching Band. He's a Celt and rumored to have come from a long line of warrior bards. He's quiet, shy, and one of the nicest guys you'll ever meet, but Carson can be as tough as nails when he needs to be.

Oliver Hector: Oliver is a Spartan who is friends with Logan and Kenzie and helps with Gwen's weapons training. He's also one of Gwen's friends now too, because of what happened during the Winter Carnival.

Kenzie Tanaka: Kenzie is a Spartan who is friends with Logan and Oliver. He also helps with Gwen's weapons training and is currently dating Talia.

Savannah Warren: Savannah is an Amazon who was dating Logan—at least before the Winter Carnival. Now, the two of them have broken up, something Savannah isn't very happy about—and something that she blames Gwen for.

Talia Pizarro: Talia is an Amazon and one of Savannah's best friends. Talia has gym class with Gwen, and the two of them often spar during the mock fights. She is currently dating Kenzie.

Helena Paxton: Helena is an Amazon who seems to be positioning herself as the new mean girl queen of the academy, or at least of Gwen's second-year class.

Morgan McDougall: Morgan is a Valkyrie. She used to be one of the most popular girls at the academy—before her best friend, Jasmine Ashton, tried to sacrifice her to Loki one night in the Library of Antiquities. These days, though, Morgan tends to keep to herself. Gwen isn't sure what Morgan remembers about that night, but she thinks that Morgan knows more than she's letting on....

Who's Who at Mythos Academy and Beyond—
The Adults

Coach Ajax: Ajax is the head of the athletic department at the academy and is responsible for training all the kids at Mythos and turning them into fighters. Logan Quinn and his Spartan friends are among Ajax's prize students.

Geraldine (Grandma) Frost: Geraldine is Gwen's grandma and a Gypsy with the power to see the future. Grandma Frost makes her living as a fortuneteller in a town not too far away from Cypress Mountain. A couple of times a week, Gwen sneaks off the Mythos Academy campus to see her grandma and enjoy the sweet treats that Grandma Frost is always baking.

Grace Frost: Grace is Gwen's mom and a Gypsy who had the power to know if people were telling the truth or not just by listening to their words. At first, Gwen thought her mom had been killed in a car accident by a drunk driver. But thanks to Preston Ashton, Gwen knows that Grace was actually murdered by the Reaper girl who is Loki's Champion. Gwen's determined to find the Reaper girl and get her revenge—no matter what.

Nickamedes: Nickamedes is the head librarian at the Library of Antiquities. Nickamedes loves the books and the artifacts in the library more than anything else, and he doesn't seem to like Gwen at all. In fact, he often goes out of his way to make more work for her whenever Gwen is working after school in the library. Nickamedes is also Logan's uncle, although the uptight librarian is nothing like his easygoing nephew. At least, Gwen doesn't think so.

Professor Aurora Metis: Metis is a myth-history professor who teaches students all about Reapers of Chaos, Loki, and the ancient Chaos War. She was also best friends with Gwen's mom, Grace, back when the two of them went to Mythos. Metis is the Champion of Athena, the Greek goddess of wisdom, and she's become Gwen's mentor at the academy.

Raven: Raven is the old woman who mans the coffee cart in the Library of Antiquities. Gwen's also seen her in the academy prison, which seems to be another one of Raven's odd jobs around campus. There's definitely more to Raven than meets the eye. . . .

The Powers That Were: A board made up of various members of the Pantheon who oversees all aspects of Mythos Academy, from approving the dining hall menus to disciplining students. Gwen's never met any of the board members that she knows of, and she doesn't know exactly who they are, but that could change—sooner than she thinks.

Who's Who at Mythos Academy— The Gods, Monsters, and More

Artifacts: Artifacts are weapons, jewelry, clothing, armor, and more that were worn or used by various warriors, gods, goddesses, and mythological creatures over the years. There are Thirteen Artifacts that are rumored to be the most powerful, although people disagree about which artifacts they are and how they were used during the Chaos War. The members of the Pantheon protect the various artifacts from the Reapers, who want to use the artifacts and their power to free Loki from his prison. Many of the artifacts are housed in the Library of Antiquities.

Black rocs: These creatures look like ravens—only much, much bigger. They have shiny black feathers shot through with glossy streaks of red, long, sharp, curved talons, and black eyes with a red spark burning deep down inside them. Rocs are capable of picking up people and carrying them off—before they rip them to shreds.

Champions: Every god and goddess has a Champion, someone that they choose to work on their behalf in the mortal realm. Champions have various powers and weapons and can be good or bad, depending on the god they serve. Gwen is Nike's Champion, just like her mom and grandma were before her.

The Chaos War: Long ago, Loki and his followers tried to enslave everyone and everything, and the whole world was plunged into the Chaos War. It was a dark, bloody time that almost resulted in the end of the world. The Reapers want to free Loki, so the god can lead them in another Chaos War. You can see why that would be a Bad, Bad Thing.

Fenrir wolves: These creatures look like wolves—only much, much bigger. They have ash gray fur, razor-sharp claws, and burning red eyes. Reapers use them to watch, hunt, and kill members of the Pantheon. Think of Fenrir wolves as puppy-dog assassins.

Loki: Loki is the Norse god of chaos. Once upon a time, Loki caused the death of another god and was imprisoned for it. But Loki eventually escaped from his prison and started recruiting other gods, goddesses, humans, and creatures to join forces with him. He called his followers the Reapers of Chaos, and they tried to take over the world. However, Loki and his followers were eventually defeated, and Loki was imprisoned for a second time. To this day, Loki seeks to escape from his prison and plunge the world into a second Chaos War. He's the ultimate bad guy.

Mythos Academy: The academy is located in Cypress Mountain, North Carolina, which is a ritzy suburb high in the mountains above the city of Asheville. The academy is a boarding school/college for warrior whiz kids—the descendants of ancient warriors, like Spartans, Valkyries, Amazons, and more. The kids at

Mythos range in age from first-year students (age sixteen) to sixth-year students (age twenty-one). The kids go to Mythos to learn how to use whatever magic and skills they possess to fight against Loki and his Reapers. There are other branches of the academy located throughout the world.

Nemean prowlers: These creatures look like panthers—only much, much bigger. They have black fur tinged with red, razor-sharp claws, and burning red eyes. Reapers use them to watch, hunt, and kill members of the Pantheon. Think of Nemean prowlers as kitty-cat assassins.

Nike: Nike is the Greek goddess of victory. The goddess was the one who defeated Loki in one-on-one combat during the final battle of the Chaos War. Ever since then, Nike and her Champions have fought the Reapers of Chaos, trying to keep them from freeing Loki from his prison. She's the ultimate good guy.

The Pantheon: The Pantheon is made up of gods, goddesses, humans, and creatures who have banded together to fight Loki and his Reapers of Chaos. The members of the Pantheon are the good guys.

Reapers of Chaos: A Reaper is any god, goddess, human, or creature who serves Loki and wants to free the evil god from his prison. Reapers are known to sacrifice people to Loki in hopes of weakening his prison, so he can one day break free and return to the mortal realm. The scary thing is that Reapers can be anyone at

Mythos Academy and beyond—parents, teachers, even fellow students. Reapers are the bad guys.

Sigyn: Sigyn is the Norse goddess of devotion. She is also Loki's wife. The first time Loki was imprisoned, he was chained up underneath a giant snake that dripped venom onto his once-handsome face. Sigyn spent many years holding an artifact called the Bowl of Tears up over Loki's head to catch as much of the venom as possible. But when the bowl was full, Sigyn would have to empty it, which let venom drop freely onto Loki's face, causing him great pain. Eventually, Loki tricked Sigyn into releasing him, and before long, the evil god plunged the world into the long, bloody Chaos War. No one knows what happened to Sigyn after that. . . .

Reapers of Chaos, the Helheim Dagger,
crushing on Logan Quinn . . .
the stakes get even higher for Gwen in

DARK FROST,

coming next June.

Chapter 1

"If you guys don't stop making out, I'm going to be sick."

Daphne Cruz, my best friend, giggled and laid another loud, smacking kiss on her boyfriend, Carson Callahan. Princess pink sparks of magic shot off Daphne's fingertips and flickered in the air around them, the tiny rainbows of color almost as bright as Carson's flaming cheeks.

I rolled my eyes. "Seriously, seriously sick."

Daphne quit kissing Carson long enough to turn and stare at me. "Oh, get over it, Gwen. We're not making out. Not in this stuffy old museum."

I raised an eyebrow. "Really? Then why is Carson wearing more of your lip gloss than you are?"

Carson's blush deepened, his dusky brown skin taking on a fiery tomato tint. The band geek pushed his black glasses up his nose and swiped his hand over his mouth, trying to scrub away the remains of Daphne's lip gloss, but all he really did was get pink glitter all over his fingers. Daphne giggled, then pressed another kiss to her boyfriend's lips.

I sighed. "C'mon, c'mon. Break it up, lovebirds. The museum closes at five, and we haven't seen half the artifacts we're supposed to for myth-history class."

"Fine," Daphne pouted, stepping away from Carson. "Be a spoilsport."

I rolled my eyes again. "Yeah, well, this *spoilsport* happens to be concerned about her grades. So, let's go to the next room. There are supposed to be some really cool weapons in there, according to the exhibit brochure."

Daphne crossed her arms over her chest. She narrowed her black eyes and glared at me for interrupting her fun, but she and Carson followed as I stepped through a doorway and left the main part of the museum behind.

It was a few days after New Year's, and the three of us were in the Crius Coliseum, a museum located on the outskirts of Asheville, North Carolina. Visiting a museum didn't exactly top my list of fun things to do, but all the second-year students at Mythos Academy were supposed to schlep over to the coliseum sometime during the winter holidays to view a special exhibit of artifacts. Since classes started back at the academy in the morning, today was our last chance to finish the assignment. It was bad enough that I and all the other warrior whiz kids at Mythos were being trained to fight Reapers of Chaos, some seriously nasty bad guys. But homework over the holidays, too? That was *so* not fair.

Daphne, Carson, and I had gotten here about three o'clock, and we'd been wandering around the museum for the last ninety minutes, going from one display to the next. From the outside, the Crius Coliseum looked like just another building, just another museum, one of dozens tucked away in the Appalachian Mountains in and around the city.

Inside, though, it was a different story.

Walking through the front door of the museum was like stepping back in time to ancient Greece. White marble rolled out as far as the eye could see, broken up by towering pillars. Gold, silver, and bronze leaf glinted here and there on the walls before spreading up to cover the entire ceiling in dazzling disks of color. Sapphires and rubies burned like colorful coals in the necklaces and rings on display, while the fine silks and other garments shimmered inside their glass cases, looking as light and delicate as spiderwebs. The museum staff even wore long, flowing white togas, adding to the effect.

But it wasn't just ancient Greece that was on display. Every room had a specific theme and displayed a different culture, from Norse to Persian to Japanese and all the lands and peoples in between. That's because the coliseum was devoted to members of the Pantheon. Gods, goddesses, ancient warriors, mythological creatures—the Pantheon was basically a group of magical good guys who'd joined forces to save the world.

Way back in the day, the evil Norse trickster god Loki had tried to enslave everyone and had plunged the world into the long, bloody Chaos War. But the members of the Pantheon had risen up to stop Loki and his evil followers, the Reapers of Chaos. Eventually, the other gods and goddesses had locked Loki away in a mythological prison, far removed from the mortal realm. Now, the coliseum showcased the various artifacts—jewelry, clothing, armor, weapons, and more—that both sides had used during the Chaos War.

Of course, what most people didn't realize was that Loki was *thisfreakingclose* to breaking free of his prison and starting another Chaos War. It was something that I thought about all the time, though—especially since I was somehow supposed to stop the evil god from escaping.

"This is cool," Daphne said.

She pointed to a curved bow inside a glass case. The bow was made out of a single piece of onyx, inlaid with bits of gold scrollwork and strung with several thin golden threads. A matching onyx quiver sat next to it, although only a single golden arrow lay inside the slender tube.

Daphne leaned down and read the bronze plaque mounted on the pedestal below the weapon. "This says that the bow once belonged to Sigyn, the Norse goddess of devotion, and that every time you pull the arrow out of the quiver, another one appears to take its place. Okay, now that's *wicked* cool."

"I like this better," Carson said, pointing to a curled ivory horn that vaguely resembled a small, handheld tuba. Bits of onyx glimmered on the smooth surface. "It says it's the Horn of Roland. Not sure what it does, though."

I blinked. I'd been so lost in my thoughts about Loki, Reapers, and the Pantheon that I'd just been wandering around instead of actually looking at the artifacts, like we were supposed to.

We stood in an enormous circular room filled with weapons. Swords, staffs, spears, daggers, bows, throwing stars, and more glinted from behind glass cases and in spots on the walls, next to oil paintings of various mythological battles. The entire back wall was made out of the same white marble as the rest of the museum, although a variety of mythological creatures had been carved into the surface. Gryphons, gargoyles, dragons, chimeras, Gorgons with snakelike hair and cruel smiles.

An ancient knight dressed in full battle armor perched on a stuffed horse on a raised dais in the center of the room. The knight had a lance in his hand and looked like he was about to charge forward and skewer the wax figure of a Roman centurion that also stood on the dais, his sword raised to fend off the charging knight. Other figures were scattered throughout the room, including a Viking wearing a horned helmet, who was poised to bring his massive battle-ax down onto the circular bronze shield of the Spartan standing next to him. A few feet away, two female figures representing a Valkyrie and an Amazon held swords and dispassionately watched the Viking and Spartan in their eternal epic battle.

I stared at the Viking and Spartan, and for a moment, their features flickered and seemed to move. Their wax lips drew up into angry snarls, their fingers tightened around the hilts of their weapons, their whole bodies tensed up in anticipation of the battle that was to come.

I shivered and looked away. My Gypsy gift had been acting up ever since we'd entered the museum.

I had psychometry magic—touch magic, some people called it. Basically, my Gypsy gift let me touch any object and immediately know, feel, and see its history. Everything from how a weapon had been used in battle to all the blows a shield had taken over the years to who had used them both in the first place. Plus, I could feel and experience everything a person had when she'd been using a specific object. The heady adrenaline rush before an intense battle; the hot fury of the actual fight; the sweet, electric thrill of victory.

My psychometry magic also let me see, feel, and experience all the memories and emotions of every person who'd ever used or touched an object—no matter how good, bad, or ugly those feelings were. If someone had been absolutely terrified during a battle, if he'd been exceptionally brave, even if he'd coldly murdered someone by stabbing the other person in the back—I could see all that and more. With just a brush of my fingers, I could discover people's deepest, darkest secrets—no matter how hard they tried to hide them.

Sometimes, though, I didn't have to touch an object to get a vibe off it, since some items had so many memories and feelings attached to them that they just radiated emotions. Or maybe my imagination was just working overtime today, since I was surrounded by so many artifacts that had been used by so many heroes and villains over the years.

I'd seen so many freaky things already at Mythos Academy, even though I'd just started going to the school last fall. Most of the time, I felt like I was just waiting for the next Bad, Bad Thing to happen. Like someone trying to kill me—again.

"Hmph. Well, I don't think that bow is so bloody special," a voice with a snooty English accent muttered. "I think it's rather boring. *Ordinary*, even."

I looked down at the source of the voice—Vic, the sword sheathed in the black leather scabbard hanging off my waist. Vic wasn't your typical sword. For starters, instead of having a plain hilt, the sword actually had half a face inlaid into the metal there. A single ear, a hooked nose, a mouth. All that joined together to form the sword's hilt, along with the round bulge of an eye. It always seemed to me like there was a man trapped there inside the silver metal, trying to get out. I didn't know exactly who or what Vic was, other than rude, bossy, and bloodthirsty. The sword was always going on and on and *on* about how we should go find some Reapers to kill.

Actually, there was just one Reaper that I wanted to kill—the girl who'd murdered my mom.

A crumpled car. A sword slicing through the rain. And blood—so much blood . . .

The memories of my mom's murder bubbled to the surface of my mind, threatening to overwhelm me, but I pushed them away and forced myself to focus on my friends, who were still staring at the onyx bow and ivory horn.

I'd brought Vic along today, because I thought he might enjoy seeing the items on display at the museum. Besides, I'd needed someone to talk to while Daphne and Carson were giggling and tongue-wrestling with each other. The two of them were so into each other that it was rather disgusting at times, especially given the sad state of my own love life.

"It's just a bow, after all," Vic continued. "Not anything important. Not a *real* weapon."

I rolled my eyes. Oh, yeah. Vic talked, too—mostly about how awesome he was.

"Well, some of us happen to like bows," Daphne sniffed, looking down at the sword.

"And that's what's wrong with you, Valkyrie," Vic said.

The sword glared at her. Vic only had one eye, and it was a curious color—not quite purple but not quite gray either. Really, Vic's eye reminded me of the color of twilight, that soft shade that streaked the sky just before the world went dark for the night.

"And you, Celt," Vic said, turning his attention to Carson. "Gwen told me that you prefer to use a staff. A staff! It doesn't even have a bloody *point* on the end of it. Disgraceful, the things they're teaching you warrior kids at Mythos these days."

Every kid who went to Mythos Academy was some sort of warrior, including the three of us. Daphne was a Valkyrie, Carson was a Celt, and I was a Gypsy, all of us the descendants of the Pantheon warriors who'd first taken on Loki and his Reapers. Now, we carried on that tradition in modern times by going to the academy and learning how to use whatever skills and magic we had to learn how to fight Reapers. And we weren't the only ones. Vikings, Romans, Ninjas, Samurais, Spartans, Persians. All those warriors and more could be found at the academy.

"Disgraceful, I say," Vic crowed again.

Carson looked at me. I just shrugged. I'd only had Vic a few months, but I'd quickly learned there was no controlling the mouthy sword. Vic said whatever he liked, whenever he liked, as loudly as he liked. And if you dared to disagree with him, he was more than happy to discuss the matter further—while his blade was pressed up against your throat.

Vic and Daphne glared at each other before the Valkyrie turned to Carson and started talking to the band geek about how cool the bow was. I wandered through the rest of the room, peering at the other artifacts. Vic kept up his running monologue about how swords were the only *real* weapons, with him, of course, being the best sword *ever*. I made agreeing noises when appropriate. It was easier than trying to argue with Vic.

Daphne and Carson continued to look at the bow, and Vic finished his rant and fell silent once more. I was reading about a ball of silver thread that had belonged to Ariadne, a Greek maiden who helped Theseus find his way through the labyrinth where the Minotaur was kept, when shoes tapped on the floor and someone walked up beside me.

"Gwendolyn Frost," a snide voice murmured. "Fancy seeing you here."

I turned and found myself face-to-face with a forty-something guy with black hair, cold blue eyes, and skin that was as white as the marble floor. He wore a dark blue suit and a pair of wingtips that had a higher polish than most of the glass cases in the room. I would have thought him handsome if I hadn't known exactly how uptight and prissy he was—and how very much he hated me.

I sighed. "Nickamedes. What are you doing here?"

"Overseeing the exhibit, of course. Most of the artifacts on display are on loan from the Library of Antiquities."

Nickamedes was the head honcho at the Library of Antiquities, which was located on the Mythos Academy campus a few miles away in Cypress Mountain, North Carolina. In addition to books, the massive library was famous for its priceless collection of artifacts. Hundreds and hundreds of glass cases filled the library's seven floors, containing items that had once belonged to everyone from various gods and goddesses to their Champions to the Reapers they had battled.

I supposed it made sense that the Crius Coliseum had borrowed some artifacts from the library—that was probably the reason the Mythos students had been assigned to come here in the first place. So they'd be forced to look at and study the items they walked past and ignored on a daily basis at the library.

Nickamedes stared at me, not looking a bit happier to see me than I was to have run into him. The librarian and I didn't get along, and I generally thought of him as a giant pain in the ass. I worked several hours a week at the Library of Antiquities as sort of an after-school job, which meant that I reported directly to the librarian. Mostly, I shelved books, dusted the artifact cases, and helped other kids find reference materials, so they could do their homework assignments. Nothing too hard or strenuous.

But back in the fall, an evil Valkyrie named Jasmine Ashton had tried to sacrifice her best friend to Loki and kill me one night in the library. Since I'd been fighting for my life, I hadn't been too concerned about all the stuff I'd damaged along the way—but Nickamedes had. I'd thought Nickamedes was going to strangle me right there on the spot when he'd seen just how badly Jasmine and I had trashed the first floor of the library during our fight. Needless to say, I wasn't one of the librarian's favorite people. The feeling was definitely mutual.

His mouth twisted. "I see that you and your friends waited until the last possible second to come and complete your myth-history assignment, along with a great many of your classmates."

Morgan McDougall, Samson Sorensen, Savannah Warren, Talia Pizarro. I'd spotted several kids I knew roaming through the coliseum. All seventeen, like me, Daphne, and Carson, and all second-year students at Mythos, trying to cram in a visit to the museum before winter classes started in the morning.

"I've been busy," I muttered.

Nickamedes let out a disbelieving huff. "Right."

Anger filled me. I had been busy. *Very* busy, as a matter of fact. Not too long ago, I'd learned that the Reapers were searching for the Helheim Dagger, one of the Thirteen Artifacts that had been used during the final battle of the Chaos War. The Thirteen Artifacts had a lot of power, since they'd all seen action during the climactic fight. But what made the dagger so important—what truly scared me—was the fact that it could be used to free Loki from the prison realm he was trapped in.

I was determined to find the dagger before the Reapers did, so during the holidays I'd read everything I could get my hands on about the weapon. Who might have made it, how it might have been used during the Chaos War, even what powers it might have. But all the books and articles I'd read didn't tell me what I really wanted to know: where my mom, Grace Frost, had hidden the dagger before she'd been murdered—or how I was supposed to find it before the Reapers did.

Of course, I couldn't tell Nickamedes all that. He wouldn't believe that I'd been doing something useful, something important, during the holiday break. No doubt Nickamedes thought I'd just been sitting on my ass reading comic books and eating cookies like I did so many nights when I was working in the Library of Antiquities. Yeah, yeah, so maybe I wasn't all that dedicated when it came to my job. Sue me for wanting to goof off and have a little fun before I had to face down another crazy Reaper who thought I was more powerful and important than I really was.

Still, despite the librarian's frosty attitude, I couldn't help glancing around the room, hoping that I'd see a guy my age with him—a guy with the most beautiful eyes I'd ever seen and a sexy, teasing grin to match.

"Is Logan here with you?" I couldn't keep the hope out of my voice.

Logan Quinn was Nickamedes's nephew and the Spartan guy who I had a major, major crush on. Okay, okay, so maybe "crush" wasn't a strong enough word to describe my feelings for Logan, but it was what I was going with at the moment.

Nickamedes had just opened his mouth when a voice interrupted him.

"Right here, Gypsy girl." A low, rumbling voice sent chills down my spine.

My heart pounding, I slowly turned around. Logan Quinn stood behind me.

Thick, wavy, ink black hair; intense ice blue eyes; a confident smile. My breath caught in my throat as I looked at Logan, and my heart sped up, beating with such force that I was sure he could hear it.

Logan wore jeans and a dark blue sweater topped by a black leather jacket. The clothes were designer of course, since the Spartan was just as rich as all the other academy kids were. But even if he'd been dressed in rags, I still would have noticed the lean strength of his body and his broad, muscled shoulders. Yeah, Logan totally rocked the bad boy look, and he had the manwhore reputation to match. One of the rumors that kept going around the academy was that Logan signed the mattress of every girl he slept with, just so he could keep track of them all.

I'd never quite figured out if the rumors were true or not, but they didn't matter to me, because Logan was just a really, really great guy. Strong, smart, funny, caring. Then, of course, there was the whole saving-my-life-multiple-times thing. Kind of hard not to like a guy when he kept you from getting killed by Reapers and eaten by Nemean prowlers.

Logan's eyes dropped to my throat and the necklace I wore there—the one he'd given me before school had let out for Christmas. Six silver strands wrapped around my throat, creating the necklace, while the diamond-tipped points joined together to form a simple yet elegant snowflake in the center of the strands. The beautiful necklace looked like something a goddess would wear. I thought it was far too pretty and delicate for me, but I loved it just the same.

"You're wearing the necklace," the Spartan said in a low voice.

"Every day since you gave it to me," I said. "I hardly ever take it off."

Logan smiled at me, and it was like the sun had come out from behind a sky full of storm clouds. For a moment everything was just—perfect.

Then Nickamedes cleared his throat, popping the bubble of happiness that I'd been about to float away on. A sour expression twisted the librarian's face as he looked back and forth between Logan and me.

"Well, if you'll excuse me, the museum's closing in a few minutes, and I need to make sure that the staff is ready to start packing up the items for transport back to the academy in the morning."

Nickamedes pivoted on his wingtips and strode out of the weapons room without another word. I sighed. Yeah, I'd destroyed thousands of books during my struggle with Jasmine in the Library of Antiquities, but I always felt there was another reason Nickamedes hated me. He'd pretty much disliked me on sight, and I had no idea why.

I put the librarian and his bad attitude out of mind and focused on Logan. He'd texted me a few times over the holiday break, but I'd still missed him like crazy—especially since I had no idea what was going on between us. Logan had recently broken up with his girlfriend, Savannah Warren, but he hadn't exactly declared his love for me in the meantime—or even asked me out on a real date. Instead, we'd been in this weird holding pattern for weeks now—one that I was determined to end.

I drew in a breath, ready to ask Logan how his winter break had been and what was going to happen between us now. "Logan, I—"

Shouts and screams ripped through the air, drowning out my words.

I froze, wondering if I'd only imagined the harsh, jarring sounds. Why would someone be shouting in the museum? A second later, more screams sliced through the air, followed by several loud crashes and the heavy *thump-thump-thump* of footsteps.

Logan and I looked at each other, then bolted for the door. Daphne and Carson had also heard the screams, and they raced along right behind us.

"Stop! Stop! Stop!" Daphne hissed.

She managed to grab my arm and the back of Logan's leather jacket just as the Spartan was about to sprint out of the room. With her great Valkyrie strength, she was easily able to yank both of us back and give me whiplash.

"You don't know what's going on—or who might be out there," Daphne warned.

Logan glared at her, but after a moment, he reluctantly nodded. I did the same, and Daphne loosened her grip on us. Together in a tight knot, the four of us crept up to the doorway and peeked through to the other side.

The Crius Coliseum was shaped like a giant wheel, with one main space in the middle and the various hallways and rooms branching off that area like spokes. The doorway we stood in opened up into the center section of the museum. When Daphne, Carson, and I had walked through a few minutes ago, folks had been milling around the exhibits, looking at the artifacts and browsing through the expensive replica weapons, armor, and jewelry in the museum's gift shop. Besides the staff, most of the other people in the museum had been second-year Mythos students, trying to get their homework assignment done before classes started tomorrow, just like the three of us.

Not anymore.

Now, figures wearing long, black, hooded robes stormed through the coliseum—and they all carried sharp, curved swords. The figures swarmed over everyone in their path, their blades slashing through the air and then into the students who'd been staring at the exhibits just a few seconds before. More screams and shouts tore through the air, echoing as loud as gunshots inside the museum, as people realized what was happening.

But it was already too late.

"Reapers," Daphne whispered, voicing my own horrific thought.

The Reapers of Chaos ran their swords through everyone they could get their hands on, then shoved the dead and dying to the floor. The museum staff, adults, kids. It didn't matter to the Reapers who they killed. Wax figures, statues, display cases, and more crashed to the floor, splintering into thousands of pieces. Blood spattered everywhere, a cascade of scarlet teardrops sliding down the white marble walls.

A sick, sick feeling filled my stomach at the bloody chaos in front of me. I'd heard about Reapers, about how vicious they were, about how they lived to kill warriors—about how they lived to kill *us*. I'd faced down two Reapers myself, but I'd never seen anything like this.

Some of the Mythos students tried to fight back, using their fists or whatever they could get their hands on. But it didn't work, and one by one, the Reapers swarmed over the kids. Samson Sorensen, a guy I knew, fell to the floor, screaming and clutching his stomach, blood spurting out from between his fingers. A few Mythos students tried to run, but the Reapers just grabbed them from behind, rammed their swords into the kids' backs, and then tossed them aside like trash.

Out of the corner of my eye, I saw another student, Morgan McDougall, duck down and squeeze in between a tall, wide pedestal and the wall. Green sparks of magic shot out of Morgan's fingertips like lightning, a clear sign of her surprise and panic, and she curled her hands into tight fists and tucked them under her armpits to try to smother the colorful flashes. Morgan knew as well as I did that if the Reapers saw the sparks, they'd find and finish her off. The pretty Valkyrie spotted me watching her and stared back at me, her hazel eyes full of fear.

"Stay there! Hide! Don't try to run!" I shouted, although I didn't think Morgan could hear me above the screams and alarms that had started blaring.

In less than a minute, it was over. The Reapers regrouped in the middle of the museum, talking to each other, but I couldn't hear what they were saying over the moans, groans, and whimpers of the dying kids on the bloody floor.

"Reapers," Daphne whispered again, as if she couldn't believe what she was seeing any more than I could.

It was almost like they'd heard the Valkyrie's low murmur because several of the black-robed figures turned and headed in our direction.